# INVERCLYDE LIBRARIES

## SOUTH WEST

## INVERCLYDE LIBRARIES

**This book is to be returned on or before
the last date above. It may be borrowed for
a further period if not in demand.**

*For enquiries and renewals Tel: (01475) 712323*

D0432843

# After the Silence

JAKE WOODHOUSE

PENGUIN BOOKS

# PENGUIN BOOKS

Published by the Penguin Group

Penguin Books Ltd, 80 Strand, London WC2R ORL, England

Penguin Group (USA) Inc., 375 Hudson Street, New York, New York 10014, USA

Penguin Group (Canada), 90 Eglinton Avenue East, Suite 700, Toronto, Ontario, Canada M4P 2Y3
(a division of Pearson Penguin Canada Inc.)

Penguin Ireland, 25 St Stephen's Green, Dublin 2, Ireland (a division of Penguin Books Ltd)

Penguin Group (Australia), 707 Collins Street, Melbourne, Victoria 3008,
Australia (a division of Pearson Australia Group Pty Ltd)

Penguin Books India Pvt Ltd, 11 Community Centre,
Panchsheel Park, New Delhi – 110 017, India

Penguin Group (NZ), 67 Apollo Drive, Rosedale, Auckland 0632, New Zealand
(a division of Pearson New Zealand Ltd)

Penguin Books (South Africa) (Pty) Ltd, Block D, Rosebank Office Park, 181 Jan Smuts Avenue,
Parktown North, Gauteng 2193, South Africa

Penguin Books Ltd, Registered Offices: 80 Strand, London WC2R ORL, England

www.penguin.com

First published 2014
001

Issa haiku ['A world of dew'] from *The Sound of Water: Haiku by Basho, Buson, Issa and Other Poets*,
translated by Sam Hamill, © 1995 by Sam Hamill. Reprinted by arrangement with The Permissions
Company, Inc., on behalf of Shambhala Publications Inc., Boston, MA. www.shambhala.com.

Set in 12.5/14.75 pt Garamond
Typeset by Palimpsest Book Production Ltd, Falkirk, Stirlingshire
Printed in Great Britain by Clays Ltd, St Ives plc

PAPERBACK ISBN: 978–1–405–91428–4
TRADE PAPERBACK ISBN: 978–1–405–91429–1

www.greenpenguin.co.uk

MIX
Paper from
responsible sources
FSC www.fsc.org FSC® C018179

Penguin Books is committed to a sustainable
future for our business, our readers and our planet.
This book is made from Forest Stewardship
Council™ certified paper.

For Zara, and my parents

# Prologue

'Move.'

The voice shot out from behind him in the dark, and the cold touch of a gun, his own gun, jammed into the back of his neck.

This was not how he imagined it would be.

He'd been shoved to the hard, freezing ground, where something – *a stone, a shard of glass?* – had jabbed into his right kneecap, a trickle of blood cooling fast. He twisted his head up towards the sky, his breath rising plumes, stars piercing the dark, and somehow the pain made it all seem more beautiful, more precious, more real.

He had to play it cool, had to make sure he didn't give in to the fear wrenching his gut, pulsing right through him. But, he thought as he fought down the rising panic, he wasn't a soldier, a commando trained to kill with his bare hands, or a martial arts expert who could whirl around, kick the gun away and deliver a fatal blow to a secret place on the side of the neck.

No, he was just a police officer, an Inspector, specializing in homicide, dealing with crime after the fact, after murder had been committed.

His work began where someone's life ended. And he'd seen enough of those to know he wasn't yet ready to be a mere job for someone else, for some other Inspector to arrive at the crime scene, piece together his life, and the events which had led to its close.

*How could I have been so stupid*, he thought, *letting them catch me?*

The people he was supposed to be chasing, bringing to justice. Who'd tied up the old couple and let them burn alive in their own home . . .

'I said *move*.'

Increasing pressure from the gun barrel, pushing on the spot – the same spot as the earlier impact just on the back of his skull – made him rise up, both knees cracking like pistols.

'Take it easy,' he said, and couldn't believe how scared his voice sounded.

He moved forward, step by step, the odd patch of ice shooting his feet away until he learnt to just shuffle along. Steel from the cuffs cut into his wrists.

He pictured the man behind him, the leather face mask with the zip where the mouth should be.

*Is this it, am I going to die now?*

Part of his mind screamed at him to engage his captor, he seemed to remember that was the key to surviving these situations, making them see you as a human being, not just a target, a kill – and where exactly did he know that from, a film? He was pretty sure he'd never received any such training from the Amsterdam Police Force – but he didn't know what to say.

'Stop.'

That voice. Harsher now, more guttural, as if the freezing air was corroding his vocal cords.

He thought of his wife, at home, her belly swollen

with the life he wasn't going to see. Doubling up, he vomited bile.

A kick to the back of his legs made him fall to his knees again. The feeling of being trapped rushed over him, crushing the air from his lungs, and making his head spin so badly he jerked sideways before managing to right himself.

It was then he heard the car, moving slowly, behind him off to the left. The sound grew, headlights streamed out of the darkness and his elongated shadow spilled forward on to the ground, a monk kneeling at prayer.

*Prayer*, he thought, *the last resort.*

He took a moment to scan his surroundings; it was a concrete drainage ditch – he'd thought as much – the shallow, sloped sides leading up to the trees which he knew must be all around.

The car stopped, engine turned off and ticking gently, but the headlights stayed, blue-white lasers slicing the dark. Doors opened then closed with soft thuds. Footsteps from the road, difficult to tell how many people, soles grinding grit against concrete, then quieter steps on grass, before more hesitant footfalls on the ditch's sides, each one carefully placed to avoid slipping.

Voices, in a language he didn't understand, grating, sinister.

He was shivering now, his whole body shaking as if every muscle had simultaneously gone haywire, but he didn't know if that was the cold or the sheer terror, or maybe both.

Someone walked round his left side and flicked a torch directly in his eyes, dazzling him. Instinctively his eyelids closed tight, protecting, even though part of him wanted to see who it was. He squinted them open just in time to see a figure in silhouette, wearing some kind of trench coat. The man's arm moved, checking the time on a large wristwatch.

Then the light was off, one word uttered behind him and the footsteps retreated, doors opened and closed again, and the car, its engine roar splitting open the silence of the night, reversed away.

He listened until he could no longer hear it.

*Was that it? Was this just a warning?*

He couldn't be sure but he felt he was totally alone now, the man who'd brought him here had departed as well. Relief surged through him, but then . . . if they'd found out about him . . .

*I've got to warn Jaap*, he thought, his knees aching, stomach loose. He forced himself up and started to turn around.

A shot rang out, and faded into the darkness.

a world of dew,
and within every dewdrop
a world of struggle

(Issa)

# DAY ONE

# I

'Just 'cause you're police doesn't mean you don't get broken into.'

Inspector Jaap Rykel glanced out of his houseboat's porthole, across dark water to the trees lining the opposite side of the canal. He could see their naked boughs, heavy with Christmas lights, each orb glowing like a strange winter fruit.

'Is there really no one else?' he switched the phone to his other ear, bent down and peered at the jimmied door again, scratches in the black paint revealing raw wood underneath. 'I mean, I know I'm on the rota for today, but as I said I've been up most of the night and –'

'I hear you, but there's no one available. And it's not straightforward, it needs someone who knows what they're doing.'

'So you're resorting to flattery now?'

'Whatever it takes.'

*It's either that*, he thought looking at the door, *or dealing with this.*

'Okay,' he sighed into the phone, 'I'll take it. But I need you to get someone over here right now to clean this mess up. And replace the lock.'

'No problem, but don't hang around. And I've sent Kees Terpstra –'

'Not Kees . . .'

'Express orders, you're to hold his hand on this one.'

'Anyone trying to hold his hand is likely to get it bitten off.'

'So fill out a form, wounded in action. Look, I've gotta go –'

'Wait, check a name for me. Friedman.'

'First name?'

'I don't know, just run it, call me if anything jumps out. And try and get hold of Andreas, I'm not having any luck.'

Jaap dropped the phone on the kitchen table. He'd only answered thinking it might be his partner, Andreas, calling to explain his text message last night.

> Call me, I'm on to something. A guy called
> Friedman is our way in.

*Maybe I should have gone with him when he asked,* he thought as he tried to call him. It just rang out again, as it had before.

He pulled up Andreas' home phone number and was just about to hit the call button when the thought of Saskia stopped him. She'd never been an early riser, and he was sure being pregnant hadn't changed that.

*I'll wait a bit,* he thought, pocketing his phone.

He spent a few minutes checking what had been stolen, and found that nothing had gone. Not even the most valuable thing he owned, his *nihonto*, the ceremonial sword he'd been given when he left Japan.

He looked at the silver dragons sinuously coiling round the black lacquer scabbard.

*It's right there on the wall,* he thought, *how could they not have seen it?*

He figured it would take a while for anyone to arrive so he pulled out his battered I Ching and the three two-euro coins he kept with it. He threw the three coins together on to the table's surface, noting down the result each time. Each throw corresponded to one line, and he threw six times to form a hexagram.

He recognized the bottom three lines, the symbol for Lake, and the top three represented Thunder.

He looked up the combination and read 'Do not argue with how things are' just as he heard footsteps clanging on the metal gangplank.

A uniform stepped through the door, bending down to avoid hitting his head, and wiped his nose on his sleeve. Jaap could see the glistening trail it left on the dark blue fabric as he slipped the coins and book back.

'What have they nicked?' asked the uniform.

'Weirdly, nothing.'

'Maybe you've got nothing worth nicking.'

Jaap pointed to the sword and the uniform studied it for a moment.

'Hmm. Probably got disturbed then.'

Jaap thought it unlikely. Most break-ins were done by drug addicts desperate for cash. Having got in they'd leave with something, disturbed or not.

'Maybe.' He shrugged. 'Anyway, I've got to go. Get the

door replaced, and drop the new keys off at the station,' he said as he stepped outside.

On deck he had to pause for a moment as he struggled with the zip on his jacket – it kept jamming just below the throat and he had to strum his hand up and down to release it – before moving off across the narrow gang-plank, swaying gently until he reached the shore.

The distant rumble of a tram came to his ears, and then the splash of an early water bird, landing in the canal off to his left. He shivered, then set out east, his steps like gunshots on the laid brick road, shooting across the water and back again.

*I hope Andreas has got somewhere*, he thought, *we need to close that gang case down.*

They'd been working on a murder which had led them to a gang who called themselves *Zwarte Tulpen*, Black Tulips. They were from a variety of ex-Soviet states, and were vicious, secretive and well-organized. As Jaap and Andreas had started investigating they'd begun to under-stand the sheer reach of the gang. In the four years since the Black Tulips appeared on the scene they'd virtually taken over the ports; if it went in or out and it was illegal you could be sure they controlled it.

And they didn't get to be the major players by being lax. In the two weeks since they'd started on the case he and Andreas had been continually frustrated by the lack of a way in. They kept hitting a brick wall. And it'd begun to feel like the wall was never going to crack.

Ten minutes later he turned the last kink in Heren-gracht, one of four canals which cupped Amsterdam's centre. He could make out an ambulance and a patrol car, their blue lights strobing. Red-and-white-striped tape reached from a house out to a leafless tree on the canal's edge, fluttering in the icy breeze which had just started up.

The scene was already bustling – he counted at least five uniforms – and as he got closer he could see they were all looking skywards like acolytes in some religious painting in the Rijksmuseum. But as his gaze rose he could see the object of their worship wasn't an angel descending from the clouds on feathered wings, but a body.

Naked.

Hanging by the neck from a pulley.

When the dispatcher had said there was a body he'd assumed he was going to spend the morning fishing someone out of the canal, a tourist perhaps, unused to the strength and availability of Dutch dope or beer. Or the two combined.

He felt his phone buzzing in his pocket, and checked the screen to see Andreas' home number.

'Andreas, where've you been?'

'Is he not with you?' Saskia's voice. 'I thought you were going with him last night?'

*Shit.*

'Uhh . . . no . . . I didn't in the end. So did he leave early this morning?'

The breeze brought a pungent hit of tar and brine off the canal.

'No, I woke up just now but he hasn't been back, and he's not answering his phone.'

*Where the hell is he?*

'I'm sure it's fine, you know what he's like when he gets stuck into a case –'

'But he's *never* stayed out all night and not let me know before.'

Jaap wondered if there was an implied criticism there, but decided she was sounding too scared for point scoring on an old relationship. And anyway, that was history now.

'Look, I'll try and get hold of him, someone at the station will know where he is. I'll get back to you soon, but in the meantime don't worry, okay?'

Once Saskia hung up Jaap called the station and got them to check the logs, find out where Andreas had gone last night.

*I really should have gone with him*, he thought as he walked the last twenty yards.

His footsteps announced him, the uniforms all turned as one, and he ducked under the police tape, noticing for the first time an old man sitting in the back of the ambulance.

One of the uniforms, Ton Baanders, was smoking by the canal edge. Flicking his cigarette into the water, the orange tip looping downward through the air, he stepped over to meet Jaap.

'Hey, how's it hanging?' he asked in English syruped with an American drawl.

'Funny guy,' said Jaap, turning his head up, wondering how difficult this was going to be. His eyes connected with the body, pale skin basted by the sodium glow of a street light, rotating slowly first one way, then back again like the soles of his feet were dancing to an unheard tune.

Jaap motioned to the old man in the ambulance.

'He the one who found him?' Because it was a *him*, that much was visible even from down at street level.

'Yeah, that's the guy. He was a bit distraught when I arrived but he's calmed down now. He seems to have something against immigrants, he was banging on and on about them earlier.'

'What's he called?'

Ton inspected his notebook as if he'd spent all morning interviewing fifty suspects with complicated names.

'Pieter Leenhouts.'

'Keep him here, I'll want to talk to him. Forensics up there?'

'Yeah, they got here on time for once. Said they'd just set up and wait for the word.'

Jaap turned back to the house where three stone steps, a faded bloom of green algae coating their surface, led to a cream front door. There were five storeys, three tall windows on each floor, and in the triangular facade a modern addition, French windows which echoed the roof's outline.

Ton broke the silence.

'Not sure I'd top myself if I could afford to live in one of these.'

'He didn't do this to himself.'

'No?'

Jaap followed the taut line of the rope from the man's neck, up over the pulley wheel and then as it sloped down, to where it ended up, jammed between the window and frame.

*Is that all that's keeping him up*, he wondered, *or is the rope attached to something else inside?*

'He could have hanged himself. Not sure he could have closed the windows behind him though.'

'See what you mean,' said Ton.

'No sign of Kees?'

'Isn't that him there?' Ton pointed back down Herengracht, past the concerned neighbours gathering at the tape, necks craning. A figure, a phone clasped to his ear, was heading towards them.

Jaap watched as Kees stopped, intent on his phone conversation, his left hand throwing out angry gesticulations.

'When he gets here tell him to come straight up. Unless, of course, he's got more important things to be doing.'

Ton grinned. 'Looks like a domestic to me.'

'Yeah, well, domestics should be kept at home.'

Inside the house a short hallway led to wooden stairs. An antique table stood to his right, on it a cigar box and a pile of letters. Jaap picked them up and looked at the first. The paper was plain, a plastic window revealing a printed name and address.

His stomach clenched.

The name was D. Friedman.

# 2

The piercing ring of the phone jerked Sergeant Tanya van der Mark awake. She pulled herself out of bed, feet against the cold tiled floor, and stumbled towards the source of the racket.

'Hello?'

'Tanya, it's Roelf, did I wake you?'

'Umm, kind of . . .' She shivered, wishing her cheap landlord would replace the chipped chessboard tiles with carpet. Roelf was the station dispatcher, which meant she wasn't getting back to bed any time soon.

'Sorry, I didn't have any choice, I'm kind of short on options here.'

'What about Baltje?'

'He's down in Amsterdam for a few days. Some stupid course about reaching out to the community.'

'So he's living it up in the big city and I'm stuck up here covering for him?'

'Yeah, life's not fair. I tell that to my kids every day, just to prepare them.'

She looked down at her feet; one on a white tile, the other on black. 'Your place sounds like a lot of fun.'

'Has its moments,' he said. 'But anyway, the reason I'm calling is we've got a fire, out by Zeedijk? And –'

'Call the fire service, they're generally better at that kind of thing.'

'– and with all these arson attacks we've had you know Lankhorst said someone needed to attend any suspicious fires.'

'Is it suspicious?'

'It's a fire, isn't it?'

Tanya tried to see the hallway clock, but it was too dark to make out either of the hands.

*It must be before eight*, she thought, *I haven't heard the rubbish collectors yet.*

'Okay,' she yawned, 'I'm on my way.'

She'd been wrestling with a dream, the familiar nightmare, when the phone had roused her. Standing there it took her a moment to separate everything out into the right compartments before returning to the bedroom and dressing quickly, her eyes squeezed to slits against the harsh electric light she'd been forced to turn on.

She drank down a glass of orange juice, just to clear the sour taste from her mouth, and went to the drawer where she kept her ID. She couldn't find it, and it wasn't in her jacket pocket either. She gave up and left the house, looking at the photo she kept on the hall table as she picked up her keys.

Her parents.

*Thirteen years this Thursday*, she thought as she stepped out into the glacial air, a hint of woodsmoke catching her nose. A cat, or maybe a fox, startled by her appearance, jumped on to her neighbour's fence, back paws scrabbling for a few seconds against the wood, before making it over and rushing through the undergrowth with a rustle which quickly fell into silence.

Tanya checked the post box, hoping for her exam results. If she made Inspector she'd be putting in a transfer request right away. But all she had were offers of faster broadband and falafel delivery.

She looked at her bike, frost crusted on the black chassis, but turned to the police car. As she got in she paused and sat behind the wheel for a moment before firing up the motor, unable to completely shake her dream. She still had them after all these years. Their power over her hadn't diminished.

She shook her head quickly, trying to focus. She didn't want the distraction, not now.

*Not ever*, she thought to herself.

Off to her right she could see the first hint of dawn, the intensity of the night sky just easing, and over the next twenty minutes as she drove through the flat landscape she watched the transformation of the world from night to day, the horizon cycling through layers of colour like a kaleidoscope.

Her destination was clear even before the satnav – silent on the long straight road north – barked at her, a pillar of smoke rising up into the apricot-tinged sky. There was no wind at all judging by how straight a line the smoke was forming and it reminded her of a column on an ancient building.

*Should that be Doric or Corinthian?* she wondered as she slowed down, and found a mud track leading towards the source, a plot of land wedged between fields with a low hedge marking out the perimeter. Small potholes in the track were frozen solid, fish eyes looking towards the sky.

Approaching what remained of the house she could see it had probably been one of those typical bungalows built, along with so much in the Netherlands, by a mad eighties architect who had all the visual flair of a blind civil servant. They were dotted around the countryside, cumbersome and out of place, and she'd always disliked them.

*One less ugly building,* she thought to herself as she pulled up, parking in the long shadow of the fire engine cast by the low sun. The fire crew – about seven in all, their hi-vis clothing dazzling in the first rays of light – were winding the hose back on to an enormous reel, each turn forcing another spurt of water out of the nozzle. It looked to Tanya like a gigantic python retching.

The first thing that hit her as she got out was the dark, heavy smell of burning, and as she walked round the front of the fire engine she could feel the heat, radiating like an oven. The building had been levelled, two corner uprights on the far left-hand side all that remained of the structure, forlorn against the sky.

It was still possible to distinguish some things, the kitchen retained its outline, a fridge severely burned – but still standing – and the bath and toilet blackened, cracked, but still recognizable.

The lead fireman saw her and started walking her way. As he reached her he offered his hand and they shook.

'Tanya van der Mark,' she said.

'Paul Lemster.' His face was weathered; a smudge of soot on his left cheek just below the eye reminded Tanya of a soldier. 'As you can see, it was pretty much done by the time we got here.'

Tanya looked around, clocking the lack of a car – impossible to live without one in this remote spot. A vegetable patch sat off to the left, neat rows of winter kale and leeks, pushing free from the tilled earth.

'The owners?'

He pointed to the remains of the building.

'Looks like a couple of adult bodies there, they didn't make it out in time. Give us five minutes to get it cool enough and we can take a look.'

'Any idea what started it? More arson?'

He shrugged.

'In my experience it's usually something minor, bad wiring or something like that. These buildings weren't built to last.'

She walked round the property, just close enough to feel the heat but without it being uncomfortable, and looked out at the surrounding landscape.

Beyond the hedge lay agricultural land, neat field after neat field, dotted with the black-and-white cows from which the region, Friesland, got its name. To the north, past more fields, a lead-grey sea brooded. She felt the bleakness, and wondered if living out here could drive someone mad.

As she followed the path of the hedge something caught her eye, just at the base. She knelt down, her left knee feeling the hardness of the frozen ground, and tried to pull out whatever it was, hidden behind the dark green leaves veined with frost. Pushing her hand further in, feeling the brittle branches scraping her skin, she managed to get hold of something smooth. Twigs broke as she pulled it out.

In her hand was a small doll, which despite the frost looked brand new. She stared at it, the white arms and legs, the crimson dress pristine, and the blonde hair frozen solid.

A distant ship's horn barged in off the North Sea.

*So where*, she thought, turning back to the burnt wreckage, *is the child?*

# 3

'. . . not fair. I gave up my job to come here with you, and now you treat me like this.'

*Like what?* wondered Inspector Kees Terpstra as he regretted answering for the hundredth time. He'd just turned on to Herengracht and could see the house up ahead, catching a glimpse of Jaap Rykel as he disappeared inside, the streak of white hair running from his right temple marking him out. If Marinette hadn't chosen this morning to have a go he wouldn't have been late.

'And you're never here either. Are you seeing someone else?' Marinette's voice rising rapidly, screeching in his ear, metal on metal.

*I wish I was*, he thought, *someone who didn't spend all their time bitching about things.*

'Or have you started again? Is that it?'

*Christ, I could use some of that right now.*

'I've got to go, I'm working a murder investigation here, I haven't got time for –'

'That's part of the problem, you never have time any more. You're always too busy' – the stridence softened – 'and we never get . . . to . . . talk.'

'Okay, okay. We'll talk tonight, when I'm back, but it's going to be late.'

He glanced up the canal to the house, uniforms milling around outside, his own breath blossoming in front of him. 'I have to go.'

He hung up before she could respond.

God, what was up with her? Ever since they'd moved here eight months ago, from the very first moment they'd pulled up outside the apartment – the apartment they'd both chosen – he'd known that something was wrong, could sense a seam of resistance, something hard, inflexible, forming in her. And okay, moving somewhere new was bound to be a bit difficult at first, he knew that, had made allowances, had given her time to try and settle in, hadn't forced her to look for a job straight away.

Despite the fact that on what he earned alone they were struggling.

And didn't she understand he had to put the hard work in now, that to rise up the ranks required a huge amount of time and effort?

He strode towards the house, taking the anger out on the ground, and had to jostle his way through a small crowd of people who'd been attracted to the red-and-white tape – insects writhing on flypaper.

A man, fat, face like pummelled dough, tried to ask him what was going on as he made his way through.

'Police business,' he snapped as he ducked under the tape and into a space free of the crowd. He could hear the man – his voice slightly high, petulant – saying something about there being no need to be so rude, and he felt like turning round and responding but managed to control himself.

Ton Baanders stepped forward.

'Glad you could join us.'

'Fuck off, *Sergeant*.'

Ton laughed.

'Jaap said to go straight up.'

Kees hadn't yet worked with Jaap, but he'd heard the stories. How he'd shot and killed someone and had some kind of breakdown, disappearing for over a year before returning to duty. Some people said he'd got into some weird eastern religion whilst he was away, that was what made him come back, carry on being an Inspector. Kees reckoned he didn't look the type, but who knew?

He headed over to the front door, wondering what it'd be like to shoot someone. Ever since he'd started gun training he'd wanted to know. Maybe he'd ask Jaap.

Just as he reached the first step he spotted someone walking down the canal towards him, texting on her phone.

For a few long seconds Kees thought it was Marinette.

His girlfriend coming to kick up a fuss right in front of everyone.

The embarrassment of that would be crushing, and he was just starting to move, head her off when he saw it wasn't her.

She had the same silvery-blonde hair, and a shapeless coat in the same drab navy blue, and her face was similar, but slightly thinner and the nose a bit more pointed. His heart, which had ramped up on seeing her, was starting to slow now he knew it wasn't Marinette.

As if sensing his gaze she looked up and stopped short, took in the scene quickly; her eyes caught Kees'. Just as he read surprise, and maybe a touch of fear in them, she turned round, and walked fast the way she'd come.

'Hey, stop!'

She heard him, and just went faster.

He was after her, having to push through yet more people at the tape – bovine murmurs of complaint filling the air – and once he was through he saw her disappearing round the corner, into Oude Leliestraat, the narrow street which joined Herengracht with its neighbouring large canal, Singel. She dodged round the bollard which kept traffic out for most of the day, and disappeared from view.

He broke into a run, the rush of cold air making his eyes water, his feet slipping on the bricks as he started off. He made it to the corner, where the dodgy falafel joint was already pumping out grease into the morning air, mingling with the damp, herbal hit from the Coffeeshop four doors down. She was about ten metres ahead now, and running. Pushing harder he gained ground and was close enough to catch a blast of camphor.

*Must be from her coat.*

She was just reaching Singel, heading for the bridge which would take her over into Dam Square, her coat flapping out behind her – thick seaweed in a strong tide – and he was nearly close enough to grab it as she flew across the road, not even looking from side to side.

But as he followed, less than a metre behind, a van – its side an explosion of hippy rainbow print – slid in front of him, and he had to change direction quickly to avoid it.

As he rounded the back, his hand slamming with a

hollow thud against the metal, he could just see her head disappearing on the far side of the bridge when his view of the world flipped ninety degrees.

His head smacked hard against the road and the person on the bike he hadn't seen because of the van, sprawled on top of him.

A screech ripped into his ears.

Everything slowed.

His head turned just in time to see a car tyre halt centimetres from his nose, kicking grit into his eyes.

He could smell rubber.

He tried to kick free, cursing, shouting, disentangling himself from the large woman who was crushing his legs, already screaming at him to look where he was going – and made it to his feet.

But even after he'd half run, half limped over the bridge, winded as he was from the fall, his left ribs aching with each quick inhale, the shock of almost having his head crushed reverberating through his whole body, and his eyes blinking furiously in an effort to clear themselves, he could tell he'd lost her.

# 4

'You called it in?' asked Jaap, eyeing Kees' face, a bruise flooding his right cheek, just under where his hair reached down to.

'Yeah, did it already.' Kees probed his cheekbone. His face was narrow, gaunt almost, and his eyes porcelain blue.

*Shame it wasn't serious enough to get him reassigned*, thought Jaap.

He'd just reached the top floor when he'd heard Kees' shout and had run back down, still reeling from the name on the envelope.

'We need to get on. The paramedic can look at it if you want.'

Kees shook his head.

'I'm fine, let's just get on with it.'

As they stepped back into the house Jaap tried Andreas again but just got voicemail.

*Where the hell is he?* he thought as they started to climb the stairs, wood creaking like a ship's rigging.

His partner's text had said Friedman could be a way in, into the Black Tulips.

*Andreas found a connection between Friedman and the gang*, he thought. *But what is it?*

Two plastic suits were waiting for them as they reached the top. Jaap scanned the room, noticing the winch in the corner holding the end of the rope.

'Give us a few minutes,' he said to the forensics.

They nodded as Jaap walked to the windows and looked out.

The body was facing away from him, feet and calves swollen with blood, looking like they belonged to a fatter man. He could see hair, slicked down on the dead man's head by the dew, the early morning light filling the tiny drops with colour. There was a poem he'd read in Kyoto, something about a world of suffering in each dew drop. He tried to remember it but gave up and turned back to the room.

The rest of the loft was dominated by a cylindrical stove, the flue reaching up past the exposed wooden beams, breaking though the narrowest part of the sloped ceiling.

Placing his hand on the rough, black surface of the stove he felt a remnant of heat. He bent down to look through the rounded glass door on the front. Soot encroached from the edges and a few glowing embers – satsumas packed in the grey ash – were all that remained of the fire.

Jaap stood and turned to the men, knowing he couldn't put it off any longer.

A plane tore a white line in the sky beyond the body.

'Get him down.'

'How? He's at least two metres out, and the rope in that thing over there' – the forensic pointed to the winch – 'is no way long enough to get him down to the ground.'

Jaap stepped back over and eased the French window open with his toe. The rope shifted, causing the body to swing. He heard a gasp from someone down below just as Kees made his way over.

'We could just drop him,' said Kees, peering down at the crowd below. 'There's a fat guy down there who'd break his fall.'

'Let's try my way first,' said Jaap turning to the forensics. 'Get something to lasso his feet, we can pull him in if one of you lets out the rope in the winch.'

The forensics set about his order whilst Jaap and Kees grabbed some latex gloves, and helped bring the body in through the window. Once inside they laid him on to a sheet of plastic and pulled him further into the room, face down.

A cluster of white-tipped pimples crested the body's right buttock.

'Nice ass,' said Kees.

No one laughed.

'On three,' said Jaap, squatting down and grabbing the body's shoulders. But as the body turned, and they laid it down on its back he could see there was something wrong.

Something jammed in the body's mouth.

He crouched down. The smell, despite the cold conditions outside, was already intense. The forensic undid the noose, revealing a neck mottled with wine-purple bruises.

'Looks like he was strangled before being hung up,' said the forensic tracing the lowest edge of markings. 'It's a larger area than the rope would cause.'

'Makes sense I guess,' said Kees. 'Easier to swing a dead body out, less thrashing around.'

*But why hang him outside if he was dead already?* thought

Jaap as he looked closer, the bruises darker on the right side of the neck. He could see the object in the body's mouth was a phone.

'Get it out,' he said as he stood, making room.

The forensic reached forward and tried to pull the phone out but it kept knocking on the inside of the body's teeth. He shifted his weight and used both hands to prise apart the jaws. They cracked and Jaap winced.

'Careful.'

The forensic just grunted and handed it to him. It was a cheap clamshell and as he flipped it open the screen lit up. On it was a freephone 0900 number which had yet to be dialled.

He passed it to Kees and pulled out his own phone.

'Give me the number.'

Jaap punched it in as Kees read it out, hit the call button and put it on speaker.

*. . . at the third stroke the time will be o-eight hundred hours and fifty-three minutes . . .*

Jaap felt something tighten in his throat.

'What else is on the phone?' he asked.

Kees spent a few moments exploring.

'No text messages, only three numbers in the address book, and the same in the recent call lists,' he said still looking at the screen, the light shining on his face, making him look pale, sick.

'Names?'

'No, just numbers.'

'Really?'

Kees nodded and Jaap looked down at the body again, thinking about Andreas' text.

*Looks like he's right about Friedman,* he thought.

'They're probably disposables, but check with the phone companies anyway,' he said to Kees.

'I'll get someone on it.'

'How about you do it?'

Kees looked at him before moving over to the window. Jaap could hear his finger hitting the plastic keys as he started dialling.

*I wish Andreas was here instead,* thought Jaap.

His own phone started to buzz; he saw the station's number.

*Finally he decides to call me.*

'Andreas, where the hell have you been?'

'Jaap, it's Elsie, I've got Smit on the other line for you, hold on.'

Jaap groaned. The last thing he needed was a conversation with Henk Smit, his boss. He'd been running the station ever since Jaap got promoted to Homicide, and was famous for driving people hard, mainly so he could advance his own career. Behind his back most of his staff referred to him simply as the eel, slippery and with sharp teeth. And not without irony, given his size.

'Rykel,' came Smit's voice after a few moments. 'I have some, uh, bad news for you. Get into the station now.'

Jaap's heart detonated in his chest.

'What's going on?'

Kees and the forensics looked at him all at once.

'Inspector Kees Terpstra can take over, just get back here now.'

Jaap stepped away towards the stairs, checking that Kees was out of earshot, lowering his voice, 'He's not experienced enough, this isn't straightforward. Is this about Andreas?'

'It's . . . uhmmm . . . yeah, it is.'

Jaap felt the room start to sink and twist out of shape, as if he'd just stepped into a Dalí painting. A bird flapped past the window, flickering a shadow into the room.

'And?'

'He's been shot.'

# 5

Tanya was standing in what she figured had been the living room.

The fireman, crouched down next to her sifting through the ash, was humming a tune she half recognized.

'So what caused it?' she asked.

'Not faulty wiring,' came the reply, his voice a rough whisper.

He picked up a few small fragments of metal, and handed one to her, still warm to the touch.

'These are bits of a canister, like the ones you buy petrol in.'

Tanya looked at them.

'Are you sure? I mean, these could be anything, couldn't they?'

The fireman shook his head.

'I found some more over in that corner as well. Accidental fires always start in one place, but if you're trying to burn something down you'll set several ignition spots, gives it a better chance of taking off before anyone can stop it.'

Tanya handed the metal back to him.

'Is this how the other fires have been started, with those same cans?'

He tossed it back, the metal disappearing into the ash with a small puff.

'Mostly, but to be honest this is how they're always done. Not original thinkers, arsonists.'

They turned to the bodies, blackened flesh like jerky, smudged bones poking through.

'And there's no sign of a child?'

'Not that I've found, and I've been through it thoroughly.'

'Maybe they'd get burnt up completely?'

'No,' he pointed to the nearer of the two bodies. 'See how much of them is left, even having been right in the middle of the blaze?'

He started brushing away more ash, moving up the shin towards the knee. Tanya opened her mouth to say something but caught a flake in her throat, making her cough.

*I hope that wasn't from one of the bodies*, she thought.

Too grim to even consider, but she couldn't shift the idea. She went back to her car, feeling her breathing quicken, which only made it worse. There was a bottle of water she'd left there a few days ago and eventually her fingers touched the cold plastic, jammed under the front passenger seat. She pulled it out, gulping down the last few mouthfuls, the water tasting flat, stale.

She'd felt something else down there as well and put her hand back in to retrieve it. Her ID card, the police logo on the back.

But when she flipped it over the picture wasn't her.

It had her name, but the image was of a woman in bondage gear, crudely cut out and plastered on top of her own. For a moment she was too stunned to think who could have done it. Then it came.

*Inspector Wim Bloem*, she thought, *what a bastard.*

They'd never got on, and despite working in the same department for several years she'd for the most part managed to keep out of his way. As one of the three Inspectors he chose his underlings, and Tanya wasn't one of them. Unless there was a particularly shitty job he needed doing.

And they had occasional verbal sparring contests, name calling, snide comments about her red hair. But just recently the run-ins had become more frequent, the sarcasm more cutting.

*He must feel threatened by me taking the Inspector exams.*

She tried to peel off the image but it was held in place with something industrial strength.

*And how did he get into my car?*

Tanya gave up. She wasn't going to even think about it now and looked over again at the remains of the house. Something was wrong with all of this. They should have been able to make it out of a single-storey building, so what stopped them?

*And what about the car*, she thought, *where is it?*

She walked back to the humming fireman who had now completely exposed the first body and was working on the second.

'Something to show you.' He gestured to the first body.

It was lying on its back, arms wedged underneath.

*That's not good.*

Pulling on some gloves she moved forward and squatted down, fighting the revulsion growing in her, making her head swirl. She reached her hand out and then hesitated, before forcing herself to touch the charred flesh. It was still warm, and for a second she had the feeling the body was still alive.

It was light, and she lifted it slightly, her hand underneath the collarbone, trying to see what had held the arms beneath the body's back.

'They must have been tied up,' she said. 'But I can't see anything.'

'Same with this one here.'

*Maybe forensics will find something,* she thought. But she didn't hold out much hope.

Letting the skeleton-body roll back – it settled down into the ash as if it belonged there, a bird in its nest – she stood up, wanting to move away.

It was murder. She had to call it in.

As she waited to be put through to the station chief, she remembered that in less than two months he was headed south, to take control of a much larger district in Maastricht.

At which point it was likely Bloem would take over from him.

*At which point,* she thought, just as a voice came on the line, *my life will become hell.*

'What have you got?'

'Murder, two adults, and there might be a missing child,' said Tanya

'Fantastic. Let me see who's free.'

She heard him put down the phone and speak to someone in the office.

'Okay, sit tight,' he said. 'Bloem's on his way.'

# 6

'I'll call you when we get something, but to be honest, with that description you gave I wouldn't hold my breath.'

Kees hung up on central dispatch.

*Amateurs*, he thought as he made his way to the ambulance where the old man was being treated for shock. He'd got the call from Smit asking him to take over the case, at least temporarily, just as Jaap had left. Kees had agreed.

*This is my chance*, he thought.

Ton was standing by the ambulance door, stopping any of the press who'd started rolling up getting to their only witness.

'What have you got on him?' said Kees.

'Pieter Leenhouts, works as the verger at the Noorderkerk –'

'That's the one on Prinsengracht, shaped like a cross?'

'Your local knowledge's improving,' said Ton as his radio shot out white noise. He turned it down.

'Any sign of the pathologist?' asked Kees.

Ton shook his head.

'Call them again, I'm getting sick of waiting.'

A paramedic was having a furtive cigarette on the far side of the ambulance, the slow tendril of smoke giving him away. Kees stepped round to ask him if the old man was ready to answer some questions.

'I think so.' He paused to blow smoke out over his shoulder. 'But he's a bit . . .' He circled his ear lazily with his cigarette hand.

'From the shock?'

The paramedic shrugged.

'Probably like that to begin with.'

Kees clambered into the back of the ambulance, where Pieter Leenhouts was sitting up on a stretcher, inspecting his fingernails, head cocked like a bird. He had a thin face, round-framed glasses with bottle-end lenses, and wispy white hair which appeared to be moving even though the air was static. His teeth, on view from parted lips, required some drastic dental work, a craggy range of chiaroscuro.

He looked up, squinted at Kees and then went on with the inspection.

'I'm Inspector Terpstra, and I'm in charge of this case.' *That sounds good*, he thought. 'You okay to answer a couple of questions now?'

'I was wondering when someone would want to talk to me.'

'Well, you've had a shock, and we didn't want to rush you –'

The old man snorted like a horse.

'No need to treat me like I'm senile.'

'Why don't you tell me what happened,' said Kees sitting down on the side bench, pushing a defibrillator tentacle away from him.

Pieter leant back slightly, assured that he was now being taken seriously. Antiseptic thickened the air.

'I come along here every morning, I start early, you see, there's so much of *his* work to be done.'

Kees groaned inside.

'I'm sure there is. So you saw the body and called us.'

Pieter finished looking at the fingernails on his left hand and transferred his attention to the right.

'The seagull.'

'What?' said Kees, thinking the paramedic was probably right.

'The seagull. It was right over there' – he pointed his finger – 'and it flew up when it heard me, my bicycle can squeak a bit you see. And that's when I saw it. At first I thought it was one of those . . . dummies. Like the ones they sell over in De Wallen.'

'A sex toy.'

Pieter shuddered.

'It's disgusting, it really is, we're letting the country turn into a cesspit, all this . . .' He waved his hand around and then half whispered the word, '. . . *sex*.'

Kees thought about the last time he and Marinette had tried to go through the motions, well over a month ago. He shook his head, trying to dislodge the memory. Which only brought to mind her earlier accusation.

*How did she know?*

'It's their fault,' said Pieter, breaking into his thoughts.

'Who?' asked Kees.

'The immigrants. They're pouring in off the boats and trains every day.' He threw Kees a look as if he personally spent time down at the docks, welcoming each and every one of them. 'They're the ones with these disgusting perversions.'

Kees could see Pieter was getting worked up.

*So much for the brotherhood of man.*

'I know. But what made you decide to call it in?' said Kees.

'I looked at it again and it seemed so . . . real.'

Kees glanced towards the canal where a barge – a glass-topped tourist vessel devoid of tourists – floated by.

'And you didn't see anyone else in the house, anyone leave, or go in?'

'No, and I've been here the whole time.'

Out of the corner of his eye he noticed Ton hovering.

'Pathologist's here,' said Ton when Kees looked at him.

'I think that's it,' Kees said, turning back to Pieter. 'One of my colleagues took your address and phone number, didn't they?'

Pieter nodded, his hands now limp in his lap.

'So I can get on now?' he asked.

'Absolutely.' Kees got out of the ambulance. 'And don't talk to any journalists,' he said over his shoulder before turning to Ton.

'Where is he?'

'*She's* over there.' Ton pointed to the front door, where a figure was just disappearing inside. 'She really laid into Gerard.'

Gerard, two years off retirement, had never made it above the lowest grade in the eighteen years he'd been on the force. Some people said it was because he really loved working the street and didn't want to get promoted to an office, that his inertia was actually a noble thing.

Kees reckoned he just wasn't that bright.

'What did he do?'

'Didn't believe that she was the pathologist, said that women couldn't even become pathologists.'

Kees laughed and Ton joined in, several people in the crowd looking round at them, as if annoyed at their levity, inappropriate at a murder scene. Kees picked one out – the fat man from before – and gave him the stare until he looked away, cowed.

*Fucking fat people*, he thought as he walked to the front door, *should keep their disapproval to themselves.*

Inside he stopped off in the second-floor bathroom, locking it behind him. He'd been rattled that Marinette had accused him of starting again. If she could see it, what about anyone else?

As he pulled the small bag out, scooped a fingernail and snorted it in one go, he figured he'd just have to take the risk.

A filament of scent – floral, musky – led Kees up the stairs, giving a new rhythm to his pulse, and his boots, leather soles held in place by flat-head nails, scraped the wooden steps.

The curved glass door of the stove gave him his first glimpse of her as it came into view at the top of the stairs. She'd squatted down by the body, her back to him, widened and distorted by the reflection.

The forensics were packing up, the noise of their movement crackling in the air like radio static. He stood and watched as she snapped on some gloves and reached for the victim's face, and the way she moved her fingers made him think of a dusty white tarantula.

'Are you just going to stand there, Inspector?' she asked without stopping her exploration, her fingers probing the neck.

'I didn't want to get in the way,' he said, advancing. 'And how –'

'Did I know you were an Inspector? Well' – she stood up and turned to him in one movement, peeling off her gloves at the same time – 'I figured it was time one turned up.'

The connoisseur in Kees ran a quick once over.

*Not bad, not bad at all.*

'That's funny, because here I was thinking that I'd been waiting for you.'

She had a husky's eyes, he read a challenge in them, and something else. Her face was lean, like her body, and her hair, pulled into a tight ponytail, shone like blonde lacquer.

'How strange,' she said as she tossed her gloves into one of the plastic bags. 'I'm Carice Stultjens.'

'Kees Terpstra.'

Her hand was warm, and there was a soft residue of powder from the glove's inside.

'So, you working undercover?'

'What do you mean?'

'The hair, not exactly the normal police cut.'

Marinette had been hinting recently he did something about it. Which had made him even less likely to do so.

'My hairdresser died, and I haven't found another one I trust,' he said.

She gave him a look, her head tilted to one side. Kees read that as a positive.

'How come we've not met before?' he asked.

She shrugged and then stepped back to the body. He joined her and looked down. The face seemed to have more colour than when he'd first seen it, the mouth was

43

still gaping where the forensic had prised it open earlier.

'I'm guessing he wasn't like this when you pulled him in?'

'How'd you mean?'

'Looks like he died yawning.'

'We had to get a phone out of his mouth,' he said. She looked at him but didn't ask.

'How soon can you get the autopsy done?'

Kees couldn't see her doing it, cutting open corpses, viscera up to her elbows, the sheer foulness of the job. It all seemed wrong, only ugly middle-aged men did autopsies, not highly attractive women like this. He caught another wave of her perfume and despite the situation, something stirred inside him.

'We've got a lot on, but I'll try for first thing tomorrow. Looks fairly simple though, I don't think there can be much doubt as to cause of death.'

She started towards the stairs. Kees found himself following her.

'Any chance of today?'

'You Inspectors are all the same, you always want it now.'

'Hey, we have needs.'

She threw him a fed-up look over her shoulder, but he didn't buy it and they carried on down the stairs.

'I guess you should give me your phone number,' he said as they made it out the front door like a famous couple leaving their own home, police holding back fans and paparazzi on either side.

'That depends,' she said, turning to him with a half-smile. He noticed her front teeth were slightly squint, one lapped over the other.

Somehow that made him like her even more.

'Depends on what?' he asked.

She reached out and brushed something off his sleeve.

'It depends, Inspector, on what you'd do with it.'

# 7

'We're here.'

Pulling up to a stop, gravel crunching under one of the tyres, the driver turned off the engine and waited. Silence filled the car's interior. Jaap looked out at the trees lining both sides of the road, barren branches like hands clawing the sky.

This was Amsterdamse Bos, a wooded area south of the city covering over a thousand hectares, with trees planted by twenty thousand citizens in the 1930s, a government attempt to raise employment after the knock-on effects of the Wall Street crash reached the Netherlands. By day it was frequented by ordinary people, walkers, dog lovers, young families.

But at night the perverts, the drug addicts and weirdos roamed.

His throat was Sahara-dry, a leg – *left, right?*, he wasn't sure – had started to shake, and his stomach felt like he'd just swallowed a litre of live frogs, their slippery bodies writhing in a churning mass, desperately trying to escape his searing gastric juices.

He tried to calm himself, slow his breathing down,

count, anything to bring his body back under control. But nothing seemed to be working.

The door, where his right hand had been gripping the handle, was opened with a soft click by the uniformed officer who'd stepped forward as the car drew to a halt, and the Arctic air rushed in, ravaging his exposed face, hands and ears.

And that helped, made it easier to force himself out of the cruiser which had brought him here, to this patch of land deep in the forest.

Then he was standing, his leg – it was definitely the left, feeling like it had its own private earthquake, ten on the Richter scale – wobbled even more, and he had to steady himself with his hand on the raw metal of the car's roof, before moving off towards the three men a few metres away.

They were looking down, away from him, like they were comparing shoes, though they must have heard his arrival in the stillness of this deserted spot.

His feet ground the frosty grass by the side of the verge, and they took that as their cue to turn and acknowledge his presence. The shorter of the three, and the only one not in uniform, stepped forward and held out his hand.

When Jaap took it in his own it was like it wasn't there, almost as cold as the surrounding air, a slight roughness the only clue that he was touching anything at all. The man's beard was starting to frost like the grass, his shoulders warming his ears.

'Inspector Rykel?'

He spoke in a voice which was quiet, soft, but still held some authority, the same voice Jaap would use – *did use* – when breaking the bad news to the wife, or husband, or indeed any relation of a murder victim, anyone unlucky enough to open the door to a sombre-faced police officer.

This was slightly different of course, Andreas Hansen was not a relative at all, but he almost felt like one. They'd been working together for over nine years. Other Inspectors joked that they were like a married couple, only without the squabbling.

No longer.

Someone had decided to fire what looked like a single shot to the back of the head, creating a Pollockesque spray on the concrete incline. None of the dark drops had escaped the frost, each was coated with the same dusting of what looked like powdered glass, reflecting the pale sun which was climbing in the sky, shortening all their shadows.

'When was he found?'

His own voice sounded strange to him, muted slightly, as if his throat was full of cotton wool.

'A driver, first thing this morning.'

*Maybe*, the hope rushed into his head, *it's not Andreas at all.*

The body was lying face down, arms at its sides like it was on a skeleton bob. The clothes looked familiar, the leather jacket like the one Andreas wore, and the blond hair, slightly too long, clumped together by blood. He wanted to say that this wasn't Andreas, sure it looked like him, but it was someone else.

But as if reading his mind the Inspector handed him Andreas' wallet and ID, the face still whole.

Jaap could hear his teacher in Kyoto, Yuzuki Roshi, saying life and death were the same thing. At the time he'd thought he'd understood. Or had convinced himself he had.

Now he knew he'd not understood at all.

'What . . . what was he doing here?'

The short officer shuffled nervously with one of his feet.

'Actually, we were hoping you might be able to tell us.'

Jaap looked down at the body again.

*Did the Black Tulips bring him out here? Or was he here following one of them and got caught?* he wondered as another thought broke through.

*God, I'm going to have to tell Saskia.*

He started back towards the cruiser, trying not to think of what he had to do next. But as he reached out his hand to open the car door another thought hit him.

The break-in.

Andreas' text.

What Andreas had discovered was dangerous to someone, most likely the Black Tulips.

So they'd killed him.

But what if they'd checked Andreas' phone and saw the text? He shuddered and thought about what that meant. It could be that the Black Tulips had found out that Andreas was on to Friedman, and killed them both.

But if they'd seen Andreas' text then they'd also know that he knew . . .

*They didn't steal anything*, he thought as he lowered himself into the car and nodded at the driver, *because they came to kill me too.*

49

# 8

'Look, we've just finished, and if there was a child, or children, or whatever, we would have found them.'

Tanya looked at the man, his thin face, thin body, a shiny round of pink crowning his grey hair, and knew that he didn't really care. Didn't care that there might have been a child in there, didn't care about the pain or the fear or the despair.

To him and his two colleagues the bodies were just another prop, a part of their job, something to be analysed, bagged up, then forgotten about. She'd got the forensics to check after the firemen had left, she didn't want to leave anything to chance. And Bloem would be here soon; any authority she had now would disappear.

'I still think we need to check,' she said and could see the thoughts in his head, as if his eyes were a direct tunnel straight to his brain – *Better humour her, don't want a hysterical woman running around* – before he nodded and walked over to his two colleagues, who'd been listening in. Tanya figured they were rolling eyes at each other.

A wind had started, coming in off the sea to the north, lifting flecks of ash into the air like tiny feathers.

As more ash blew and Tanya turned away she had a

thought. There was a house, and a petrol station, about a kilometre back along Zeedijk, which she'd passed earlier.

She glanced over, at the forensics back at work, and made a decision. It would take them at least another half-hour to go over everything again, more than enough time. And anyway, what was she going to do, stand here just to make frostbite a certainty? And was she going to confront Bloem when he arrived about her ID card? She knew it was him but of course had no proof.

He'd already called and told her not to do anything until he got there.

*Well, tough.*

In the car she turned on the radio, the landscape so flat and desolate any distraction, even the inane chatter of the local radio, would be a comfort.

'. . . was in fact a Homicide Inspector.' She reached for the dial and cranked the radio up. 'The police have so far neither officially confirmed nor denied this although we are expecting a statement shortly. Back to you in the studio.'

'Thank you, Nicolotte, we'll rejoin you for the official statement, but in the meantime let's have some more music.'

*What was that about a Homicide Inspector?* she wondered as she clicked the radio off. She thought about calling the station, but then told herself to concentrate on her own job.

By the time she pulled off the main road, parked and got out of the car the wind had increased, slamming in off the sea, grabbing the car door from her hand before she had a chance to close it herself.

*Who'd want to live out here?* she thought as she pressed the doorbell, and stood back waiting for someone to answer, pulling the collar of her coat closer round her throat. The door swung in, opened by a young woman with short blond hair and hyperthyroid eyes. From behind the woman Tanya could hear the shrieks and screams of children at play.

*She's about my age*, thought Tanya. *Are those her kids?*

She was called Geertje, she said, and she lived here with her husband and three children. She didn't know the neighbours that well, an old couple called Van Delft, and she was shocked that they were dead. But she was adamant they didn't have a child. Tanya thanked her, got back in her car and headed to the petrol station.

*If they didn't have children*, she thought as she drove, *then why have a brand-new doll? Maybe it was for a grandchild, when they visited?*

Whoever had set light to the house would have had to come past the petrol station; the western approach was nothing more than a dirt track which led to bleak sands, and the North Sea. There was a chance someone there had seen something.

A slim chance, but then her job was built on slim chances.

The station stood alone in the landscape, and she felt the desolation again.

*If I've passed I could transfer out of here*, she thought as she hit the indicator.

Turning into the forecourt she was checking for cameras, and yes, there were four. Judging by their angle and elevation at least three of them might just catch some of the road, enough to tell if a car passed sometime early in the morning. If she was really lucky they might even have had to fill up.

Inside the shop a young man, teenager really – with hair his parents would consider way too long and the eyes of a stoner – sat flicking through a magazine dedicated to car tyres. He looked up as Tanya approached.

'Which number?'

'I didn't get any petrol, I'm with the police, I wanted to ask you some questions.'

He swallowed, and tried to look cool.

'This place is open twenty-four hours right?'

'No, we like close at ten? Hardly anyone passes this way after about nine-thirty, kind of dead really. But the guy who runs it wants us to be open, just, like, in case?'

His tone of voice showed that he didn't agree with that particular business decision.

'What about the CCTV, I notice you've got cameras outside?'

'They're on' – he scratched his head – 'all of the time. Dunno why though, I don't think we've ever been robbed.'

*It's hardly worth doing*, she tried to tell herself even as the words came out of her mouth.

'I need to see the CCTV tapes.'

'Errr . . . I'm not sure how to do that.' His voice tight-roped between the treble and bass of boy and manhood, his eyes blinking furiously.

'Maybe your boss?' she prompted.

'Yeah, right. Yeah, he'll know.' He picked up the phone.

'Yeah, it's Harri, there's like this policewoman here, she wants to see the CCTV tapes?'

He listened, brows furrowed in concentration, slowly

scratching a patch of red skin just by his right ear before holding the phone out to her, which she took, catching a wave of his damp odour as she did so.

'Who is this?'

'I'm Gerrit Cloet, I run the petrol station. Who are you?'

'Sergeant van der Mark' – she could feel Harri's eyes on her – 'and I need access to your CCTV tapes.'

'What's this about?'

'There was a fire on Zeedijk, I need to check if any cars passed late last night or early this morning.'

There was a pause; she could hear sounds in the background, gunshots, theme music.

'Okay, put Harri back on and I'll talk him through how to set it up.'

Five minutes later she was sitting in the cramped back office, peering at a tiny black-and-white monitor. Harri had loitered once he'd found the tape in the safe and set it up to play, but she couldn't bear the smell in such an enclosed space, and asked him if he shouldn't be watching the front of the shop?

The tape started, according to the time stamp at the bottom right, at 18.38. She figured that whoever started the fire would have waited until the roads were clearer, and pressed the fast forward button. Lines streaked horizontally across the screen, and the scene shifted between the five camera angles – the fifth was in the shop itself – about one a second. By the time she'd got to midnight she slowed the tape down and started watching.

Nothing. No movement, no cars. Nothing.

Then something, a fox. Then nothing.

*This could take hours*, she thought.

She should really get this back to the station and have someone else sit there looking through it. She flicked it forward in quick blasts, until her eyes were going fuzzy and her head began to ache.

Harri's voice startled her.

'Would you like something? Coffee?'

The thought of coffee made her realize how hungry she was. Coffee on an empty stomach was not something she was willing to do but when she turned to look at him there was a kind of hope mixed with embarrassment in his eyes.

'Yeah, that would be great. And if you've got something like a sandwich?'

Three minutes later he was back with a rye and Gouda wrapped in plastic and a cup of something which had all the appeal of dilute engine oil.

'Anything else, I'll just be out there,' he said before closing the door again.

She didn't know exactly what wild teenage imaginings were running through his mind, but it was clear what the general topic of them was.

*Why are men always like that?* she asked herself.

As if on cue her phone rang. She expected it to be Inspector Bloem asking where she was, but it was Wilhelm. Wilhelm who just didn't get that their relationship was over. It was four months since she'd chucked him out, and in that time she'd still not worked out exactly why she'd done it.

Things had been going well, they'd been living together for just coming up to a year, and he'd certainly not changed, or let her down, or cheated on her . . . But it was always the same, she reached a point where she just couldn't see the point of carrying on. Whilst training at the academy she'd had three relationships.

All three had ended the same way.

And all three men had taken it badly.

She let it ring and turned her attention back to the screen, wrestled with the sandwich wrapper and started eating, washing each bite of the impossibly dry sandwich down with coffee.

Time stretched out, she heard a customer come and go, Harri asked her a few more times if she needed anything but he was disappointed each time and had now given up, and she was on the verge of giving up herself, packing it in and taking it all down to the station. She glanced down at her watch; she needed to get back to the scene, Bloem would be arriving any time now, and she reached forward to eject the tape.

And then, when her eyes flicked back to the screen, there was a flash of something on camera one.

She reached for the controls and rewound, going too far and having to wait a few moments. There it was, a car, the time showing as 02.19, heading in the right direction. It was going slowly. The head pointed towards the petrol station. She paused the tape and stared at the screen. She could hear Harri talking to a customer behind the door. Coffee and rye curdled in her stomach.

The image was black-and-white, but she could see the driver was wearing a mask.

There was a zip where the mouth should have been.

# 9

On the way back, just as they were pulling on to the main road, Jaap ordered the driver to stop, shoved the door open and stumbled out just in time to throw up on the verge. Traffic rushed behind him, exhaust saturating the air, and he wondered what he was going to do now. He could hardly believe it, could hardly believe that Andreas was dead, murdered.

*But he was an Inspector*, Jaap's mind kept repeating, *he shouldn't have been killed.*

Then he thought of the hexagram, Lake and Thunder, and shivered.

Climbing back into the cruiser and pulling the door shut he nodded to the driver that he was okay, acid coating his mouth, his stomach loose. They nosed back into the stream of traffic and Jaap's thoughts turned to what he had to do next.

He had to tell Saskia what had happened.

He couldn't leave it to anyone else, and he couldn't do it over the phone.

And he needed to find out what it was Andreas had discovered on Friedman.

By the time they made it back into Amsterdam, his

57

throat raw from the excoriating bile, he felt exhausted, drained, lost, last night's lack of sleep weighing him down. He forced himself to pull out his phone and dial Kees.

'I'm just arriving back at the station, where are you?'

'I'm out, top end of Herengracht.'

The car in front braked suddenly, lights flaring like devil eyes, and his driver responded, flinging Jaap forward until his seat belt jammed.

'I've got to talk to Smit,' said Jaap after he'd sat back, 'after that you'll have to take me through what you've got.'

'I may need a little longer –'

'Just come back, you've got uniforms out there, right?'

'Yeah . . .' There was a pause, like Kees was taking a drag on a cigarette. '. . . yeah, I have. Okay, I'm heading back.' His tone said he wasn't happy.

The driver dropped him off right in front of the station, and he went straight to Andreas' desk, three away from his own. In stark contrast to the other Inspectors in the department whose desks weren't even visible for the piles of old case notes, mug shots, half-empty coffee cups and festering boxes from the Indonesian takeaway just over the street, Andreas had liked to keep things neat. One orderly pile of papers and a laptop.

Jaap was about to open it up when he heard Smit's voice from the corridor outside, talking to De Waart.

Jaap and De Waart had joined at the same time, and been paired together right from the start, cutting their teeth on minor cases. There'd been no need for rivalry, but De Waart was cocky and had spent each case they worked on together trying to undermine Jaap, jostling for position. Until the case where De Waart, trying to make sure it was his collar, messed up and let the killer escape abroad. Jaap never revealed what happened.

But after they'd both been publicly bollocked by Smit he wished he had.

They no longer worked together.

Jaap quickly darted away from Andreas' desk back to his own. He'd been thinking on the journey back, he wanted to take Andreas' case, though he knew that would never be allowed. But so far only he knew that his new case was linked and . . .

Something moved in the corner of Jaap's vision and he turned to see Smit's considerable girth easing through the doorway. Smit looked around before locating Jaap and heading over, resting a buttock on the corner of Jaap's desk. Jaap feared it wasn't going to hold.

'Terrible thing this.' He shook his head. 'I still can't believe he's gone.'

The image of Andreas, face down in the ditch, flared up, as it had been on and off since earlier, each repetition just as vivid, HD quality.

'There are some things I need to talk to you about, to do with Andreas,' continued Smit before peering down his nose at his watch. 'I've got to brief city hall in forty minutes, but when I'm back later I think you and I should have a chat.'

He hesitated for a moment and put a hand on Jaap's shoulder, giving it a squeeze.

'Okay?'

'Yeah,' replied Jaap, unsure why the physical gesture from his boss unsettled him so much. 'What time?'

'I'll get Elsie to let you know when I'm back,' said Smit, hefting himself off the desk, one of the metal legs creaking. 'It all depends on how much of a grilling I get, a dead policeman is not going to make them happy. And I'll get someone to tell Saskia.'

'No, I'll do it.'

Smit looked at him for a moment then nodded.

'If you're up to it, it's probably best coming from you.'

Once Smit left Jaap stood up, wanting to get to Andreas' laptop, but as he stepped towards the desk he saw Kees walking in. Jaap sat down again and Kees dragged a chair with him, the legs screeching on the floor. His bruise had developed further.

'Okay, so what have we got? ID? Word from the phone companies?' asked Jaap.

Kees took him through what he knew; the victim was Dirk Friedman, a diamond merchant with a business on Oude Nieuwstraat.

'Did you go there?'

'I interviewed the main staff, wasn't much of interest. They all thought he was great, couldn't believe it was him, you know, the usual.'

'Nothing of interest?'

'Well, there was one thing. Carolien van Zandt, she's the general manager, mentioned that she'd left something in the office on Thursday last week and when she'd gone back to pick it up she heard Dirk Friedman arguing with this guy called Rint Korssen? Apparently he owns a stake in the business, so he doesn't work there day to day but kind of drops in now and then.'

'This woman, Van Zandt, did she say what they were arguing about?'

'She claimed not to have been able to make it out.'

'And you checked up on this guy, Korssen, was it?'

'He's in Rotterdam, said he'd be back on the first train tomorrow morning.'

'Anything else?'

'Not really, I checked Friedman's diary, just to see. The last entry was on Sunday morning, he had a meeting at eleven a.m. with some charity called Vrijheid Nu, and I've lined up his lawyer to make an official ID, once the morgue gives clearance.'

'The charity was open on a Sunday?'

'I called them, the guy who he was meeting is called Hans Grimberg, he'd gone in specially to meet Friedman.'

'What does the charity do?'

'Something to do with abused children.'

'We'll need to talk to Grimberg, he might have been the last person to see him. And the phones?'

'The numbers are all pay as you go, no way to trace who bought them.'

'Did you get the logs?'

'They said they'll fax them over.' He glanced at his watch. 'I doubt they'll be here yet.'

'What about the house?'

'Nothing much there. The door wasn't forced though so he knew the killer.'

Jaap suddenly thought of his houseboat, the door broken – he hoped the officer had got a locksmith in to fix it up by now.

'Okay, chase the phone company, I've got some calls to

make, and get as much info as you can on the company Friedman owns, we'll go there but I want to be prepared.'

Kees got up to leave, then paused a second as if making up his mind about something.

'Listen, I'm really sorry about Andreas, I know you two were . . . close . . .' He paused before continuing. '. . . but I've got it under control here, so if you want to . . . um . . . just take some time, that's cool?'

Despite everything that had happened, despite all the fear and revulsion and anger, Jaap's instincts told him he was being worked. The studied calm of Kees' voice was proof enough that he was really hoping to be in charge of this.

'Thanks, let's see later. Chase for those logs, I'd like to see them when I get back.'

Jaap watched Kees leave. He'd transferred in from somewhere south about eight months previously, and it was clear he wanted to go places. And, to Jaap, it looked like he didn't care how he got there. He hadn't worked with Kees before, but a few of his colleagues who had didn't much enjoy the experience.

*I hope*, he thought as he started back towards Andreas' laptop, *he's not going to be difficult.*

A voice called his name from behind him.

*What now?*

Jaap turned to see the uniform from earlier. He told Jaap he'd got the door replaced and the locksmith had transferred the old lock over – the lock itself hadn't been damaged, just the door and frame. Jaap thanked him and pocketed the key.

*Lucky I didn't go home last night*, he thought as he sat down and opened up the laptop, wondering what linked Friedman to the Black Tulips. Did they do business together and they were afraid Friedman, under pressure from the police, would talk?

He and Andreas had evidence that the Black Tulips smuggled guns, drugs and women for the sex trade, maybe they ran a sideline in conflict diamonds too. Or Friedman's business was a front, a way to launder some of their big profits into clean money.

The screen came on and asked for a password. Jaap knew it, punched it in, and started looking for recent files on the desktop, hoping Andreas had left something here which would help.

He spent a few minutes searching, a sick feeling pooling in his stomach as time and again he came up with nothing. There was nothing on the laptop, no old case files, no emails, nothing.

It had been wiped.

# 10

'Just there,' said Tanya, pointing to the screen.

The screen paused and both of them, the tech guy and Lankhorst, leant forward. They were in Lankhorst's office, a small room just off the main open-plan section. It smelt of bleach.

They studied the image in silence for a few moments.

'It's not much to go on really, unless we can get the plates,' said Lankhorst.

'No, but the very fact that he was there, heading in the right direction, at that time in the morning, has to count for something? And what kind of a freak drives around in a mask like that anyway?' said Tanya.

He looked back at the screen. 'That's the only way to get there, isn't it?'

'The only other way would be by boat.'

'Is there any way to get this magnified a bit?' Lankhorst asked.

'This isn't the movies,' said the tech guy. 'You can't just zoom in and get high-res images, those cameras just aren't set up for it.'

He tapped a few keys, moved frames backward and forward until he settled on one and enlarged the image. But they couldn't really make out the plates, a smudge of letters and numbers. They spent a few minutes trying to work out the various combinations it could be before Tanya noticed something on the screen.

'What's that on his neck?'

'A shadow?'

She leant in.

'No, it's more like . . .'

The heating clicked on, a radiator responding with a series of bangs, Morse code.

'. . . it's like a birthmark,' Lankhorst finished, still peering intently.

Tanya moved closer to the screen.

'It's not a birthmark, it's too . . .'

'So what is it?'

'A tattoo,' she said still staring at the screen. 'It's a tattoo, shaped like a spider.'

'Okay, check it out, then let's meet in twenty minutes.'

Tanya made her way to her desk, pulling up the *Herkenningsdienstsysteem*, the national database that had a record of everyone who had ever been arrested. Which sounded great until you realized that all the info had been inputted in such a haphazard manner that finding people was far harder than it should have been.

She filtered for tattoos on the neck in distinguishing features as a first shot, result 127. Way too many to go through. She tried to narrow it down to Leeuwarden, which returned zero hits. By the time she had to meet Lankhorst she'd managed to get a list of twenty-five. She printed off their records and took the papers back to Lankhorst's office, where he was waiting.

A ceiling light flickered.

'So, let's start. What do you think happened?'

'Given that nobody was tied up and left to burn at any of the other fires,' said Tanya as she sat down opposite him, 'I think we're safe to assume that it's not the same people, unless they were doing trial runs.'

'I think it's unlikely.'

'So do I.'

The door opened and she looked up into Bloem's face. He was smiling.

'Come in, Wim, we'll go through this all in a minute, I've just got to make a call.'

'So *that's* where you are,' said Bloem once Lankhorst had left. 'I thought you were supposed to wait for me on Zeedijk?'

'I found something,' she said directing him to the screen. Bloem kept his eyes on her.

'What is it?' he finally asked.

As she explained, pointing out the tattoo on the man's neck, she could feel Bloem's eyes boring into her.

'And?' he said, fake yawning.

She thought about her ID card.

*Don't give him the satisfaction.*

Instead she turned to the tech guy.

'I think I lost my ID card, I can't find it anywhere, could you get me another?'

He nodded as Lankhorst stepped back in.

'Where are we at?' he asked.

Tanya put her hand on the records she'd got from the database.

'I've got twenty-five people here with prior arrests and tattoos on their neck.'

'Any look right?' asked Lankhorst.

'I haven't had a chance to look.' She pulled them towards her, passing each one on to Lankhorst as she'd glanced at them.

'Ugly bunch,' remarked Bloem, who was looking over Lankhorst's shoulder. 'I wonder if anyone's done a study on looks and criminality? It would certainly make it easier for us, just arrest all the ugly people.'

*Thing is*, thought Tanya, *if we did arrest people for looks you'd be first to be pulled in.*

She handed another sheet across and looked down at the next one.

The same spider tattoo, on the same side of the neck. She slid it over to Lankhorst. He held it up to get a better look.

'Follow this up,' he said after he'd studied it for a moment. He handed it back to her. 'Looks like most of his arrests have been in Amsterdam. If you need to go down there, let me know.'

He looked at Bloem and Tanya. 'I'm sure you two will make a brilliant team. Give me an update by the end of the day?'

Tanya went back to her desk, Bloem telling her to write up her initial report. But she sat down and read record seventeen. The man with the tattoo was called Ludo Haak, prior arrests for aggravated assault, armed robbery, and extortion. There was nothing on arson or murder, and the last offence had been over eight years ago. Seems like Haak had cleaned up his act.

But as she scrolled further down she noticed the last time the record had been accessed.

Friday.

Last Friday.

She checked the name of the person who'd looked at the file, Inspector Andreas Hansen, from Amsterdam's Western District Homicide Squad.

'I thought I said do the report?' Bloem's voice shot out from behind her, making her jump.

'Yeah, but I've got something interesting here –'

'There's this thing called chain of command, you heard of it?'

Tanya thought about her exam result. She felt sick.

*Please can I have passed*, she offered up, *then I can transfer out of here.*

Once she'd sensed that Bloem had stepped away she picked up the phone.

'Hey, Sergeant van der Mark from the Leeuwarden station. I'm looking for Inspector Andreas Hansen? Yes, I'll hold.' She looked down at the photo of Haak. Was he the killer? Was this the guy who'd tied them up and burnt them to death?

'Inspector Rykel, can I help?'

The man's voice was deep, but soft. Tired maybe.

'I was trying to get hold of Inspector Hansen.'

'What's it about?'

'I've got a suspect in a case I'm working, they're on file with several previous, and Inspector Hansen was the last person to look them up on the system.'

'When?'

He sounded more interested now.

'Last Friday.'

'What's the suspect called?'

68

'Ludo Haak.'

'And what's he suspected of?'

'Murder, two people got burned in their own house last night.'

'Give me your number, I'm going to call you back.'

Once she'd given it to him he hung up. She didn't need to have passed the Inspector exam to tell by his reaction that something was going on.

A phone was ringing in the office, no one was picking it up. The clock on the far wall said it was past eight, it must have stopped. Her early-morning start was catching up with her, the stale air of the office like some kind of narcotic, and she got up, figuring she'd get some more coffee before tackling the car, yawning as she did so.

'So who is he?'

Tanya turned to see Marek, the most junior member of the team. Recently Tanya had got the feeling that he might have taken an interest in her. He kept appearing out of nowhere, and his eyes tended to linger on her longer than she felt comfortable with.

'Who?'

'The guy who's keeping you up so late?'

The image of her foster father flashed into her brain.

*That's who keeps me awake at night*, she thought, *ruining my sleep.*

'Early start.' She pulled her keys off the desk and put them in her pocket. 'That's all.'

The phone was still ringing.

'Yeah, I hate those.' He paused. Tanya had a sinking feeling that a question to which the answer was 'no' would soon be making an appearance. 'Listen, I was wondering –'

The phone stopped ringing, fazing Marek slightly before he continued: 'if you'd –'

'Tanya?'

A shout from Roelf, sitting in the outer office.

'Yeah?'

'I've got someone called Geertje on the line for you, she says you spoke to her earlier, something about the fire?'

'I'll take it, transfer it here.'

She picked up her desk phone, feeling relief, sensing Marek's disappointment. As she got the speaker to her ear Geertje was already talking, her voice agitated, breathless.

'Geertje, it's Sergeant van der Mark ... I'm sorry, I missed that, could you start again?'

Tanya could hear Geertje's kids in the background, screaming loudly at each other, no longer playfully.

'I spoke to Arend, my husband? About what we talked about, and he said that he'd seen them in town, at the weekend' – Tanya could see Bloem swaggering back into the room like he owned the place – 'and they had a child with them, a little girl.'

# 11

*I can't believe he's still on the case*, thought Kees as he slammed the phone down on his desk.

When Jaap had been called away from the house on Herengracht Kees had been phoned by Smit, who'd asked him to take over.

Then, later, Smit had called again, bumping him back down to playing second . . .

Behind him the fax sprang to life, and he turned to see the phone logs he'd requested finally coming through.

*I'm going to need a bit of help getting through these*, he thought, and headed to the toilets, taking a scrap of paper off his desk with him. He didn't usually do this at the station, but what with Marinette, and getting knocked over, he figured he could use a boost.

It was payment – at least that's what he told himself as he rolled up the paper and snorted the coke off the back of the toilet – for the disappointment of the situation. It hit his system and thirty seconds in he felt more positive, more focused. He crumpled and flushed the roll of paper, and rubbed clean the dirty porcelain.

He checked his phone, hoping for a message from

Carice Stultjens. He'd started a text conversation about having a drink.

*Not strictly a top priority when it comes to the case*, he thought, *but hell, why not?*

The bruise, witnessed in the harsh bathroom light, had been startling, and he thought about the woman who'd run away. Was fate playing some cruel trick on him, making him chase someone who, superficially at least, looked like Marinette? Someone he was starting to feel less and less inclined to see anything of at all?

It wasn't his fault she'd changed since they got here, the move had been decided on by both of them, they'd agreed it was the right thing to do for his career, and she was excited about the prospect of moving somewhere else.

It wasn't like he'd dragged her kicking and screaming against her will from the rural backwater they were living in before.

But it was true that she wasn't the only one the city had changed. It had done something to him as well, exerted some pressure or influence which had made the pilot light of ambition flare.

And yes, he'd been working long hours, and maybe neglecting her a bit. But then it was easy to neglect a mopey bitch, which, in his eyes, was exactly what she'd become.

Back in the office the fax was still spooling slowly, so he turned to his computer, scanning through every female under the age of thirty-five arrested in the last year in the whole of Amsterdam. There were quite a few.

And, he reflected as he moved on to the next set, not many of them were very attractive, certainly nothing like the pathologist, Stultjens. She didn't seem the mopey type. In fact there was something about her, about the way she'd looked at him earlier . . .

*This is hopeless*, he thought, reaching out and turning his computer off, *I'm never going to find her this way . . .*

But he had to find her, she knew something, something which might well lead him to close the case down. And that was a result he'd like to get.

Maybe he should get someone to do an e-fit, he could ask the neighbours if they'd seen her.

'Hey, Martijn.' A man just on the unhealthy side of portly looked up. 'Is there someone here who does e-fits?'

'Yeah, there's a guy in the tech department who's good at them – can't remember his name – but if you ask he can do all sorts of stuff.'

'Like?'

'Like, you know . . .' He cupped his hands just under his chest. 'Really top quality, you'd never know it had been done on a computer. Looks just like in a magazine. Any position you want.'

'Seriously,' said Kees as he got up, glancing at the phone records on the fax and deciding they could wait, 'you need to get out more.'

Martijn's laugh followed him into the corridor.

Kees called the tech department on his cell and got through to the guy Martijn had told him about. He was giggling when he answered the phone. Kees didn't know why but he found it slightly sinister. They agreed to meet in twenty minutes. The tech department was in another building, and Kees decided to walk it, the coke giving a shine to the bright but freezing day.

He arrived and was directed to the first floor, where a man with long hair tied back in a ponytail nodded at him.

'You the guy who does e-fits?'

He nodded. 'Hope you haven't got a difficult one for me?'

'It's a female at least.'

'Thank god, I hate having to stare at men's faces for hours on end.' He motioned to the chair next to him. 'So what does she look like?'

Kees described her as best he could, and the image took shape on screen, the changes morphing slowly as he requested them. But after twenty minutes he was getting frustrated, there was something wrong with the cheekbones, or was it the eyes? And the mouth, the mouth wasn't right at all, or, come to think of it, the chin.

'This doesn't look anything like her.'

'Hey, I'm not fucking Rembrandt you know, I'm just doing what you tell me to do.'

Kees' phone buzzed in his pocket and he pulled it out, willing it to be Carice Stultjens. But it wasn't.

'Okay,' he said holding up the phone for the e-fit guy to see the image of Marinette, taken in happier times, which lit up the screen. 'She looks a bit like this, can you use that as a start?'

# 12

Jaap's hand shook as he pressed the doorbell. Saskia opened the door, one hand supporting her swollen belly as if it might fall, and looked at him, eyes probing his.

Her face crumpled.

'No,' she sobbed. She lunged forward, her arms flailing, 'you should have been with him.'

Jaap grabbed her, pinned her arms and held her tight. She squirmed against him. Then the tears came. Her body shook.

He'd never felt so sick.

He manoeuvred her into the house, and managed to sit her down on the sofa. For a moment he'd been worried she was going to pass out – the shock had seemingly stopped her breathing and her face had whitened whilst her eyelids flicked. He got her a drink of water, tipping the glass into her mouth, two streams dribbling down the sides of her lips.

He went through to the kitchen to fill the glass up again. The water was freezing and as he swallowed some a sharp pain stabbed him right in the forehead.

Saskia was still sobbing next door, and he didn't know what to do. He'd had the training in grief counselling that cops had to undertake, but what at the time had seemed pragmatic now appeared to be useless.

So he went and sat beside her, his arm round her shoulder, whilst she cried it out.

'I loved him, you know?' she said finally.

Jaap squeezed her shoulder. 'I know. He loved you too, I could tell.'

'How did he die?'

'Saskia –'

'Just tell me!'

She turned to him, shrugging his arm off her shoulder, her mouth set hard. She'd always been prone to rages, that was one of the reasons it'd not worked out between them. Jaap had been curious as to how Andreas had dealt with them, wondering if she was different with him. But he'd never asked.

'He was shot.'

'Who by?'

'We don't know yet but –'

'So what are you doing here?' Her voice was rising, and her face was heating up. 'Why aren't you out there finding out?'

'I'm –'

'Just go,' she turned away from him. 'I want you to go right now.'

# 13

'So what do you think has happened?'

Jaap had left Saskia after calling a friend of hers – he didn't think she should be alone – and had gone straight to Gert Roemers, head of the computer crimes unit. On the way over Jaap had been trying to clear his mind, trying to get a grip on what was going on.

But his mind wouldn't clear.

Roemers was staring at the screen, his face and hands softly illuminated in the dark room.

Rumour had it that Roemers' wife had thrown him out over three months ago and he now slept by his desk in the basement which housed his unit. The room certainly smelt like someone was living there, a kind of soft funk which was on the verge of blooming into something unpleasant, though Jaap couldn't see what he'd actually sleep on. Unless he used the dirty, padded swivel chair he was sitting in now.

'You're sure that there was stuff on here?'

'There should be years of case files on there, basically every report he's done was done on this computer.'

'Maybe he kept everything on an external drive?'

Jaap tried to picture Andreas' desk; he was certain there was no external drive.

'No, it was all there.'

Roemers looked at him with raised eyebrows.

Jaap, trying not to get angry but unable to stop the irritation creeping into his voice: 'It *was* there.'

Roemers' hands shot off the keyboard, raised to his shoulders like someone had just told him to stick 'em up.

'Okay, okay. I'll have a dig around and see what I can find, but you'll have to leave it with me overnight.'

A thought hit Jaap: he remembered Andreas telling him that he'd got some service which backed up his computer online. Andreas had been excited that it could sync two computers.

Jaap had thought it sounded like hell. He didn't even have a computer at home, but if he did there was no way he'd want it cluttered up with old case files. He was about to mention it to Roemers but then thought better of it.

'Soon as you get something, call me.'

'Uh huh.'

Jaap turned to leave and had just made it to the door when Roemers, face still communing with the screen, spoke.

'Sorry about Andreas.'

Jaap stood there a moment, hand on the door handle, his throat swelling up like there was something inside.

He left, unable to trust his voice.

# 14

'Is there anything we can use?'

Kees had brought the phone logs to him in the canteen. Jaap had suddenly felt he needed food, replacement for what he'd lost earlier, but the bowl in front of him hardly qualified. It didn't look even vaguely edible, and he pushed the unidentifiable meat stew away, his appetite gone as quickly as it had appeared.

'The three numbers in Friedman's phone are all pay as you go, no trace of who bought them. I've got call logs for all three and Friedman's. They don't send text messages at all and the calls are really short, usually only around ten seconds or less.'

'And do they call anyone else?'

'No, just the four numbers, it's a closed circle.'

'So they're disciplined.'

'Yeah, very. There is a kind of pattern though, and it looks like Friedman is at the centre. He made the most calls to these two numbers here.' Kees pointed to the sheet. 'And he usually called them. They rarely call him.'

'Is it definitely his phone?'

'Only his prints on it.'

Jaap nodded.

'How long do the lists go back?'

'About a month, they don't keep them any longer. But this third number here?' He pointed again. 'This one only calls Friedman's number, and only a couple of times.'

Jaap stared at the sheets. This was classic drug-dealer behaviour, limit the circle, limit the risk.

'Have you got location results?'

'Only for the last forty-eight.' Kees pulled a sheet from the bottom.

'Friedman's was in Amsterdam, as was this one here, the third one was out somewhere up north, and the fourth one looks like it was turned off, it didn't check in with any cell towers anywhere.'

'Up north where?'

'Somewhere in Friesland. Maybe they were cattle rustling.'

*Where was it Sergeant van der Mark called from?* thought Jaap.

'Let me see,' he said reaching for the sheet.

The cell phone had been in Amsterdam all Saturday and most of Sunday morning, then it was turned off, and only signed in with a cell tower just past midnight in Friesland, then by eight this morning it was back in Amsterdam.

Van der Mark's murders had happened last night.

'Leeuwarden's in Friesland, right?' he asked Kees.

'Yeah, pretty sure it is.'

*Could that number*, Jaap wondered as he stared at the sheet, *belong to Ludo Haak?*

He glanced at Kees, but decided he was going to keep that secret for now. If Kees found this case was linked to

Andreas' death he wouldn't put it past him to go running to Smit with the news. Then Jaap would be off the case.

And that he wasn't willing to risk.

He had a link to Andreas' killer, and he wasn't going to let it go.

'Friedman's the centre,' said Jaap going back to the logs, 'Directing these two, and he answers to this one. Whatever he was directing, it looks like someone didn't like it much. The fact that whoever killed Friedman left the speaking clock's number on his phone, well ...' He paused, tapping the desk with a finger. 'I'm going to need you to turn over this guy's life, we need to know everything we can about him.'

He wrote a number on a scrap of paper.

'Call this number and speak to Teije. Tell him I sent you and that you need him to get Friedman's finances, business and personal.'

'Is he police?'

'No, which is why he can do things the quick way.'

'Yeah, cool.'

Jaap looked across to the only window in the office, a large seagull having just landed on the window sill, tucking in its wings, cocking its head from side to side.

'You think whoever owns these numbers is next in line?' asked Kees.

Jaap watched as the bird turned round on bright orange feet, a dribble of shit splashing on to the lead sill before it launched itself with a leathery flap of wings.

'Looks like it. The problem is, how do we find them first?'

Kees went to his desk and started making calls, and Jaap bashed out a quick report summary for Smit.

Whilst he waited for it to print he unlocked his desk drawer and looked down at his gun, a standard issue Walther P5.

His hand hovered for a second, just the sight of it bringing back a day seven years ago.

A day he'd fucked up.

Badly.

He picked the gun up, feeling the weight, the texture on the grip.

He could feel his finger pumping eight times.

The ringing in his ears.

Blood smearing on the wall as the two bodies slid down slowly.

Andreas had sorted it all out, messing with the positions, covering for Jaap's mistake.

*He was there for me then*, thought Jaap as he felt the gun's weight, the feeling of power, *and last night I failed him.*

Jaap turned the gun over and thought about what had happened next, the gradual deterioration. He'd felt like he was a jigsaw on a wall. And the bits started to fall out, one by one. It was then the white streak had appeared in his hair; he remembered the morning a few weeks after the incident when he'd first noticed it glaring out at him in the bathroom mirror.

He carried on for six months, his relationship with Saskia deteriorating, before one day he just couldn't get out of bed.

Literally.

Saskia had moved out by then, but Andreas dropped round wondering why he hadn't turned up for work.

He got Jaap to talk to a shrink. The shrink didn't help

him. But he did write a recommendation that Jaap be taken off active duty until such time he was deemed fit for work.

They said the rest would make things better. That and the pills they gave him.

The rest didn't help, if anything it made things worse, and the pills didn't do much either. Principally as he flushed them down the toilet each day, the little blue sphere bobbing in the turbulent water before disappearing.

After two months at home Jaap couldn't bear it any more. Dragging himself out of bed following yet another sleepless night he packed a bag and went to Schiphol airport.

He picked a flight at random, and spent the next few weeks moving around, staying only until he felt compelled to move on, each new destination again picked at random.

By the time he found himself in Kyoto he'd run out of money.

And out of willpower.

Wandering round the city, the first snow of winter falling, and darkness thickening, he took shelter at a small temple in the Ukyo-ku ward.

He felt like he couldn't move any more, and lay down outside.

They discovered him several hours later and took him in. He woke the next day in a tiny room.

He was politely asked to move on. He didn't have the energy to argue. But he didn't have the energy to go either.

After a few days a monk, Yuzuki Roshi, took pity on him, and got him a job in the temple kitchen. Payment was food.

And several hours of sitting every day.

Non-negotiable.

So Jaap sat, and months later, after the plum trees had blossomed, after their petals had fallen, after the sticky summer heat had subsided and the insects that buzzed round his face had shrivelled up and died in the first frosts of autumn, he knew that he had to go back.

But on the flight home he'd sworn to himself that he'd never carry a gun again.

And here he was holding it in his hand.

After a moment's hesitation he returned it, locked the drawer, retrieved the report from the printer, and headed to the floor above.

Smit wasn't ready for Jaap when he arrived at his office so he called Sergeant van der Mark.

'Hey, sorry it took so long to get back to you, I've got a bit of a situation on my hands.'

'That's okay.'

'What I didn't tell you earlier was that Andreas Hansen was killed last night –'

'God . . . I'm sorry.'

'And I think Haak is involved.'

'How?'

'I'm not sure, but we're going to need to go through what we've each got.'

'There's something else. The couple that were killed had a child, and it's missing.'

Jaap saw Smit standing in the doorway, looking at him. He knew Smit didn't like to be kept waiting.

'I'm going to have to call you back.'

'Yeah, fine. I might even be in Amsterdam tomorrow, I

really need to find out about Ludo Haak, so maybe we could meet?'

'Sure, let me know what time you'll be arriving.'

Jaap looked over at Smit as he put away his phone, wondering how much he'd heard.

Smit ushered Jaap into his office. The room was furnished in a style which was clearly meant to convey power and seriousness, but ended up looking like a set for an eighties film about Wall Street greed.

Rumour was that Smit was aiming for Chief of Police – he'd spent the last six months trying to get everyone's clearance rates up, which presumably would form part of his bid for the top job. If Smit did move up, the position of Station Chief would become free, and Jaap figured he would be best placed to take on the role.

*Though there's always De Waart*, he told himself. *What if he goes for it too?*

Smit sat behind the ostentatious dark wooden desk and Jaap took the seat opposite.

'How are you holding up?' started Smit.

'You know, pretty shaken.'

'We all are,' he said shaking his head, 'we all are. Do you need a few days' leave?'

Jaap knew this was coming and had prepared.

'Well, I was hoping I could take on Andreas' case?'

Smit looked at him as if he were an idiot.

'You know I can't allow that, if the press found out . . .' He let it hang. 'And anyway De Waart is taking the case.'

'De Waart?' Jaap tried to keep the disbelief out of his voice.

Smit's tone slid down the temperature scale.

'Yes, De Waart. I know that he and Andreas didn't get on, but he's a professional, he wants to see justice served as much as anybody else in the department.' He paused, and when he started again his voice had warmed up a bit. 'Maybe I can get you a few days' leave, I can always let Kees run your case.'

Jaap had been thinking about the break-in at his houseboat. Luckily he'd been out when whoever it was broke down his front door. If he'd been there then who knew what could have happened. But then again, if his sister Karin hadn't called in a total state – six months back from Afghanistan and nowhere near over what she witnessed – then he'd have gone with Andreas. In which case Andreas might still be alive.

*Or we'd both be dead*, he thought.

'Well?' asked Smit.

Jaap thought of Andreas, his brain splattered over the concrete, and he thought of Saskia, carrying Andreas' child.

He was going to nail whoever was responsible, he had to.

And being on leave would make it more difficult, even if he was going to have to hide what he was doing from Smit.

'There was something else. Andreas' laptop has been wiped clean. I think whoever killed him did it.'

'Why?'

'He must have had some information on there, something to do with the case we were working' – Smit was giving him the fish eye – 'and my houseboat was hit last night. And do you know what was stolen? Nothing. Whoever busted my front door down took nothing.'

Smit, elbows on the table, steepled his fingers, sniffing

surreptitiously at the tips. There was something there which he was deriving a certain amount of pleasure from. His eyes fell to the report Jaap had put on his desk. Jaap waited.

'You and Andreas, you were getting somewhere with this case, the gang, Black Tulips I think you said they were called?'

'Yeah, I think we were really close.'

Smit thought for a moment.

'I wouldn't normally ask this, but as we're a man down I want you to carry on with the Herengracht case. From what I've seen here' – he tapped the report – 'I agree with you, there's a good chance whoever killed Friedman is going to try and get to the people who own those other numbers. If that's the case I can't afford to let Kees run it on his own.'

*Those people might be my only chance to find out who killed Andreas*, Jaap thought, *I've got to get to them before the killer does. But I still don't know why the killer left the phone in the first place.*

'And I'll need you to brief De Waart on what you know first thing tomorrow,' continued Smit. 'But this has got to be clear, you go nowhere near De Waart's investigation.'

'Okay,' Jaap said, getting up, Smit's smile like a shark spotting a lone seal bobbing on the surface of the ocean, 'I'll stay right out of it.'

'And Jaap?'

'Yes?'

'I know you had to take time out a few years ago, so if you start to feel the pressure . . . well, just let me know, okay? We can't have another . . . mishap.'

# 15

Tanya stood, ankle deep in the ashes, and followed the white light of her torch beam as it swung slowly back and forth. She'd been here for at least half an hour and had nearly covered the whole area, but so far there had been no child's bones, or indeed anything else of interest. Not even the sound of an owl or a seagull to break the silence.

The night was clear, and the darkness, punctured only by a handful of stars, showed how far from a major city this corner of the Netherlands was.

She shivered and wished she'd brought a hat with her, or at the very least some gloves.

*What am I doing here*, she wondered, *what am I going to find that everybody else has missed?*

Finally she managed to convince herself to leave and she headed back to the car, the smell of burning catching in her throat from all the disturbance she'd caused. She was just reaching out to open the door when she thought she saw – or did she hear? – something off to her left, in the far corner of the plot. She kept still, holding her breath while she tried to peer into the darkness, willing her eyes to work better.

*Is that her?* the thought hammered at her. *Is she here?*

She aimed her torch in the direction of the noise and flicked it on.

There was something there. Her chest felt like it had been whacked by a speeding truck. The torch beam caught something, movement, by the hedge almost exactly where she'd found the doll.

Before she knew what she was doing Tanya felt the wind in her hair and her limbs pumping as she sprinted back towards the burnt-out house. She didn't have time to go round and so ran straight through what remained of the ash, causing it to fly up all around her.

Her eyes were stinging and she couldn't see but she kept on, pushing hard, her lungs willing her not to breathe in. Moments before she was about to make it out the other side she caught her foot on something and went down hard, slicing her knee on a part of what must have been the same object she tripped on.

She picked herself up and tried to carry on, forcing herself through the hedge, the scratches nothing compared to the pain in her leg. Once through she couldn't see anything. Training the torch out in an arc she figured she'd be able to catch sight of the person – because she was sure it *was* a person – but despite the landscape being flat there was nothing.

*Were they taller than a child?*

She paused and listened, but the only sound she could hear was the blood rushing in her ears, a sound like a massive waterfall, and the dull thump of her heart, which seemed to make the landscape around her pulse in time.

Which way had they gone, and what had they been doing there? And how long had they been there watching her? Were they out there somewhere now, observing her still from the cover of a ditch, or flattened out in a rut in a field? Again she swung the torch around and again she came up with nothing. And it was then that she began to feel exposed.

*All that's good for*, she suddenly realized, *is showing where I am.*

She flipped the switch on her torch and turned round, scared suddenly and pushed back through the hedge, the crackling loud in the still night, the sharp branches clawing at her like evil hands.

She could feel a presence behind her the whole way back to the car, and even turned twice fully expecting to see a face, or a raised arm whose hand clutched a hammer or knife. The feeling got so strong that she ran the last twenty metres back to the car, threw the door open, jumped in and fumbled with the key, unable to get it in the ignition. Then it was in, sliding into place, and she yanked it to the right, the engine not firing up until the third attempt.

She swung the car round in a tight circle and slammed her foot down so hard she was afraid she'd break the accelerator.

# 16

'And he didn't say where he was going?' Jaap asked.

Saskia shook her head. Her rounded belly touched the table in front of her.

He'd come back, aware that she was all on her own. He thought of all the times he'd been here with Andreas and Saskia, in this very kitchen, enjoying a meal, each other's company.

And that time last year, when Andreas had been away. He felt even worse about that now.

Everything looked different, as if Andreas' absence had altered the room.

'I can't do this on my own,' she said, tears rolling down her cheeks. Jaap moved round behind her, holding her shoulders as she sat in the chair. He could feel her shaking, the damp heat of her tears.

Holding her brought back memories of when they'd been together, before they realized they just couldn't make it work. Ironically it was her and Andreas getting together which had brought them closer than they'd ever been as an item.

'It's going to be okay,' he murmured to her, hearing how empty the words were.

'So where were you last night?' she asked as the sobbing subsided.

'I had to go see Karin, she called me in a total state and you know there's no one else –'

'Jaap, forget what I said earlier, I don't blame you.'

'I should have gone, but Karin was . . .'

Her hand found his.

'Andreas shouldn't have gone on his own, it's not your fault.'

The fridge juddered, clicked off, and he could hear a plane, coming in to land at Schiphol, humming through the sky outside.

'I need to check Andreas' computer,' said Jaap. 'I think there may be something on it I need.'

'It's in the study,' she said, her voice thick, choked.

Jaap walked though and flipped the light on. He could still feel where Saskia's hand had lain on his own.

He was just about to fire up the computer, but stopped and looked for the router, which he found under the desk. He turned it off – he didn't want it syncing with a server and wiping everything off this one as well.

Result.

Everything was still there.

He opened the case file on the Black Tulips; the last entry was early Sunday morning, and it was just a phone number. He looked up the area code and found it was from Friesland, up north.

*Where Sergeant van der Mark called from. Is her case linked to the Black Tulips too?*

He shut down the computer, then hesitated for a second before turning the router back on.

*Let's see how smart De Waart is*, he thought as he left the room.

'Do you know who did it?' she asked as he returned to the kitchen.

'I . . . not yet but I'm going to find out. But there's something I've got to tell you.' He pulled a chair up and sat, looking at her. 'I can't be officially on the case, they won't let me. The thing is . . .' He paused, searching out her eyes. '. . . they've assigned De Waart to do it.'

'De Waart?' She straightened up. 'But he hates Andreas, blames him.'

'I know, but there's nothing I can do about it.' He found himself scratching a small dark stain on the table with one of his fingernails.

Andreas and De Waart had been in a chase which led them out towards Haarlem. It was foggy and Andreas was driving. As the visibility diminished he said he was going to stand down, but De Waart insisted they carry on. Less than a minute later, when something shot out in front of them in the fog, Andreas swerved and flipped the car.

The seat belt meant Andreas got away with minor bruising, but De Waart didn't have his on.

The impact broke his leg in three places and left him with five pins, a limp, and a hard-on for Andreas.

'So he's going to come and ask you some questions – just don't tell him that you've been talking to me.'

'Does he know about us, that we were together once?'

'Probably, I don't know, but it doesn't matter.'

'What if I refuse to speak to him?'

93

'I don't think that would be a good idea.'

Her head went back down.

'The funeral's set for Friday morning. I can't believe he's gone,' she whispered. 'I can't believe he's gone.'

Jaap sat in the night's stillness.

He'd learnt how in Kyoto. It had seemed impossible at first. *Just sit*, his teacher had told him, but when he did the very thoughts he was trying to escape kept churning, multiplying like cockroaches. It nearly drove him crazy. Until, a few months in, they'd started to fade, the images went from Technicolor to sepia to black-and-white. And sometimes, for just a brief few moments which nevertheless seemed almost timeless, a stillness, a vast empty space filled his mind. At those moments he was free.

After leaving Saskia he'd gone back to his houseboat, and although exhausted was unable to sleep. He'd got up, gone through to the main living area, and settled on the mat and cushion he kept in the corner furthest from the door which led up on to the deck.

He focused on the breath as it entered his body then left it, again and again, feeling the cold air's sharpness against his nostrils on the in-breath, its softer warmth on the out.

Gradually the torrent of thoughts receded from his mind's foreground. They were still there, forming, trying to hook his attention, demanding that he engage with them, but he kept his focus on the sensations caused by the movement of air, until he felt almost as still as the world around him.

These were the moments when everything was different, when he couldn't tell where he ended and the world began, when he felt connected.

There was no *he* and nothing to be connected to.

Time was irrelevant, time didn't exist.

When he finally opened his eyes hazy moonlight was pooling on the floor in front of him.

He rose, his legs stiff and his back sore, and he got the feeling there was something he'd missed during the day. Something that he should have checked, something important.

But, as he climbed back into bed, pulling the cover up over him against the cold, he just couldn't think what it was.

# 17

As the plane lifted off the ground Jan Zwartberg settled back into his seat and closed his eyes, the dimmed cabin lights making it difficult to read. He could have reached up and activated the little spotlight above his head, but when it came to it his arms just wouldn't obey the command issued by his brain.

He was exhausted – the last few days had rushed past quickly: he'd managed to achieve what he'd set out to do, had got a few more contacts, interested parties who liked the look of the unique service he offered – and as the plane steadily rose he sank down into sleep, contrary motion.

The feral smell of the on-board meal woke him, the fold-down tray loaded with a baking hot plastic container. Peeling back the lid he saw what looked like a prop for a cheap slasher movie and, revolted, pushed it away.

No use trying to get back to sleep now. He'd picked up a late edition of *De Telegraaf* at the departure lounge and he reached into the seat pocket where he'd jammed it as he boarded, the air-con nozzle shooting a cold stream down his neck as he did so.

A stewardess came round and offered drinks; he took a

whisky, just to help him relax a bit, unwind, help work out the kinks in his neck and shoulders, and to celebrate, treat himself. He opened the paper, the ink already staining his fingers – and why couldn't they invent an ink which didn't do that, and whilst they were at it what about making newspapers smaller, so that you didn't end up having to fight with them, especially if you were in a small space?

He started reading. Enjoying the earthy tang of the drink he scanned the front page and then moved on to the next, where, as he saw the headline, the latest mouthful of whisky he'd taken sprayed out of his nose, searing the delicate mucus membranes, making them feel like he was breathing fire. The paper was dappled with tiny spots of single malt.

The title, 'Amsterdam Diamond Merchant Murdered', had got his attention. He scanned the article at speed but there was no mention of a name, the journalist clearly having very little real information. But it did say the victim had been discovered at their house on Herengracht.

He placed the plastic cup back down on the tray table, his hand shaking so badly that the remaining whisky slopped over the edges, creating little pools of golden liquid which glinted in the half-light. Everything was racing now, mind, heart, bowels, and he felt claustrophobic, like he needed to smash open the window and breathe some real air.

Eventually – by the time the captain had come on the speaker, heralded by angelic soft ascending bells, and told them all to buckle up as they were starting their descent, and would the cabin crew mind preparing for landing? – he'd managed to calm himself down and convince himself that he was jumping to conclusions. There were countless diamond merchants in Amsterdam, and many of them probably lived on Herengracht. After all, what was the point in making money if you couldn't enjoy it? So there was no reason to panic just yet.

As soon as they landed he pulled out a clamshell phone and placed a call.

The phone rang out, his hand sweating against the cheap plastic.

He pocketed it again, and told himself that he'd find that everything was okay, that it was someone else, just a coincidence.

And it was this thought which sustained him through the landing, through passport control at Schiphol, sustained him all the way through the cab ride back into town, sustained him right up to the moment when he closed his front door behind him, and slid across the two deadbolts, each locking into place with a loud clang.

# DAY TWO

# 18

De Waart was trying to pick something out of his teeth with the corner of a tram ticket.

Earlier Jaap had seen him bringing in an arrest and he'd reluctantly agreed to meet in the canteen. When they'd sat down De Waart had un-holstered, putting his gun on the table by the small jar filled with packets of mustard.

'Damn thing's giving me a rash,' he said scratching the side of his chest. 'The doctor said it might be nickel, but no one can tell me if these things have even got nickel in them or not.'

'Can't help you with that,' said Jaap, turning to check the clock on the wall. 'You wanted to talk to me?'

'Yeah. So this gang, the Black Tulips,' De Waart said as he pulled the ticket out and inspected a grey blob on the corner, 'you and Andreas were after them because . . . ?'

Jaap was feeling impatient, he wanted to get on, but Smit had insisted he brief De Waart. And if he didn't he knew where De Waart would be heading to complain.

*Everything's linked*, he thought.

He'd tried to empty his mind before heading out earlier, hoping whatever he'd glimpsed during his session last night might appear again.

But it hadn't worked, his thoughts untamable, and he'd found himself turning to the I Ching. Yuzuki Roshi came from the Obaku sect, and had made a lifetime study of the Book of Changes, even though his fellow monks saw it as little better than Chinese superstition, not a fit subject for a Japanese Zen master. He'd taught Jaap how to read the hexagrams and whilst Jaap had not initially seen the attraction, he'd gradually found himself using it more and more, drawn to it in a way he couldn't explain.

This morning he'd thrown the coins and formed the hexagram for Fire and Thunder.

'Quiet withdrawal overcomes obstacle to truth.'

He'd never felt less like quietly withdrawing in his life. But he'd been doing this long enough to know that he shouldn't dismiss it totally.

'I thought you were in a hurry?' asked De Waart.

'Yeah, sorry,' said Jaap.

He could smell something cooking, something greasy, something being fried in oil used a thousand times already. His stomach turned.

'I was just thinking . . . there was a homicide up at the docks. We knew the Black Tulips were responsible. They smuggle in drugs, arms, women for the sex trade, whatever they can make some money at. The problem was we couldn't get close to them, they're a tight group and we hit a brick wall.'

'And you think that Andreas had got somewhere, found something out which might have helped.'

This was what Jaap had been waiting for. He'd been turning it over in his mind, should he tell De Waart or not? The problem was he didn't trust him. De Waart was a player, he'd worked his way up not by being a great detective – he wasn't even a good one in Jaap's eyes – but by sucking up to the right people at the right time. He had a knack for it, like it was hardwired into him, always looking for the angle when he should have been doing his job. Jaap had watched him over the years, deftly manoeuvring himself, using people.

*If I tell him about Friedman*, he thought, *I'll get taken off the case.*

'It's just a feeling I have, maybe I'm just being paranoid, but the same night he was killed my houseboat was broken into –'

'I heard, and they didn't steal anything, right?'

'Right.' Jaap checked the clock again. 'Look, I've got a case on where we're pretty sure the killer is going after some other people so if –'

'Did Andreas call you over the weekend? Maybe he'd found something out?'

'He tried a couple of times, I missed his calls. I did try to reach him later, but I couldn't get through,' he said as he stood up. He figured he should mention the number he'd got from Andreas' home computer, but that would complicate things too much. 'Look, I'm sorry but I really need to get on.'

De Waart stood as well, and offered his hand. Jaap was surprised but took it anyway.

'Smit is keen for me to run this one, so if there is anything else you will let me know?' asked De Waart.

Jaap hoped his palm wasn't about to start perspiring.

'Sure,' he said, 'anything comes up, you'll be the first to know.'

De Waart thanked him and turned to leave.

'Hey,' said Jaap handing him his gun. 'Not sure you should leave this lying around.'

'Shit, you're right. Mind you,' he said as he holstered it, 'if I can't stop the damn thing making me itch I may have to do without.'

Once De Waart had left the canteen, Jaap dashed up the stairs, and went to his desk. He fired up the database and got Ludo Haak's record. Under known associates there was a name he recognized, Coenraad Akster.

He'd come across him in a case a few years back, and Coenraad had agreed, if Jaap didn't bust him for possession, to pass certain information back. Jaap had felt slightly bad about it – the possession charge would never have stuck in any case – but when Akster consistently came up with nothing he rapidly forgot about him.

Jaap looked for his current address, expecting it to be, like Haak's, unknown. But there was an address, out in the tenements. He wrote it down.

Then he unlocked his drawer, took out his gun and fitted the shoulder holster.

He'd sworn he'd never carry one again.

But that was before Andreas had been killed.

And the break-in.

*I'm going to have to get used to it*, he thought as he went to meet Kees in the cafe opposite the station.

On the short walk over he called the phone company, giving them the number in Friesland and asking for full details. They'd get back to him, they said.

*I'm going to need to check Sergeant van der Mark's still coming today*, he thought as he hung up.

When he arrived, Kees was sitting at a table towards the back, cup in hand, looking like he'd been up all night. The bruise on his face had darkened since yesterday.

Jaap slid into the seat opposite him, having placed his order with the waitress.

'We need to work out who owns these phones, any ideas?'

'We don't even know why Friedman was killed. We could just call them, explain they're in danger?'

Jaap shook his head.

'Normally I'd agree, but they were clearly hiding something, Friedman was running something illegal. It had to be high stakes for them to have gone to this much trouble with the phones. If we call them they're just going to disappear.'

The waitress brought his order, *matcha* from Japan that he'd had to sweet talk the cafe into buying for him, and Jaap watched Kees' eyes linger on her slim figure.

He pulled out a sheet with the numbers on and drew a diagram, the first unknown number at the top with an arrow down to Friedman's number, then two more branching from Friedman to the remaining two unknowns.

'It's clear from the logs that whoever owns the first number is the one really in charge, Friedman answered to him, then issued orders to the other two. That's the one we really need to focus on.'

Kees pulled out his phone and started tapping keys.

'Important?' asked Jaap. 'I wouldn't want to get in the way or anything.'

Kees put his phone away and Jaap continued.

'Have you shown the numbers to the manager at Friedman's business? Van Zandt, was it?'

'No, I'll ask her if she recognizes any.'

Jaap took a sip of the dark green, foamy *matcha*. He could tell Kees was wondering what it was.

'Right,' he said putting down the cup, 'we need to talk to this guy Rint Korssen. I want to go over to the business on Nieuwstraat, and we should set up a meet with this charity Friedman visited on Sunday. As it stands whoever met him there was the last person to see him, they might be able to tell us something. Friedman's lawyer is going to make the ID official at the morgue today?'

'Yeah, he'll be there at ten a.m.'

'Okay, I want to be there for that. Did you get a TOD from the pathologist?'

'She didn't really want to commit, she still hasn't done the autopsy, but from the temperature she said any time between eight on Sunday evening and about one in the morning.'

Jaap swirled his cup, took a final sip, stood up.

'Okay, let's go see Rint Korssen, you can call Van Zandt on the way.'

His phone buzzed and he answered. The phone company, with the name the number was registered to, Van Delft.

*The question is*, he thought as they got into the car, *what did Andreas want with whoever Van Delft is? And why was he looking up Haak?*

# 19

Chief Inspector Henk Smit peered into the room through the glass pane set high in the door. It was full – every journalist in the Amsterdam area had answered the call, a story like this was irresistible – and he felt the familiar anticipation of public address.

*Rats to a sewer,* he thought as he took a deep breath and pushed the door open, strode to the table set with a glass of water and a microphone and sat down, the bustle which his entrance had caused – cameras being readied, notebooks flipped open, throats cleared for the shouting of questions – dying back as he did so.

The lights were blinding, and he shifted his head, trying to find an angle where he didn't have to squint.

Expectation bristled.

He pulled the microphone closer, a vicious whine cutting the air, and he flinched, along with everyone else in the room.

The news that Inspector Andreas Hansen had been found dead, in inexplicable circumstances, had reached him yesterday morning, and had leaked out within the hour. Journalists jammed the phone lines and his decision to put the press conference off until today was to give the investigation a chance to get somewhere.

*It would have looked great if I'd been able to hold a conference to say the crime was already solved*, he thought.

But now that didn't look like it was going to happen he couldn't hold off any longer. In his experience, built over years of handling the media, the longer they were kept waiting the bigger the turn-out.

He wouldn't be surprised to see himself on the midday news.

He wouldn't be displeased either.

'Thank you all for coming along today,' he started, before pausing and waving a hand in the air. 'Can we get some of these moved?'

People sprang around moving spotlights, no one wanting to be responsible for any delay, until he signalled that he was comfortable, and he took a moment to look round at his congregation before going back to the mic.

The speech he'd written yesterday evening, and spent the last fifteen minutes rehearsing so he could deliver it without notes, began with a brief reaction, shock of course, to the murder of a colleague, and quickly moved on to how they were going to deal with an attack on a trusted public servant. The words flowed, and the audience were attentive, some scribbling quickly into notebooks, some holding recording devices, and the red lights on the TV cameras along the back gave him hope that he *would* make the midday.

He wrapped up, then threw it open for questions, picking out some favourite journalists, those who, in exchange for early access to certain cases, tended to show the department in a positive light.

'Can you tell us what your theories are?' asked a petite

woman in the front row who Smit knew as the chief crime reporter for *De Telegraaf*.

'We're dealing with a fluid situation here' – he gestured with his hands – 'and at this stage all I can tell you is that we're pursuing several, potentially interesting, leads.'

'Is there any indication that this is terrorist linked?' queried a thin man with a pencil moustache and a nervous tic, sitting three rows back. Smit had only seen him a few times before and didn't know which paper he worked for.

'Well, at this stage –'

'Wasn't he into child porn?' a voice shouted from the back.

Silence crushed the room.

Smit squinted to try and see who it was, but the figure was standing right next to a spotlight aimed in his direction, and it was impossible to make out his face.

'And you are?'

'Patrick Borst, *De Adelaar*' – he knew the rag, the type of tabloid which regularly ran stories about alien abductions, secret conspiracies and pet love-ins. How did people like this even get a press pass? – 'and I think your man was involved in child pornography.'

Smit was suddenly attune to every tiny air movement in the room. He hadn't risen to be Chief Inspector by ignoring his instincts, and right now his instincts sensed danger.

Then anger.

This was going to be on the news, and here was someone, some grubby hack who worked for a sensationalist newspaper, about to crap all over it.

'I'm not sure I follow you, but in any case' – trying in his manner to imply that nothing worthwhile had just happened – 'we are vigorously pursuing several active leads and expect to make considerable headway in the next few hours. We will call another press conference when we have an update.'

He reached forward and flipped the microphone's switch to off, before standing and heading for the door, everyone on their feet, baying like a pack of hounds.

# 20

'It's got to be around somewhere,' said Jaap looking in the glove compartment. 'Check the boot, would you?'

Kees got out and checked.

'Nothing here,' he said after a few moments.

'Well, I'm not paying the fine. When you take the car back check who had it last, and why they didn't leave it.'

'Probably took it home, I heard someone say they did that.'

The badges exempting unmarked cars from parking tickets had been introduced as a cost-cutting measure. The fact that they blew the car's unmarked status hadn't crossed the minds of whichever genius had come up with the scheme.

'I need to make a call, then we'll go,' said Jaap, slamming shut the glove compartment door.

He dialled Karin, his beautiful, confident sister, who'd been working as an army medic for ISAF in Afghanistan. She'd been so excited to be deployed, and he'd seen her off.

Eight months later she came back.

But she hadn't really returned.

They kept her on meds and gave her therapy, but she still had attacks which only Jaap's presence seemed able to calm. And on Sunday she'd called, and he could tell by her voice that she was worse than usual. Which was why he didn't go with Andreas.

But she wasn't answering her phone now. He knew that sometimes she didn't get up until well past lunchtime.

'Okay, let's go,' he said to Kees as they started out.

The air, honed overnight like a knife, cut into his face. Earlier Jaap had noticed ice starting to creep in from the canal edges, crooked fingers reaching out for each other. Another few days of the same weather and the fingers would meet in the middle and it might even become solid enough to skate on.

'What background have you managed to get on Korssen?' Jaap asked.

'No record, but that's not really a surprise. He's rich, he has to be to live here. And he invests in businesses, often ones which need some kind of help. Carolien van Zandt said that Friedman's business was in trouble a few years ago and that Korssen got on board to help out.'

They lapsed into silence as they walked and Jaap thought back to Saskia. She'd taken it hard. But then who wouldn't? Everything was going well, she was with someone she loved and they were about to have their first child. Then her whole world exploded.

*I should have gone with Andreas*, he thought as they found the address, *then he might still be alive.*

As they stood in front of the building Kees whistled. The house was a late-nineteenth-century structure and the back would look over Vondelpark, a position which could make even the most level-headed Amsterdammer say *Hey* to the green-eyed monster.

'Doesn't look like he's short of cash,' Kees said as he

pressed the bell, holding his finger on the button, tip turning white from the pressure.

Two-tone bells oscillated back and forth.

Jaap could feel Kees' impatience, though he got the impression that was more to do with the fact he'd thought the case was his.

After a few moments the door opened, and a figure, taller than Jaap, wearing a light pink-and-white striped shirt tucked into the kind of jeans that looked messy but cost a fortune, stood there looking down at them.

'Yes?' His tone of voice implied that a major inconvenience was taking place.

'Rint Korssen?'

A siren zoomed behind them, the pitch drooping as it passed by.

'Yes, are you the police?'

'Inspector Rykel. And this is Inspector Terpstra.' Korssen glared at Kees, who'd only just taken his finger off the bell.

'Come in.'

He stepped aside and once they'd moved over the threshold into the warmth Korssen closed the door behind them.

'Straight through to the end,' he said and Jaap walked, followed by Kees, his shoes feeling like they were scratching the highly polished walnut floor.

*Sure he can afford to get it fixed*, thought Jaap.

The back of the house, as he'd suspected, looked over the Vondelpark, but what he hadn't expected was that the whole building had been remodelled on the inside, and instead of being made up of several different rooms as it would originally have been, there was now a modern, cavernous space.

And the far wall, instead of being brick with a few windows, was a huge sheet of glass giving not so much a view of the Vondelpark, but a feeling of being in it.

Korssen followed them, gestured to a table at the kitchen end of the room and asked if they'd like a drink.

Jaap refused, but Kees had accepted and they now had to watch as Korssen prepared the drinks from a stainless-steel machine which looked like it needed a degree in mechanics to operate.

Jaap took the opportunity to assess him. He was a large man, but not in any way slow. His skin was that of a Scandinavian nudist. Toned arms showed he worked out, and on first glance you might mistake him for a trim forty-year-old. But on closer inspection, a slight bulge of middle-age spread, and the skin on the backs of his hands not being as taut as maybe it could be, led Jaap to believe he was more likely at the upper end of his fifties.

He appeared self-assured – he didn't feel the pressure to talk, like most people who were confronted with two police Inspectors usually did to hide their nervousness – like a man happy with his place in the world.

Once he'd brought the coffee, served in the most delicate porcelain cups Jaap had ever seen, he sat down opposite and finally turned his attention to them.

'What do you think?' he nodded to the cup in Kees' hand. 'I've got a friend who imports this stuff, hideously expensive of course, but like they say, life's too short to drink bad coffee.' He took a sip and sighed before continuing. 'But anyway, Jaap, you're obviously here because of Dirk. Big shock to us all. When I heard from Carolien I was . . .' He paused, an ostentatious search for the right word with eyes roving the ceiling. '. . . devastated.'

His voice, changed now from its earlier aggressiveness, had the languid speech of those accustomed to getting their own way.

*Why are these people always so arrogant?* wondered Jaap.

Was it because of their success, or were they successful because of that very arrogance, that quality of self-belief, their assurance that they were better, cleverer, stronger and more ruthless than anyone else?

Whatever it was, Jaap didn't like it.

'What was your relationship exactly? I hear you got involved with the business a few years ago, when it was in financial trouble?'

'Dirk didn't start out life as a businessman. He was actually a teacher, physical education, I seem to remember, and he inherited the business from his uncle. Totally out of the blue apparently. So there he was one minute running round a field blowing a whistle at some brats playing football or whatever, and the next thing he's handed the keys to a business turning over millions of euros. And all credit to him he did become a great front man, though quite how he managed it I don't know. His previous career choice wouldn't have led anyone to believe he had the charm or guile needed for that kind of role. But finance was not his strong point, counting goals was probably about the extent of his abilities, and then his divorce cost him more than he could really afford, and he'd taken money from the business to cover it. Big mistake, as that meant he couldn't meet some of the business's obligations.'

Jaap watched the self-satisfied smile reach Korssen's lips, two slugs parting after sex.

'And so you stepped in?'

'I was introduced by a mutual friend whom Dirk had asked for a loan. Which he'd refused of course. But he knows that I'm always on the look-out for investment opportunities so we were put in touch.'

'I'm guessing that you didn't offer him a loan though.'

'What am I, a charity?' he laughed. 'No, the terms were very clear, I took a controlling interest in the business.'

'What did Friedman think of that?'

Korssen shrugged. 'He wasn't jumping for joy, if that's what you mean, but he was days away from the business collapsing, having to lay off all the staff, so he didn't have much choice.'

'Was the business in trouble because of the recession?'

Korssen took another sip and then dabbed at his lips with a napkin.

'No more than anyone else. There has been a bit of a slow-down, but really it was financial mismanagement, by Dirk, which caused the problem.'

Jaap sat back slightly in his chair. By the sound of things he would have thought Korssen would be the one in line to be bumped off, not Friedman.

'So what happens now?'

'You mean to the business? Well, we had a clause that in the event of either of the shareholders dying his estate would inherit the shares.'

'In Dirk's case who would that be?'

'You'd have to talk to his lawyer about that.'

'Apparently he doesn't have any children?'

'Not that I know of.'

'Current girlfriend, partner?'

'Again, I don't really know. He divorced before I met him. But like I said, we weren't close personally, we met once a month to discuss business and that was it.'

*I bet*, thought Jaap, *those meetings were a whole lot of fun.*

'There is one thing though,' continued Korssen, as if just remembering. 'I saw him at a restaurant last week, Tuesday I think it was, and he was with someone, a man. And he seemed really uncomfortable, nervous almost. Don't know why really, I don't care what sort of road he treads outside business hours, as long as it doesn't affect his work.'

'Is that what you had your argument about?'

'And which one would that be?'

'The one on Thursday evening, at Friedman's office.'

'You are well informed. Or rather, partly well informed. We had a discussion at the office, it's true, but nothing out of the ordinary. It's the kind of thing which has to go on in a business every now and then, work out differences, and I'm sorry to say that Dirk was never very good at taking orders – too pig-headed – which is why he ended up in financial difficulty in the first place.'

'So the argument was about what, specifically?'

Korssen sighed, glanced at his watch.

'We've been planning an expansion for a while now, but Dirk kept putting up reasons why it wouldn't work. Russians are enjoying a new prosperity, and we need to have a presence there.'

'And he didn't agree?'

'He was coming round to see my side of things.'

'You can give us the name of this restaurant?'

Korssen gave it to him and Jaap wrote it down, not one he knew. In all probability one he'd never be able to afford to know either.

'And if it was you who'd died?' he asked Korssen.

'What do you mean?'

'Who would inherit your share?'

Korssen looked at him for a moment, nothing changing in his gaze.

'I'm not sure how that's really relevant?'

'It's relevant.'

For a moment Jaap thought he wasn't going to answer.

'In the event of my death my share would pass to my brother, though he doesn't know that.'

'Can I take it you're not married or in a relationship then?'

The smile which blossomed this time was real and he laughed the laugh of an alpha male, the leader of the pack whose duty it was to always come first in whatever endeavour he undertook.

'I have what you would call a rich and varied social life.'

'Meaning that you get through women quickly.'

'You make it sound so cold, but yes, there is . . .' He coughed gently. '. . . a rapid turnover.'

*He's totally in love with himself*, thought Jaap, *but is he a killer?*

He got up to leave, pushing the chair back, Kees doing the same.

'Last question, where were you Sunday night?'

'At an event.' Korssen slipped the watch off his wrist, the right, Jaap noticed, and slid it across the table. 'One of my other investments is Helmstok.'

Jaap looked at the watch. It was huge, with all sorts of, as far as he could tell, useless extra dials and numbers littering the face. Telling the time on one of these would be problematic at best.

'We were launching a new watch, and we had a party at the Hotel De L'Europe.'

'And you were there all night?'

'It started at eight but I was there from about four making sure that everything was in place, and at the event, which was very successful, by the way, there were at least a hundred and fifty of Amsterdam's richest people.'

'And what time did you leave?'

'Probably about one in the morning. You understand that there was a certain amount of champagne being drunk so it's hard to be totally exact, but I was with a close friend afterwards, I went to her place, stayed for a couple of hours, and then got a cab home.'

'You'll be able to give us the cab company's number, and that of your close friend?'

Jaap saw his eyelids flicker.

'To be honest I can't really remember, I picked one up just outside her place, in the Jordaan.'

'Did you call for it?'

'No, I'd decided to walk but then I saw a cab and thought I'd rather do that. I had had a few drinks after all.'

'So in that case why not just stay there with your friend, whose details I'd like by the way, rather than coming home?'

'I love women, Inspector,' said Korssen, stretching his arms over his head, making something click, 'but I've reached the age where I like to sleep in my own bed, you know?'

# 21

Tanya was sitting on a bed.

A hospital bed.

Her jeans were draped over the back of the chair in the corner of the room. A mobile screen – folds of institution-green fabric against the far wall – partially obscured a frosted window which looked, if she guessed right, out over the car park.

She felt slightly embarrassed by her underwear, firmly in the designed for comfort not looks category, but when she'd dragged herself out of bed, her leg throbbing with each heartbeat and hot to the touch, she'd had other things on her mind.

She had so much to do, talking to Geertje's husband about the child he saw with the Van Delfts, and then getting down to Amsterdam, a good two-hour drive, to meet Inspector Rykel.

She'd wondered about bandaging the leg up herself, but once she'd flicked the light on and looked at it properly she decided it needed a professional and drove herself straight to the hospital, every time she braked a new shot of pain running up her leg.

The junior doctor was, she had to admit to herself – at

least on the basis of the last twenty minutes – just the kind of guy she would be happy to spend some time with, if, of course, she was looking.

Which she wasn't.

Definitely wasn't.

But still, it was a real shame she'd not put on something at least a little more glamorous, if nothing else just for her own sense of pride. He'd spotted her tattoo, the two-headed snake coiling up her inner thigh, though he'd not commented.

She'd had it done when she was seventeen, an act of defiance which hadn't gone unnoticed at home. And later, every man she'd been with had been fascinated by it, though she'd never told any of them its real significance.

As he pushed the needle into a spot just above her knee she flinched, her leg jerking upwards, hitting him in the shin.

'Sorry.'

'No worries, it's practically impossible to stop that reflex. I did have a patient a few years ago though, a really old guy, and he didn't react at all to any injection, it was like he couldn't feel anything.' He pulled the needle out, dropped it into the foot-operated bin, and then started swabbing the wound. 'So one day he was lying down, and I was going to give him the injection as normal, but instead I pinched his other arm, and you know what?'

'He felt it?'

'He didn't just feel it, he jumped out of his skin.' He pushed back, riding the wheeled stool to the desk behind him, where he picked up the sterile stitch kit and then glided over to her again.

'Turns out that he was in a camp, during the war? He'd

actually been used for what they called "medical experiments" and he'd taught himself not to feel the needles they kept shoving in him. Like he literally couldn't feel them, blanked it out of his mind somehow, and it stayed. But anything else, stubbing his toe or getting a paper cut, he really felt it.'

'Amazing. Is that true?'

He looked up, mock shock in his eyes, then he smiled.

'Hey, you're the detective, you tell me.'

She gave him a look.

'Well, okay.' He stood up and peeled off his latex gloves. 'You're good to go, I've stitched it up, they'll dissolve so you don't need to get them removed.'

He was out the door but stuck his head back in.

'And I also put something else on there, a little extra.'

She looked down, and sure enough, on the bandage which was now covering the wound, there were scrawled a name and phone number.

As she pulled into the street where Arend had his workshop, searching for number 19 among the small industrial units, the sun lifted above the building at the end of the road, making her grab for the sun visor.

After Geertje's call yesterday evening all the fear that she'd felt before flooded back. She'd *known* there had been a child, but Bloem hadn't taken her seriously. And thinking about it, maybe that was her fault, maybe she should have pushed it more, stood her ground, not let him waste most of her day with what amounted to little more than stupid errands.

An oily crow jabbed at something on the road, then launched itself into the air.

She found 19 and pulled the car to a stop just outside. Frost covered the concrete and she could hear the sound of a saw, buzzing somewhere off to her left.

The man who swung the door open – the metal screeching along the concrete floor – was short, shorter than her, with a head of loose black curls, and a jumper so splattered in what looked like mud it was hard to tell what colour it had started out.

'Arend?'

'Yeah, you must be Sergeant van der Mark? Come in.'

She followed him down a corridor into a wide-open room, the glass ceiling saturating the area with light.

'So you're a potter?' she asked, making sense of all the equipment, and the two kilns at the far end of the room.

'Yeah, hardly anyone does this kind of thing by hand any more, but you get such a superior finish that machine-made just doesn't do.' He picked up a round, delicate black bowl and handed it to Tanya, the swooping curves reminding her of a tulip with wilting petals.

'I started about eight years ago, just me on my own, and now I've had to take on two apprentices to help with the work load.'

'Beautiful.' She handed it back. But she was not here to look at pottery.

As if reading her mind he placed it down and said, 'But you're not here for this. When Geertje told me about your visit yesterday. . . It made me remember about seeing them with this child, and I thought it was strange but then kind of forgot about it. I mean, we didn't really know them, they could have been looking after someone else's kid, or maybe a grandchild of theirs, though we thought they didn't have children. So it wasn't really any of my business.' He picked a bit of clay off his sleeve, and crumbled it between forefinger and thumb. 'But then when Geertje told me about your conversation . . .' He shook his head. 'I hope that they were just looking after her for the day. It would be terrible if she'd died in the fire as well.'

'We're pretty sure that she didn't.' She looked across at one of the kilns, the mouth revealing a deep, orange glow inside. 'But that means that we need to find out who she was. Where exactly did you see them?'

'There's that cafe, on Gouverneursplein? The one by the art gallery?'

She knew the place, it was where she'd told Wilhelm that things weren't working out between them.

It had not been a pretty scene.

'I'd just dropped off a new piece for a customer round there on Saturday and saw them coming out. At first I didn't recognize them, I guess the fact they had a child threw me, but as I walked past I could tell it was them.'

'Did you talk to them?'

She could hear footsteps behind her, coming towards them.

'No, it was weird, it was like they'd seen me and didn't want to be noticed. I mean, we hardly knew them, but even so, we're kind of the only neighbours they've got . . .' He shrugged, then greeted the owner of the footsteps, who walked over to the right-hand kiln. 'But, who knows, I guess they were just really private people.'

'What time was this?'

'Would have been about ten, ten-thirty?'

'And you're sure the child was with them?'

He nodded. 'No doubt. Eva van Delft was doing her coat up for her.'

'And what did she, the child I mean, look like?'

'I couldn't really see her face, her coat had one of those hoods with fur all around the rim, but I'm pretty sure she had red hair, like yours, kind of long.'

*Bloem's going to have to listen to me now,* she thought, a tendril of excitement wrapping round her stomach,

'Anything else noticeable about her? What sort of age do you think she was?'

He screwed his eyes up, before opening them again.

'About five or six I'd say, same as my two.'

'Can you think of anyone who'd want to burn down their house?'

He shook his head before answering.

'No, I mean, we didn't really know them so it's not like we even knew who their friends were, let alone any enemies.'

Arend's colleague dropped something; the loud clatter made them both jump.

'So you think they had friends?'

'Well . . .' He ran a hand through his hair. '. . . now you mention it, not really.'

She thanked him and made her way back to her car. As soon as she got moving her phone went.

Bloem.

'I thought I told you to check this,' he said when she answered.

'Check what?'

'The house, who owned it.'

'You didn't.'

'Well, I did. But anyway, I've done it now and it turns

out the Van Delfts were only renting, so I need you to go and talk to their landlord.'

'Listen, I've had confirmation that the Van Delfts had a child with them over the weekend, so I really think we need –'

'Just go and talk to this guy, I've spoken to him and he's expecting you. And come back here when you're done.'

He gave her the address on the east side of town, which Tanya was pretty sure did live sex shows.

*Surprised he didn't want to go there himself*, she thought as she hung up and swung the car around.

As she pulled into the half-empty car park ten minutes later, crushed beer cans littering the ground like miniature ships on a grey frozen sea, she spotted a guy, beer gut bulging under his tight designer T-shirt.

Her dashboard thermometer read one degree; maybe it was the hair on his arms, so hairy he appeared to be at least two steps back down the evolutionary ladder, that allowed him to go outside without more on.

Once she'd parked he ambled over, she lowered the passenger side window, and he introduced himself as Saar Kloots. He looked like the kind of guy who would leer at her whilst she was out with friends.

*I can't even remember the last time I went out with them all*, she thought.

Not wanting to go inside to talk she reluctantly leant across and opened the passenger door. He got in, bringing both the cold and a strong aftershave, polluting the entire airspace in the car within seconds. True to form his eyes slid up and down her body – a reptile on a rock –

before he settled into the seat, legs splayed as wide as was possible, nudging the gearstick.

'Work?' asked Tanya, nodding towards the club, a red neon sign advertising 'Live Sex' pulsing above the door.

'Purely pleasure,' he grinned. 'I have someone who looks after the day-to-day running of my properties, so I've got more leisure time than I used to.' He coughed a tight cough and continued. 'What happened?'

'We're not too sure at the moment, but the building went up in flames sometime yesterday, and the Van Delfts didn't make it out in time.'

'Do you know how the fire was started?'

'Not yet.'

'I'm going to have to get on to my insurance people. Have you got some kind of report that I can give them?'

'My main interest is in the two people who died there,' she said trying to get as much reproach in her voice as possible. He didn't seem to care that two people had burnt to death in one of his houses. 'What can you tell me about them? How long have they been there?'

'I can't really remember, about three or so years I reckon. But I've been having problems with them. Serious problems.'

'Really?'

'Non-payment of rent. And that totally fucks me off, I mean I'm not a charity, I've got to pay the mortgage on that place, and if they don't pay the rent I can't. Leaves me in a bad position.'

'So what did you do?'

'First I dropped in on them, just for a friendly chat' – Tanya had her doubts – 'and when things didn't get better I had to get my lawyers involved. We're actually due to go to court next month, get this settled once and for all.'

'Did they have a child?'

A man walking past on the pavement turned to stare at them. She could read in his eyes and the slight smile which tugged at the corners of his mouth he'd pegged them as a couple having an argument.

Girlfriend-catching-boyfriend-at-sleazy-sex-joint.

'You know, now that you mention it, I remember. There was a child there, a little girl, I asked them about her and they were kind of coy about it. But I pushed them, they hadn't mentioned anything about having a kid when we signed the tenancy agreement.'

'And what did they say?'

'That they'd only recently adopted her.'

Adopted. The word hit her like a boulder. The doll had been for an adopted daughter. So where was she now?

'Maybe they torched it on purpose, just to get back at me.' Kloots' voice broke into her thoughts, a kernel of anger in his voice.

'And killed themselves as well? Sounds like that would be more of a favour to you?'

'Point taken.' He reached down and scratched his crotch slowly, his overlong nails sounding like they were shredding the denim. 'Maybe they got caught up in it by accident?'

'I'll need to talk to your lawyers about this, but if you think of anything else let me know.'

'Yeah, okay.' He opened the door and swung a foot out. 'Don't suppose you want to join me for a drink inside?'

Tanya stared at him until he swung out the other foot and stood up.

'Okay, I get the message,' she heard as he slammed the door shut.

By the time she made it back Bloem wasn't around so she looked up adoption agencies. There was a local branch in Leeuwarden, which she called, but a recorded message told her that it was closed and to direct all enquiries to the Central Adoption Agency in Amsterdam. The recorded message didn't extend the courtesy of telling her the number, so she had to search online.

Bloem came in just as she'd managed to speak to someone who was able to confirm that they had the Van Delfts on their system, but that if she wanted more info they'd have to pull the file.

'Van der Mark, in here.'

Bloem indicated the incident room.

She joined him, the air of the room dense with stale sweat.

'What have you got?'

'I spoke to the landlord, and he said they did have a girl, they'd adopted, and I just got off the phone from the adoption agency in Amsterdam, they have the Van Delfts on file.'

'And there was no trace at the scene, we're sure she wasn't just . . . burned up?'

'I asked the forensics several times, they said no. I think we should put it out there.'

'With what, a vague description of a young girl without a name? Unless you got that info from the adoption agency?'

'They wouldn't give it to me over the phone, some child protection legislation, but they said if I go in person, with a warrant, they can let me have a look.'

He stared at her.

'I just don't buy it. Why would someone kill them and take the child?'

The door opened and Lankhorst walked in.

'Where are we up to?'

Bloem cleared his throat.

'We're concentrating on finding out who actually started the fire. I can't find any reason why someone would want to murder these two, they were just an old couple who kept themselves to themselves. I think we need to look at the possibility that it might have been suicide.'

'Do you really think they'd tie themselves up though?' she asked. Bloem shot her a look.

'I don't believe any rope was found?'

'No, but the position of their arms, they couldn't have just lain there like that by accident.'

Bloem just glared at her.

Lankhorst turned to Tanya. 'And the kid? Where are we at?'

'They adopted, I'm going to go to Amsterdam to try and get a name, and I'll meet with Inspector Rykel, the one who knew Haak?' she felt Bloem's eyes might actually start a fire on her skin.

'What kind of age was she?'

'About five or six, it seems.'

'Check the schools, see if the name Van Delft comes up. Update me before I leave today. Anything else?'

They both shook their heads, Lankhorst left, and Tanya headed towards the door in his wake.

'Sergeant van der Mark.' She turned back to see Bloem lounging back in his chair, twirling a pen between his fingers. 'A word of advice, I'm going to be in his position soon, so if you want to get ahead . . .'

He cupped himself through his jeans with his spare hand, and stared at her.

*Why are men such assholes?* she wondered as she held his gaze for a few beats, then turned and left.

# 22

Jaap felt the tension in the room as soon as he stepped into Smit's office.

*What's the matter with him?* Jaap wondered as he watched Smit stride from the window and assume the throne behind his desk.

He didn't invite Jaap to sit.

'Is there something I should know, about Andreas?' Smit's voice confirmed something was wrong.

'I . . . I don't know what you mean.'

'What I mean is . . .' Smit leant forward. 'Does he have any "extra-curricular" activities that I should be worried about? Because I just gave a press conference and a lunatic journalist from a tabloid asked me if Andreas was into child porn.'

'What?'

'And if I've been out there' – he jabbed a finger towards the corridor – 'waxing lyrical about an officer who turns out to have been a rotten apple then the repercussions for everyone in this department are going to be severe.'

'I've no idea what's going on, Andreas wasn't into por—'

'Are you sure? I've got his record here, and about five

132

years ago he ran a child porn case, and I'm wondering if he acquired a taste for it.'

'No way.' Jaap shook his head. 'There is *no way* that Andreas was into that.' His voice rising but he couldn't help it. 'And I can't believe you'd even consider it. Who was this journalist?'

'Now *that* I'm not going to tell you – if you start putting pressure on a journalist then this thing is going to be worse than it already is. And I want to stress that you're not to be involved in the investigation in any way. You have your own investigation to run and if I find that you're getting in De Waart's way' – his voice raised, his eyes like bullets – 'your career is going to take a swift trip down the shithole, is that clear?'

A car horn blared from the street below.

*Andreas is being buried on Friday*, Jaap thought, *and now this.*

'I really –'

'Is,' said Smit emphasizing each word like he was chipping them from stone, 'that clear, Inspector Rykel?'

# 23

Kees kicked a can, which skittered across the bricks and over the edge into the canal. He heard it hit ice.

After they'd left Korssen, Jaap had fobbed him off with the jobs of interviewing Friedman's ex-wife, checking up on Korssen's alibi with his lady friend, Heleen de Kok, and, worst of all, trying to find out who Friedman's dining partner had been. De Kok wasn't answering her phone, but he did manage to track Friedman's ex to an address in Haarlem. Which meant at least an hour's drive. The restaurant wasn't open this early so he'd have to leave that till later.

*Typical, he gives me the shit jobs, just like all the others*, he thought as he made his way to the car pool, which was fifty metres away from the station on Prinsengracht. But just as he got there his phone rang, Smit requesting an immediate meeting.

'Kees, good of you to come,' said Smit as Kees arrived.

*What the fuck's he talking about*, wondered Kees as he sat in the chair indicated by Smit's plump hand, *he's the one who ordered me here?*

'My pleasure, sir.'

'Tinged with a bit of disappointment, no doubt?' Smit

lowered himself into his chair – hands on the arm rests, elbows in the air – as if his backside were made of porcelain and needed to be treated with care. 'A young Inspector like you would have been hoping to take that case on himself.'

'Well, yeah, I did figure Jaap would be pulled from it, given the circumstances.'

Smit nodded slowly, as if Kees had just said something profound.

'It isn't about ego, this job.'

Kees hid his disbelief; the man sitting in front of him was reputed to have the largest ego in Amsterdam.

'It's about making sure the guilty are brought to justice in the quickest way possible, it's about teamwork, it's about results.'

*Where's he going with all this crap?* Kees nodded, feigning interest.

'I've been looking over your file.' He picked up a folder from his desk and flipped through it. 'Great results, near the top of your class at the Netherlands Police Academy, and excellent references supporting your transfer here. Settling in well?'

*That was just because they wanted rid of me.*

'Yes, thank you, sir.'

Smit put down the folder and adjusted it so it squared with the edge of the desk.

'You know, when it comes to progressing in the police force, all these things' – he waved his hand over the folder as if trying to disperse a noxious scent – 'are a great start, but they *are* only the start. I read your reasons for transferring, that you thought you were able to contribute more in an urban setting, meaning, presumably, that where you were things were a bit slow?'

'Zeeland is not exactly Amsterdam, sir.'

Smit shuddered, a slight chill, or the mention of Zeeland, affecting him.

'No, I can imagine, agricultural crime isn't what you signed up for. Someone of your skills should be here, in the city.'

He leant back in his chair and studied Kees, his porcine eyes boring deep. Kees held his gaze until Smit nodded, as if agreeing with some internal voice.

'Jaap will be working the case, this you already know.'

Kees knew.

Smit's desk phone started ringing; he glanced towards it but didn't pick it up.

'But because of Andreas' death I would like you to . . . keep an eye on him.' He paused and picked up a pen, rolling it between his fingers. Kees thought he looked like he was rolling a joint. 'Just to check that he's okay.'

'Sure, no problem.'

'He wanted to be put in charge of the investigation into Andreas' death . . .'

*If I'm reading this right, he's asking me to make sure Jaap doesn't investigate it on his own.*

'It's things like these, little favours, which can really help a career . . . take off.' He stood up, the interview clearly at an end. Kees stood as well.

'I read your report first thing this morning, anything changed since?'

'We're looking at ways for tracing those numbers, I think whoever owns them is in danger. Jaap didn't agree but I'm going to work on that angle if that's okay with you?'

'Good. Give me an update every day, more frequently if something comes up. And we're on the same page here, are we?' He threw him another look, which Kees read as the significant sort.

'I think so.'

Smit nodded.

'Good,' he said. 'Very good. And Inspector? Get a haircut.'

# 24

'Did he agree?'

De Waart had been standing down the corridor from Smit's office, waiting until Kees had left.

Smit nodded.

'I think he's on board.'

They'd been discussing the case earlier; it was bad enough being an Inspector down, but to then have that same Inspector's reputation being questioned so openly in a press conference was intolerable to Smit. If there was any truth in it at all then he could kiss goodbye to moving up to be Amsterdam's next Chief of Police, the board would shift him sideways at best. And if he allowed a close working colleague of Andreas Hansen's to take the case there would be headlines screaming about institutional cover-ups. Then he'd never get where he wanted, where he *needed*, to be.

He'd worked his way up from the street, and he wasn't prepared to let it all fall down now.

'So what's the latest?'

'You knew Hansen's laptop has been wiped?'

'Rykel told me last night.'

'Well, we checked the security tapes on the office – the only person to go near it in the last twenty-four hours was

Rykel. The only person prior to that was Inspector Hansen, on Saturday afternoon.'

Smit stared at him for a few moments.

'Okay, I want hourly updates on this, and the second you get anything, you let me know.'

De Waart turned for the door, but before he stepped out he paused.

'What is it?' asked Smit.

'I was just thinking,' he said, scratching at the side of his chest, 'what do we do if it turns out Rykel is involved?'

# 25

Jaap was sitting in a car outside the morgue, phone glued to his ear.

His eyes had strayed to the building, a large concrete block which seemed to be sucking all life from the surrounding area in an attempt to reanimate its inmates.

'You should have seen him, his eyes nearly popped out of his head. I tell you, it's not often you see Smit like that, and he recovered quickly, but . . . it was pretty funny.'

Jaap, who in another situation might well have been able to enjoy the story of his superior officer's discomfort, wasn't able to respond that enthusiastically, a fact that Niels, Jaap's tame journalist, picked up on.

'Look, sorry, I know you must be going through hell right now.'

'Which is why I called you, I need the name of that tabloid hack, the one who made the accusation.'

A pause, just breathing.

'I thought maybe you were calling to tell me something.'

'Like?'

'Well, like if there was any truth in what that guy said?'

'Are you kidding me? Andreas was not involved in that kind of shit, I can guarantee you –'

'Can I quote you on that?'

'Come on, I just need his name. I'm not going to beat him up or anything.'

Niels sighed a stage sigh.

'Yeah, okay, let me look at my notes, I wrote it down as he wasn't one of the regulars, I'd never seen him before.'

Jaap could hear shuffling, and music. Some eighties pop song that he couldn't quite place.

He tuned the music out and started trying to make connections.

He had Andreas' death, and Friedman's. Andreas had thought Friedman was their way into the gang, the Black Tulips, and the anonymous phones showed that Friedman was up to something illegal. But who then had killed them? Was it the same person? Or was it ordered by someone higher up, and farmed out to different people? And what had Andreas been doing with the number from Friesland, where Sergeant van der Mark had seen Ludo Haak? And Andreas had pulled Haak's record a day before he was killed.

He had to start making the connections.

But they just weren't forming.

He also needed to talk to Sergeant van der Mark, but she still hadn't let him know exactly when she'd be down.

The phone was getting hot against his ear just as Niels came back on.

'Okay, got it. He was called Patrick Borst, and he works for *De Adelaar*.'

'Thanks, Niels.' And he just managed to stop himself from adding, 'I owe you one.'

Not something he really wanted to say to any journalist, tame or not.

'No worries, and Jaap?'

'Yeah?'

'If you do end up beating him to a pulp, promise me I'll get an exclusive?'

Jaap hung up then dialled *De Adelaar*, asking to speak to Borst. He had to repeat the name a couple of times.

'I'm sorry, but I can't find a number for him, do you know which department he works in?'

'I know he reports on crime stories.'

'Okay, let's see,' said the woman. 'No, I'm not coming up with anyone here of that name.'

'Can you put me through to the HR department, this is really urgent.'

After a few minutes on hold, a thought began to form, a thought he didn't like. A voice came on the line, so croaky he couldn't tell if it was male or female. He explained that this was an emergency, and he had to get in contact with one of their staff.

'We definitely don't have anyone of that name on the payroll.'

'What about freelancers, you must use them as well?'

'I checked, nothing there either. Maybe you got the name wrong?'

*Or maybe*, thought Jaap as he killed the call, *he doesn't exist.*

He got out of the car and walked into the building, the disinfectant like a slap in the face. A man was waiting outside a door; the dull grey paint embellished with a yellow male stick figure. Some joker had drawn a white outline, a crime scene halo, round it. He was short, late fifties, and wearing the grey suit and refined blue herringbone shirt of a lawyer. Making up in girth what he lacked in height, he looked around briefly and then caught Jaap's eye, his mouth pulled into a forced smile.

'Inspector Terpstra?'

'Inspector Rykel.' Jaap held out his hand. 'I work with Inspector Terpstra.'

The man waddled over to where Jaap was standing, and they shook hands, the lawyer's hand so moist that Jaap felt like he wanted to wipe his own afterwards.

'Lars Heiland. Terrible thing, this.'

'I believe you were his lawyer?'

'You must get used to that in your profession, using the past tense.'

Shrugging, 'It comes with practice.'

*Does he really want to discuss grammar?* thought Jaap

'I can imagine, though in this case I'm afraid you weren't quite right. I am *still* his lawyer, even if he is dead.'

*He does.*

They made it to the viewing room and found the body laid out under a white sheet. The bright clinical light only accentuated the feeling of revulsion which everyone who entered the morgue felt. All except, of course, the staff, who were perfectly at home with death, and gave it no more thought than their charges ever did.

The scene looked like something out of a seventies sci-fi programme, minimalist white tiles, glinting stainless steel. At Jaap's gesture a bald white-coated man, with vivid red cheeks obscene in their expression of life, appeared and lifted back a corner of the sheet just enough for Heiland – still smiling – to see the face.

The lawyer nodded – the smile had wilted now as if the muscles in the corners of his mouth just gradually gave out – and he dabbed at his lips with a handkerchief.

'Yes, that's him.'

The orderly re-covered the body and Heiland spoke again, but almost to himself.

'Such a shame, so young.'

He shook his head as if trying to dislodge something from his ears.

He didn't look that young to Jaap, mid-forties at least, if not fifty.

'How old was he?'

Heiland looked up as if he'd forgotten where he was, and when he saw Jaap the smile returned. Jaap could see that it was the ingratiating smile of the eternal sycophant that so many lawyers resorted to in their life-long bid to convince people their services were required.

Or maybe he was being too harsh, Heiland might never have had to identify a dead body before and was simply finding the situation difficult.

'Forty-seven. And he's done so much good, giving to charity, but he never got what he –'

Jaap's phone rang, the loud noise startling him, making him aware that they'd been talking in quiet voices. Respect for the dead.

'Hey, it's Sergeant van der Mark, you said to give you a call?'

'Yeah, where are you?'

'I'm going to be in Amsterdam in about two hours, have you still got time to meet?'

Jaap gave her an address and said he'd be there at 2 p.m. He turned back to Heiland.

'You were saying, he never got something?'

'All he really wanted,' said Heiland, breaking off to swallow, 'was a child. A child of his own.'

Once the papers had been signed and Heiland had taken his leave Jaap pulled out his phone and dialled Saskia. She didn't answer so he left a quick message, asking her call him as soon as she could.

He wanted to warn her about the allegations against Andreas before she found out for herself from the TV or radio. Then he went in search of Valentien Breed, a short, stocky woman – a victim of traditional Dutch cooking – who had been working at the morgue ever since Jaap had been coming there, and was seemingly inured to death like no other, transporting corpses on their trolleys as if she were doing her weekly shop in Albert Heijn. He found her and made his request.

'I'm really not supposed to do that.' She looked at Jaap as if he were disappointing her.

'I know, but I would really appreciate it.'

'I mean, I know he was your friend and all, but you're not the officer on the case and you shouldn't be able to see the body before the autopsy has taken place.'

'Look, I know, but it's just that . . . I want to see him before . . .' . . . *before they cut him up*.

She reached out and rubbed his arm.

'It's all right, love, I understand.' She led him to the examination room and unlocked it. 'I'll wait out here, don't be too long.'

Closing the door behind him he felt the chill that kept

the bodies from decomposing, and shivered. There were five tables in the room, but only one body was out, Andreas, on the centre table, the altar of an ancient cult which practised human sacrifice. He glanced up at the chart on the wall to his left; Andreas' name was written in black with '12.15' scrawled next to it in red pen.

*I need to get this over with*, he thought noting the time. Soon someone would be along to prep.

He pulled in two or three deep breaths, the disinfectant stinging his nostrils, and then, feeling like he was stepping off the edge of the world, moved forward, his right foot slipping away slightly on the tiled floor.

It was worse than he'd feared, no way of identifying him from his features, the bullet having taken a good portion of his face off when it exited, probably around the left cheekbone, though it was hard to tell. This was a closed-casket job.

Even worse for Saskia.

In Kyoto he'd learnt about form and emptiness. How they could be viewed as the same, as two parts of one whole. He'd thought he'd understood.

Now he wasn't so sure.

He couldn't bear it and pulled his eyes away only for them to settle on the clothes and his personal belongings laid out in neat little bags on the table to his right. The bags weren't labelled up yet, which meant that someone was about to come back and catalogue all this.

He slid on a pair of gloves from a box on the wall, extracted Andreas' phone from the bag and powered it on, looking at the calls list. Aside from his own number there was one which jumped out. The number he'd got from Andreas' computer, a call lasting just over ten minutes on Sunday morning.

*Heiland said Friedman wanted a child*, he thought, *and Sergeant van der Mark's missing one. Is that the connection here?*

After a few seconds he watched his finger, shaking, navigate the menu, then delete the text message about Friedman.

There was a line.

And as he slipped the phone back into the bag, he knew he'd just crossed it.

# 26

As Kees drove, his conversation with Smit kept playing in his head, changing slightly with each re-imagining.

He'd watched himself, rising up through the ranks, quickly becoming Smit's favourite, the hotshot officer who was assigned the best cases, and by the time he reached the turn-off to Haarlem he'd mapped out his whole career in Technicolor, the images vivid in his mind.

And he wasn't surprised that Marinette hadn't featured in the movie of his future life at all.

In fact the woman who had been at the door – an expensive house near the Vondelpark, one of those large buildings he drove past on the way to the station every morning, not dissimilar to Korssen's place – to greet him home with smouldering eyes was pretty close, he realized with a jolt, to the pathologist, Carice.

*She is*, he admitted to himself as he drove down the road scanning numbers, *pretty hot*.

Which made her response to his text all the more exciting.

He found the house, parked up on the far side of the road – the only free space left on the street – and let the silence settle in around him for a few moments as the engine died away.

An old man with a dog, some kind of mongrel, shuffled round the corner and the pair made their way towards him. The dog was limping – one of its hind legs, or maybe its hip, wasn't working properly – so they moved in fits and starts, the old man occasionally tugging at the lead.

Another car passed on the road, and Kees cracked the door open, filling the interior with cold air, wet against his skin. As he got out he caught a glimpse of his face in the rearview mirror and wondered if the face he could see there was the face of a snitch.

The house was large, set back from the road and built predominately from red brick. Five polished marble steps led to a front door. Two box trees with long slender trunks and immaculately pruned branches stood guard.

He'd called ahead; he knew that really he should have been in front of her when she was told about Friedman's death, but he didn't want to drive out all that way and find she wasn't in, find she was at work, away on holiday, or any other of the many reasons why someone might not be at home during the day.

She answered the door, and though her eyes might have held the slightly misty, liquid quality of the recently bereaved, her manner wouldn't give a casual observer any idea that she had recently lost a husband, even an ex. She was a slight woman, short blonde hair and a figure that, when she wasn't pregnant as now, Kees noted as his eyes travelled downwards, could be confused for a slim man from the right angle.

'I'm Paultje,' she said as she motioned him in and showed him through to a room at the back of the house, impeccably decorated, white marble floors, low furniture and a large red dragon standing by one of the sofas, the scales picked out with gold leaf.

'Beautiful, isn't it?' she asked when she saw Kees looking at it. 'I picked it up when my husband and I were on our honeymoon in Beijing. They have amazing craftsmanship there, and Japan too. They really take care of things, not like here where everything is done in a rush and as cheaply as possible. But then again they seem to have a different regard for human life, especially in China, or at least they did when we were there.'

She paused for a moment, seemingly confused.

'Sorry, I'm talking nonsense, it's just a bit of a shock. Will you sit?'

She motioned with a delicate twist of her wrist, her open palm showing the chair allocated for him, and then sat herself on a sofa, arranging the cushions against her back so she was upright.

'You said he was . . .' She looked down at the floor for a second before her eyes rose again. '. . . murdered.'

'I'm afraid so. Do you know anyone who he'd argued with, anyone who had threatened him?'

'Other than me?'

'I'm guessing that given your . . .' He cleared his throat. '. . . present condition you probably wouldn't have been up to it.'

She felt instinctively for her stomach, laying a hand just on the top of the curve.

'No, hard enough getting up the stairs at the moment let alone running around killing ex-husbands.' A weak smile, not reaching the eyes. 'Would it surprise you to know he was a difficult man?'

'In what way?'

'He was very domineering, he always wanted things his own way, and he was very secretive, he'd sometimes not talk for what seemed like days, just the basics, yes, no, I love you, all on autopilot.'

'Is that why you split up?'

'Have you ever split up with someone?'

'Many times.'

*And I'm heading that way again.*

'Then you'll know what it's like. There's that feeling you start to get, when you look at them sometimes and you suddenly realize that you're not attracted to them in the same way you were once. Something they do irritates you, makes you want to avoid catching their eye. That's when you know it's over. It's just a question of how long you keep on deluding yourself.'

'So there wasn't anything specific?'

'There were many reasons, the main one was that he really wanted a child, but it just never happened. He got really agitated about it, we went to all sorts of doctors, had tests done, everything. And each time the results came back fine, but it just didn't work. Then he started talking about adopting a child but by then our relationship was over, I'd known it for a while, but it took him longer to realize. And I think that made me actually get up and go – the fact that I'd been ahead of him, that he'd not figured out that something was wrong just made it more important that I left. That and the porn.'

'Porn?'

'I found some. On his computer once. He tried to lie about it, say it wasn't his, that he didn't know how it got there. This was towards the end anyway, and I don't know if he'd always been into that kind of thing, or if it was recent. But it was like the final straw.'

Kees wondered what proportion of the male population had some kind of porn stashed on their computer. He figured it was pretty high.

'What type of porn, anything out of the usual?'

'I don't really know what usual is, but it looked to me like the women in it were made up to look like teenagers. You know, pigtails and bright nail varnish, that kind of thing.'

*So Friedman liked them young*, Kees thought.

'Did he have any financial worries?'

'Not that I knew of, he always seemed to have enough money, and he always talked as if the business was going well.'

'And what about friends, is there anyone who I should be talking to?'

'He was always seeing people, meeting them, taking them out to expensive restaurants, for the business he'd always say, but I don't think he had any actual friends at all.'

Kees was wondering what he was doing here. It was a complete waste of time, she didn't know anything, and it clearly couldn't have been her. He should be back in Amsterdam getting on with more important things.

*Like spying on Jaap.*

'When did you last see him?'

'Ages ago, I think it must have been August, September maybe.'

'Where?'

'In the newspaper, there was something about him

becoming a patron for some charity, a children's charity, I think it was. Made me laugh, I figured he still hadn't found someone to have a baby with.' She massaged her stomach again, running her hands over it, a gypsy woman with a crystal ball.

'Especially,' she said as her hand stopped, 'as the problem was clearly his, not mine.'

# 27

Jaap sat on a creased leather sofa in the reception of Vrijheid Nu, the last appointment in Friedman's diary. Green palms, moved by the aircon, were scraping their fronds gently against the wall, and the receptionist was filing her nails with a dry rasp.

Subdued abstract paintings hung above her and a water cooler hummed softly.

The receptionist's phone rang and she answered, cradling the phone between her shoulder and head whilst she started to apply nail polish. The intense chemical smell rapidly gave Jaap a headache.

As if his head hadn't been aching already.

Borst didn't exist, that much was clear. After *De Adelaar* claimed no one worked there he'd called the station and got them to check the press pass list, and wasn't surprised to find Borst missing from it.

Was this the Black Tulips further trying to muddy the water, create a diversion away from the real reason Andreas had been killed? To accuse a cop of being involved with child porn was smart, from their point of view. It would throw the top brass into panic, the thought of the headlines alone, justified or not, would be enough to rile them into a state of near frenzy. The pressure would be to shift the focus of the investigation.

Jaap suddenly felt he was in a better position not being in charge of the case.

'You can go through now.'

On the other side of the door there was a large open-plan office, a similar size to the station, but filled with half the people. And each luxuriated in a desk several feet apart from that of their colleagues. A young man stepped forward awkwardly, holding his hand out to be shaken but he seemed to judge it wasn't appropriate, changing his mind and withdrawing it just as Jaap reached out.

'I'm Teunis van Marwijk, assistant to the director. He'll be along shortly, if you'd like to follow me?'

He ended up in a smaller office off the back, a window on to the street, and a glass wall looking on to the main area. At Teunis' insistence he sat at a round table, and declined his offer of coffee. Teunis seemed slightly nervous.

'Can you tell me what this charity does exactly?' Jaap asked just as Teunis appeared to be on the verge of leaving him.

'Well, it's for children who've been victims of abuse. We help with everything we can, both for the parents, unless they were the abusers, of course, and for the children.'

'So this is a step after the social services?'

Teunis grimaced.

'The social services pass most of this on to us, they can't cope.'

'Who can't cope?'

The question came from the man at the door, dressed

in dark blue jeans and crisp white shirt buttoned tight at the neck but with no tie.

Teunis jumped at the voice and turned round.

'I was just telling them about the social services . . .'

'Oh, I see. Well, he's right, they really can't cope.' He advanced into the room and Jaap stood to shake hands. 'Hans Grimberg, pleased to meet you.'

Jaap guessed his age to be around thirty, young for someone in his position, though the dark circles like bruises below his eyes, *almost the same colour as the bruises on Friedman's neck*, he thought, made him look older. From his accent he placed him as being from somewhere south.

Like Andreas.

He'd been from down south as well, though his accent had changed quite rapidly when he moved to Amsterdam.

Jaap could see him, lying on the table at the morgue. He tried to erase the image.

Grimberg sat down, Teunis hanging back for a few moments, before Grimberg thanked him, the dismissal clear.

'So what can I do for you?'

'I'm afraid we have some bad news. Dirk Friedman was found dead yesterday morning.'

'Dead? How?'

'He was killed.'

Jaap watched as Grimberg absorbed the news, his face going slack for a few moments before he regained control.

'I don't know what to say . . . do you know who killed him?'

'Not yet, that's partly why I'm here, I believe you had a meeting with him on Sunday?'

'Yes, he was here, sitting right where you are now.'

Jaap found himself shifting in his chair and stopped abruptly.

'And was there anything wrong? Was he acting strangely?'

'Not at all, he seemed his normal self.'

'And what time did he leave?'

'Umm . . . I'd have to check when the appointment was for.' His face pinched with concentration.

'According to his diary it was at eleven a.m.'

'Yeah, that sounds about right, so he would have left by about quarter to twelve at the latest.'

He was staring down at his hands, clasped together on the table, the angle of his neck making his voice indistinct.

'Did he mention anything unusual?'

'It was a fairly normal conversation, we're . . . we *were* planning a fundraising event, in March, and we had a few details to go over.'

'Why Sunday?'

'He'd had to cancel early in the week, and we had to meet up so I suggested Sunday. So when you say he was discovered yesterday, was that when he was killed?'

'Sunday evening, maybe early Monday morning, we're waiting for the time of death from the pathologist. The thing is, as far as we can tell at the moment, you might well have been the last to see him alive.'

Grimberg forced a laugh, a goat choking on the cud.

'That's usually a bad sign, right?'

Jaap shrugged.

'How long have you known him?'

'About seven, eight months maybe.'

'And how did that come about?'

'He wrote to us, or no, maybe he rang first ... I'm pretty sure, he rang, and said he was interested in somehow being involved with the charity, so we arranged to meet.'

'And you didn't know him before that?'

'I'd heard of him, not sure where, he wasn't famous or anything ... I think I must have read something about his business in the paper.'

Jaap took out a notebook from his coat pocket and flipped through it.

'So what was the outcome of your initial meeting?'

'Well, like I said, he wanted to be involved, become a patron. He initially made a donation, but then he had the idea to do an event, he was going to host it, tap into some of his rich clients.'

'Do you not get public funding?'

Grimberg sighed, and leant back in his chair.

'We used to. Then two years ago it was cut. So we're totally dependent on raising our own funds. And to be honest we're struggling' – his voice dropping, a quick glance towards the glass wall, as if afraid his staff might hear. 'This event we were planning. It was probably going to be the last chance to get some real exposure.' He shook his head, resigned. 'I guess that sounds callous, here he is dead, and I'm worrying about money. But the thing is, what we do for these kids – and we cover the whole country here, every abuse case is referred to us, and some people find their own way – is essential. It's not something you can get over easily. I guess some people think that with a bit of counselling they can get over it, that as they're kids they'll be able to somehow shrug it off . . .' He leant forward. '. . . but it can affect their whole lives, everything they do, what job they get, how they interact with people, whether they end up in trouble with the law, everything. There are studies that show the brains of abused children are actually different – there's an area called the hippocampus?'

Jaap nodded.

'Well, abuse can re-wire it. It's scary.'

Someone knocked on the glass door and motioned to Grimberg.

'Look, I've got a meeting, is there anything else I can help with?'

'Did you ever have reason to suspect his motives?'

Jaap couldn't be sure but he thought he detected a stiffening in Grimberg's shoulders.

'How do you mean?'

'You know, a single man, a childless man, interested in helping out with children?'

Grimberg seemed to think about it.

'He did mention that he didn't have children, and that's why he wanted to help. I didn't ask him *why* he didn't have his own.'

'Presumably you'd run a CRB on him?'

'No, why would I? He wanted to raise money, he wasn't going to have anything to do with the children themselves.'

Jaap thought about it. The question of children was coming up in this investigation far too often for his liking. He stood and pushed his card across the table.

'I think that's it for now, if you do think of anything . . .'

Grimberg picked it up and held it for a few moments then looked up at him, and Jaap wondered for a second if he was going to ask him for a donation.

'I hope you find the person responsible.'

The same person who'd knocked on the glass door had now opened it, sounds of office life flowing into the room, a kettle rumbling to the boil, voices, a phone cut off mid-ring as someone answered.

Jaap looked at Grimberg, at his grey eyes set slightly too wide on his face.

'We're working on it.'

# 28

'And which night did you say?'

The maître d' was managing to squeeze an immense amount of disdain and dislike into every word, his mouth pinched as if Kees had brought in the stench of a fermenting sewer.

The restaurant was plush, all dark purples and gold, and a few people in suits were finishing off late lunches, their faces saturated with wine. Kees had found it on a quiet square just south of the Concertgebouw, Amsterdam's nineteenth-century concert hall. It was so exclusive it didn't even advertise itself as a restaurant, just a number on an expensive-looking door.

'Tuesday,' Kees responded, staring back at him.

'Well, I'm not sure we are allowed to give out –'

'I already showed you my ID, so if you've got something written there' – he jammed his finger on to the reservation page the maître d' had been studying – 'you'd better tell me right now.'

The maître d' jumped, pouted and spun the book round with a flourish so Kees could read it. A few heads turned his way.

*I bet he's a fag,* thought Kees as he scanned down the times, the handwriting cramped and precise. No Friedman, but there were only four tables set for two that evening. He pulled out a photo.

'Which of these tables did he sit at?'

Sulkily the maître d' pointed to the slot for table seven; the name on the reservation was Jan Zwartberg.

Jaap's phone went straight to voicemail, Kees left a message and headed back to the station. Just as he arrived at his desk Jaap called him back.

'I've got Friedman's dining partner, someone called Jan Zwartberg.'

'Okay, go back to the station to run the name and –'

'Yeah, I'm doing it.' *I am an Inspector,* and before he could stop himself he was asking, 'What have you been doing?'

Jaap paused before answering, his voice colder than before.

'Just call me if you get anything.'

*I've been out to Haarlem and back,* Kees thought as he hung up, *and what's he been doing?*

Was this the first sign that Smit's suspicions had been right? But even so, the problem was, he now realized, how was he going to prove it? Especially if Jaap was going to send him off on stupid errands? And thinking about it, was Jaap already suspicious, was that why he sent him off to Haarlem, so he could be alone?

*So how,* thought Kees as he ran his eyes down the list, looking for Zwartberg, *am I going to get him to trust me?*

# 29

Jaap spotted her, or someone he figured was her, sitting alone at a table mid-way back, red hair glowing under the downlighters shaped like inverted tulips, a bike helmet on the table in front of her. When they'd arranged to meet he'd thought of this place, a bagel joint he and Andreas would often go out of their way to pick up food from, tucked on a narrow pedestrian street about a block away from where the red-light district really started to kick off.

He wouldn't be coming here with Andreas again.

'Sergeant van der Mark?'

She looked up at him and he noticed her eyes were green, her skin pale. He introduced himself as he sat down, taking in her biker leathers, and motioned for the waitress to take an order.

'So you've got Haak down for two murders and a kidnap?'

'Yeah, I've got a witness who says this couple adopted a girl, but there was no body at the scene.'

She pulled out a photo and slid it across the table.

Jaap picked it up. It was a CCTV image showing a young girl wearing a jacket with a fluffy collar. The image had been cropped so he couldn't make out the background.

'Where's this from?'

'Someone saw the couple with her at a cafe in Leeuwarden, I got the image from a bank's CCTV across the square.'

'You're sure this girl was kidnapped?'

'There's no other explanation, we've had dog teams out but they've found nothing. And I've just been to the adoption agency here. The couple, the Van Delfts, tried to adopt a few years ago, but were turned down.'

Something started to pulse in Jaap's head. Heiland had said Friedman wanted a child, and he was sure Haak was one of Friedman's associates. Andreas hadn't been working any other cases, so why else would he've been looking at his record? And he'd put a call in to the Van Delfts, but why?

'So they went to another agency?'

'No, they can't. It's all government controlled, so once they were turned down they couldn't just go to another office and try again.'

'So what led you to Haak?' he asked.

'The tattoo, on his neck? You could just make out there was something there, so I searched the database and came up with Haak's record. You've got to wonder how stupid you have to be to get such a distinctive tattoo done.'

'Yeah, crazy right? You've run this through missing persons?'

'Yeah, but no match was found.'

Jaap nodded, thinking about how much he should tell her. He'd always prided himself on reading people, and he got a good vibe from her. He took a deep breath.

'I'm working a case at the moment, and I think Haak is involved.'

He pulled out the diagram of the phone numbers he'd drawn for Kees earlier.

'See this number here?'

Tanya nodded.

'I think this belongs to Haak, and I know from the phone company records that this phone was up your way on Sunday evening.'

She stared at the paper for a moment.

'The thing is, the guy who had this number here' – he pointed to Friedman's – 'was also killed Sunday night, and it looks like all four were working on something together.'

'Kidnapping?' said Tanya

'It could well be.' Jaap thought of the Black Tulips.

They smuggled women.

What was to stop them kidnapping children, either for export or for the domestic market?

'I've been working a case on this gang, the Black Tulips, and they smuggle in women for the sex trade. I'm wondering . . . Have you looked at the finances of the Van Delfts?'

'No, I haven't had time. But I knew they were having trouble paying their rent.'

'Maybe you should get hold of them. If they didn't adopt legally . . . well, maybe they bought the child? Could be why they were having cash issues?'

'Bought?'

'Well, how else are you going to get one, short of kidnapping?'

Tanya breathed out. 'I . . . It could be. And maybe they didn't pay all the money owed, and whoever sold them the girl wanted her back . . .'

Jaap watched as the emotions polluted her face.

'That's just sick.'

The waitress appeared.

'You want anything?' Jaap asked Tanya.

She shook her head.

'We're good thanks,' he said.

The waitress glared at him for a moment before leaving.

'Which leads us on to Haak,' said Jaap once she'd gone. 'If these lot' – he pointed to the sheet – 'are smuggling in children, and distributing them, then Haak could be the bag man.'

The scream of an espresso machine, a cat hissing in pain, made Tanya jump. Jaap looked over to where the barista, a young dark Latino type with an overly manicured beard, was foaming up some milk.

He looked at the paper again. He wondered if the first number, the one who only communicated with Friedman, was Rint Korssen. Korssen had put money in Friedman's legitimate business, but that didn't stop them running something illegal on the side. And Korssen had talked about Russia; the Black Tulips had Soviet origins.

'The trouble is, I think everyone who owns one of these is a target.'

He told her about the phone with the speaking clock's number on it and watched as she took in the news.

'So Haak could have her and someone is trying to kill him?'

'It looks that way . . .'

Tanya sat still for a moment, staring down at the paper.

'And there's one more thing.' He pulled out his phone and showed her the number he'd got from Andreas' computer. 'Recognize this?'

'No.'

'It's a number registered to Van Delft, I checked the address, on Zeedijk.'

'Shit . . .' She breathed out. 'Where did you find it?'

'Listen,' said Jaap checking his watch, 'there's a guy who might know how to get to Haak, want to come? I can tell you about the number on the way. Your bike secure?'

'Yeah, the guy at the car pool let me park it there.'

As they walked to the station Jaap filled her in on the number's origin.

'So what did Andreas want with them?' she asked.

'That's what we need to find out,' he replied as he signed out a car. 'And I think you should get the photo of the girl to Interpol, check against their lists.'

He glanced up and saw De Waart at the far end of the corridor just as he picked up the keys.

'I want a word with you,' called out De Waart.

Jaap gave the keys to Tanya.

'Get the car ready, this won't take long.'

She departed with a quizzical look at him; she'd picked up De Waart's tone of voice.

'What do you want?' asked Jaap as he turned back to De Waart.

De Waart stepped closer, trying to use his bulk to intimidate.

'I'm warning you,' he whispered. Jaap could smell something rotten on his breath, 'Stay out of my way.'

'I'm not in your way De Waart.'

'No? Then why do I hear you're looking for that journalist?'

Jaap cursed Niels, he must have a deal going with De Waart as well.

'No harm done, I haven't even spoken to them yet.'

'Yeah, well, make sure you don't, I don't want you fucking this up for me.'

'Just relax, all right?'

They glared at each other. People were looking at them; further down the corridor someone shouted, 'Go on, kiss him', causing an explosion of laughter. A striplight was flickering overhead, the sound like an electric wasp.

'Did you think I'd find out about your and Andreas' little secret, is that why you did it?'

De Waart let it hang, like his pestilential breath, which just wouldn't dissipate.

'What are you talking about?' said Jaap, trying to keep his voice level.

'You wiped his laptop, to hide whatever fucked-up shit you were both into.'

'You've totally lost it.'

For a moment Jaap thought they were going to end up in a brawl.

He felt his muscles tense in readiness, his palms itched to slam into De Waart's chest, push him back against the wall. They stood for a moment like two wild beasts sizing each other up before lowering their heads and cracking horns. Jaap remembered the morning hexagram's message to withdraw.

Then De Waart stepped back.

'If I find you messing around in this,' he called out as he moved away, his limp causing his left foot to drag over the scuffed floor tiles, 'I'll have you fucking crucified.'

# 30

As Kees pressed the button, a peal of soft bells floating from within, he could sense his nose beginning to drip – it was getting colder, the air now felt like something out of an Alaskan winter – and he was just wiping it away when the door opened to reveal a tall woman, just as he'd imagined one of Korssen's lady friends would look like.

She extended her hand and he tried to surreptitiously wipe his own clean on his leg before clasping her warm, fragile fingers, her nails a flurry of red lanterns.

And then he was over the threshold and the door closed behind him, the hallway warm, dark, and scented with something rich and exotic, perfume drifting in plush waves past his nose. He followed her up the stairs, and if he couldn't stop himself from admiring her figure, the slender legs merely hinted at under the scarlet dress which clung to her hips and plunged right down in a huge curved 'V' exposing the creamy skin of her back, then so what, he was human.

Flesh and blood.

They reached the first floor, where she led him into a room as lavish as her scent, pointing to a deeply upholstered leather chair. He sat, watched by the woman, Heleen de Kok, who had remained standing but had leant on the edge of a table, her legs placed in such a way that a slit – which he hadn't noticed before, in the left side of her dress – opened and revealed, like curtains parting at the theatre, the star of the show, her thigh.

He looked around, partly in an attempt to tear his eyes off various parts of her, and took in the picture on the wall, a massive oil painting of a woman being fucked by a swan.

There was a strong smell of pot.

'So, you're a friend of Rint's?' she asked, her voice sultry.

'No, but I need to ask a few questions.'

She raised an eyebrow, and it was like she was on stage, an actress, fully aware of how to communicate with the smallest physical gesture.

'Oh, but you're not here to arrest me, are you?'

The phrase, accompanied by a tilting of the head and holding out her two arms, delicate wrists together, forcing her cleavage – framed by a cascade of blonde curls – into his view, was meant to sound coy, but she couldn't hide a sliver of uncertainty.

'I just need some information, so there's no need to carry on with the act.'

She looked at him for a moment, a cat watching a mouse, then crossed to the chair opposite and sat down, still with elegance and the knowledge of how to make a man look at her, but with less obvious show.

'I'm sorry, when you mentioned that Rint had given you my number I misunderstood.'

'That's okay, I need to check something with you, and I wanted to do it face to face.'

And what a face – he was already glad that he'd made the effort. Kees watched as she settled back, crossing one leg over the over, the slit in the dress opening, and her hand closing it back up.

'So what is it I can do for you, officer?'

'Inspector. You can tell me where you were the night before last.'

'Oh, that's easy, I was with Rint, at the Hotel De L'Europe.'

'Until what time?'

'Well, we left around half twelve, and then we came back here.'

'And what time did he leave?'

'It wasn't that long after to be honest, he'd drunk quite a lot and . . . well, you know how it is, how alcohol can have a *dampening* effect.'

He smiled in spite of himself; the very fact that Korssen had to use a prostitute – a very high-class one, but a prostitute nonetheless – was funny, but that he then wasn't even able to perform was too good.

*Do you get a discount for that?*

She smiled as well, two kids sharing a secret behind an adult's back, and then they were both laughing, and it felt good, made him feel free, uplifted. He hadn't laughed for what felt like months, and so what if it was partly the residue of pot in the air and he was sitting here with a prostitute when he should have been out chasing after murderers?

So what?

'So,' he started after he'd managed to stop laughing, 'what time did he really leave?'

'It was no later than half one, that's when I went to bed.'

Korssen had said he'd left the event at one, then come here.

He'd been lying.

Kees looked at her, mirth making her even more attractive. He'd never paid for sex, had always enjoyed the conquest, the feeling of power it gave him when the woman gave in.

As they inevitably did.

'Are you sure?'

She looked him in the eye and started to giggle again, her hand covering her mouth like an oriental courtesan.

'Totally,' she said when she managed to stop. 'I charge in quarter of an hour blocks.'

Kees looked at her.

He wondered how much cash he had left in his wallet.

# 31

'. . . and you think you can just barge in here? Yeah? Big fucking cop? Fuck you.'

Jaap tweaked the poet's arm slightly higher up his back towards his shoulder, grinding his face further down into the carpet – so stained it was hard to tell the original colour. It appeared to be moulting in patches, like a diseased dog.

He and Tanya had found Akster in a standard dingy council flat, social housing at its worst. It smelt of vomit, gas, and some floral scent which Jaap couldn't quite place.

He didn't like using strong-arm tactics, but when people drew knives on him just as he was asking questions he had to react, and was thankful that Akster, judging by the warm alcoholic stench rising off his breath, was drunk.

'I didn't barge in, you opened the door and let us in, remember? Or is your brain so addled by whatever it is you're on you can't even remember that?'

The response was a spit, which backfired as Akster's mouth was too close to the dirty fibres.

'So I'll ask again, where can I find Ludo Haak?'

'Fuck Ludo.'

'I don't give a shit about your love life, I just want to know where I can find him.'

'FUCK YOU!' – accompanied by a burst of wrestling and squirming, causing Jaap to jam the arm even higher.

'Listen.' Jaap bent down and spoke in his ear. 'Either you tell me where Ludo is right now or I take you in for assault. You know what happens to people who assault police officers, don't you?'

Less squirming, just heavy breathing.

'So I'm going to ask again. Where' – he started to push the arm even further – 'is Ludo Haak?'

Voice tense, strained. 'I don't know, I haven't seen him for, I don't know, months.'

'Cut the shit, you used to work with him. I know that, you were even arrested together for the same robbery.'

'Yeah, well, that was then. Things change.'

'Okay, what changed?'

'He wanted me to help him out with something, he'd some plan to make a lot of money.'

'And?'

'And I said no, sounded too dangerous to me.'

'Dangerous how?'

'Weird shit, you know? Like making porn movies, and he said something about kidnapping someone –'

'Kidnap who?' Tanya asked. 'Was it a child?'

'I don't know, yeah, it might have been, but when I said I wasn't in he didn't tell me any more, and he said that if I ever told anyone he'd kill me.'

'When was this?'

'A while back, I can't remember, a few weeks maybe.'

'Where can I find him?'

'Look, I don't want trouble and –'

Jaap yanked his arm even higher up his back, he could

feel it was close, something would give if he went any further.

'Where can I find him?'

'Let go!'

'Tell me what I need to know, then I'll let go.'

'Okay.' His voice tight from the pain. 'But don't tell him you've spoken to me, he's got powerful friends these days.'

Jaap released it a bit. All the air went out of Akster's chest, Jaap could feel it deflate. His phone had started buzzing in his pocket, he ignored it.

'Trust me on this, I've got far more important things to discuss with him than you. Who are these friends?'

'I think he hangs around with some people, foreigners, up by the ports, he's got some work there.'

'More specific?'

'I don't really know much about them, I think they're Latvian or Albanian, or Russian. Something foreign anyway, I've heard they call themselves the dark tulips.'

'Black Tulips.'

'Yeah, whatever. Mean fuckers, they'd take you out just for fun, and they do weird shit to the people they kill as well.'

'Where will I find him?

'I don't know, I really don't. And can you get the fuck off me now?'

Jaap could see that was as much as Akster knew.

'Only if you promise not to do anything stupid.'

Akster nodded, his cheek rubbing the carpet, and Jaap released his arm, standing up and back at the same time.

'This your place?'

'Kind of.' Sullen, sitting up, twisting his shoulder and arm in a circular movement.

'I'd get someone to come check the gas, and don't smoke till you do.'

Once outside Jaap checked his phone, he'd missed a call from Kees.

'Korssen's prostitute friend said that he'd left no later than half one. So he was lying,' said Kees when Jaap asked him why he'd called. They were driving past Dam Square, still full of tourists despite the freezing cold.

'Which puts him right in the time frame for Friedman's death.' Jaap switched the phone to his other ear, one hand on the wheel. 'Good work. We're going to have to have another chat with Rint Korssen.'

'And Zwartberg, Friedman's dining partner. His address is up at Brouwersgracht, number seventy-three.'

'I'm close to there now, I'll cover that. You track down Korssen, find out where he is, and Kees?'

'Yeah?'

'Call me when you've got him, I want to be there when he's arrested.'

*I want to see his reaction*, he thought as he hung up, flicked on the sirens and lurched the car forward.

'Looks like you joined us just at the right time.' He glanced across at Tanya as she re-did her ponytail, snapping the band into place.

*She's not bad looking*, he found himself thinking.

'I hope so.'

They were there in four minutes. Jaap extinguished the siren and parked right outside. The house was older than Friedman's; Brouwersgracht was in the Jordaan, a full century older than the central canal district, but just as expensive. Until recently the Jordaan had been a working class district, but had turned trendy during the boom years. Maybe now the Netherlands were in a triple-dip recession it was destined to return to its roots.

They got out and ran to the door. Nobody answered the bell.

He pushed it, and it swung open.

Both he and Tanya drew their weapons, before stepping quietly inside. The hallway was dark, the only room on the ground floor empty.

They found him on the first floor. Naked, lying on the floor, a purple stole with two white and gold crosses at each end round his neck.

His mouth was slightly open. Jaap holstered his gun, pulled out some latex gloves, and wiggled the phone gently out of the body's mouth. It was identical to Friedman's. He didn't need to open it up and look at the number on the screen, but he did anyway.

*Why is the killer leaving these?*

'What is it?' asked Tanya from behind him.

'This,' said Jaap dropping the phone back into Zwartberg's mouth, where it clattered against his teeth, 'is us being too late.'

# 32

Tyres shrieked against asphalt.

'Is that Kees Terpstra?' asked Tanya as their car stopped, rocking forward.

'You know him?'

'Yeah.'

She didn't sound that enthusiastic. He didn't blame her.

They jumped out of the car and ran towards where Kees was waiting by Korssen's house.

'Not here?' Jaap shouted as he neared.

'No. What about Zwartberg?'

'Dead. With a phone, just like Friedman.'

'Shit.'

Kees looked at Tanya then turned to Jaap.

'What's she doing here?'

'Helping us.'

'Nice to see you too,' said Tanya.

Jaap looked from one to the other. He didn't have time for this right now.

'Just put it aside, whatever it is. Zwartberg's phone had a call this afternoon from the phone that had only called Friedman before, I think it could be Korssen,' he said.

'Makes sense, I just spoke to a neighbour who said he

178

bundled into a cab not long after we spoke to him earlier,' replied Kees.

'Have you traced it?'

'I put a call out, so far nothing.'

'It's got to be him. He lied about the timing then does a runner. Let's get in.'

'I've got just the thing to open this up.' Kees sprinted over to the patrol car he'd come in, yanked open the boot and brought out a standard-issue battering ram.

'I made sure the car had one of these, just in case.' He was grinning, like he was about to start enjoying himself.

Two swings and they were inside.

The open-plan living space was just as it had been when they'd seen it before. They took the large spiral staircase, and nearing the top they could hear the sound of a TV or radio.

All three instinctively drew their weapons, and crept forward, gently placing each foot heel to toe.

There were four doors on the landing. The sound was coming from the third along to the left. They paused either side, listening. Nothing but voices, some talk show with talentless celebrity morons giggling and preening. Jaap nodded to them both and counted down from three with his fingers.

The door flew inwards with such force that it sprang back and knocked Kees' outstretched gun as he leapt forward. The sound of the shot made Jaap instinctively drop to his knees, even though he knew it was Kees' gun which had fired.

There was no extra noise from the room, or anywhere else in the house.

Kees, embarrassed, pushed the door open, and entered followed by Tanya, then Jaap. The room was brightly lit, the sound coming from an enormous television hanging on one of the walls.

'Shit, now I'm going to have to fill out one of those stupid report forms.'

'Don't forget the bullet, dig it out.'

Jaap turned the TV off. Kees was already checking the unmade bed, and Tanya the walk-in closet towards the back of the room.

Near the back she came across a dark wooden chest, a reproduction antique, out of place with the ultra-modernity of the rest of the house.

It was locked.

'Anyone want to open this?' she asked.

Kees stepped forward. Jaap could tell he liked this kind of stuff, but then who didn't? Most detectives got some kind of a thrill from breaking things. It was so immediate, unlike most of their work.

Kees had to resort to smashing it against the wall, the lid finally splintering in two. He ripped it back and then emptied the contents on to the floor.

Whips, DVDs and a whole load of other objects whose use Jaap didn't even want to think about spilled out.

Kees poked around with the toe of his boot, separating various bits of black leather to reveal a face mask.

'Looks like he's into exotic toys.'

'That mask,' said Tanya, her voice tight. 'That's like the one Haak was wearing.'

# 33

As Kees walked into the bar, scanning for Carice and finding her, the back of her blonde hair coppered by the mood lighting, he wondered, for a split second, if he should be doing this.

Music pulsed, a couple at a table off to his left erupted with laughter. Then the pathologist turned, raised her eyebrows and looked at her wrist before swivelling back to the bar, and her drink, and he knew the answer.

The appearance of Tanya helped with the decision. He hadn't seen her for two years, and there'd been a brief moment when he'd felt all the anger rush back. That was not good. Especially as they now seemed to be working together.

He felt the small plastic pouch he'd picked up on the way over and slid on to the barstool next to her, shrugging off his coat as he did.

'Hey.'

'Hey, are you always in the habit of keeping women waiting?'

He thought of Marinette, waiting at home for him.

'Heightens the expectation.'

'Hmmm, might not be such a good idea.' She looked him up and down. 'Expectation can be *too* heightened.'

'You saying I'm a disappointment?'

'Only visually.'

'Not so hot yourself,' he replied, motioning *same for me* to the barman.

She laughed, and flicked her hair back. The music shifted beat. The rowdy couple behind them were getting even louder. It wasn't laughter any more, it sounded more like screaming. Just as they turned Kees saw the man spring up from the table and the woman hurl a half-full glass of beer at him. It bounced off his chest but wasn't so lucky with the floor.

'You bitch!' the man shouted, his voice hoarse. 'You crazy fucking bitch!'

She was up at him now, and before he could react she grabbed him by the shoulders and rammed her knee into his crotch. He doubled up with a cry. The music stopped, everyone else in the bar was watching the couple. The place seemed frozen.

'Shouldn't you go over there and put a stop to all this?' Carice whispered into his ear. 'You're the cop, after all.'

'Off-duty cop,' he reminded her and they watched as the woman shoved the man over, toppling him on to the shards of glass on the floor, and swayed for the exit. Then people were helping him up and Kees and Carice turned back to each other.

'That reminds me, you know the body?' said Carice.

'Friedman?'

'Yeah, him. He'd had the . . .' She made a scissors motion with her fingers.

'Castrated?'

She squinted at him. 'You were there yesterday, at the scene, weren't you?'

'Yeah, I –'

'And even you would have noticed if he'd been missing something vital. He was lying naked, and I'm sure you guys must all check each other out.' She raised an eyebrow. Kees felt sucked in.

'Yeah, okay, so what do you mean . . .?' He did a clumsy snip of his own.

'You know, a vasectomy.'

He stared at her for a moment, and then found himself starting to laugh, a machine chugging to life.

'You mean,' he said, having to break off again for another round of laughter, Carice looking at him, 'he was shooting blanks?'

# 34

Jaap stepped out from Zwartberg's front door.

After searching Korssen's place, Jaap, Kees and Tanya had gone back to Zwartberg's. They'd gone over the scene but it hadn't turned up anything. Kees had left earlier, looking like he was in a hurry. Jaap glanced up at the sky.

The moon peered down at him like a sick eye.

'I need a drink, how about you?' he asked Tanya as she joined him outside.

'Yeah, that'd be good.'

They found a bar, an old-time place which didn't play music, and ordered: Tanya beer, Jaap water. They were too exhausted to do anything but look at the drinks when they arrived at their table. Jaap watched the head spilling over the side of Tanya's glass, forming a puddle on the dark wooden tabletop.

'You don't drink beer?' Tanya asked as she finally raised the glass to her lips.

'Lost the taste for it a while back,' said Jaap.

He always found people reluctant to accept he didn't drink alcohol, and through experience worked out the best way for them to accept it was to imply he'd had a drinking problem. He was a cop after all, so most people figured he had one anyway.

They sat in silence for a while, both absorbing what had happened over the last few hours.

'How does this all fit together with Inspector Hansen's death?' Tanya asked.

Jaap took a sip of water before answering.

'Andreas and I were working a case together, trying to get to this gang I told you about.'

'The one Akster mentioned, the Black Tulips?'

'Right. They killed someone and we'd been on the case for a while now, and Andreas had discovered a way to get to the gang, right before he was killed.'

'So they did it, to stop him exposing them?'

Her phone rang and she pulled it out. Jaap watched as she hesitated before answering. She had a brief conversation, explaining where she was before listening. Jaap could hear the voice but not the words. Whoever it was sounded angry.

'Trouble?' he asked once she'd hung up.

'That's the guy I work with, he's . . . well, let's just say we don't get on. And he's ordered me back to Leeuwarden.'

'Got a better lead up there?'

'No. But he doesn't like that I might be on the right track.'

She took a huge gulp of beer, the glass hitting the table as she lowered it too fast.

'Anyway,' she said, 'you were saying, about Andreas?'

'Uhh . . . yeah, I think they killed him because he was getting too close. But they didn't just stop there. The person he'd found was Friedman.'

'Your first body.'

'Exactly. The problem is, nobody else knows the two cases are linked, if they did I'd be pulled off this one straight away,' he said.

'Kees doesn't know?'

'No. Partly as I reckon if he knew, I'd be off the case real quick, and partly ... well, you've clearly met him before.'

Tanya nodded; she looked embarrassed.

'We were at the academy together, we had a thing for a little while,' she said.

'And it didn't end well, I'm guessing.'

'They didn't make you a detective for nothing then.' She smiled.

*She's really cute*, thought Jaap as he finished his water.

A waiter walked past telling them they'd be closing soon.

'Did Andreas have a partner?' asked Tanya.

'Married three years and expecting a baby in a few weeks.'

'That's just awful.' She shook her head and fiddled with the glass. 'Did you know her well too?'

'You could say that, we were together for a couple of years. And before you ask, no it wasn't a problem when she and Andreas started seeing each other.'

'I wasn't going to.'

'You'd be the first not to. People thought it was strange, but we'd been together and it didn't work.'

'So you're still friends?'

Jaap thought back to the night last spring when Andreas had been away for a few days. Andreas had called Jaap and asked him to look in on Saskia, she'd seemed to be down about something. Jaap had called her and gone round that evening.

Then he'd stayed the night.

He'd felt guilty about it for weeks afterwards. Working with Andreas every day hadn't helped.

But when Andreas didn't say anything he figured Saskia hadn't said anything either. So he'd tried to forget it, figuring that most people ended up sleeping with their ex at some stage.

'We got on better when she was with Andreas than we ever did on our own,' he said.

*Though that may change now*, he thought, *she might still blame me for not going with him.*

He rubbed his eyes.

'You look tired,' she said, 'maybe we should call it a night.'

'Exhausted, in fact. Are you going back up?'

Despite his fatigue he hoped she wasn't.

She looked at her watch.

'Way too late, but I can't anyway. I've got to be here to find Haak. And the girl.'

'I could do with the help, do you want to give me your superior officer's name? I'll talk to him in the morning, see what I can do.'

'He won't like it, but you're welcome to try.'

'You got somewhere to stay?'

'I booked a hotel, somewhere by the Rijksmuseum.'

*That's kind of a shame*, he thought as he offered to drop her off.

They drove in silence, both consumed by their own

thoughts, and agreed to talk first thing. Jaap dropped the car back at the station and started walking towards his houseboat.

He called Saskia, aware that he'd not spoken to her all day. She was doing okay, she told him, she'd had various friends round during the day and evening, and he promised to drop in tomorrow.

Jaap hung up and stopped short four houseboats along from his own.

Street lights dripped light along the canal edge.

Had he seen something, or was he just being paranoid?

He found he was holding his breath, and he only released it when he spotted the glowing tip of a cigarette in the darkness less than twenty metres from his houseboat, no figure visible.

Moving forward as slowly as he could, he tried to place his feet carefully but on the third step he hit something, a crushed drink can, which scuttled along ahead of him. The glowing tip lurched wildly, hung in the air for a moment, then fell to the ground.

A motorbike roared. Jaap was running but the trail of noise was receding fast.

Then it was gone.

When he went to bed, after having tried to sit and clear his mind, and failed, he jammed a chair against the front door.

It wouldn't stop anyone getting in, but it would make enough of a racket to give him some warning.

He hoped.

# DAY THREE

# 35

'Three things,' said Jaap as Kees made it into the room, a full fifteen minutes after Jaap had told him to be there. Kees looked even worse than yesterday, his eyes bloodshot and the bruise on his cheek yellowing round the edges. He sat down across from Tanya.

Jaap had drawn on a white board the same diagram of the phone numbers he'd done on paper yesterday, thinking about the hexagram formed when he'd thrown the coins earlier, just before leaving his houseboat.

Mountain over Water, 'even a fool can attain wisdom.'

*I could do with a bit of wisdom right now*, he thought as he turned to the board.

'The first is this. Friedman's dead.' He drew a line through the number. 'So is Zwartberg' – another line, the pen squeaking – 'which leaves us with these two.'

He circled them.

'This one here we're sure is Ludo Haak, and this one looks like it's Rint Korssen. Now there's two ways of looking at this. The first is that Korssen is the killer, and he's killing them off to avoid us getting to him. Or it's someone else connected with them who we don't know about yet, and Korssen realized what was going on and decided to get out before he got hit as well. Either way we're running out of time.'

Kees yawned, and scratched a spot on his jaw.

'The second is that stole round Zwartberg's neck.' He tapped his pen against the crossed-out name. 'Kees, I'll need you to check the local churches and see if anyone recognizes it, or Zwartberg.'

Kees grunted.

'Third, Korssen. Have you got anywhere with him?'

'He got a cab to Centraal station about half an hour after we left his house.'

'You checked the trains?'

'Yeah, but there are way too many, no way of knowing which he got. He could be anywhere in Europe by now.'

'They should never have signed up to Schengen,' said Tanya.

Jaap nodded agreement.

'We'll need a European arrest warrant, I'll sort that out, and I'll get a freeze on his bank accounts. We might get lucky if he tries to use a credit card. And I'm also putting out a call on Haak. Tanya, I'll get you put down as the contact point on that one.'

She shifted in her chair.

'The thing is I've been ordered back –'

'Shit, I forgot to call him, I'll do it right after we've finished here. Kees, any news on the woman who ran away?'

'I got an e-fit done, and it's out there, but no one's called in.'

A knock at the door, and a uniform popped his head round the frame.

'Smit wants to see you' – this directed at Kees – 'and there's a call for you, someone called Teije?' he said as he turned to Jaap.

'What line?'

'Seven,' he said before closing the door again.

'Okay, lets get on with it,' said Jaap.

Kees left and Jaap turned to the desk.

*What does Smit want with Kees?* he thought as he picked up the phone.

# 36

As Kees stepped towards Smit's office, he was still trying to get his thoughts in order, separate out the jumble that was going on in his head. He'd woken, back aching from the hard bed that Carice had in her flat. His mouth felt like someone had sprinkled salt on his tongue and he had a strange buzzing in his ears, thousands of tiny insects.

Coffee hadn't helped. Neither had a half-line – just the leftovers he managed to shake from the bag – rubbed into his gums. He'd checked his phone; his text to Marinette last night explaining he was going to be out all night on a case remained unanswered.

Kees knocked and went in. There were two people in the room, and that helped bring everything into focus, a shot of adrenaline clearing out the system. Smit was sitting behind his desk, and Inspector De Waart in a chair just off to the side.

Both had smiles on their faces.

'Come in, come in,' Smit said, despite the fact that Kees, as far as he could tell, was already in. He felt there was a creepy, false cheer about the way Smit was talking. 'You know Inspector De Waart of course.' Kees nodded. 'So let's get down to business, please take a seat,' said Smit.

'Inspector De Waart is in charge of the investigation into Inspector Andreas Hansen's death,' continued Smit and De Waart nodded slowly, 'and wanted to ask you a few questions. I've told him that you are . . .' He coughed into his hand. '. . . looking after Jaap at this difficult time.'

Kees' stomach contracted. He'd already made up his mind, he was doing this for his career, but now that he was actually here he could feel a sick reluctance to start grassing on a colleague.

Especially as he was now being asked to do so not just in front of Smit but another Inspector as well.

Meaning the chances of this getting out were suddenly doubled. If word got around — and what did they always say in those mafia movies, you can always smell a rat? — then his career would effectively be over. He'd be shunned, despised. It was one thing answering to Smit, quite another having De Waart involved as well.

De Waart spoke for the first time, his grainy voice lower than Smit's.

'I'll just give you a brief outline of where we are currently. As you know, Andreas Hansen was found dead with a single bullet wound to the back of the head by the side of a road in Amsterdamse Bos two days ago. There was very little at the scene to give a reason or any idea of why he'd been there, other than footprints showing that at least three people had also recently stepped on the verge.

'Then, as you'll no doubt have heard, at the press conference announcing his death a journalist made an accusation which we've had to take very seriously.' Smit nodded emphatically to emphasize De Waart's speech. 'Namely that he was somehow involved with child pornography.'

Smit took over. Kees wondered if they'd rehearsed the routine.

'And I don't need to tell you how damaging to all of us things like that can be.'

'No,' replied Kees.

'So we started looking into it,' continued De Waart, 'we had to, and found that before he was killed, Andreas Hansen, or somebody else, had wiped his computer clean of everything. Which makes me think that he was aware something might well be going to happen to him. I should just mention that Jaap Rykel took Andreas' computer to the tech lab shortly after his body was discovered, claiming that the computer must have been wiped by a . . . what was it?'

'A Russian gang that they'd been investigating earlier in the year,' completed Smit.

*They have*, thought Kees, *rehearsed this.*

'Exactly, a Russian gang, as if they wouldn't just take it and burn the thing if they were really worried about what was on it. So we're left with two possibilities: either Andreas himself wiped it, or Jaap did after he'd found out about Andreas' death to help cover for his friend. Which would mean that . . .'

'Jaap knew what Andreas was into, and may even be involved himself,' finished Smit.

They let Kees absorb what he was being told.

*Could Jaap really be involved with something like that?* he wondered.

'So you see, our conversation from the other day is more relevant than ever. Do you have anything to report?'

The buzzing returned to Kees' ears, only stronger.

Louder.

# 37

'Right here.'

Teije bent over Jaap's shoulder and jabbed a transaction in a sea of transactions which had been highlighted in pink, the ink smudging slightly towards the end of the stroke. Jaap'd had a text from his sister Karin on his way to Teije's place; he decided he was going to drop in on her after he was done with Teije. Which didn't look any time soon.

'And that relates to these' – Teije thrust another bit of paper into Jaap's view with two transactions, also pinked – 'which add up to the first amount. These people were clearly good at whatever it is they're doing, there's a fair amount of money sloshing around here. But when they came to moving it?' He shook his head. 'Amateurs, total amateurs.'

Teije had spent his career working for global corporations advising them on tax, or tax avoidance to give it the full, unofficial, title. And as such knew every trick in the book.

And then some.

'So in effect money was coming in from here –'

'Yeah, it's going to take a bit longer to trace *exactly*

where that is coming from, I think Switzerland, which may complicate things a bit . . .'

Jaap's phone rang; it was Inspector Bloem.

'Inspector Bloem, thanks for calling back.'

'I got your message, what can I do for you?'

'I'm working a case which looks like it might be linked to yours, Sergeant van der Mark contacted me –'

'I know.'

'Well, we're getting somewhere, and I think Tanya can contribute –'

'Sergeant van der Mark should be back here already, I ordered her back, are you saying she hasn't left?'

'No, she hasn't, but I've got two dead bodies, and possibly two more on their way, and I need her here. And, as I said, we have a suspect in common so we'll be advancing your case at the same time.' He shifted gear, aware after his confrontations with Smit and De Waart that he seemed to be making enemies. 'I'd really appreciate your help on this.'

Jaap could hear Bloem's breathing, the heavy rasp of tar-laden lungs. Teije made the drink motion to him but Jaap declined.

'Okay.' His tone of voice said otherwise. 'She can stay for one day, after that if you haven't got anywhere then she's coming back, no extension.'

'Thanks.' The words nearly stuck in his throat. 'We'll keep you updated.'

'Damn right you will,' said Bloem. Jaap heard a click, then silence.

He put his phone away.

*Maybe*, he thought, as he turned his attention back to Teije, *I could swap Kees for Tanya.*

'Sorry,' he said, 'so the money comes in and then goes out to these three, Zwartberg, Haak, and this one, which is a smaller amount.'

'Yeah, that one I've traced now, it's going to someone called Paulus Fortuyn, I've got two addresses here.'

Jaap looked at it, one in Haarlem and one in the red-light district, and pulled out his phone.

'Kees, it's Jaap, where are you?'

'Just at the station, I was –'

'I've got a name, Friedman was paying a Paulus Fortuyn. Get a squad car to this address in Haarlem' – he made Kees read it back – 'and then meet me at 35 Bloed-straat in' – he checked the clock on the wall – 'twenty minutes, got that?'

'Got it.'

'And Kees?'

'Yeah?'

'If you get there before I do, wait, don't go in without me.'

# 38

Tanya knew she shouldn't have answered when she saw it was Bloem calling.

'What I want to know is what you did to get your new boyfriend so hot for you? On your knees were you?'

Tanya found her jaw was tight.

'I think you need to work out where your priorities are, because right now I'm not sure I'll have a place for someone like you on my team.'

*I think you need,* Tanya thought as she hung up, *to go fuck yourself.*

She was waiting to meet Inspector Guus Visser from the Eastern District, who'd called twenty minutes after Jaap had put out a nationwide call on Haak. Visser had a lead on Haak and had offered to pick her up at the station. As she sat she remembered what Jaap had said yesterday about Interpol. She borrowed a computer and pulled up their website, finding the missing-persons section.

There were thousands of images, from people all over the world, young, old and everything in between. Each one a tragic story which would never be told.

*This will take me for ever,* she thought.

She picked up the phone, eventually getting through to

someone who said she could send the photo over to them, but the chances of anyone there getting round to trawling through the pictures looking for a match was slim to none. Without a name, she was told, she might as well forget it.

She slammed the phone down on the desk, and started clicking through the pages, scanning for the girl. As her eyes jumped from photo to photo her mind started raking over what she knew, and what she and Jaap had talked about last night.

She'd asked herself if people really did that, pay for a child who in all likelihood had been trafficked for that purpose, kidnapped, taken away from their parents? How could you live with that? Live with the knowledge that somewhere out there were a mother and father, crying in the night for the loss of their child, lives destroyed for ever with the uncertainty, the cruel hope which would taunt them, scrape at them, force them to think that each day might be the day when their child was found, safe and well?

It was the same hope she'd felt for years, maybe still felt even now, that her parents would turn up, despite knowing that was impossible. And the same hope she used to feel each time she was forced into bed by her foster father, that this time would be the last.

It was sick, and if the Van Delfts had done exactly that then they'd got what they deserved, payback for the misery they'd caused. But then maybe they were victims too, perhaps they were naive enough to believe what they were told, that the child they were buying was actually an orphan, rescued from some repressive culture or regime where they wouldn't have survived on their own. Coupled with their desire to have a child, they might have convinced themselves they were doing good.

Just as she'd been deluding herself all these years, pretending it had never happened, and that she'd be able to lead a normal life if she just buried it deep enough.

Deep, too deep.

Or maybe not deep enough.

She'd been clicking through pages as she thought, her finger and eyes working independently of her brain.

She clicked through to the next page, twenty-seven of god-knew-how many, and there she was.

Mid-way down.

Tanya pulled out the photo she had of her. The angle was different in each, and the photo onscreen was of a younger-looking girl. But the basic bone structure was the same, and her hair was red.

*This is her*, she thought, her breathing fast all of a sudden. *This is the girl.*

She quickly read the details.

Adrijana Fajon had gone missing just over two years ago, from Slovenia.

Tanya reached for the phone; her fingers seemingly not under her control, she misdialled twice before she got it right on the third time.

When she got through to someone she requested the full file, and the woman promised to get it over to her on email within half an hour.

As Tanya hung up her mind was racing.

'Now I know who you are,' she said, looking at the photo again, comparing them to make sure she hadn't made a mistake.

'Hey, are you Van der Mark?'

The voice startled her. She turned to see a man, short, with a thin face and sharp eyes.

'Yeah.' She rose and they shook hands.

'A colleague of mine saw the call on Haak, he knows someone who might be able to help.'

'Is he not coming?'

'He's on a case, can't spare the time. Talk to photos often?' He winked.

They left the building and got into Visser's car, where the radio was on low. He leant forward and turned the dial up as he pulled away from the kerb.

'... *Police have yet to confirm that the latest murder in the Jordaan is linked to the murder on Sunday of the businessman Dirk Friedman, but sources close to the police hint that there is a connection. And staying with the police, Inspector Andreas Hansen, also found murdered on Sunday, is alleged to have been involved with child pornography. For the latest we'll go to our reporter Annette Groot.'*

*'Thank you, Pieter. The allegations, and we must stress that they are only allegations at this stage, were made in this morning's edition of* De Telegraaf *and other papers, and seem to point to material found on Inspector Hansen's computer whilst investigators were trying to piece together the mystery of his death. We asked the officer in charge to comment but he was unavailable. However, we were given a short statement saying that the investigation was ongoing and that more details would be released later on. Over to you, Pieter.'*

*'Thanks, Annette, sport now . . .'*

'Bad shit that, if it turns out to be true,' Visser said as he swung the volume dial round to off.

'The guy I'm working with, he knew him. He was his partner.'

'Yeah, who?'

'Jaap Rykel, he's the one who put the call on Haak out?'

Visser shook his head.

'Haven't met him. Amazing how many of us there are really. I guess in an ideal world we wouldn't need any police, we're just a symptom, you and I.'

He waved a finger lazily in the air between them, then looked across at her and asked, 'Not a good thought?'

'Not really.'

'My dad told me not to go into the police, said it was like putting your finger over a crack in the dam. In a way he was right, but I've been doing this for over twenty years now, and, well, I'm still not sure I was right, or if he was.'

'What did he do?'

Visser swerved to avoid an old man on a bicycle who'd suddenly cut in front of them. The old man shouted something at them. Tanya noticed his teeth were half black.

'My dad?' he laughed, shaking his head. 'He was a doctor, guess he knew something about the futility of it all. Seriously though, what else are you going to do with your time? And if you manage to solve even one crime that's got to be worth it. Especially if solving that crime means finding an abducted child.'

She looked out the window, the rows of shops filled with Christmas displays, looking tired now, forlorn. She shivered, the damp cold reaching a hand down her neck. She thought back to the faces she'd seen on the Interpol site.

Tanya had fallen asleep in her hotel room with the picture of the girl in her hand, and the doll she'd found at the scene of the fire, determined she was going to give it back to the girl. The girl who she now knew was called Adrijana. She'd dreamt she was little again, her foster father coming for her, and she was unable to escape.

'Yeah, I guess,' she said, watching a man being pulled along the pavement by a small dog. 'Just as long as I find her alive.'

# 39

'Hey,' Karin said as she opened the door. They hugged and she invited him in.

'I can't stay, I just wanted to check up on you, see how you were,' said Jaap.

She was standing there in flannel pyjamas which were baggy at the knee, and her hair looked like it hadn't been washed in days.

'It comes and goes. I feel a bit better today.'

Jaap noticed her eyes were filling up though, and she looked away. He hugged her again.

'I've got to go, just give me a call, whenever you need, okay?'

He felt her nod, her head resting on his shoulder, and then he released her. As he turned to leave she spoke again.

'Thanks, Jaap, it means everything to me, you know that, don't you?'

Time for his eyes to well up.

His phone rang. It was Roemers.

'Have you got anything?'

'I've been working on that laptop you asked me to look at, and your friend Andreas?' Jaap could hear raised voices and the sound of a glass bottle hitting brick off to his left. 'He had some seriously tropical browsing habits.'

# 40

Kees looked up at the building, four storeys in total on a pedestrian street. The ground floor was taken up by prostitutes in their glass-fronted cubicles, some sitting on tall stools waiting, and some with the curtains closed, a client inside.

He looked at them.

Dogs for the most part, he decided, but one of them made him think of Carice.

The women themselves reacted differently to their prospective clients; some sat, almost demurely, perched on their stools, others gyrated up against the glass, their flesh tinged, almost bruised, by the lighting which gave the area its name.

They were tall, short, thin, fat; every taste, ethnic or otherwise, catered for, though from what he'd seen on the short walk from Dam Square, beauty was the possible exception.

*Jaap did*, he thought, eyeing the one who was looking more like Carice the longer he stared, *tell me to wait though that's probably not what he'd had in mind*.

The sun was beginning to rise over the roof, a gold coin edging upwards, the light reaching the ground in the narrow street. He checked his watch; he'd been here for nearly half an hour, the cold starting to bother him.

*Where is he?*

The door, wooden and worn, black paint chipped off in places to reveal an earlier coat of blood red, had two buzzers on the wall next to it.

*Fuck it*, he thought, *might as well do it myself.*

35b yielded nothing so he tried 35a, and after a half a minute a voice, too crackled by the intercom to sex, came on.

Shortly, after Kees had explained what he wanted, the door opened to reveal a squat woman with no neck and blonde spiky hair.

'We need to get that thing fixed.' She nodded to the intercom. 'Drives me mad. But anyway, you said you're police?'

Kees showed her his ID and watched whilst she scrutinized it.

'So what can I help with?'

'Do you live here?'

'Technically no, but it sometimes feels that way.' She ran a hand back through her spikes. 'I run a centre for recovering drug addicts, and we're short-staffed, no one wants to know about this kind of thing. It's all very well your lot trying to stop the people who deal hard drugs, but to be honest you're not doing a good enough job. The people who come here are pretty much ruined.'

She'd worked herself up, her face hard with anger.

'Hey, I just work in the murder squad,' he said, wondering if he'd ever need this kind of service.

She looked up at him for a few moments before her hard features softened slightly.

'Sorry, it's just when you see what I see every day it can get to you.' She rubbed an ear where a stud glinted. 'Anyway, you wanted to know about the upstairs?'

'Yeah, who lives there?'

'Some guy, I don't see him very often.'

'This centre you run, it's open twenty-four hours?'

'God no.' She shook her head. 'If we could afford it we'd do it, but . . .' She shrugged.

'So the addicts only come in the day?'

'They know they can come in for support any time from eight a.m. to six p.m., six days a week.'

'I'm going to need to have a look.'

'Knock yourself out.' She stood aside to let him in and then closed the door. 'Take the stairs to the top.'

The top floor had a short landing ending in a door. Locked, but it looked easy enough to force. As the flat of his foot slammed into it he was rewarded with a splintering sound, more on the second time, and then it swung open on the third.

It was dark inside, and he ran his hand up and down the wall trying to find a light switch. When he couldn't find one he stepped in, and extended the search, eventually finding something about a metre away from the doorway.

He flicked it but nothing happened.

*What was that?* he thought as he heard, or felt something, some movement of air perhaps, and a hint of something he recognized. Camphor.

And then, before he could react, the rushing of air behind him grew before pain exploded in the back of his head for a millionth of a second.

# 41

Visser pointed across the road to a block of flats.

They reminded Tanya of a documentary she'd sat through recently – too tired to get up and turn it off – on ex-Soviet states and the criminals who were extending their reach all over Europe. She wished she'd paid more attention.

*Was it Ukraine,* she found herself wondering, *or Uzbekistan?*

Grey, depressing uniformity, each tiny window a desolate eye, reflecting the bright sun. But not even that could bring them to life.

The stench of urine seared her nostrils as they climbed the graffiti-encrusted stairwell. Each step echoed off the hard surfaces like small explosions and tiny bits of grit ground between the concrete and the soles of her shoes, setting her teeth on edge. When they were standing in front of the right door Tanya noticed she was holding her breath. Visser noticed too.

'Not used to the smell?'

He breathed in deeply, his chest inflating, a man standing on the prow of a yacht heading into a light breeze, and then laughed at the look that her face must have been pulling.

'I can't actually smell a thing, had a car accident a few years ago and it just vanished.'

'Right now I'd be happy with the same.'

Visser knocked.

She could hear faint voices, and then silence. He knocked again, louder and more persistent this time, but that didn't seem to do it either.

So he took a deep breath and hammered on the door.

'Open this door or I'm going to break it down right now,' he yelled.

The intensity made Tanya jump. He turned and winked at her.

'I'm fluent in the local dialect.'

Footsteps and a creak heralded the opening of the door. Tanya could see a thin, bearded man peering at them through the crack. There was a chain on the door.

He looked Tanya up and down, then his eyes shifted to Visser.

'Yes?'

'Police. I'm looking for someone, a colleague of mine said somebody here might be able to help,' said Visser moving forward.

'No one here,' said the man, closing the door.

It stuck on Visser's foot.

'That's a nice chain,' said Visser. 'I wouldn't want to have to break it.'

The man's eyes, dark as granite, looked at Visser for a few moments. Impossible to read what he was thinking, then he nodded.

'Okay, you need to move your foot first.'

Visser pulled it back and the door closed. They could hear the sound of the chain clinking.

But the door didn't open.

'Hey,' said Visser pushing the door. 'Open this up *right* now or I'm going to break it down.'

Nothing.

He sighed, and turned to Tanya.

'Dumb fuck,' he said. 'It's not like he can go anywhere. You any good with locks?'

'No.'

'Me neither.' He turned back to the door, took a few steps back and launched himself forward. After the fourth battering a voice, different from before, called out.

'Stop, I'm going to open it.'

'Just as well,' whispered Visser, rubbing his shoulder.

The door was opened by a bearded man wearing a grey tracksuit, fluorescent yellow strip running up each leg and down the tops of the arms.

A pristine turban, white as a wedding cake, encased the top of his head.

'Very kind of you,' said Visser.

'My cousin, he didn't think,' replied the man. 'Come in.'

He stepped aside to let them pass. The flat turned out to be every bit as depressing as Tanya'd imagined from the outside. Dark, small rooms with single unshielded light bulbs and virtually no furniture. The smell was a cloying mixture of chemical room freshener and smoke, and wasn't much of an improvement on the latrine-like quality of the air in the stairwell.

In the main room, square with one window over-looking an identical building less than four metres away, three other men, in similar tracksuits and beards, sat cross-legged on the worn-down carpeted floor, a card game in progress.

They all looked up when Tanya and Visser came in, and Tanya tried to work out which of them had been at the door first.

Tanya had seen this kind of set-up before.

There'd been similar scams being run in Leeuwarden. Council tenants renting out their flats to immigrants, who packed in many more than the flats were designed to comfortably hold.

Which meant that the money was enough for the original tenant to rent a place of their own and still have enough left over for drugs.

'Which one of you is Tariq?' Visser asked.

One of the men on the floor inclined his head slightly.

'A colleague of mine said you might be able to help, Inspector Volk?'

Again the inclined head, like his beard was weighing him down.

'We're looking for someone called Ludo Haak, Volk said you might know where to find him.'

'We've never heard of him.'

'Don't give me that shit,' said Visser. 'I know he's done some work for you, probably still does. Maybe he's hiding somewhere in here? Perhaps I should get a team up here to have a search around?'

'You won't find anything here.'

'It's amazing what you can find if you want to,' said Tanya to Visser. 'And then we get accused of planting stuff. Unbelievable, isn't it?'

A brief conversation, the unfamiliar syllables shooting back and forth in the air between them, then the man on the right laid his cards face down and started speaking.

'I think we'll be able to help.'

Visser, hint of sarcasm in his voice: 'Thank you.'

The same man pulled out a phone from his trousers, flipped it open and pressed a speed dial.

The person at the other end, the voice just audible in the quiet air, spoke the same language, and the conversation was brief. He closed the phone and placed it down with exaggerated care next to his cards.

'I've asked someone, they will call me back in a few minutes, but in the meantime we will continue. Please sit.' He picked up his hand, and Tanya and Visser ceased to exist to the four men.

Tanya looked at Visser – the last time she'd sat cross-legged on the floor her parents were probably still alive – and he shook his head. So they stood there, watching the game, which appeared to unfold at a glacial pace, until the phone rang and the man held it to his ear, listened for a moment and hung up having not said a word.

'I think you will be able to find him, tonight, at a flat not far from here. He collects rent on Wednesday every week.' He pulled out a notepad and pen from his other pocket and wrote down the address, folded the paper in half and held it out for Visser to take.

She held her breath on the stairwell on the way down, having to gasp air once she'd got far away enough from the building.

'Who were they?'

'The Arabs? According to Volk, they control half the

drug trade around here. You wouldn't know it to look at them, they never seem to spend any money on anything.'

'Maybe they send it home to their families?'

'Yeah, could be.' He paused for a moment as they got in the car. 'Mind you, I can see why they need to deal in drugs, don't they have several wives each where they come from?'

Tanya pulled the car door closed and clicked in her seat belt.

'Interested in that kind of thing?'

'God no.' He fired up the car and pulled away from the kerb. 'One is more than enough.'

# 42

'So he went inside?' asked Jaap.

'Yeah, I mean he had ID and everything. I didn't feel I could stop him.' Her breath rose like smoke.

Jaap was late as he'd had to detour to the tech unit, Roemers showing him the sites Andreas had visited, one of which, according to Roemers, probably downloaded the virus that had wiped the laptop clean. Jaap had asked if someone could have hacked into the computer and placed the list of visited sites there. Roemers had said yes, but it was unlikely.

'Don't worry,' he said to the spiky-haired woman who'd answered the door to 35 Bloedstraat. 'He *is* police, it's just I told him to wait for me.'

The prostitute's booths lined both sides of the street like glass coffins and whilst waiting for Kees, Jaap had watched at least seven punters wandering up and down, window shopping.

There were men who went about it brazenly, and they'd tried to catch Jaap's eye, to share some experience that men who frequented prostitutes clearly had, and others shuffled around, as if their wives or mothers might pop out of one of the windows just as they were peering in, though the call of sex was clearly too strong to allow them to turn tail and take flight altogether.

All for a few moments' fleeting pleasure.

Yuzuki Roshi had told him once that you can never find what you're looking for. Jaap felt like walking over to the men and telling them that. He could see himself, standing with a placard, a crazy man.

He knew the arguments for legalized prostitution, that containment was better then pushing them underground, that the prostitutes were safer here – they even had their own union, the Sex Workers Union, which was supposed to look after their working conditions and pay – but the reality was that many of the foreign women had been trafficked here, with the promise of waitressing or nannying jobs, only to be slapped in the face with the harsh reality on their arrival.

By gangs like the Black Tulips.

A mobile cleaning crew came past, a woman spraying something which smelt like bleach on the ground.

'How long ago was this?' he asked.

'Ten, fifteen minutes.'

*Why didn't he wait?*

'Okay, let's have a look.'

Up on the top floor, the metal stairs clanging on his ascent, he could see that someone had broken in, the door battered, hanging off its hinges. He'd tried calling Kees several times as he'd stood outside but his phone just kept ringing.

Anxiety churned his stomach.

Pulling out his gun and checking the clip, the action still fluid despite lack of practice, he nudged the door open with his toe, which swung back to reveal darkness. He stepped forward. The floor creaked underfoot. Holding the gun with one hand he tried to find a light switch with the other.

The first one didn't do anything, but further along the wall his hand found a second, and when he flipped it light blazed from the ceiling, illuminating a large loft space. He scanned the room quickly, squinting his eyes against the onslaught of light but found no immediate threats. He holstered his gun and started exploring.

It looked like a repository for small theatrical sets, a series of three-sided boxes each with its own theme. An ancient Greek palace, something which was meant to look like the interior of a Sioux's teepee with furs everywhere, a dungeon scene, and the furthest one a mock-up of a Chinese opium den, in front of which a video camera stood on a tripod.

*I don't like the look of this*, he thought.

There were costumes too, racks of them at the far end, hats with large feathers flowing into the air, leather cat-suits, Nazi uniforms. The air smelt of paint and dust, and something else.

*Stale cigarette smoke, and is that mothballs as well?*

He headed for the camera, and turned it on, pressing the button with a bit of cloth, a blue silk scarf he picked up off the floor.

The screen flashed on, and he had to bend down slightly to see it, the opium den visible on the backlit screen. He tried to see if there was anything in its memory, but gave up after a few moments. Next he checked the desk on the opposite side of the room, partially hidden by a freestanding screen festooned with a wild print of jungle creepers.

*I've been wrong about this whole thing*, he thought.

The hexagram he'd got this morning had been for Mountain and Water: 'Even a fool can attain wisdom.'

Sometimes the I Ching scared him.

A laptop, a few more digital cameras, and an ashtray filled with twisted butts, each emerging like a diseased plant from the grey ash-soil. He tapped a few keys on the keyboard and was surprised when there was a sudden whirring, a soft click, and it sprang to life. He looked at the screen, a blank desktop with about twenty folders, each with a date.

*I'm not sure I want to see this*, he thought even as his hand was reaching out.

He clicked on the most recent, just five days ago and found several files, which he clicked on again. A window opened and a video started playing.

Jaap watched for a few moments

Then he reached out with a shaking hand and closed it.

He'd been right.

He didn't want to see it.

# 43

Kees woke.

Total darkness, his head pounding. He was on his side, on a floor. As to where that floor was he had no idea. He tried to move his head, but he clearly wasn't ready for that; the pounding, already monumental, increased tenfold, making his stomach contract hard, vomit shooting out of his nose.

As the rough liquid burned and he desperately tried to force air out to clear his nostrils he wondered why his mouth had filled up but not released.

Then he understood; he was gagged. He had to breathe out hard, almost inhaling some of the burning sick when he ran out of air, before his nose was fully clear, and his hands could pull the sopping wet gag down to his neck. Jaap had told him to wait, and he'd stupidly ignored the order. He blacked out again, and when he came round next had no idea how long it had been.

He tried to look around, moving slowly this time, but it was still so dark he couldn't see a thing. The air was heavy with his own vomit and for a moment he thought he was going to throw up again, but just managed to control the contractions.

On the third attempt he managed to sit up, his head banging against something hard just above him, and he blacked out again.

# 44

The loft was swarming, uniforms, techs, people taking photos, and all of them clad in plastic suits, the sound of each person's movements building up to white noise. Jaap was wearing one too, and despite the cold was beginning to sweat. Though it felt more of a cold sweat, feverish, sickly.

And to top it all no one knew where Kees was. The woman downstairs hadn't seen him leave, he wasn't answering his phone, and the station had no record of his movements.

*Why didn't he just wait?*

He was standing in the kitchen area, looking down at a pile of photos one of the forensics had found in a cardboard box. He felt a presence to his left and glanced up.

Tanya stood, her eyes locked on the photos. She looked ill.

'Disgusting.'

Jaap could hear, could *feel* his voice, unsteady, wobbling on the edge between anger and something else.

Something more akin to despair.

Tanya reached out and touched his arm, her grip was tight. Jaap wondered if she was holding on to stop herself from falling over.

It was well over an hour since he'd seen the video on the laptop, watched the man appear in an oriental costume, a long red robe, round matching hat, and a fake drooping moustache. And then he noticed the child, the girl who was lying on the opium eater's bed under a red satin blanket.

He didn't need to watch to know what was going to happen next, but something had held him there for a few seconds too long, before he closed the laptop, and he sat, a feeling of such emptiness it was as if he'd swallowed the whole vastness of the universe in one go.

Then the emptiness started to coagulate, to grow, urgent contractions racked his stomach, and he just made it to the bathroom, vomiting pure bile, electric yellow against the white porcelain, muscles straining hard in fits, until there was nothing left.

Washing his mouth out under the tap, then tipping his head back and gargling, trying to rinse the burning out of his throat, all he could think about was what he'd seen, the few seconds playing in a continual loop, running across his brain like sandpaper.

He'd never dealt with a case like this, but he knew a few Inspectors who had – Andreas was one of them – and to a man they'd all come out the other side thinner, harrowed, a look that never quite went away.

'How many are there?' Tanya asked, reaching out for a photo.

'Who knows, hundreds.'

He'd elected to go with the photos and leave the videos on the laptop for someone else; he'd thought maybe they'd be less disturbing – they were more stylized than the videos, more obviously posed, artistic in some evil way – but now he wasn't sure.

'We need to get these people.' Tanya's voice sounded, thin, shaken.

'Pretty much all of them are wearing masks, they're going to be impossible to identify. The ones that aren't I've put in a pile over there.'

Tanya picked them up and flicked through. 'We can run them against known offenders in the database, I guess.'

'And if that doesn't get us anywhere then I'm going to give them to the press.'

'Hang on . . . shit . . . you're not going to believe this.'

She handed Jaap a photo where an already familiar scene was being played out.

'Look, off in the corner.'

He peered closer, having to tilt the photo to get some light on it. There was a mirror on the set wall, and reflected in it, like a fleeting glimpse of the devil himself, was half a face.

Half of Ludo Haak's face.

A voice cried out from the back of the room. Jaap looked over; one of the forensics was kneeling down by a large box, an antique trunk which must have been a prop for one of the shoots.

'We've got a body here!'

When Jaap made it to the trunk he looked down, a body curled up inside.

It looked like Kees.

# 45

'You have got to be clear on one thing, if I give you an order you have to follow it, you hear me?'

Jaap was having trouble keeping his voice calm. They were sitting round a table, the cream Formica surface pitted by overuse, piles of photos turning it into a cityscape.

A sip from the bottle of water he'd picked up on the way in drove a spike into his forehead.

'Going in there on your own was stupid, you're lucky whoever knocked you out didn't put a bullet in the back of your head.'

Kees' eyes jumped around the incident room, before connecting.

'Yeah, I'm sorry, it's just I wanted to get on, you know? And there didn't seem to be anyone inside. The door was locked.'

Jaap watched him squirm. He didn't enjoy it, but right now Kees needed to be reined in, for both their sakes.

'So you have no idea who it was, you didn't see them, they didn't talk?'

Kees shook his head. 'Nothing, I was trying to find the light switch, I kind of sensed something was behind me then I blacked out.' He rubbed the back of his head gently, and winced. 'I know I fucked up, looks like I got punished for it as well. But I hear what you're saying, I'll stick to orders from now on in.'

The room was stuffy, badly lit, and the air stank of the station toilet next door. Disturbing splashes filtered through the paper-thin partition wall.

The Indonesian takeaway's revenge.

The door opened and Tanya stepped in, her face pale, muscles hard. She'd been watching the videos.

At the scene one of the tech guys had gone through the laptop and discovered something which had made Jaap's veins freeze up. It looked like the videos were accessed over the so-called darknet, where most of the web's illegal activities took place. But even worse, the tech reckoned some of the abuse was streamed live, and, judging by some instant message logs he'd found on the laptop, was actually being directed by paying customers.

Tanya tossed a still screenshot on the table.

Jaap picked it up. He could see a girl with red hair.

'I think that's her,' she said, her voice hoarse, 'it was shot just under a year ago.' And I found one with Haak in, made just two weeks back.' She started pacing back and forth along one side of the room. 'We've got to get him.'

Jaap watched the blaze in her eyes. He rubbed his face with his hands, trying to work this out.

He'd been wrong about this right from the start. These were revenge killings, the killer had left the phones as he'd wanted to expose the link between them, show what they had been up to. But who was it? A victim, a member of a victim's family? The thing was, seeing what he'd seen today, he could hardly blame them.

'This isn't that gang killing them off like we thought,' said Tanya echoing Jaap's thoughts. He could feel Kees' ears pricking up. 'It's a victim.'

'Yeah, it's got to be one of their victims. And whoever it is we're looking for might well be in here.' Jaap indicated the pile of photos. 'By the looks of things these go back years, so they could be an adult now.'

'Or it could be a parent or relative who found out?' said Kees.

'The thing is, I think these kids here are smuggled in, and then sold on, so they're on their own here. And you let someone who knows about this get away,' she said, turning to Kees.

'Jeez, and here I was thinking you'd just be happy I wasn't dead,' retorted Kees, smirking.

'You think this is a joke?' She stepped towards Kees.

'Let's just cool it,' said Jaap, 'we've just seen some shocking –'

Tanya banged her fist down on the table.

They looked at her. Jaap could see she was struggling to contain something.

Then she stormed out, slamming the door behind her.

'She takes things too personally. Always did. We saw each other for a bit, took it bad when I ended it,' said Kees.

*Not what Tanya told me*, thought Jaap. He wondered about going after her, before deciding to let her cool down by herself.

'I don't want to know about that. What I do want to know about is what we can do about this? We need to start . . . Kees, you with me?'

Kees had leant back, massaging his temples.

'Yeah, just my head, I'll be fine.'

Earlier Jaap had got a medic to give Kees a once over, even though Kees protested he was okay. Jaap had heard the medic tell Kees that if he felt dizzy, or had any other strange symptoms, in the next forty-eight hours he should get to a doctor.

It was then Jaap realized he'd been hoping Kees would need to go for some tests, get him off the scene. The swelling on the back of his head looked painful, and Jaap had seen him swallowing more painkillers than the instructions normally advised.

Kees stood up and walked round the table. Jaap looked down at the photos in front of him.

Friedman, according to his lawyer, had been desperate for a child of his own, and was also the patron of the charity for abused children.

How could that be? Unless it was some kind of weird atonement for what he knew was going on, a self-administered absolution.

'Friedman's wife, she said she'd found some porn on his computer, right before she left him,' said Kees.

'Yeah? And just when were you going to tell me this?' Jaap found himself shouting. 'This isn't some fucking game, you know, this is real.'

'I . . . it just didn't seem important at the time.'

'Unbelievable,' said Jaap, shaking his head. He thought back; he didn't remember seeing a computer at

Friedman's house, but then he'd been called away to identify Andreas.

'You checked his computer?'

'I don't think there was one at his house.'

Kees looked uncomfortable now. Less cocky.

'Get someone to go to Friedman's, maybe there's a laptop somewhere that was missed. And also find out where exactly he was a teacher before he inherited the business, see if there were any reports of abuse.'

Whilst Kees made the calls, Jaap wondered what else Kees hadn't told him about.

Or what else he might have missed.

'Any news from the patrol car?' he asked when Kees had hung up.

'Which one?'

'Are you with me here? The address in Haarlem, Paulus Fortuyn?'

'Yeah, right, they're there, outside the house. Waiting for orders.'

'Got a contact?'

'Marc Steenbergen, here's his number.'

Jaap knew him, they'd been at the academy together, friends who'd lost touch as they went their different ways. He'd have thought Marc would have made Inspector by now. Something had clearly gone wrong.

'Marc, it's Jaap.' A slight pause forced him to add, 'Rykel.'

'Hey, Jaap, how are you? Must be, what, eight, nine years?' He didn't sound that pleased to hear from him.

'More like twelve, isn't it?'

'Nah, I was talking about how long I've been sitting

around in this car with no idea what I'm doing here. Which I'm now assuming has something to do with you.'

'We've got a bit of a situation here, sorry you weren't kept up to speed but things were moving fast.'

'My boss was livid, called me up and said some rude cocksucker from Amsterdam called him up and barked orders at him.'

'I didn't make the call.' Jaap eyed Kees.

'Well, whatever. I'm here now, so what's up?'

'What's there? A residential address?'

'It's hardly a fucking cathedral.'

'Any signs of life?'

'Morgue-like.'

'You got someone there?'

'Me and my buddy Hendrick. Say "Hi", Hendrick.'

'Okay, sit tight, anyone tries to leave, hold them. I'm going to get over there as soon as I can. Anything changes, call me.'

'Message received. And Jaap?'

'Yeah?'

'Bring some food, I'd like a bagel with that aged cheese they do, and Hendrick here wants a box of doughnuts. And coffee, two coffees.'

Jaap hung up.

'Friend of yours?'

'Not any more it seems.'

Kees rolled his shoulders and moved his neck from side to side, Jaap could hear gristle.

'I need a coffee, you want one?' Kees asked. 'Or that green stuff you drink?'

*What's this*, Jaap thought, *a peace offering?*

He shook his head as Kees got up and left. His hand reached for the water bottle, to see if it had warmed up. It hadn't.

He began on the second-oldest lot. The photos, some of them taken with a Polaroid, had colours fading into a sepia wash.

They were different, apart from their age, not staged, mainly taking place in what looked like a bare room. But the abuse was the same, the same positions, the same body parts, the same thing over and over again. The only thing which changed was the faces.

And then, about thirty in, his hand, which had been mechanically taking them from one pile and moving them to another, stopped. There was something that he recognized. He brought it closer.

There was a child – a teenager really – wearing jeans but no top. He was sitting on a bed, face two-thirds to the camera.

*That can't be . . .*

There was a man too, but he still had his clothes on; this was the first in a sequence which unfolded over several photos. He reached the end, and the boy's face was, in the final shot, fully visible.

He recognized that face.

It was Andreas.

# 46

On his way to the canteen Kees slipped into the toilets, found a cubicle, locked it and slumped down after lowering the seat lid. His head was still throbbing; the painkillers hadn't killed much of the pain, and he was wondering if coke would help. Not that he had any.

*So much for trying to get Jaap to trust me*, he thought as he reached into his pocket and pulled out a slim purse, worn red leather, and flipped it open.

He'd found it under his hip when he'd come round in the trunk, Jaap's grip on his arm shaking him back to consciousness, and even though he was only loosely aware of what was going on he'd slipped it into his pocket as Jaap had helped him out. Too bad Tanya'd been there to see it all.

He'd been sure she was enjoying it.

Nanoseconds before he knew he was going down he'd placed the smell – mothballs, camphor. The girl who looked like Marinette and had run from Friedman's house on the first day. It had been her who'd knocked him out, and she must have dropped the wallet when she shoved him into the box.

There was nothing that would identify her directly, no

ID. He flicked through the contents, 150 euros in ten-euro notes – coke money now – a card for a taxi firm, a receipt for a journey taken yesterday, and folded up behind that a dry-cleaner's receipt, for the same day.

The dry cleaner had a name, and an address.

He pocketed it again, and went to get the drink he desperately needed.

# 47

Ludo Haak sucked in his cheeks, pulling cigarette smoke deep into his lungs. He held it there for a few seconds before releasing a steady stream through pursed lips, head tipped back. The dirty kitchen surrounding him belonged to one of the council flats he was in charge of collecting the illegal sublet money from. But there were currently no tenants, he'd kicked them out yesterday, just after he'd collected the monthly rent, two weeks early.

He'd had to.

He needed a quiet place, and he figured by tomorrow, or the weekend at the latest, he could fill it again. There were no end of immigrants who were willing to pay for this, cramming in as many as they could, scrimping and saving what little money they earned on their shit jobs, just so they could send some back to the rest of their family in whatever shithole they'd crawled out of in the first place.

It would actually work out better. He could pocket the difference between the rent from the old tenants and the new, a whole month's rent he wouldn't have to pass on. There was something in this.

He should do it more often.

And thinking of extra cash, there was a job he had lined up. They wanted that cop dead. And he was the man to do it.

A faint sobbing came from the bathroom, the only room in the flat with a lock on the door – *and what kind of a place had a lock on the outside instead of the inside?* – where he'd put the girl.

Which was a pisser, because he really needed to go. He stood up, grinding his cigarette out on the tabletop, and made his way to the sink. He pulled his trousers down, turned and managed to sit on it, balancing on the edge, the metal rim cold against his flesh and the tap poking into the small of his back.

*The new tenants can clear this up*, he thought.

When he was done, he had to use one of the kitchen towels to wipe himself – kind of smeary, he figured it must be the stress – he checked his phone. Someone was supposed to be calling him soon, to arrange the pick-up of the girl, the girl who'd bitten him yesterday as he'd brought her here. He examined the wound on his left hand, the teeth marks visible in red swollen flesh.

Jan hadn't been there to collect her, and he'd not been able to get hold of that creep Dirk either. Then he'd seen on the news that Dirk was dead, and he'd got a call to say the plan had changed. He was to find somewhere safe to hold her until today, when he would hand her off to someone else.

And he'd got ragged on at the same time, saying he should never have sold her, should have had her shipped out like all the rest.

But he didn't have all day to hang around, he had shit to do, and where was this asshole anyway?

As if on cue his phone rang and he answered.

'Yeah?'

'You've got her?'

'She's here.'

'Okay, I'm going to give you an address, you'll need to take her there now. Come by car and put her in the boot, don't let anyone see her. Or you.'

*Fucking asshole*, he thought as he listened to the address, *what does he think I am, some kind of moron?*

# 48

*15.16*

'I just can't believe it.'

The head of Vrijheid Nu, Hans Grimberg, looked like he'd been gutted, filleted and served up on a slab.

'I mean, he sat there telling me how he wanted to help, and then I find out he was involved in this . . . this . . . are you sure it's him?'

Grimberg looked back and forth between Jaap and Tanya, who were standing in front of his desk, as if one of them would suddenly smile and tell him it was all a big joke.

'There's no doubt. He was involved,' said Jaap.

'So what was this, coming here to offer help and money? Was it like trying to make up?' He stared at Jaap, his eyes on fire. 'As if giving money to us would cancel it out? Was that it?'

'I don't know, I don't suppose we'll ever know. But I need to find his killer.'

Grimberg shot out of his chair and paced back and forth behind his desk, his head shaking, he was muttering to himself, so quietly that Jaap couldn't make out the words.

'And you think that whoever killed him was a victim of his?'

'It's a possibility.'

'Don't you think they would have suffered enough?' he asked suddenly swinging round. 'If you've got proof of what he's done then why does it matter who killed him?' His voice closing up, rising like he was being strangled. 'And what if that was a kid of yours, what would you do if you found out? You'd go round and kill the bastard, that's what you'd do. But you'd get away with it because you're police, you could cover it up.'

'It's not that simple. There's a girl who's been kidnapped, and if we don't find and stop whoever killed Friedman, then we'll lose our chance to save her.'

*And get Andreas' killer.*

Grimberg's eyes lasered into him, before flicking away. He walked over to his chair and slumped into it.

'You know what? People like that, they deserve to die' – he slammed his hand down on the desk, knocking off a pile of papers which flurried into the air – 'they deserve to die like fucking dogs.'

'Look, we're all upset about this. And if the person responsible was abused by him then I don't want to bring them in either, but there's a life at risk.'

Grimberg sat, dead still now after the pacing, his eyes fixed on Jaap.

Jaap continued. 'Friedman used to work as a sports teacher and I've got someone checking up on where. I remember you saying a lot of these cases aren't even reported to the police –'

'And you want to check our records,' Grimberg butted in. 'See if there is anyone from wherever it turns out he worked?'

'It'll be the quickest way of seeing if there is a match, something we can follow up.'

'No. Our records are confidential, they have to be otherwise people wouldn't ever come to us for help. Look . . .' He paused, ran his hand through his hair. '. . . people live with this, and some come to terms with it. Some though, despite what help we give them, keep it inside, stay silent for years and years. It's only after the silence is broken, by themselves, when *they're* ready, that proper healing can happen. Breaking into that too soon can be highly detrimental to their recovery.'

'I realize that, but in this case there is a little girl who we might be able to save, and that's got to be worth something, hasn't it?' asked Tanya, anger, or something Jaap couldn't place, in her voice.

'I've got a duty of care to these people, they've been damaged, in some cases irreparably. I can't just have you charging around –'

'What it comes down to is this.' Jaap leant forward over the desk, planting his balled fists on straight arms to support him. 'I'm investigating three murders and a kidnapping of a child. I'm trying to stop anything else happening to her, something worse. You've seen what abuse does to people, so give me access to your files and maybe we can stop another victim coming through your door. I can get a warrant for this, but we need to see it now.'

Grimberg just stared at him, then looked down at his hands.

Tanya spoke up, her voice more controlled this time.

'You have the chance to help save a little girl, I don't see how you can refuse to help us.'

Grimberg chewed his lower lip.

# 49

Jaap had split up their duties: Kees was to focus on Friedman and Zwartberg, whilst Jaap got to run around with Tanya.

*Fucking typical,* Kees was thinking as he made his way to Friedman's house, the cold air not improving his mood, *he makes a big show of including me in what he's doing, then fobs me off with the shit work. I bet he's fucking her too.*

The interior, when he got there, was no warmer than the air outside. Kees flicked on a light switch and the hallway was revealed. A massive oil painting, a pastoral landscape with eighteenth-century wigged noblemen and rustic shepherds, hung on the wall in a gilt frame.

Below the picture two slender vases with a blue floral pattern on a white background and a surface which looked like cracked ice. And supporting them, a dark wooden side table, their reflections slightly blurred on the polished surface.

*I hate all this old shit,* he thought to himself before heading forward.

His temples had been pounding since he woke, a mushroom cloud exploding over and over, and each step only made it worse.

He spent the next twenty minutes searching the house,

but, just as he'd said, there was no laptop. As he left the building something caught his eye, just by the doormat.

Kees bent down to pull it out, the tiny corner of paper revealing itself to be a business card. He felt the roughness of the textured paper against his fingertips, and turned it over. It was completely plain with a string of numbers and letters, the embossed shiny surface of the black ink catching the light, running across the centre which didn't seem to make any sense at all.

XT56SUGK9DYUSNGH

He pocketed it and went back to the station. Next on his growing list was to check up on the stole of Zwartberg's. As far as Kees understood, it was kind of like a football scarf, different churches had different patterns, so if he trawled round enough churches someone must be able to recognize it. He'd have to make a list of places to visit, starting with those in the Jordaan.

But when he got to his computer it was the card he felt drawn to. There was something deeply wrong with it.

Sitting at his desk he stared at the numbers and letters. It just didn't make any sense.

'. . . and then she says, "but that's too big to fit in my hole".'

Laughter erupted from a few desks away, a joke he'd heard at least four times already over the last few days, doing the rounds of the office like a viral infection.

He hadn't even found it that funny the first time.

A business card usually had a name and contact details on, so this wasn't a business card. What was it for? Was it some kind of password or code? But if so why have it printed on a card?

He wrote out the letter and numbers and tried to rearrange them into something meaningful, but, having never been any good at crosswords, he gave up after a few minutes.

A yawn prised his jaws open, forcing his head back. He closed his eyes.

Voices he'd been half hearing came into focus.

'. . . so it'll be Rykel, not De Waart?'

'That's what the rumour is.'

'I guess he'd make a better Station Chief than Smit, but he's a bit young, isn't he? That would piss off Felco and Bastiaan.'

'Yeah, but Felco is pissed off anyway, I've never met anyone like that, and they couldn't make Bastiaan Chief, he'd blow the department budget in like a week.'

'He'd probably bet it all on one match –'

Kees' eyes flicked open. Jaap to be Station Chief? If that was true then he'd really messed up.

Shit!

Why had he done it? He could feel the moisture on his palms. How could he have been so stupid? He got up, had to move, think it through, and he headed off, needing to do something to neutralize the unease.

'Hey, Kees?' Martijn's voice from behind him.

'Yeah?'

'Did you know about this, Jaap being next in line?'

He turned to look at him, the bulk concentrated round his stomach making his shoulders and head seem tiny.

'No, I hadn't heard.'

'You're working a case with him, aren't you?'

'Yeah . . . yeah, I am.'

'Looks like your chance to impress then.'

Kees swallowed.

'Yeah, I guess it is.'

Later, once he'd calmed down – the only way that Jaap would ever know was if Smit or De Waart told him – he went back to his desk and looked at the card again. A thought had occurred to him, and he fired up his laptop. He typed the collection of letters and numbers printed on the card into a browser, prefacing it with 'www' and ending with '.com'. He hit return and waited for the page to load, but a 'could not connect to server' message appeared. But, trying again, this time with '.nl', yielded a result.

His phone rang.

'Inspector, this is Sergeant Boekestijn. You're the contact point on e-fit 4751?'

A simple page appeared, asking him to log in or register.

'You've found her?' The pulse in his veins sped up, and he shifted forward in his chair, typed in a made-up email address and hit 'Submit'.

'Yeah, got her down in holding now, but she's not happy.'

As Kees hung up another screen, 'Thank you for your registration, your download will begin shortly', flashed up, and the download window started showing the progress bar, fifty-seven minutes remaining.

Down by the holding cells – strip lights blinking and buzzing making him feel sick – he asked the duty officer where she was.

'She's in there, refused to speak to us.'

Kees pushed the door, walked in, and stopped short,

completely unable to breathe. There were four women, two prostitutes and an alcoholic by the look of them, but it was the one on the end of the bench that caught his attention.

'You bastard,' Marinette hissed. 'Is this your idea of a joke? I'll get you sacked for this.'

*Fuck*, he thought, *those fucking, fucking idiots.*

'There's been a misunderstanding, they weren't supposed to arrest you –'

'Of course they weren't, but you made them.' Her face was twisted up, lines appearing where there were none before, blood pulsing under her skin like a rash.

'No, listen to me. There's someone we're looking for, she just looks like you, and they've got the wrong –'

Before he could do anything she was up off the bench, her hand hitting his left cheek, the sting bringing tears to his eyes.

The other women cheered.

# 50

*Wednesday, 4 January*
*17.05*

Tanya checked her watch, but it hadn't changed much from when she'd last looked. It was still a few hours before Ludo Haak was due to collect rent from whatever group of immigrants had fallen into the trap of illegal subletting.

But here she was, sitting in a car across from the apartment building anyway. Jaap had agreed to meet her later before he'd rushed off to Haarlem, but she'd felt drawn here, a voice nagging at her, telling her that Haak might turn up early, and if she missed him . . . Well, that didn't bear thinking about.

She'd only been to Amsterdam a few times over the years, day trips where she took in the canal district with its wealthy houses, boutique shops, jewellers, high-fashion leather handbags and artisan chocolatiers whose wares would have to be very sweet to get rid of the bitter taste their price would create.

Commerce polished the veneer of respectability, a sense that all was right with the world. But out here in the suburbs things were different.

This was the Amsterdam tourists rarely saw.

This was the Amsterdam of poverty, drug addiction, social and racial segregation. She thought back to what

244

Visser had said, his pessimistic view. Then she thought of the girl with Haak.

The girl with red hair, Adrijana Fajon.

She thought of him ordering her to get undressed, of his pale body, the tattoo like a livid scar, the feeling of desperation, lack of hope, fear and revulsion.

She knew that feeling all too well.

Her fingers tightened on the wheel.

She shook her head, tried to focus on her breath, anything to clear what was going on in her mind. Her heart was slamming in her chest like a monkey trying to escape a cage.

The file had come through much later than promised, but she'd read it before leaving the station. There wasn't much, parents an art teacher and cleaner who'd reported her missing from a cafe in the centre of Ljubljana. Someone at a nearby table had keeled over with a heart attack, and in the confusion Adrijana simply disappeared. The police had been notified, run their investigation, and, failing, had passed it on to Interpol within a couple of months.

At Interpol her image just sat on a webpage.

Tanya had managed to get the name of the man in charge of the original investigation in Ljubljana, and had sent him a message. So far he'd not got back to her.

A car, blacked-out windows and shiny hubcaps – classic drug-dealer motor – was slowly crawling down the road towards her, rhythm pounding from speakers which would have cost more than she earned in a month.

If the owner had even paid for them, that is.

It pulled to a stop right by her and the window, in which

she could see her face reflected, slid down halfway. A hand appeared from the dark interior, the middle finger raised, a large gold ring with a skull and wings catching the dying light.

The car moved on.

She was in an unmarked, and she wasn't in uniform. But they could spot her just the same. Maybe waiting here wasn't such a good idea. As she reached for the ignition key she noticed a tremor in her hand.

# 51

Kees was heading out of the station; the news of what had happened would be spreading like wildfire, and he wanted to get clear of its path.

He also wanted to get to the dry cleaner's, see if he couldn't get a lead on the woman who'd knocked him out.

'Kees, I was hoping to have a word with you.'

He turned to see De Waart coming down the front steps. Cigarette in one hand, a styrofoam cup in the other, steam rising like smoke signals.

All day he'd had the uneasy feeling he was being watched. Who would be watching him he didn't know, so he'd tried to dismiss it. But when he'd walked into Smit's office earlier and found De Waart there, dismissing it got a whole lot harder. He didn't like that De Waart knew what he was doing, that De Waart now had a hold over him.

The police force was no different to anywhere else when it came to politics. There were people who tried to avoid it, turned up and hoped that doing their job well would be enough. And then there were people like De Waart, people who could sniff out an angle, people who wouldn't hesitate to use knowledge, justified or otherwise.

And what little he knew of De Waart told him that he was one of the players.

Fair enough, Kees was too, but he didn't like the position this put him in one little bit. Smit letting it slip that Kees was ratting for him was highly unlikely, but De Waart?

Well, De Waart he didn't trust.

'I'm just heading out.'

'Where?'

'Just out.'

'Anything I should know about?'

'Not really.'

De Waart narrowed his eyes.

'You know, I'd have thought you'd have been able to tell us more this morning, because let's face it,' he said turning his head, trying to make eye contact, 'this is a good opportunity for you to make new friends.'

'My social calendar is kind of full as it is.'

De Waart laughed, and slapped him on the shoulder.

'Come on, I'll walk with you, wherever it is you're heading.'

The sun was falling, dragging darkness behind it. He glanced at the ice, a hard skin on the canal. A van slowly crossed a bridge; Kees recognized it as the same one which had got in his way the day he chased that bitch.

The one that looked like that other bitch.

De Waart was talking, and Kees had to tune back in.

'. . . so do you think it could have been done?'

'Uh . . . Yeah, I don't see why not,' answered Kees trying to work out what he was talking about, he was having trouble concentrating.

'That's what I thought, so I started to think, maybe it was erased on purpose, you know, to hide something?'

'Yeah, could be.'

De Waart turned his head to look at him for a moment, as if trying to decide something. They passed a young couple, faces jostling together, long hair and clothing so similar it was hard to work out which was the girl. Then Kees realized they were both girls. He thought of Carice.

Carice and Tanya.

He felt himself stiffen.

'Okay, so if you come up with anything you'll let me know?'

'Yeah, sure,' Kees said, 'of course.'

'And seriously, it's good to have friends around here, especially as things are going to be changing soon.'

They shook hands, both playing the crushing game, and De Waart turned and limped back the way they'd come.

It took him fifteen minutes to reach the Oudezijds, the medieval heart of the city, which had deteriorated since into seediness, his mind occupied the whole time with images of Carice and Tanya, powerless to stop them.

The dry cleaner's was wedged between a novelty sex-toy shop for the tourists and another selling Asian porn DVDs, and inside an old man was sitting, sewing buttons on a shirt.

The air was hot and stank of chemicals.

Somewhere out back an iron hissed like a snake.

Kees gave him the ticket, flashed his ID, and told him what he wanted.

The man, grey hair combed over a shiny scalp, peered at it, and then shook his head.

'Doesn't tell me much, it says a coat, and the cost.'
Kees pulled out a print-off of the e-fit.
'That's Helma.'
'Surname?'
'I don't know, but I sometimes deliver to her house, it's just round the corner.'

# 52

Jaap's eyes were on the road.

But all he could see were the pictures of Andreas.

He wondered if they'd ever go.

It was dark, stars appearing in the gaps between the sodium lights which rushed past him on the motorway.

Andreas was thirty-two when he died, so the photos must be at least fifteen, maybe seventeen, years old.

*I never suspected he'd been abused,* he thought, *does Saskia know?*

Andreas had grown up near Groningen and Jaap needed to find out if Friedman, or Zwartberg, or even Haak, had ever lived there. Or Korssen.

Since he'd seen Andreas' body sprawled out in Amsterdamse Bos he'd not been himself, emotions had been running loose, changing too quickly for him to really know what they were, flashes of feelings he couldn't identify.

And now this, proof that his partner, his friend, had been abused. Proof that he'd been carrying a secret around with him, letting it gnaw away at his insides, and all the time Jaap had had no idea.

Yuzuki Roshi had once told him that although pain was

inevitable, suffering was optional. All well and good when you're cloistered away from it all.

*But now?* he asked himself.

He pulled off the motorway and followed the instructions the satnav kept giving him, not really noticing his surroundings. The voice told him that a further hundred metres and a left turn would take him to his destination. It was a broad street, an affluent area with large houses, vehicles to match. Halfway down was a car which stuck out, too battered, not shiny enough, the police department unused to staking out in rich areas.

Jaap could see two heads. He parked and walked towards it, getting into the back seat. The car smelt like cars did on stakeouts.

Bad.

Marc turned his head.

'Got my bagel?'

'They were out of bagels.'

His partner – Jaap couldn't remember his name – snorted.

'Well, anyway. Nice to see you again,' said Marc twisting his shoulders and head round the headrest, the seat creaking. 'So what have we got going on here?'

'Which one is it?'

The partner pointed to a house three down from where they were, lights on in the downstairs windows, Christmas lights flashing in a dark window on the next floor. Now you see Santa, now you don't.

'The guy who lives there also owns a place in Amsterdam, and someone's been shooting porn there,' said Jaap.

'Bring any of it along? Might help ease the boredom a bit.'

'It was child porn.'

'Oh . . . shit.'

All three watched as a people carrier drove past them and parked on the opposite side. The driver, a woman in a fur coat and with long blonde hair, herded four kids into the house next door to Fortuyn's.

'Having kids these days,' offered Marc. 'Risky business.'

Jaap thought of Saskia, of her and Andreas' baby.

*Fatherless before even being born.*

'I'm going in. Marc, come with me.'

When they got to the door and pressed the bell a man opened it.

'Yes?' he asked, tired eyes going suspicious.

He was young, about Jaap's age, but his shoulders were slumped forward, as if he were expecting a blow to slam down at any moment. Some kind of war film seemed to be playing in the background, explosions and rapid gunfire.

'Paulus Fortuyn?'

He nodded.

'We're going to have a little chat, can we come inside?'

In the corridor Jaap noticed a photo of Paulus, an attractive woman and a young child. It was taken on a boat, a yacht floating on a bright turquoise sea, a wooded island in the background. All three were smiling, squinting towards the camera.

*Who took the photo?* wondered Jaap.

The main room at the back of the house contained a young boy, the same as in the photo, and the source of the explosions, a large screen hooked up to a console, the images moving fast.

'Miki, can you turn that off now?' asked Paulus.

'Dad . . .' The word stretched into a moan. '. . . I'm just getting to where the main enemy camp is, I can't stop now.'

'Let's go in the kitchen,' suggested Paulus.

Two pizza boxes greeted them, a large slice with thin strips of peppers lay congealing in the top one.

'Does 35 Bloedstraat mean anything to you?'

'I own it. Why, has something happened?'

'You could say that, I was there earlier today, and what I saw I didn't much like.'

'What?'

Jaap reached into his jacket and tossed a photo, one of the more recent ones, on to the work surface Paulus was leaning against, his hands on the edge, fingers white. He picked it up, and Jaap watched as his face crumpled.

He handed the photo back with an unsteady hand.

'So you don't know anything about this?'

'Of course not, I just rent the place out, I had no idea that guy was going to be doing this . . . this . . .' He couldn't seem to find the word and gave up. A baby started crying upstairs.

Marc nodded towards the ceiling. 'You want to get that, or is your wife around?'

'No, she died giving birth to him.'

He left the room.

'Nice one,' whispered Jaap.

Marc looked uncomfortable, didn't meet his eyes.

Jaap looked around. It was clear that Paulus wasn't coping that well; the kitchen was a mess. Apart from the pizza boxes, more spilling out of the bin, the surfaces were dirty, festooned with crumbs, orbs of jam and tomato sauce, and a tin opener, still with the round disk attached, lay by the sink.

Jaap's phone rang, De Waart's number.

*Christ*, thought Jaap, *what does he want?*

'Yeah?'

'Listen, I think we should have a chat, I've come across some stuff, and . . . well, it looks like I may have been too hasty.' De Waart sounded uncomfortable.

'What is it?'

'It would be better if we can talk this through, face to face?'

Jaap gave him the name of a bar most of his colleagues used and told him he'd be there in an hour and a half. Agreement came from De Waart as Paulus returned, the crying upstairs having stopped. He sank into a chair at the kitchen table and looked at his hands.

'You want a drink?' he asked Jaap.

'Do you?'

'There's some whisky in the cupboard there.'

Jaap nodded to Marc, who retrieved the bottle and three glasses.

Jaap stared at him until he put two back.

'You'll want to know about who I rent it out to, I've got his details somewhere,' said Paulus once Marc had poured him a glass.

'Dirk Friedman?'

'No, some other guy.'

'How long have you rented it out?'

'Five years? Maybe six, my wife inherited it, and we decided to rent it. The rent just about pays, or rather paid, the mortgage on this place.'

'Paid?' Then Jaap understood. 'Life insurance?'

'Yeah, they paid out.' He shrugged. 'You sign those bits of paper and you pay the money every month, but you know it's never going to happen. And then it does. There was a problem with the baby, turned round at the wrong time and the doctors? They said it was nothing to worry about.'

Paulus took a long sip, and pushed himself up from the table.

'I'll get you that name.'

He returned a few minutes later with a red ring-bound folder, which he opened out on the table.

'It should be in here somewhere, all the original correspondence. My wife ... she was good at organizing things.'

Jaap couldn't think of anything to say, so he watched Paulus flip through the pages, occasionally stopping before moving on. Once he'd reached the end he looked up shaking his head.

'It's not here, but our lawyer will have a copy of the original tenancy agreement.'

Jaap took down the details and just as he was thanking Paulus a huge explosion reverberated from next door. Jaap figured it meant either the game was over or the boy had got through to the next level.

# 53

Kees was speeding along the last short stretch of motorway towards Schiphol airport, the road virtually clear,
radio on loud. He didn't really need to be going this fast,
just as he didn't need to have the lights flashing, or, for
that matter, the siren screeching, long sinuous wails
streaming out behind him punctuated with short bursts
of static like rapid gunfire into the night.

But hell, he'd had a shit day.

The stinging slap, delivered with real force by Marinette
in front of several uniforms, had already made it to the
status of station legend – he was going to be the butt of
jokes about domestic violence for the rest of his career.
He could see the whole thing now.

He'd tried to ignore it, but all the while he kept playing
the scene, over and over, prodding at the wound until the
call which propelled him into the car came through. And
now he was racing through the dark, the speed calming
him.

He'd taken the call whilst Jaap was off in Haarlem, and
he'd not been able to reach him on the phone. It was from
someone at border patrol, Schiphol branch, to say that
they had received one Rint Korssen, detained in Hamburg

under the European Arrest Warrant and put on the first available plane back to Amsterdam. But things hadn't been so efficient at this end, and it was only just past seven when Kees finally heard about it despite the fact that Korssen's plane had touched down a little after one o'clock. He glanced at the sign, coming at him quickly, one more exit to go.

Ten minutes later, siren and lights now extinguished, he pulled up at the airport police base, where three patrol cars were parked outside, their windscreens already glistening with frost.

Inside he had to talk with a brain-dead night receptionist who just couldn't get his head round what was going on, until finally, and reluctantly, he got through to someone who could help. He passed the desk phone to Kees and turned back to his small TV, a believer at his altar.

'Are you Rykel?' said the voice on the line.

'No, I'm Inspector Terpstra, but we work together.'

'I'm sorry, but the warrant was issued under the name of Rykel, so I'll only be able to release the prisoner to him.'

'Are you shitting me? We work together, I told you that, and I've just driven out from Amsterdam.'

'Guess you should have checked first.'

Kees slammed the plastic receiver down on the desk three times in rapid succession, making the receptionist jump, and then glare at him, before he took it back to his ear.

'Did you hear that? That's what's going to happen to your head if I'm not leaving here in ten minutes with the prisoner I came to pick up.'

In the end it took more like twenty-five.

Korssen was being held in a unit on the far side of the site, and Kees was just wondering if he was going to have to go on a rampage and get someone higher up the food chain on to it, when the doors by the receptionist opened and in stepped Rint Korssen, hands cuffed behind him, and a police officer gripping his upper arm, pushing his right shoulder up to his ear, making him look lopsided. Korssen looked at Kees, and was about to speak but something flashed in his eyes and he held his tongue.

Kees stood up, signed the bit of paper thrust at him by the officer and turned to Korssen.

'Welcome home, sir,' he said. 'Welcome home.'

# 54

A cop bar. Cheap beer to help wash away the taste of the day, loud music to help drown out thought, and so dark that you couldn't see how depressed your fellow cop drinkers were.

Jaap hated the place, hardly ever came here, but he didn't want to go back to the station, the room full of photos, and the laptop containing countless videos, waiting for him like a death sentence.

He was going to have to go back to it, trawl through to see if there were any more of Andreas, but he needed to put it off as long as he could.

De Waart wasn't there when he arrived so Jaap found a table where he could see the whole room, and was as far away from any speakers as possible. A group of five uniforms were celebrating something at the bar. One of them was the uniform who'd sorted out his door.

Once he'd returned from Japan, and decided to rejoin the police, he started looking for a place to live. The old flat he'd rented, out past the Amstelpark in an area of renowned architectural monstrosity, just didn't appeal any more.

Initially he'd trawled round property after property, but it became apparent that he wasn't going to be able to

afford much in the centre of town, rents were strato-
spheric, and buying was not an option.

Just as he was on the brink of resigning himself to living further out Andreas had called to say he'd busted a
grizzled American who'd been living the dream in Amsterdam since the late seventies and had got a bit loose with
his drug possession.

The guy had tried to talk his way out of a charge, claiming he was trying to sell up and go back to the States,
where he'd inherited, unexpectedly, a small fortune, and
pointed out the handmade 'For Sale' sign on his houseboat on Bloemgracht.

Andreas reckoned the American would be open to
offers, given that he wanted to leave and didn't want a
drugs bust slowing down the process, and Jaap was round
there like a shot.

The deal only took a few days to conclude.

It took longer to get rid of the smell once he'd moved
in, a deep funk of something Jaap eventually worked out
was a combination of pot, no surprises there, and fenu-
greek.

He was starting to wonder where De Waart was when
he looked up and saw him limping in. De Waart scanned
the room and nodded to Jaap's raised hand, stopping off
at the bar on the way over.

He brought over two beers, and handed one to Jaap as
he sat down.

'I forgot,' he said when Jaap didn't touch it. 'You don't
drink, do you?'

Jaap shook his head.

De Waart shrugged, pulled the glass back and drained

it in one go, wiping his mouth with the back of his hand and letting out a theatrical sigh.

'Guess I can squeeze another one in.'

*I'm sure you can*, thought Jaap.

'As I said on the phone, I maybe should have listened to you more in the beginning.' He swirled beer round the second glass. 'I've found some stuff which ties in with what you were saying.'

'I'm listening,' said Jaap, not wanting to make it easy for him.

'Firstly though, I wanted to apologize for the other day, I got out of control, and with all the shit you were having to deal with I should have laid off. So . . .'

'Forget it,' said Jaap.

'Okay, so down to business. You said Andreas' death was to do with the case you were working on before, and I dismissed that. I was wrong, but you have to understand, I was getting pressure from above on this as well.'

'Smit?'

'Yeah, he said you were not thinking straight. You know, after you . . .'

'After I what?' asked Jaap.

'Well, that shooting, and your . . . uhh . . . episode.'

'Come on, just say it.'

'Okay, after you cracked up and went away somewhere to sort yourself out. Look, I respect that, I think it makes you a stronger cop. I know some of the other guys think whatever you're into is weird, all that eastern sh . . . stuff, but they can't deny you get results. And I know how close you and Andreas were and I just figured it could be clouding your judgement.'

'And you didn't like Andreas at all.'

'Look, we had that thing, the accident.' His hand strayed down to massage his leg; Jaap wondered if it was unconscious or for show. 'I'll be the first to admit that. But he was still one of us.'

De Waart's phone started ringing, he glanced at the screen and put it away again. 'Anyway, that's all beside the point.' He paused for another sip. 'It got me thinking, what you'd said, so I did a bit of digging of my own. This gang you were working on, they operate out of the ports, so I had a word with someone I know up there and he told me that he'd heard some chatter, about the gang being nervous and needing a problem taken care of.'

'When was this?'

'About a week ago.'

'Who's your source?'

'Just this guy. I helped him out with something a while ago, and he passes me the odd bit of information.'

Someone dropped a glass by the bar, a cheer went up from the uniform quintuplets.

'So what are we having the discussion for?'

De Waart looked at him, as if humouring a small child.

'I just wanted you to know that I'm on it . . .' He leant closer. '. . . and also to see if you'd got anywhere with it yourself, anything which could help?'

'What makes you think I've been working on it? Smit told me not to, so I didn't.'

De Waart laughed as if Jaap had told the funniest joke in the world, then stopped himself, the laugh cut off before it could flourish.

'Okay, I'm sorry. What I'm trying to say is that if it was

me I would have ignored the order. You're a good cop, Jaap, you fight for what's right, I've seen that. And in this situation no one is going to blame you for wanting to be involved in Andreas' case. I just want to find these bastards, and I was hoping you'd be able to help me.'

Jaap was tired.

Beyond tired.

He thought of the image he had in his pocket of Andreas as a teenager. His insides were wound so tight they might snap at any moment. He was carrying this all on his own.

Maybe he could use some help.

Maybe he should tell De Waart everything.

'Okay, so where I'm –' started Jaap just as his phone rang. He pulled it out and saw it was Kees.

*Just in time*, thought Jaap as he answered.

# 55

Once he'd left Korssen in one of the holding cells in the basement Kees had finally managed to get through to Jaap. The music blaring in the background had meant he'd had to repeat himself a couple of times before Jaap got it. He told Kees he'd be there in twenty minutes and not to question Korssen till he arrived.

Kees had felt like pointing out that he'd been the one to drive all the way out to Schiphol and back, so if he felt like asking a few questions he would, but resisted.

The office was quiet, a couple of new red names on the murder board showing why. He texted Carice, then turned to his computer, remembering the download he'd started before having to collect Korssen.

The screen was dark; he clicked the mouse button a few times before it flared to life. The download window wasn't there, and there didn't appear to be a newly downloaded file. After a few moments' searching he found that there weren't any files at all, there was nothing on his computer.

Everything had gone.

# 56

'. . . and he said that Andreas was mixed up in child pornography. Jaap, I can't take this. I don't understand what's going on.'

Saskia's voice, coming through the hands-free kit in the car, sounded distorted, alien. Even so, he could tell she was scared. Really scared. He flicked the indicator and pulled left on to Leidsestraat, heading for the station. Leidsestraat was ostensibly traffic-free, given over to trams and pedestrians, but Jaap didn't feel like going the long way round. And who was going to stop him?

'Listen, De Waart doesn't know what he's doing –'

'Andreas was never into that, he wasn't. You have to tell him, you have –'

'I don't think he's going to listen to me right now.' Raising his voice, angling his head towards the mic by the rearview mirror. He noticed a motorbike one car behind him, its headlight blinding. 'Listen,' he continued, 'I think I may be getting somewhere with this case, and I'm going to be able to prove that Andreas wasn't into that . . . stuff. It's just going to take a little while. I'll be round later, I'll let you know more then.'

*The thing is*, he thought as he ended the call, *I'm not sure I'm getting any closer at all.*

He checked the rearview again.

The bike was still there.

# 57

'Is this some kind of joke?' said Korssen.

'Do you find something funny about murder and child pornography? Because I have to say I don't,' Jaap shot back.

The interview room was lit with a single bulb, unshielded, and the air was stale with sweat and fear. It was like a stage set, the sparseness of it all designed to give a guilty mind nothing to latch on to, nothing to distract itself.

He knew how effective emptiness could be.

He'd faced it in Kyoto, wrestled with it. He wasn't sure now if he'd won.

'But what have I got to do with that?'

'I don't know, which is why you're here, and we're having this little talk. But what I do know is that your business partner winds up dead, an associate of his, who he's running a child porn business with, is also killed, and after we talked, you do a runner. If you were in my shoes, what would you think?'

Something tightened in Korssen's face.

'Get me my lawyer.'

'Where's Ludo Haak?'

'Who the fuck is Ludo Haak?'

'I think you know.'

'I'm not saying another goddamn thing until you get me my lawyer.'

Jaap stood up.

'Find him a cell,' he said to Kees, and went for the door, turning back once he'd opened it and was half outside, 'and see if you can find a busy one, don't want our friend here getting lonely.'

Once Korssen was settled in – Kees had found a group of tourists for him to stay with, tattooed tossers on a stag night which had ended in the usual brawl – Jaap called Tanya, agreeing on where to meet. But before they left Kees mentioned something which caught his attention.

'Totally wiped?'

'Yeah, all my reports and stuff, gone.'

Jaap checked his watch, it would be tight, but he needed to get the laptop over to Roemers, find out if it was the same as Andreas'.

'I'm going to drop it off with Roemers to have a look at. You head over to meet Tanya, I'll catch you up.'

Kees unplugged his laptop and handed it to Jaap.

'And Kees?'

'Yeah?'

'Keep it civil between you two, okay?'

# 58

'So you think it's a victim killing off Friedman and the people he worked with?' asked Tanya, looking out of the car window. None of the four street lights were working, the only illumination coming from windows, stark light from unshaded bulbs. They were sitting in an unmarked, watching the building entrance, hoping that Ludo Haak was going to make an appearance soon.

Jaap stretched his legs out as far as they would go under the dashboard and yawned. Kees was parked three back, and Jaap had decided he'd rather wait with Tanya.

Obvious, really.

And not least as he was getting bad vibes from Kees. He seemed to be reckless. And angry.

Jaap knew about both.

And he knew they were not a good combination.

'It looks like it, the phones make that pretty clear. But there's a whole load of things I don't get.'

'Like where's the girl.'

'And how come Andreas is dead. If it was a victim killing these guys off why would they kill Andreas as well.'

'The news reports –'

'Fuck the news reports, all that shit about him being into porn, it's just not true.' He breathed out slowly, aware that he'd snapped. 'Sorry, it's just . . .'

She reached a hand out and touched his.

'I know, it's okay,' she said.

'The thing is, I'd spoken to Andreas on Sunday, he asked me to take a ride with him, he thought he was getting somewhere on that case I told you about. And there's a good chance if I'd gone . . .'

'You can't think like that.' She squeezed his hand. 'Maybe if you'd gone with him you'd both be dead now.'

Jaap toyed with telling her about the houseboat break-in, and the motorbike, but decided against it. He was exhausted again, and he was just getting used to sitting there with Tanya's hand on his own.

*It's been so long . . .*

Her phone started ringing; she took her hand away and pulled out her mobile.

'I think it's the investigator, from Ljubljana,' she said before answering it.

Jaap listened to the conversation, in English. Tanya's was better than his. He tried to stretch his legs out a bit further but there wasn't room; he found the lever down by the side of the seat, but it was jammed.

Tanya had shown him the file from Interpol and the photo of Adrijana. The resemblance was there, but it wasn't what anyone would call a 100 per cent match.

'When was this?' asked Tanya after a few moments. She listened some more, then thanked whoever it was and hung up.

Jaap looked at her, he could tell she was shaken.

'Adrijana's parents.' She swallowed and looked out the window. 'They killed themselves three weeks ago.'

He paused to watch a young Algerian come out of the building, stop to light a cigarette, hunched over the flame, his face flickering for a second, then walk up the street away from them, the tip of the cigarette like a firefly.

All his training in Kyoto had been to try and accept suffering. Yuzuki Roshi had said that was the only way to be free of it, annul its terrible power. It had all seemed so simple there, cloistered away from day-to-day life, from relationships, from people and the evil they did.

But now it wasn't simple.

He reached his hand out to Tanya's, she gripped it, her face still averted.

Then he noticed a figure emerging from a car which had just pulled up outside the building, a hood making him look like an executioner.

'Is that him?' asked Tanya, her voice strangled with emotion.

Jaap strained to see his face but couldn't get an angle.

The hooded figure took one last drag from a cigarette and then threw it on to the ground, blowing the smoke up into the night. He stepped through the doors and disappeared. Jaap and Tanya both reached for their door handles at the same moment. He checked the rearview to make sure Kees was alert. His head was back against the headrest. Jaap couldn't tell if his eyes were open or not.

'Let's go and find out.'

Jaap walked back to Kees' car and rapped on the

window. Kees jerked forward, opening his eyes, then got out.

'I need you alert. Wait at the foot of the stairs, Tanya and I are going up.'

There were nine storeys, and it was on the seventh that they heard the shouting, a woman with a foreign accent telling him she didn't have the money, and a man's voice, presumably Ludo Haak's, telling her that he didn't give a toss, he wanted to be paid, and if she didn't have the cash he'd take it in other ways.

They rushed up the next set of stairs, Jaap spotting the open door three down the corridor. As they pushed their way in they saw the figure shoving someone to the floor. Jaap ran forward, but the man, still wearing his hood, must have had some sixth sense.

He slammed his elbow up into Jaap's face, jarring with the force of a freight lorry against his jaw. There was no pain at first, just shock from the blow, and where his head kicked back against the wooden doorframe.

Tanya lunged forward but he knocked her back, she tripped over one of the steps behind her and fell awkwardly, her leg twisted.

Jaap ran after him and could see him taking the stairs four at a time. He followed, a rushing in his ears like a waterfall, head feeling light from the blow. They'd started on the eighth, and the figure was a floor ahead of him already. He could hear the ricochet of his steps below, slamming off the hard surfaces like firecrackers. Jaap had to close ground before they got to the car, and he tried to push himself to go faster.

He turned the last corner to see the hood flying back,

caught in the wind like a full sail, before the figure ducked into the car, the door slamming shut. Tanya was right behind him, her breath loud in his ear.

*Where is Kees?*

Jaap sprinted forward, his heart pounding against his ribcage and his lungs burning, getting to the kerb just as the car pulled out into the street, clipping the car parked in front.

Then he saw Kees, he was off to the left, not where Jaap had told him to wait, running towards them, the cigarette he'd been smoking leaving a trail of red sparks as he flicked it away and reached for his gun.

No one had been shot at – Jaap didn't even know if the man was carrying a gun, though it was probably a safe bet that he was – and Kees shouldn't be doing this. The rule, drilled into raw recruits from day one, was ONLY SHOOT WHEN SHOT AT. He shouted out to him, but Kees couldn't hear with the roar of the car.

Or he chose not to.

Jaap watched as Kees, still running, raised his gun.

The first bullet hit the back windscreen.

The glass cobwebbed.

It was hard to tell what happened with the second. The car swerved, smashing right into the front end of their own. Jaap heard metal crunch.

Kees was closest, only metres away, the gun still in his hand, Jaap shouting not to shoot again.

The car was trying to reverse, tyres smoking, the engine at full revs, the two vehicles' bumpers locked together, before one of them gave, the car shot back and Kees had to dodge sideways to avoid eating metal.

Jaap was running, Tanya by his side now. She was yelling something to him but the words were getting lost in the air, not connecting properly with his ears. And he could tell she was limping, forcing herself forward before it became too much and she dropped back.

Kees was within reach, skirting, reaching out for the door handle, when the car lurched, the gear change from reverse kicking in, and it took off, Kees running alongside, his shouts covered by the shriek of tyres.

By the time it skidded round the corner with a long drawn-out screech of rubber, it had left him behind.

Jaap had jumped in their own car, trying to get it moving, the ignition firing on the third attempt, but the steering wheel wouldn't shift. He yanked it hard, nothing. The crash must have jammed the wheel, maybe forced the axle, all the while the thought running through his head like a mantra, *Get him, get him, get him.*

Tanya's hand yanked the door open, grabbed the radio and called it in, the plates would be on the system within seconds.

But, as she hung up, they both knew it was too late. Kees was walking back along the road, gun still in hand; he looked like he was cursing. Faces had appeared at windows, only to disappear as quickly.

Just shadows and phantoms of the night.

They didn't want trouble.

And seeing things was definitely trouble.

Tanya looked across at Jaap, bent forward, his forehead on the wheel.

The car would be found in a similar area in a day or so, torched. The driver would not.

'It wasn't him,' she said getting her breath back.

He looked up at her, his brain pulsing, damp heat rising up out of his clothes, his jaw feeling like it had been crushed.

'You sure?'

'Yeah.' She looked down the street, watched Kees. 'There wasn't a tattoo on his neck.'

Jaap hit the steering wheel.

# 59

'Why has no one caught whoever did this?' asked Saskia.

Jaap reached out to touch her, calm her, but she shrank away.

A horned moon spiked the sky in the window behind her, and lower in the darkness the neon of Amsterdam glowed.

'I'm working on it.'

'Don't keep saying that!'

'You don't think I want to find them too?' Rage flared in him like phosphorus pulled from water. 'Huh? You think I'm spending my days screwing around?'

He turned away. He'd been doing a good job of controlling his anger since Andreas' death, partly as he had something to focus on, but it was starting to burn. Two deep breaths then he continued, 'I'm sorry . . . I'm sorry.'

He could hear her start to cry again behind him, and he turned and went to her, cursing the Black Tulips, cursing Andreas, but, most of all, cursing himself.

# DAY FOUR

# 60

*Thirteen years ago today*, thought Tanya as she opened her eyes.

She tried to push the thought away before it turned into a cascade of what ifs.

What if her parents hadn't gone out that day?

What if she'd never been orphaned?

What if her foster father hadn't . . . ?

It was no good. The same old thought patterns, wearing away at her like water carving a channel through rock. She stretched and got out of bed, yawning, her eyes feeling puffy, enormous.

The rumble of trams had bracketed her night, and unfamiliar noises kept waking her. There'd been the raised voices of drunks, planes descending with their dull roar and something – *rats?* – scurrying around in the roof above her.

The bed, like the hotel, was cheap. It creaked with the slightest movement and sagged in the middle, and when she woke, grit in her eyes and mouth dry from the metallic beer she'd drained from the mini-bar, her spine felt like it had been pummelled with a metal rod, swollen and stiff.

And the cold probably hadn't helped either. She checked the radiator, it was turned to on, but the amount of heat coming off it would struggle to melt an ice-cream.

The shower was, thankfully, hot, the thin needles of water helping to loosen her back muscles. She wondered what Jaap was doing, thought about how hard it must be having to sneak around investigating the murder of a colleague, a friend.

Of course, the rules were there for a reason. It would be all too easy to let emotion take over, cloud judgement to the point of making serious mistakes.

*But then*, she thought, trying to get the nasty pearlescent liquid from the half-empty bottle to lather in her hair, *he seems pretty in control, far more than I'd be.*

Though what would happen if he actually caught whoever was responsible? Would that threaten the case in court? Would a defence lawyer make a meal of it – vigilantism, broken procedures – allowing them to create a chance for their client to walk free?

And how would that impact her case?

*Do I*, she thought as she rinsed what little foam she'd managed to create, *have to get there first?*

She could see he was hurting.

There was something in his eyes which she'd noticed but had been unable to place.

And she liked him. He was different, though she couldn't put her finger on what it was. In any case he wasn't like Kees, which could only be a good thing. She could feel her presence made Kees uncomfortable, and she wondered if that was what had made him pull his gun and shoot last night.

*Lucky for him he missed*, she thought.

Whilst they'd waited for someone to pick them up and

tow the car, Jaap had taken Kees aside, far enough away from her so that she couldn't hear the words, but close enough for her to know he wasn't reciting poetry. There would be questions asked and surely they would suspend Kees.

She hoped so, she knew how volatile he was, how he might jeopardize her case. And she also hoped it wouldn't put her into conflict with Jaap. There was something about him . . . She remembered the feel of his hand . . .

Out of the shower she towelled her hair dry and reached for the tiny white plastic hairdryer mounted on the wall.

Click.

Nothing.

The receptionist, once he'd actually answered the phone, seemed to promise to get one sent up, but given the language barrier – she wasn't sure where he was from but it sure wasn't close by – there was room for doubt.

She wrapped her hair in the damp towel, reeking of strong chemical laundry detergent, and her mind drifted back to Jaap.

Ease of communication was something she didn't have in her day-to-day life any more, if she'd ever had it at all. But talking with Jaap in the bar the other night, and then when they were waiting for Haak, had proved it was possible. Given the right situation or, more importantly, the right person, she could loosen up.

*I really need to get out of Leeuwarden,* she thought.

There'd been a message from Bloem, and she'd not even listened to it.

She glanced out of the window, the sky bright like

283

liquid glass, a seagull wheeling round one of the spires on the Rijksmuseum.

*Somewhere out there*, she thought with a shudder, *is a man who knows what happened to Adrijana.*

She pulled out the two photos, one from the CCTV and the second from Interpol. The news that Adrijana's parents had committed suicide had almost been too much to take, she hadn't processed it yet, couldn't process it.

She looked at the photos; both reminded her of her younger self. Before her own parents died.

*Thirteen years ago today.*

She wasn't able to hold it back any more.

The smell of the schoolroom was seared into her mind. They'd been making papier-mâché face-masks, covering balloons with the sticky pulp, the glue smelling strong and slightly savoury, almost like wood shavings, thickening the air. The head teacher – a temperamental woman whose mere presence could stop dead every kid in the school – came in and started talking in a low voice to the teacher, both sets of their eyes flicking towards her like whips.

They could all tell that something was wrong. Chatter died down, and the next memory Tanya had – she had never been able to recall how she got there – was of being in the head teacher's small office, rain hammering on the window, which looked out on to the desolate concrete playground, feeling sick to her stomach.

And scared, so scared that she didn't know what to do, couldn't move, almost couldn't breathe.

Her parents had been involved in a traffic accident; a truck driver high on amphetamines – she only learnt that later when, at the age of eighteen, she requested the report

– drove straight into the back of their tiny green car, ramming it against a concrete divider on the motorway.

The report had photos from many angles, the car crushed like a Coke can, the bloodstained road surface, figures in hi-vis jackets indistinct in the fog that had gradually – if she understood the sequence correctly – descended after the accident, and a mug shot of the driver.

She'd stared at the photo, trying to pour all her hatred, all her fear and anger and grief, into it, as if by doing so she could become free.

But it hadn't worked, and had served only to implant his image into her brain, so that even now, years later, she was convinced that she'd recognize him on the streets.

And on the streets he would be. Tanya'd got two dead parents, but, according to the same report, he only got four years, death by dangerous driving.

The foster homes were next, the strange smells, the strange new customs, the strange ways that other families had of doing things.

But with time she hardened and a gradual recovery took place so by fifteen she appeared no different from any of her school-friends, another teenager wading through the painful currents of the teenage condition.

Only things had started happening.

Things which suddenly made her an outsider for the second time in her life.

A knock dissolved the thought, and she stepped across the tiny room, the threadbare carpet rough on the soles of her feet, opened the door, and took the plug-in hairdryer offered to her by a fat, unsmiling maid with a complexion like the residue from a deep-fat fryer.

As she dried her hair she thought again of the previous night. Whilst they were talking, waiting for the guy who turned out not to be Ludo Haak, she'd suddenly had the strongest urge to tell Jaap about her foster father, how he used to come to her when his wife, her foster mother, was out. How he manipulated her, kept her silent.

And she nearly did, despite the fact that she'd only just met him, and despite the fact that she'd never told anyone else, none of her boyfriends, none of her friends, no one. But the habit of silence – lurking in the back of her mind like a dark, lithe beast – sprang on her at the last moment, and she gave in, almost with a feeling of relief.

And that was not good. She realized that she was never going to be free, would never be able to be herself, until this was resolved. What the Americans called closure. *The real question*, she asked herself as she left the room having dressed, turning to lock the door with the oversized brass key fob, *is do I deal with it myself?*

# 61

'Humiliated, I was fucking humiliated, in front of business associates. Do you know the damage that will do to me? To my business?'

Same room as last night. Korssen looked rough, stubble infecting his face. His lawyer sat next to him with glowing skin and a fresh-pressed suit, hair slicked back like an otter's.

'I don't. And more to the point I don't really care, because you lied to me about the timings on the night in question.'

'You know what? I'm going to sue, I'm going to sue the department, the whole police force if I have to, but most of all I'm going to sue you, you piece of shit.'

His lawyer, torn between the possible fees he could charge for such an extravagant venture, even if, as he knew, it was destined to fail, and making sure his client didn't antagonize anyone further, reached out to touch his hand, calm him.

'I think what my client is trying to say, Inspector . . .' He paused to check his notes. '. . . Rykel, is that you've jumped the gun somewhat here. You requested a European Arrest Warrant – and frankly I'm surprised that it was granted given the highly, shall we say, scant evidence presented –

for my client, who was promptly arrested by the German authorities. I thought the police had to follow certain procedures, due diligence? But perhaps we can get this cleared up quickly?'

'I'm not saying a fucking thing,' said Korssen.

Kees, silent up until now, said, 'We'll see about that.'

Jaap's turn to calm someone down, this time with a frosty glance. Kees wasn't as in control as he should be, and if he didn't pull it together Jaap was going to have to do something about it.

'As you say, it was granted, which means someone else higher up thought it worthwhile. So I want to know why your client disappears off to Germany after I pay him a visit to ask about the murder of his business partner. If he can explain that then there is no problem.'

Korssen glanced at his lawyer before speaking slowly, trying to keep control.

'I've already said, I was there to meet with some business associates.'

'Doing?'

'One of the businesses I'm a major shareholder in is looking to partner with a firm there, I was going to meet the board before we took the next step.'

'What sort of business?'

'We create partnerships between the private sector, government and local authorities, get schools built, hospitals, that kind of thing, though thanks to you I can safely say that months of work have now been ruined.'

*So as well as being a rich businessman*, thought Jaap, *he's also a saint.*

'Why did you leave in a hurry?'

'The meeting was brought forward at the last minute, it was originally supposed to be the following week.'

'I'd like to talk to the people you met.'

'When you do, maybe you can tell them that it was a complete balls-up on your part, and that I had nothing whatsoever to do with it. That way I might just be able to salvage something from this mess.'

'I'd still like to know what your argument with Dirk Friedman was about.'

'Can I get these stupid things off?' said Korssen rattling the cuffs, a sound like cutlery in a drawer.

'Not until you give me a good reason.'

Korssen shifted in his seat.

'I own or part own about fifteen businesses and I don't have time to keep on top of the accounts. My old account-ant left, and I'd hired someone new. Her role is to go through each business on a quarterly basis and report to me, just to check everything is on track. Obviously I'm constantly in touch with the managers of each, but I like to see hard numbers as well. A few weeks ago she came to me with some concerns that she had about Dirk's busi-ness, and we spent a bit of time looking at it. It might have been nothing, but that's what I pay her for, so I gave her the go-ahead to look back over several years and see what she could find.' He paused. 'I need a drink.'

'This isn't a bar. What did she find?'

'I really need a drink.'

'Get him a drink,' Jaap said to Kees.

Kees left, slamming the door after him.

'She wasn't sure at first,' continued Korssen when the sound had stopped reverberating round the room, 'but by the end it looked like there was money being washed through the books.'

'How much?'

'Not a lot, eighty, hundred grand a year.'

'And this money was going where?'

'Getting paid out to a couple of consultancies, marketing consultancies.'

'And how come you'd never seen it before?'

'The previous guy didn't spot it, but Maartje had worked as a forensic accountant before working for me so she was trained to spot these things.'

'And you argued with Friedman over this?'

The door opened and Kees brought in a cup, putting it down roughly in front of Korssen, coffee spilling over the edge.

Korssen took a sip, made a face and put the cup back down.

*Not the same as the coffee from his exalted machine*, thought Jaap.

'I went to him with a question, and he claimed not to know anything about it, so I said I was going to contact the consultancies to find out exactly what they were billing us for, and that was when he got jumpy. He said he'd look into it, no reason for me to worry, he'd let me know what he found out.'

'And you agreed?'

'Yeah, I knew that something was up, so I let him think that I'd leave him in charge of it, but I got her to do some digging and the more she looked into it the more it was obvious that something was going on, had been for some time. And money laundering is a serious offence, as a director of the business I would be held accountable, even if I didn't know about it.'

'People have ended up in prison for less.'

'Looks like I have anyway.'

'This is a conversation we should have had the first time round.'

He shrugged.

'So you then confronted him, the argument?' continued Jaap.

'Exactly. He went wild, started talking all sorts of crap, but really I think he was scared, that was the impression I got.'

'And did you follow up on the consultancies themselves?'

'Tried to, phone numbers on their invoices didn't work, and the couple of addresses I went to didn't exist either.'

'So that's the money going out, but to be laundering, it must have been coming in from somewhere?'

'Christ, you're wasted in the police. Yeah, there were bogus sales being processed, so we were writing an invoice for diamonds we'd never sold, and then that same money was being paid out to the consultancies.'

'Like for like?'

'No, it was better hidden than that. There might be two sales which added up to the same amount going out, but once you saw the pattern it was pretty clear what was going on.'

'And who was processing the sales?'

'As far as we could see they were all internet sales, from the same person in Germany.'

'But surely someone processes them? If a sale comes in

off the internet then someone has to actually send them out?'

'Yes, but all of the sales were from one customer, and the instruction, again given by Friedman several years ago, was that all these orders had to be passed on to him, saying that he'd get them sent out personally.'

'And then he buried them.'

'Exactly.'

Jaap sat back.

'Ever heard of someone called Jan Zwartberg?'

'No, should I have?'

Jaap slid a photo across the table.

'Oh, this guy, this is the one I saw Dirk with, at the restaurant, I told you about it. Is he Jan Zwartberg?'

'Was.'

'Was?'

'He's dead, most likely killed by the same person who killed Friedman. And this one?'

He produced a photo of Haak, still watching for a reaction. Or a too obvious lack of reaction.

'Never seen him.'

Jaap slid another photo across the table. Korssen looked at it, his face curling with revulsion.

'Christ, what's this?'

'This is where that money you were wondering about came from. Friedman and Zwartberg owned a little business on the side.'

'I know nothing about this.'

Jaap stared at him, at his eyes. He tried to read them but Korssen was hard to read.

'What about the Black Tulips?'

'What black tulips, what are you talking about?' Korssen shot back.

*Does he look nervous?* wondered Jaap. *Or am I just hoping he does?*

'Just a gang, you know, people who smuggle illegal stuff into the country. Guns, drugs, and it seems, based on this, children.'

'I don't know anything about this. If Friedman was involved in something like that I don't see what it has to do with me.'

Jaap noticed Korssen had switched to Friedman, not Dirk.

*Trying to distance himself.*

'And this?' He reached down to the bag Kees had prepared earlier and pulled out the leather face mask; it flopped on to the table, the zip clattering against the surface. 'We found it at your house.'

'You've been in my house, you piece of shit. My private life has got nothing to do with you.'

'No, you're right. Just as long as this is between consenting adults then it doesn't have anything to do with me. But if this has anything to do with children, then it most definitely becomes my business,' said Jaap.

He pushed the chair back, metal scraping on the concrete floor, and stood, pulling both photos and the mask back.

Then he produced the phone they'd found in Zwartberg's mouth, wrapped in an evidence bag.

'You got a phone like this?'

'No, should I?'

They hadn't found one at the house, and Korssen had

been searched when he arrived. But it didn't prove anything. Easiest thing in the world to ditch a mobile phone.

'Give me the number of the people you were seeing in Germany.'

The lawyer, who'd faded into the background, cleared his throat.

'It seems to me that you don't need to hold my client whilst you do that.'

Jaap had already stood and made his way to the door, his hand on the handle. He turned back and looked at them.

'Procedure.' He shrugged, like his hands were tied. 'Due diligence.'

# 62

'Kees, I need you here now,' Jaap shouted down the stairs.

He'd seen Kees rush off as soon as they'd left the room Korssen was being held in. He had to update Smit in twenty minutes and had too many other things to do without waiting for Kees.

'Yeah, I've just got to –'

'Now.'

As he walked to the main office he thought back to last night. He'd been ready to file a report on Kees, pulling and discharging a weapon without sufficient reason was a serious offence, though it was more the lack of control it showed that worried him.

He'd even started typing it out on his laptop, but after staring at the black words on the white screen he found himself highlighting the text and his finger inching for the delete key.

In the end he'd left a message with Smit; it was probably best handled off the record.

He stopped by the murder board, checking all the new red names. Last night had yielded a bumper crop – a total of five were showing.

Red ink. Blood spilled.

Two were as yet unidentified, the Inspectors' names listed below each.

'Is he there?'

He turned to see Tanya, her face raw from the cold outside, the skin round her eyes particularly red.

But she still looked good.

Better than good, and despite everything going on he felt something tighten inside.

'Could be one of these two.' He pointed to the unidentifieds, trying to shake off the feeling.

'I hope not,' she replied.

'Did you get the Van Delfts' finances?'

'The bank's going to fax them through this morning. Should tell us if they really did pay for her or not.'

Kees skulked over, and Jaap led them into the incident room.

'We're running out of time,' he said as they sat down. 'We've got to get on top of this today. Kees, where are you at with Korssen's alibi?'

'I spoke to someone in Hamburg, they're going to send someone out today to check it out, but they said it wasn't going to be a priority.'

'Did you tell them what we've got going on here?'

'Yeah, but they didn't seem that concerned, said that they had problems of their own.'

Jaap thought for a moment he could get a flight there himself, but dismissed it, it would take a massive chunk out of his day.

'We've got Korssen here. If he's the one responsible for the killings then all we need to do is find Haak; Korssen can't kill him from his cell,' said Kees.

'No, but he might not actually be doing it himself, he could have hired someone,' said Tanya.

'I agree,' said Jaap, 'we can't take that chance. Hassle the Germans, I want to be able to confirm whether Korssen's alibi is false or not. If it is then we can go back at him hard. I wasn't convinced by his performance back there, he's arrogant and thinks he's better than us. But given what we found yesterday at that loft we've got to consider the possibility that he wasn't responsible, we might even be doing him a favour by holding him inside where no one can get to him.'

He thought back to the photos and the videos they'd found at the loft.

'Judging by the amount of material we found there, our suspect pool just widened tenfold, so we've got to focus on Friedman's and Zwartberg's background and cross-reference it against the list which Grimberg is supposed to be getting to us this morning. Tanya, could you chase him up, I suspect he may still be dragging his heels.'

'Sure. What about Haak, he's either been got to or run, and Adrijana . . . ?'

'We'll get his photo out to whoever picked up the two unidentifieds last night, check if he's one of them . . . Kees, you're bleeding.'

Kees reached up and wiped his nose with the back of his hand.

A trail of bright blood glistened across his skin.

He fumbled around in his pocket until Tanya handed him a tissue. He held it to his nose and tipped his head back.

*Was that from being knocked out yesterday, or something else?* thought Jaap. He checked the time, not wanting to even think about it. About other causes of nosebleeds.

*It would explain a lot though*, he thought.

'Okay, Kees, meet me here at eleven, I've fixed up a meet with the vice squad. They can help us check through the photographs, see if they recognize anyone, and Tanya, let me know as soon as you've got that list.'

'Will do.'

Kees and Tanya left. Jaap glanced out of the window.

A plane glinted silver in the gas-flame-blue sky.

*The question is*, he thought getting up, *is Korssen the one, or have we got the wrong man?*

As he walked down the corridor to Smit's office he glanced out at the canal, ice covering it totally. He had to wait a few minutes; Smit was on an important call according to Elsie so Jaap called Fortuyn's lawyer, who, it turned out, was away on holiday.

The legal secretary, her voice like she had a clothes peg on her nose, told him that all files were kept off site, which meant it would take a couple of days to access it. Jaap gave her till lunchtime to produce the file. If they could find whoever paid the rent on 35 Bloedstraat it might help speed things along. Especially if it was Korssen. Then he called Roemers.

'Are they the same?' he asked as he got through.

'What?'

'Andreas' and Kees' laptops, were they wiped by the same thing?'

'Oh, yeah, didn't he tell you?'

'Who?'

'Kees, I spoke to him first thing this morning. That site he tried to log on to wiped the computer and put a similar browsing history in as Andreas'. So it was the same virus which did both.'

'Did you tell him it was the same as Andreas'?'

'Well, yeah, why not, you're working together right? And it's his computer.'

He hung up, his mind racing. Kees now knew what he was up to. But he hadn't mentioned it.

Which would have been the normal thing to do.

'Inspector Rykel. Come in.' He looked up to see Smit filling the doorway.

Inside, a fresh pot of coffee sat on Smit's desk. He didn't offer Jaap any as he poured his own.

'Where are we at?' asked Smit settling back in his chair, blowing steam off the top of his cup.

'So far we've got the two victims linked. Friedman and Zwartberg were running a child porn business. And this business goes back, we've found photos which are fifteen-plus years old, and a third person, Ludo Haak, is also involved. We've also got what I think is the fourth member, Rint Korssen, had him sent back from Germany yesterday. He ran right after we talked to him the first time.'

'Anything on him?'

'Nothing concrete, but we're working on it. Also Zwartberg had a stole round his neck. We're checking churches for a possible link.'

Smit sat quietly for a moment. Jaap could hear his breathing. Asthmatic whistling.

'Haak, where's he?'

'Missing.'

'So he's in the frame?'

Jaap had tried to rehearse this conversation in his head, knowing how easy it would be to let slip how it linked to

Andreas. If Smit caught even a whiff of that Jaap would be off the case in an instant. And he still didn't trust that De Waart, despite his apparent change of heart, was going to pursue it as relentlessly as he was.

Of course, if Kees had told Smit about his conversation with Roemers, the two laptops being wiped the same way, then it was going to be over quickly.

When he'd thrown the coins before leaving his houseboat earlier he'd got

Heaven and Lake, 'progress comes from quiet discipline'.

*Quiet I can do*, he thought.

'Could be, but we're also working on the possibility it might be one of their victims, looking for revenge. This thing has been going on for years, so they could be mid-twenties, maybe even thirty. And this is just the documented stuff.'

'How did they distribute? Internet?'

'All done on the darknet, impossible to trace.'

'Been down to Vice?'

'We're going to sort through the material first, then we'll hand it over to them, see if they can find any matches.'

Even though he knew that was a mammoth task Vice would not be happy to have dropped in their laps.

'You've got a call out on Haak?'

'It's out there, we're even checking the fresh stars this morning' – the stars of the show, the victims. Jaap hated the phrase, but it was so endemic in the department that he inevitably used it himself.

'Your message said you wanted to talk about Kees?'

Jaap steeled himself. He'd had images of getting Kees taken off and replaced with someone else, but now that Kees knew what he was up to . . .

'Uhmm . . . yeah, I just wanted to say he's doing fine.'

Smit looked at him, eyes sharpening.

'You called and left a message requesting a meeting just so you could tell me he's doing fine?'

'Well, you know. I wasn't convinced at the beginning, but, like I said, he's doing well.'

Smit stared at him for a moment before taking another sip.

'Okay, keep me posted.'

Just as Jaap got to the door Smit spoke again.

'By the way, I had a call from someone in Leeuwarden. They weren't very happy about you commandeering Sergeant van der Mark. Next time you think of doing something like that you should come to me first.'

# 63

Kees now had proof.

Jaap was investigating Andreas' death, and he reckoned that if he told Smit there was a good chance he'd be put back in charge of the case – there was no one else free to do it.

He glanced up at Sint Nicolaaskerk, one of the few Catholic churches in a city built by Puritans. It rose high over the surrounding buildings, its twin towers and massive cupola jutting up into the sky, thin fingers of cloud meshing together behind them. His head was beginning to ache again, and he thought back to the previous night, with Carice.

The sex, as far as he could remember, had been great. A real buzz, both of them high.

But he wasn't high now.

Now he was in the crash.

And he needed something to help. He reached into his inside pocket and pulled out the tiny plastic bag.

Empty.

No wonder his head hurt, there'd been enough for four people. He looked around, and finding no one, licked his finger, ran it around the inside of the bag, and then rubbed his gums. He crumpled the bag up and dropped it in a litter bin. Something rustled under the layers of trash.

Kees wondered if rats could get buzzed on coke.

He imagined a rat, eyes zoned out, rushing along the road at supersonic speed, neon lights blurring, people screaming. As he stepped forward towards the entrance he realized he was laughing.

Inside, the light was dim, the painted, gilded woodwork looking tired, old. A figure with a shawl over its head – kneeling in one of the dark wooden pews near the front – was so still it could have been a statue.

He could hear men's voices, singing, and an organ weaving notes in between. There were three of them, by the chancel, wearing thick coats and scarves. They were clustered round a small portable wooden organ, where a fourth man was pressing the keys in a slow, solemn way. They broke off, and started discussing something before starting up again.

The church was physically different to the one his parents had dragged him to every Sunday throughout his childhood, but there was something about the atmosphere that was the same. Maybe it was the quiet, or the dusty smell of incense which was already pricking his still tender nostrils. The bleeding had stopped but he was feeling like it might start again.

Whatever it was, it brought back the long hours of boredom, the old women with hair on their chins and eyes which peered at you as if you were the devil incarnate. He remembered one time, after Mass, when one of the women caught him and a girlfriend at it, hiding in the hedge. She yanked him by the ear and told him that he was a wicked child who would go to hell. Kees, hurting, tears forming from the pain, had looked up at her, the fanatical gaze, and said, and he didn't know where the words came from, they just did, 'Devil's whore.'

His footsteps reverberated round the space, mixing with the music which kept stopping and starting, and a man, drawn by the sound, emerged from a door at the far end. He was wearing a black cassock with the obligatory white collar clasping his thin, fragile neck, and his face, akin to that of a medieval gargoyle, was all bones and hollows.

When they were close enough to talk he welcomed Kees – in whispered tones designed not to upset the singers – and introduced himself as Father Vegter. Kees responded by taking out his ID and asked for somewhere they could talk, not tempering his volume, making the man flinch.

Father Vegter turned and walked back to the door he'd come from and Kees followed him through to a corridor ending in a small, and surprisingly well-equipped, modern office. *Looks more like a business than a religion*, thought Kees.

'Please, take a seat.' He gestured to a swivel chair of black plastic and red fabric, and sat in an identical model on the far side of the desk. 'So what can I help you with?'

'I'm looking for someone who knows something about this man.'

The priest took the photo which Kees slid across the table and peered at it, holding it at arm's length and squinting. He nodded slowly, but didn't say anything.

'What makes you think I would know anything about him?'

'I think he may have been a priest. We found this at his

home.' He passed over another picture, the stole laid out on a table. 'So you do recognize him?'

Father Vegter studied the picture.

'No, I can't say I do, should I?'

'His name was Jan Zwartberg.'

The priest paused, casting his eyes upwards for a few moments as if God would provide. But in this case he didn't, as after a few moments more – moments in which Kees started to think about what De Waart had been asking him about yesterday, a niggling unease appearing from nowhere – he shook his head.

'Sorry, it doesn't ring any bells. If you could leave the photo I could show it to the other fathers here, someone else might remember.'

'If someone does recognize him give me a call.' He handed over his card. 'So if he was a priest, how would I find out more about him. You must have records?'

'There will be records, most likely they'll be kept at the administrative centre, in Haarlem.'

Kees insisted on the phone number and wrote it down, then got up to leave.

*Waste of time*, he thought. *I should tell Smit about the laptop, maybe then he'll pull Jaap and put me in charge of the case.*

'Oh, Inspector.' Father Vegter waited until Kees turned back. 'If you ever want to talk, about anything at all, then my door is always open.'

His eyes sought out Kees', and for a moment Kees had the feeling that this man could see right into his mind.

Panic clutched his throat, and he turned and left without saying a word.

Outside in the freezing cold he noticed his palms were

still sweating. He should get back to the station, request a meeting with Smit. But he found himself heading towards an alleyway near the Oude Kerk, the old church in the centre of the red-light district.

An African stood, moving from leg to leg, coat bunched up round his shoulders. He saw Kees coming and acknowledged him with a brief flick of his eyebrows.

'How much?' he asked Kees, keeping his eyes roving up and down the alley.

'The usual.'

'Man, you're getting through this shit. Not that I'm complaining.'

'What can I say, you've got good stuff. Listen, I haven't got any cash on me right now, I'll pay you back tomorrow.'

His dark features tightened.

'Uh uh. No can do. Payment up front or not at all.'

'Hey, c'mon, you know me.'

'Yeah, but it don't matter. I can't do that.'

Kees' turn to look up and down the alley. He stepped closer.

'You know what. You're right. I won't pay you back. You're going to give me a free sample. Or would you like to have a trip down the station?'

'And if I tell them you're a customer of mine?'

Kees shrugged.

'Who they gonna believe?' he asked pointing a finger to his chest, imitating the man's accent. 'Me?' Then jabbing it into the dealer's, 'Or you?'

# 64

Ludo Haak was occupying more and more of Tanya's thoughts.

He was infecting her brain with a kind of hate she knew she should try and rein in before it became destructive. She was starting to see his image when she closed her eyes, the spider tattoo flexing its legs.

*That's not good*, she thought.

The possibility that someone may have got to him, extracted revenge for what he'd done, wasn't worrying her, or not overly even though every sinew in her body wanted to get her hands on him herself. No, that was fine in itself, the revenge would be just.

What wasn't fine was if her chance of finding Adrijana had expired with his last breath.

Of course, they had no proof that he was dead. He might have not turned up last night as he knew someone was out to get him – surely he'd be aware by now that Friedman and Zwartberg were dead – and had holed up somewhere, or some other business had taken him out of town. If he was willing to travel all the way up to Leeuwarden then anywhere else in the Netherlands wasn't off limits.

Maybe there was another child he was going to abduct.

But that didn't make sense; what use would he have for another one now that the porn business was broken, exposed? And that led her on to the most chilling thought of all, *What use would he have for Adrijana?*

She refocused on the screen, where she'd been trawling through the databases, hoping that there might be something, anything, to point her in the right direction, but so far she'd drawn a blank.

And then word had come back that the two unidentifieds weren't Haak.

She ended up at the initial arrest report, the image of the tattoo showing in the profile photograph.

The full frontal showed his eyes.

Dark, evil eyes.

She wondered about his parents. Hard as it was to imagine that someone like this had parents, they might know where he was. If, that is, they were still alive. They could easily have died, of drug overdoses in some slum, stabbed in a drunken brawl over nothing, or maybe expired from the sheer wrenching shame of having produced a son like Haak.

*Or maybe he was like me,* she thought, *maybe he had foster parents, or his own parents abused him, maybe he's repeating a pattern.*

But that didn't excuse anything. Look what she'd been through, and you didn't see her running round the countryside tying up old couples, burning them to death in their own homes and abducting their child, even if that child had been bought illegally.

And that was the other angle she needed to get into,

but if, as Jaap suspected, the Black Tulips were responsible for smuggling in children as well as sex workers and drugs and arms and god-knew-what-else, then Haak was still their best bet of putting a stop to this.

Right now he was their only link up the chain.

Parents. She'd focus on the parents first, even though the surname Haak was a dispiritingly common name she discovered when she typed it into the *Herkenningsdienstsysteem*. Haak's record had a place of birth, just outside of Leiden, so she concentrated on any Haak living there now. It was a total long shot, there was no way of knowing if they still lived there, but she had to start somewhere.

Once the results were up she hit print, then picked up the phone.

# 65

Vice had a floor all to themselves.

They were cut off from the rest of the building as if what they dealt with needed to be contained.

Which in a way it did.

Jaap had done two months there, the minimum that any Inspector had to do before they were put on Homicide, and it was two months he'd hated, had almost made him question if he was doing the right thing, if he shouldn't pack it all in and find a different line of work.

As he and Kees stood by the door, waiting for someone to answer, Jaap remembered that although the images had been a catalogue of human depravity, just about any strange act you could imagine, and mostly stuff that any normal person would struggle to ever dream up, he'd not seen any involving children. He had the feeling that would have changed in the intervening years.

Once they'd finally been let in – Kees' joke about why it took the harassed-looking man so long to answer the door not going down well at all – they were shown to a smaller office off the main section. There was no natural light, all the windows blacked out, and the air felt dense with concentration, computer fans whirring.

Jaap knew the man who stood to greet them, the same man who'd run the department when he'd been there, Reinier van Oorschot. He had the same rugged face, though the two worry lines riding up his forehead seemed deeper, more canyon-like, and the blond hair which had covered his head was now a failed crop, patches of scalp showing through like bare earth. Jaap couldn't believe he was still here; most people went crazy after a few years, if they could even stick it out that long.

'Jaap, good to see you.' His tone said otherwise.

They shook hands and Jaap introduced Kees, then explained what it was they needed.

'I'm sure they're all going to be thrilled to have a whole load of new images to look through,' he said when Jaap had finished.

'Yeah, I figured they would be.'

'And you want to see if we've come across any of this stuff before?'

Kees made a noise which sounded like a snigger.

'You were here before high-speed internet, or at least before it was widespread, weren't you?' Reinier asked, ignoring Kees, used to tasteless jokes about his work.

'Yeah, it was pretty much all stills then.'

Kees rubbed his nose as if he was about to sneeze.

'Well, now it's videos, HD, and there are even some in 3D coming out of Asia. I mean, can you image some pervert beating himself off in front of his computer wearing 3D glasses? Sick, fucking sick is what it is.'

A mobile phone on his desk buzzed twice. Reinier checked his voicemail.

'There are some videos here as well,' said Jaap when

Reinier had finished listening to his phone. 'The thing is we know where this stuff was being made, and we know it was being distributed on the web.' He motioned to Kees, who brought out a card and handed it to Reinier. 'If you try and log on to this it wipes your computer, like there's a level of security built in. Gert Roemers is working on it, you might want to give him a call, check where he's got to.'

Reinier snorted. He took the card and looked at it.

'It's a web address, use .nl,' said Kees.

'Roemers is useless,' said Reinier dropping the card on to his desk. 'I've got people here who can get round this kind of thing. This is mostly what we do now, track shit like this on the internet, we're probably more advanced here than the tech unit. The thing is, the vast majority of stuff is hosted in places abroad we can't get to, so even if we do get to the source there's pretty much fuck all we can do about it.'

'Yeah, I know . . . but it would still be really useful if your guys could see if any of this looks familiar.'

'After a few weeks it all looks familiar, you know that, but we'll give it a go. Anything in particular?'

Jaap's phone buzzed into life. He looked at the screen, saw it was Karin. He stood up, stepped out of Reinier's office as he answered.

'Hey,' he said, hoping that she didn't need him to go round there right now. 'You okay?'

'Yeah, I'm doing okay,' she said. 'I was just wondering if we could meet. There's something I'd like to talk to you about.'

'I'm right in the middle of something, not sure I'm going to be able to get round there for a while. Is it urgent?'

'No, we could maybe do tonight?'

'Yeah, tonight would be good. I'll call you when I'm free. And you're sure you're okay?'

'I'm okay. It's . . . never mind. I'll tell you tonight.'

Jaap hung up and went back to Reinier's office. Karin had sounded different, more like her old self. Maybe something had happened, maybe she'd turned a corner.

He walked over to Reinier's desk.

'I forgot to say, it looks like they were doing this over the darknet –'

'Like TOR?'

'What's that?'

'It's a way of making sure no one can trace your move-ments online, basically the signal is sent through a number of –'

'Yeah, the tech said it was something like that. But the worst thing is that they seemed to stream some of this live, and people could pay to have certain things done . . . '

Reiner shook his head.

'Wish I could say I'd not heard of this before, but we've seen it more and more recently . . . '

Jaap reached into his coat.

'These four here' – he splayed the images of Friedman, Zwartberg, Haak and Korssen – 'any of these show up, I'd like to know. Especially this one,' he said tapping the photo of Korssen.

# 66

Tanya had taken a break from phoning.

It was getting her nowhere, and she remembered the stack of fax paper with the Van Delfts' financial records which had been purring off the fax earlier. So she'd switched tasks. But already her eyes were ballooning, beginning to tire of looking at tiny numbers.

*I'm not sure*, she thought, flicking over a few pages, *this is going to get me anywhere.*

Then, three more pages in, she found something, 4,000 euros, drawn out from their current account, along with 7,000 from their saving accounts, over a period of five days, all in cash.

Jaap had been right, they had bought the child.

She didn't know which was worse, the feeling of sickness rising up into her throat like a hot greasy slick or the anger making her brain expand, or her head shrink, or both.

How could they, how could anyone do that?

The anger was getting the better of her now, a burning rage lighting her up like a firework on a dark night. She sprang up from her desk, and half walked, half ran out of the room, several Inspectors looking up at her as she passed, down the two flights of stairs, and out into the street, nearly knocking over two uniforms who were bringing in an unshaven man. Blood dripped from a lip swollen like a soft fruit.

She moved fast, pounding the pavement with her feet, raw anger pulsating inside her like some bulging parasite. Her thoughts churned and there was a roaring in her ears, disorientating, making her want to reach up and pull them off. She moved past people without seeing them, across roads, in front of a tram, on autopilot, unable to escape from the rage.

Gradually though, helped by the constant movement, she started to become more aware of the noises around her, the normal background hum of the city, traffic, a car horn, the planes overhead coming in on their final approach to Schiphol airport.

Stopping on a bridge spanning Prinsengracht, she leant on the metal railing and looked down to the ice, hard and cold, the counterbalance to her emotional state. Her mouth held a strange taste, bitter like endive, and she wondered if it was some chemical effect left over from the fury she was only just now recovering from.

Its intensity, now that it was passing, shocked her. She was not prone to rage, but there was something about this which was getting to her.

And she knew what it was, it all felt far too close to her, tied up with the problems she'd faced in her life.

But really faced wasn't right. Turned away from would be more accurate, and maybe now she was suffering for that, the bottled anger being drawn to the surface by the case itself like a splinter. She had to get a grip, had to get on with it, find the child, and then she could deal with her own problems.

And as she turned away, she knew, suddenly, the answer to the question she'd asked herself earlier.

*I'm going to have to deal with it myself.*

And she shuddered, unsure if it was from fear or something else, something closer to anticipation.

# 67

'So I was wondering if you'd had any more thoughts, on Andreas?'

De Waart had cornered Jaap as he'd got back from Vice. Jaap had the feeling he'd been waiting for him.

'Because I'm sure that you might have the key to this thing?' said De Waart.

Jaap had toyed with telling De Waart everything last night, but Kees' call telling him about Korssen had, in a way, saved him. There was something about the way De Waart had suddenly turned on the humility and charm which had rung an alarm bell deep in Jaap's brain.

'Look, I've got this case which I'm working flat out on, and in all honesty I've been trying to think of Andreas as little as possible.'

'Sure, sure,' he said nodding his head up and down. 'But like I said last night, if you do remember something, anything at all I'd like to hear.'

'Thanks, I'll keep that in mind.' Jaap glanced at his watch. 'I've gotta go, but I'll call you.'

# 68

'So you're saying that you knew this man, and that he was asked to leave the church because of *complaints about his conduct*?' Kees mimicked the voice of the Father crackling over the line.

He'd been working the phone, using the number of the administrative centre he'd got from Father Vegter, having to struggle up each layer of the chain but not getting any further than confirmation that Jan Zwartberg had been a priest, more than twenty years ago. Then, just as he was about to call Jaap, Father Vegter called him. A colleague, Father Jurgen, remembered Zwartberg, and Kees had just listened to his story.

'No, I didn't say that. There was a complaint, but he left of his own accord.'

'And you thought that absolved you from telling anyone, like the police maybe?'

*Am I shouting?* thought Kees as he noticed several heads turning his way.

Five minutes after shaking down his dealer he'd been wiping his nose in a cafe toilet as the rush came on, like being swept up in a wave of energy, transforming everything, even the hiss of urine hitting steel in the next cubicle.

'And what were those accusations?' he asked trying to keep his voice down, not wanting any of his colleagues to notice anything was wrong.

He'd yet to tell Smit what he'd found out about Jaap, but just the fact that he now had something to tell had started to change how he looked at the whole thing. People had been looking at him strangely when he got in, a few sideways glances, people's eyes darting like startled fish when he looked at them. There was no way they could know. But he still felt unease.

'I honestly can't remember –'

'Bullshit!' More heads. 'Are you telling me that he wasn't asked to leave because someone complained that he had been sexually abusing someone?'

A pause in which Kees could hear the blood thundering in his ears, roaring like a hurricane.

'It was never proven, and the person who made the accusation later withdrew it.'

'Glad to see your memory has returned, but I know how this kind of thing works, someone makes a complaint, then they are forced to retract it, pray for the sinner's soul' – *fuck, I'm shouting again,* he thought, trying to modulate his voice – 'am I wrong?'

'Sin is universal, and it is our lord who stands in judgement –'

'Save it for someone else, where was he posted?'

'I'm not sure if I can give it –'

'If you don't find it I'm going to have to come down there and get it myself.'

'That won't be necessary, if you give me your number . . .'

'I'll hold.'

319

*Hypocritical religious scumbags*, a voice in his head kept repeating, over and over, until another thought broke through the barrage, *Maybe I shouldn't have had those two lines.*

'There seems to be a problem, we don't have a record of it, but I can give you the number of somewhere that might.'

'Go ahead.'

He wrote it down and hung up without another word. Then he stared at the letters he'd scrawled across the page, something beautiful about the dark ink against the white paper.

*God I hate these people*, he thought as he once more reached for the phone.

# 69

It was just like Kees to lose it.

Tanya could hear him shouting into his phone from right across the room. She hoped she could get this done with before he did. They'd not had a chance to talk, though she got the feeling Kees wanted to.

Which was something she wanted to avoid.

She was on her twentieth call, the phone ringing for over a minute before someone picked up.

The woman's accent, educated, and the confidence with which she answered the phone had made Tanya think this was going to be another dead end, but the date of birth she gave to the woman had an effect.

'Yes, that's when Ludo was born. Has there been an accident, or is he in trouble again?'

How to answer that? Your son is responsible for killing two people, abducting a young girl whose parents have now killed themselves out of grief, and being involved in horrific child pornography?

'We need to ask him a few questions, that's all.'

The woman on the other end sighed heavily.

'We tried with him, we really did. But from day one,

right from the moment he was born, there was something about him, he was different to our others.'

'You have other children?'

'Two, another son and a daughter, and they've both turned out well. Heinrich is an environmental campaigner and Feltje works as a graphic designer and is getting married next month, so it can't be because we're bad parents.'

'No, I'm sure it's nothing to do with that.'

*And I know all about bad parents*, she thought.

'I mean, we tried everything. Took him to behaviour specialists, educational specialists, we even took him to a faith healer, that's how desperate we were. And the only thing that happened was that things got worse.'

'I really need to talk to him, do you know where he lives?'

'Me? His mother? No, I don't know where he lives. I haven't even spoken to him since he was let out of prison last time, or rather he hasn't spoken to me.'

'What about your husband?'

'The same, we've both tried to learn to let go, we know we tried to do everything we possibly could, but we can't keep holding ourselves responsible.'

But Tanya could tell from her voice that she still did, that she probably woke at three in the morning, her heart throbbing, a sick feeling rising inside.

'And your other children, do they have any contact?'

'No. We've had to accept that he's not part of our family.'

'Would you be able to give me their contact details, just in case?'

Silence stretched out down the line.

'They get upset by it, I'd prefer not to have them involved.'

'So would I, but from the sounds of things they're grown-ups too, and this is really important.'

'You don't have children, do you?'

'What has that got –'

'Because if you did you'd know that their age doesn't matter. To me they're still my children, and it's my job to protect them.'

Tanya responded before realizing she was talking to a disconnected line.

She toyed for a moment with requesting a local patrol to put in a physical appearance, but then decided she should be able to trace both of them herself. She just hoped they'd be more useful.

She sensed someone behind her, and swivelled in her chair to see Kees, standing there with a coffee in one hand and an unlit cigarette in the other.

'Like to join me for a break?' he asked twirling the cigarette between his fingers. She noticed he wasn't smiling and reflected that there was possibly nothing on earth she'd rather do less at this precise moment.

'I quit.'

Kees held up the cigarette

'Really? Good for you.'

She sighed. Seeing as it was her day for facing up to things . . .

'Okay, I'll grab a drink, but I can't be long.'

## 70

'What I want to know,' said Jaap massaging his temple, where a distinct pulse had started up, 'is how this was all operated?'

After leaving Vice, Jaap had gone to the tech department. Reinier may not have thought much of Gert Roemers' abilities, but he'd had a head start at least.

On the way over he'd got the feeling he was getting somewhere, a picture starting to form, but it was still too blurred to make much sense of it. He needed time alone, somewhere quiet to just clear his head. But that didn't look like it was going to happen.

What he did know was that everything kept leading back to children in one way or another.

His murder victims were child pornographers, an associate of theirs, Haak, was wanted for murder and child abduction – presumably she'd been destined to end up on some video and only Friedman's and Zwartberg's deaths had prevented that – and to cap it all Andreas was a double victim, murdered, previously abused.

And then the person who ran it, the fourth phone number. Was it Korssen?

'It's kind of simple really. They charge a subscription fee, hundred and fifty euros a month, for unlimited access to what's on the site, and trust me, there's a shit load of stuff on there. But the worst thing is like their premium package. That's the one where it's basically rape on demand, and –'

'Yeah, a tech at the scene thought that was what was going on. And I spoke to Reinier over in Vice, he's seen that kind of thing before.'

'Seriously, I've seen some pretty nasty shit, but this . . . ' he choked off.

Jaap shrugged. He was as worked up about it as anyone, even more so, but he couldn't deal with others' outrage on top of his own. At least not right now.

'And these payments, we could trace them?'

Roemers' turn to shrug.

'You could try, but I bet you anything you like they're all made with pre-pay credit cards, untraceable.'

'There must be some way?'

'Nah, if they used those then it's a dead end. You might get lucky, but I would have thought anyone paying for this kind of stuff is going to be real careful, they don't want to get busted.'

'And everyone accessing this was doing it over the darknet, so there's no way to trace IP addresses?'

'Right, it's impossible.

'And what about the backend, is there any way to trace who was actually uploading it, managing the whole thing?'

'Look, this is professional, right? These people have covered their asses. It'll take some time to get right back to the source, and even then that's not going to tell me much. And I thought you'd got the men who were doing this anyway?'

'Not all of them, there's one left, maybe more.'

'Sick fucks,' said Roemers.

Jaap's phone rang, he saw it was Kees.

'German's just confirmed,' said Kees once Jaap answered. 'Korssen's alibi is solid.'

'How solid?'

'Rock.'

Jaap hung up.

'Bad news?' asked Roemers.

'Kind of,' said Jaap, getting up to go. 'Just keep looking. If you get something let me know straight away. And call me, not Kees.'

# 71

'You're sure it was him?' asked Tanya.

She'd grabbed a coffee in the canteen with Kees, nervous he was going to talk to her about their past. But it had turned out he didn't really have anything to say. He'd stared at her a bit, that was all. She actually found herself wondering if he was all right; maybe all the knocks he'd had over the last couple of days had done something to his brain. After a few painful minutes of staring at cups and taking sips she downed the rest of her coffee and headed back to the phones.

'Absolutely, we haven't spoken for years, but I can still recognize his voice,' said Haak's brother.

'And what did he say?'

'As soon as I answered he said something like "I've got her."'

'Got who? This was Monday morning, right?'

'Yeah, first thing on Monday. I said hi, then asked him what he meant?'

'What did he say?'

'Nothing, he hung up.'

'And it couldn't be someone else?'

'No. I'd recognize his voice anywhere, there's no doubt it was him.'

'Have you got the number he called from?'

'Uhh . . . yeah I should have, he called me on my mobile. In fact I remember looking at the number before answering. I didn't recognize it and wondered who it was. Let me put you on speaker.'

The background noise increased suddenly, and then his voice returned, reading out a number. She thanked him and killed the call. Twenty seconds later an internet search told her the number belonged to a bar and nightclub called '57', the address of which was east of Centraal station, on the waterfront.

Twenty minutes after that she was outside the nightclub. The front doors made of smoked glass and steel with the number '57' in shiny chrome, one figure per sheet of glass. She stepped inside, flashing her badge at the bouncer, all neck and tiny eyes, who'd started towards her as she entered.

It was a large, open space, helped by the huge windows looking over the bleak harbour, low chairs clustered round small tables dotted around the floor – ten of them were occupied, too early for the crowds which would turn up well into the night – and a bar which ran the entire length of one side of the room, open glass shelves glinting with strange-coloured liqueurs and magnums of champagne.

Stairs off to her left led down to where the dance floor must be. A lone barman wearing a black shirt and rolled up sleeves, polishing glasses and keeping an eye on the closest group, a gaggle of women swaying and cackling as ethanol worked on their brains.

She walked over to the bar and the barman – he must be what? Twenty-three, twenty-five? – looked up at her. He had blond curly hair and a pointed goatee.

'Hey' – his eyes slid up and down her body – 'can I get you anything?'

'Just the manager.'

He raised an eyebrow.

'Do you have an appointment?'

'No, but –'

'Then I guess you won't be seeing him.'

'I don't need an appointment.'

She took out her ID, slow, calm, and held it up to him, raising her eyebrow in return.

'Is that you?' the goatee laughed.

Too late Tanya remembered she'd not managed to take the bondage woman off her ID.

*Fucking Bloem*, she thought as she put away her ID and opened her jacket to show off her gun.

'Just get him,' she said.

He shrugged, as if to say all the same to me, put down the glass he'd been working on and walked down to the far end of the bar and out to one of the groups, three men all sitting forward in their seats, hunched. His head bent down, towards the bald head of the man whose back she could see, and whispered in his ear. The bald seated man twisted round, following the barman's arm pointing straight at her.

The goatee walked back, told her she could go over, and picked up the glass again, giving it one more wipe and holding it up to the light to check for grease spots. Music, soft jazz, only just at audible volume. She was going to find out why Haak had been using the phone here, and a rush of hope coursed through her.

When she got close she could see the cards on the table, cut whisky glasses refracting light. He turned as she neared, cold aggressive eyes and a face gnarled through many a street fight, and rose to meet her.

One of the seated figures, whose face had just become visible as he moved, was looking up at her, a face she'd been staring at onscreen – her heart burst to life in her chest – the tattoo on his neck even more repulsive in real life.

Ludo Haak.

Sitting there playing cards and drinking whisky like he didn't have a care in the world.

He looked up from his hand, and read something in her eyes. She wasn't dressed in uniform but she obviously looked like a cop because before she could react he was up out of his chair, knocking the table over.

Glasses flew through the air. Smashed into shards on the ground. Cards fluttering down after them.

Then she was past the bald man, shoving him roughly as she tried to gain on Haak, who was heading for the door, head down, arms pumping like he was working a punch bag. She put everything she had, directed all the power into her legs, worked them like smooth pistons.

There were shouts in the air but they didn't seem to make sense, she couldn't decipher them.

He tried to steer round the table of women, so drunk they were the only ones in the room not to have noticed that something was going on, and one of them, telling a story, flapped an excited arm out to illustrate a point. The arm hit Haak just as he flew past, causing him to swerve and crash into another table.

Tanya was on him before he could get up, trying to cuff him, but he grabbed her wrists and flipped her over on to her back, her head whacking the floor, whiplash in her neck. He pushed his head towards her, his breath coating her face with a poisonous mist, his mouth moving, yellow teeth bared, but she couldn't hear the words.

And suddenly she wasn't there on the floor of a nightclub wrestling with a criminal, she was fifteen again, on her bed, her foster father forcing himself on to her, into her, revulsion flowing through her veins.

Tanya could hear a woman screaming, then realized it was her. Every muscle tightened and found new strength.

Jamming her knee up into his crotch, she felt the rubbery softness, and managed to push him off as his grip lessened. Struggling to her feet she pulled her gun, fury burning in her like a nuclear reactor.

She pointed it at him, grasping with two hands.

Cold metal, the sounds of the room coming back to her, someone screaming – a woman – a long high-pitched whine. And this time it wasn't her.

Her finger twitched, then the muscle contracted as if forming a fist. The trigger resisted, then clicked just as the barman's arms wrapped round her chest and throat, wrenching her back as the sharp crack of her gun rang out.

For a split second it seemed as if everything was still, then one of the vast glass sheets looking out over the harbour, turned from completely clear to a vast tapestry of tiny cracks, before dropping in a million pieces.

More screams, there was movement, people running, and on her ear the hot breath of the barman, whispering to her.

'Stupid bitch.' She could feel his goatee tickling her skin.

She didn't have time to think, just react. She slammed her head back and felt cartilage crumble, and then she was free, the barman howling, cursing loudly. Her back hurt where it had caught on the bar's edge, and she was struggling to get air down her throat, which felt bruised, constricted.

Haak was getting up and she leapt forward, kicked him down to the floor, foot to chest. She trained her gun right at his head and stepped back.

'Turn over!' her voice strange to her, louder, fuller, more aggressive.

Haak looked up, and then slowly did as he was told, keeping his eyes on her. She cuffed him.

Then she pulled back her right foot and kicked him in the ribs.

# 72

'. . . and he did occasionally take Mass up here, at the Sint Nicolaaskerk, but really he was based near Maastricht at a Catholic school. And Friedman worked at a school in Heerlen.'

Jaap had just arrived having got Tanya's excited call. He was itching to get in there and interview Haak but he found Kees waiting for him.

'That's real close to Maastricht.'

'Exactly.'

'Did Tanya get that list from Grimberg?'

'I don't know, I just saw her taking in Haak.'

'I'll ask her now. Good work.'

He didn't know if Andreas had been brought up a Catholic, but he was sure that Kees would find Friedman worked there, and that Andreas' name would be on the list of pupils. He'd have to deal with that when it came up.

Tanya was standing outside the door, leaning against the wall, apparently texting someone. She looked up at him and smiled.

He could see marks on her neck.

She was tough, even though she didn't look it. He liked that.

'Hey, how are you?' Her voice slightly hoarse.

What did he say, that he wanted to rip off her clothes, wanted to bed her, get animal, or that he was fine and they should get on with interviewing Haak, and what was wrong with him anyway? Why this surge of feelings?

'You okay?' She looked at him concerned.

'Yeah, sorry, I think things are kind of getting on top of me . . .' He took a breath. 'Have you spoken to him yet?'

'No, I've been waiting for you, I got him moved to a room on his own.'

'Your neck, is it all right?'

'Yeah, I think so.' She touched the worst side gently, as if trying to hide an unsightly blemish. 'Shall we?' She motioned to the cell door less than ten feet away with her head.

Her eyes were clear, hard even. He knew that look, that was the look of adrenaline spiking the system, it was the look all Inspectors had when they thought they were on the cusp of solving a case. It was the look she was probably seeing in his own eyes right now.

'Did he have a phone on him?'

'He had two, one of them was the third number. And he had a call from the fourth one yesterday.'

'Did you get the list from Grimberg?'

'No, I couldn't get hold of him.'

'He's stalling, he just agreed in order to get rid of us. Okay, let's do it. And don't let him know you're looking for a girl.'

Ludo Haak was sitting at a metal desk, his hands cuffed and chained to the loop in the centre. The single exposed bulb, which left a line in Jaap's eyes after he'd stupidly glanced at it, wasn't doing anything for Haak's complexion. His skin was yellow, dark circles round his deep-set eyes only amplified by the overhead light. He was dressed in jeans and grey hoodie, a distorted skull leered on his chest. The tattoo rippled like it was alive as he turned his head towards them.

'You fucker,' he spat out, his voice somehow choked.

Jaap pulled up a chair opposite him, Tanya stood by the wall.

'Tell me about Inspector Hansen.'

Jaap was watching him closely, and he saw Ludo's eyes, still trained on the metal desk in front of him, flicker.

'Never heard of him.'

Here was the guy who, he believed, had shot Andreas in the back of the head.

In cold blood.

Here was someone who abducted little girls and used them on porn films, who tied up and left an old couple in a burning building.

He could feel something inside him, something hot, beginning to fizz through his veins. He slammed his fist down on the table.

'Hey, fuck you!' Haak shouted, his arms jerking involuntarily, chains scraping, harsh against the table top.

'Where's the child?' Tanya starting in. Haak slowly twisted his shoulders and head to her, as if he'd never seen her before, as if she'd sprung up out of the floor like a wild vine.

'Where's who?'

'The child, the one you took from the Van Delfts. You know, after you killed them?'

'Fuck you!'

'We have you on camera.'

Silence.

Jaap's turn.

'What about Dirk Friedman and Jan Zwartberg? You remember them? Looks like you three had quite some thing going on there. How did it work? You supply the children, and all three of you assholes took turns to star in your sick videos, is that it? Then you posted this all to some website hosted somewhere abroad and watched the money roll in, is that it?'

No response.

Jaap pulled out the paper with the four numbers on it, unfolded and smoothed it out on the table.

'See this?'

Haak grunted.

'Who does this number belong to?'

'I don't know.'

'Okay, let me tell you what I think. I think this here' – he stabbed the fourth number on the sheet – 'is who you answer to, and he works for the Black Tulips.'

Jaap could see he didn't like that.

'I don't know any Black Tulips.'

'Lying is an art, you ever heard that said?' Haak just looked at him. 'Well, it is, and I can tell you, you're no good at it, you're not even an amateur. So I'll ask you again, how are the Black Tulips involved?'

'I'm not telling you shit. You ain't got nothing on me. And I want my lawyer.'

'We'll get you a lawyer, just tell me where the kid is.'

'I don't want *a* lawyer, shithead, I want *my* lawyer, and I'm not saying shit till he gets here.'

Jaap had never beaten up a suspect, something that some of his colleagues were good at, boasted about even. He'd always prided himself on upholding the law, not stooping to the same level as the thugs they so often had to deal with. But right now? Right now he wanted to reach out and pummel the shit out of him, slam his head on to the desk, knock him back into the concrete wall until he told him what he wanted to know.

As if sensing what was running through Jaap's mind Tanya stepped forward.

He noticed the movement in the corner of his eye and took a deep breath. Without saying anything else he got up to leave just as the door flew open and De Waart stormed in.

'I need to talk to you, now,' he hissed.

Once Jaap had closed the cell door behind him he turned to De Waart.

'What's up?'

'What's up? You've just arrested my suspect, the guy who I think was responsible for Andreas' death, and you've probably fucked with my chance of getting a conviction, didn't you hear Smit when he said you weren't to go after Andreas' killer?'

Jaap was getting sick of De Waart.

'He's a suspect in my investigation, which has nothing to do with Andreas. When I've finished with him I'll hand him over to you.'

De Waart stared at him, then turned and walked.

'We'll see about that.'

Jaap watched him limp out of the office. He realized he'd been clenching his fist and he released his fingers, staring at the white crescent moons in his palm.

# 73

Kees rang the bell – as far as he could tell it hadn't actually made a sound – and was surprised when the door flew inwards a few moments later. He'd tried yesterday but there'd been no one in, and Jaap had kept him so busy today that he hadn't been able to get back out here, to the address where Helma supposedly lived.

It was clear the man who'd opened the door was on his way out, jacket, neck wrapped in a dirty woollen scarf, and a stained fedora, pulled low over his face. He was about sixty and had a slim parcel wrapped in old-fashioned brown paper and string cradled in his left arm.

The man, at least a head shorter, looked up at Kees and stopped dead.

'I'm s-s-sorry, can I-I help you?' The voice was wasp-like, thin, irritating.

'I'm looking for Helma?'

His eyes narrowed.

'Who's a-asking?'

Kees flipped out his ID and shoved it forward.

'I am. Can I come in?'

'Actually I was just on my way to the p-post box' – he motioned to the parcel – 'and I wanted to g-g –'

338

'You can go to the post box after we've talked.'

'B-b-but –'

'Now,' growled Kees making the old man jump, and then scurry back inside, muttering something Kees didn't catch under his breath. He followed him through a dingy hallway filled with cardboard boxes to a room at the back of the house, where he sat down on a sagging sofa, still clutching the parcel as if it were a baby and Kees the baby-snatcher-in-chief.

Kees glanced around. The room was dark. The air smelt as though it had been breathed many times without being refreshed, and the furniture was so old it could almost be fashionable again.

If it hadn't been so tatty.

'So where is she?' he asked.

The man, who'd been staring down at the floor – eye contact was not something he seemed at ease with – flinched, but didn't answer. A cat, entirely black apart from a white patch on a hind paw, slunk into the room, skirted Kees, and hopped on to the old man's lap, where it turned and watched Kees warily.

'I don't know who you m-m-mean,' he whispered as he adjusted to accommodate the animal whilst still looking at the floor. Then he giggled.

'You think this is funny?' roared Kees. He jolted, the cat hissed.

'I-I-is she in trouble?'

He was stroking the cat's head, each pass of the hand pulled the cat's lip up exposing sharp canines.

'Yeah, she is. And I need to speak to her right now. So where is she?'

'I don't know, I don't know,' he said shaking his head from side to side like he was trying to dislodge something, and it seemed to work, at least on his stutter. 'I don't know, I don't kn—'

Kees was watching him, the weird rhythmic stroking of the cat and the way he was still clutching the parcel.

'What's in that parcel?'

His hand stopped stroking the cat and gripped the parcel even tighter.

'N-n-nothing.'

'Show me.'

'It's just a present, for . . . for . . .'

Kees strode forward and grabbed it. The old man tried to hold on to it but Kees pushed him back roughly.

The cat sprang up and scratched him across the back of the hand, three welts which bled instantly, before disappearing like a black flash.

Cursing he ripped the parcel open, through the wrapper and the cardboard box inside, stuffed with clouds of cotton wool. He up-ended it and a collection of small marbles clattered out on to the scratched wooden floor, and rolled away in every direction. The old man shrank into himself on the sofa, shoulders raised, his head rocking gently.

*Fucking creature*, Kees was thinking to himself, *I'll probably have to get a rabies jab. Or is it tetanus?*

Back outside, heading back to the station on foot, he felt bad about scaring the old man, he clearly wasn't with it.

Probably had dementia or something.

Kees had searched the house and had found a second

bedroom with some women's clothes in the cupboard, but it didn't look like she'd been there for a while. He did, however, find a letter, stuffed into one of the drawers in the dressing table, which gave her full name, Helma Martens.

He thought about what he'd done to the old man, who must have been her father. There'd been something about his posture, the way he held himself, which had just made him want to hit him.

And that was not something he could avoid, that feeling, unworthy though it was. But he should have been able to stop himself acting on it, hold back, stop the anger, or at least control it. Anyway, it wasn't the coke that was bringing this anger to the fore, in fact maybe it was that he needed some more right now. That might have helped.

*Maybe I should wait a bit*, a voice in his head advised, just as another, more sinuous, counselled the opposite.

He thought back to the previous New Year. He and Marinette had gone to Maastricht to stay with a couple of friends – *her friends* – and they'd ended up in a club where he'd first snorted coke.

It had been an eye-opener.

He'd smoked dope in his teenage years, still did some weekends, especially when Marinette and he first got together, but coke was not something which had ever appealed to him, and his choice of career had always made him refuse.

But he'd just heard a few days before that his application had been successful and that later on in the year they'd be able to move to Amsterdam, a move which had taken on a dreamlike status for them both.

And maybe, now that he thought about it, the problem between them had been there even then, maybe all their planning, their projections of what life would be like, how much better it would be once they moved, were really a symptom, covering the present by living in the future.

In any case, the people they were with knew some other people, and just after midnight Kees found himself bending over a mirrored table in the deepest corner of the club – no air, just pounding, rhythmic music filling the void – with a rolled-up hundred-euro note just by his nostril, the white line stretching out in front of him like a forbidden road.

It hadn't been like he was expecting. The rush was different to anything he'd ever felt before. And even though the next day, when he woke – sprawled over the bed in his clothes, his head throbbing in an echo of the pounding music – he swore he'd never do it again, he knew he was lying to himself.

The next weekend, when they were back home, he'd suggested they go out again.

Marinette looked at him but agreed.

They hadn't talked about it – he knew that she disapproved of people taking coke, hell, *he* disapproved, he was a police Inspector on the up – and they didn't talk about it till two months later, when she sat him down and told him that if he didn't stop she'd leave him.

He was contrition itself, and he promised that it was just a temporary lapse, nothing more, and that he'd never take it again.

The next night he called her to say he was at a crime scene and that he'd not be back till early in the morning. Within half an hour he was snorting in the back of his patrol car having picked some up at a known drug spot. When he crashed the car into a ditch an hour later, seconds before his head hit the steering wheel, he knew he was in trouble.

And he stopped.

Just like that.

Took control and refused to let the craving take over. He'd had a lucky call, he claimed the car had been stolen whilst he was picking up some food, his head injury occurring when he caught the thieves at it, one of them slamming his head against the nearest wall.

He wasn't sure if his colleagues actually believed his story or not – car-jacking a police vehicle might happen in some hellish American inner city but it sure as hell didn't happen in Zeeland, the Netherlands – but there was no serious investigation into the incident, and the two perps were never found. Case closed.

But just three months ago he'd felt something, a slight tingle, somewhere deep in his brain. At first he thought it was to do with his relationship with Marinette, her descent into a person he didn't recognize.

She'd always been a bit dark, a bit prone to silence, but he'd figured that was because her job, teaching primary school kids, required so much energy and enthusiasm during the day that by the evening she'd want to be quieter, more reflective.

And he'd liked that about her.

Now, though, he didn't like it.

It had got worse, he could see that, and he knew she should be working, that staying at home all day would drive anyone crazy.

He'd tried to talk to her about it, gently at first, but he'd been rebuffed each time. That was when he realized that the tingle wasn't anything to do with her. He'd tried to ignore it, pretend that it wasn't there, tell himself that it was just a passing urge, even though he knew it wasn't, knew that it was only a matter of time before he succumbed again.

As he reached the station, he saw Smit's silhouette standing at his office window two floors up, talking on the phone.

*I've got to get a grip*, he forced himself to think, *get on with this.*

# 74

'There's been a lot of kicking today,' said Saskia, resting a hand on her stomach.

Jaap had been leaning forward, staring at the floor, the weight of his head driving down through his hands to his elbows, and then knees. He shifted upright, arching his back, and looked at Saskia, propped up on the bed. She had three pillows behind her back, and the television was on, flickering light across her face, the sound muted.

They'd been talking about the funeral tomorrow and it had made Saskia cry again.

He was running late; he needed to get back to Tanya, decide on their strategy for when they questioned Haak, after his lawyer'd been. And then see Karin. He'd spoken to her half an hour ago, and they'd agreed to meet just past eleven. He wanted to know what it was she was going to tell him, but she'd not given anything away, saying it would be better in person.

But he couldn't leave Saskia on her own.

'Andreas was so happy when I told him. It was like something changed inside him . . . did you notice?'

Jaap nodded. He had noticed. He remembered the day Andreas had told him. He'd not been able to place exactly how Andreas was different over the coming months, but there was definitely something, a shift, albeit a subtle one. So subtle that Jaap had wondered if he was imagining it, and had tried to dismiss it. But he couldn't get rid of the sense that things weren't going to be the same, once the baby came.

*Was it jealousy?* Jaap wondered. *Was I scared of losing him as a friend?*

'I think he was more excited than I was, at least at first,' said Saskia when Jaap didn't say anything. 'He was so pleased he was going to be a father.'

Jaap glanced at Saskia then back at the floor, imagining the baby swelling and growing inside her. The baby which would now be growing up without a father.

And all he could think about was what he'd seen at the loft, how, in the end, some children's lives turned into hell.

# 75

'This is it,' said Tanya as they slowly walked towards a small house with a broken hotel sign nailed to the front door.

'Not exactly the Dylan, is it?' Jaap said.

They'd been going over what they had prior to Haak's lawyer arriving the next morning. The frustration that they couldn't just get on with it was hitting them both when they'd decided to call it a night, and Jaap had offered to walk her back.

The street was dark, the nearest street light not working, and the road was quiet. She turned to him, about to wish him goodnight, and their eyes connected.

He moved his head forward and she could feel her heart start to hammer.

Their lips touched.

Jaap's phone went off in his pocket.

# 76

Jaap groaned and reached for his phone. Pulling away from Tanya, he could sense her scent lingering.

He answered and a woman's voice came on the line. It took him a few seconds to recognize it as his sister's.

'Jaap ... I really ...' He could hear her gasping for breath. '... help ... your place ...'

# 77

Air was shredding his lungs as he sprinted along the last stretch of canal.

He could see his houseboat ahead of him, twenty metres at most.

His mind was jammed with questions. What was wrong? What was she doing there? Why wasn't she answering her phone?

The front door was half open, and there were no lights on inside. He stormed in, calling her name.

Then he stopped dead.

He could see her, slumped on the floor.

His *nihonto*, the handle quivering in a streak of moonlight, was plunged into her stomach.

# 78

De Waart was first.

Jaap had stayed at the houseboat. He'd sat and looked at Karin's body, each breath feeling like a lifetime.

De Waart stood awkwardly before reaching out and putting his arm on Jaap's shoulder.

Jaap could feel warm trickles on each cheek.

'We'll get them,' De Waart said. 'I swear to you we'll get them.'

# DAY FIVE

# 79

A gull, its cry plaintive, circled overhead.

The sky was hammered lead.

Brown earth, excavated yesterday, glinted with frost.

The rage which had burned inside Jaap last night had by morning forged something cold and hard and he was surprised at how calm he was now.

Whoever killed Karin had been waiting for him. She must have gone round and let herself in, something she used to do before she went away. Which meant she'd been getting better.

*Is that what she'd wanted to talk to me about?*

He realized he'd never know.

Perched on a gravestone, a crow gave out a throaty rasp.

The fact that someone had been waiting for him meant that whoever was behind Andreas' death was scared he was getting somewhere.

He looked across to where four men were bringing the coffin just as he felt his phone buzz in his pocket. He took it out, saw it was Roemers, and moved away from the hole in the ground.

'What have you got?'

'I worked on this thing all night, just wanted you to know.'

*And I've been up all night trying to figure out who killed my sister.*

'But have you got something?' said Jaap, swallowing his thought.

'Yeah, I think I have. Like I said, it was all hosted abroad, multiple locations, impossible to trace, but there was one slip-up. Basically I was able to find a back way into one of the servers and –'

'Just tell me what it is.'

'A computer here in Amsterdam is connected. And it looks like it has been for several days now.'

'Can you locate it?'

'I'm trying right now.'

'Call me as soon as you've got it.'

He snapped his phone shut, the noise too loud for the occasion, and rejoined the small group.

Saskia was standing next to him. He hadn't even told her about Karin. He figured she didn't need to know when she was burying Andreas.

A sharp wind started up, nosing round the gravestones, pushing into their faces like a malevolent force. The pall-bearers were making their way towards them, towards the hole in the ground around which a few of Andreas' colleagues were standing. There would have been more, but the allegations were too much for most – it had been all over the papers again this morning – and they'd chosen to take the safe line, not be involved in any way.

Andreas' parents weren't there; his mother had died years ago, and Jaap remembered dropping Andreas off at a nursing home out by Haarlem whilst they were working a case there. Andreas had said his father had Alzheimer's. Jaap had stayed in the car whilst Andreas visited, coming back out only a few minutes later, looking tired.

By the time the pastor had finished his service – some crap about eternal life which Jaap had tuned out almost as soon as his drone-like voice had started up – the wind had died down, leaving a preternatural stillness.

Jaap stepped forward and, scooping up a handful of earth, tiny pellets frozen solid, held his hand out over the hole before releasing his fingers, the thin stream scattering on the polished surface with a noise like gunfire.

It seemed a ridiculous, melodramatic act, seen a million times onscreen, only this time without the stirring orchestral score or the sweeping camera work and he'd felt self-conscious, and then he felt guilty for feeling that.

He could smell somebody's perfume – *who wore perfume to a funeral?* – heavy and cloying, and it was then, as if the scent were a trigger, that the tears came.

Jaap turned and started walking. It had started to snow, tiny flakes at first, then larger, floating down like feathers.

He'd stared at the hexagram this morning on his table, Earth and Fire.

Darkness, maintain light.

Then he'd swept the coins off the table so fast they'd shot across the room and hit the wall.

# 80

Tanya had got to the station first thing, just in time to see Haak's lawyer turn up. She'd paced around, glancing at the clock every few seconds, working herself up, her whole body wired. Eventually the desk sergeant told her she should go and get some breakfast and he'd call her the moment Haak's lawyer was out.

So here she was, sitting a table with a dog staring up at her, jaws open, eyes like polished ebony. She could smell its hot, foetid breath, wheezing out in short bursts like it needed an asthma inhaler. After a few moments, when it became clear that she wasn't going to share her bagel – the egg mayonnaise smelling as bad as the dog's ragged exhalations – it waddled round 180 degrees, small steps, and padded away to another table to try the same trick.

The rear view, two legs jostling two tight, furry balls back and forth, was even less attractive than the front.

She'd watched it do the same routine at four separate tables before it got to her, and only at one had the tactic paid off in the form of what looked to be a leftover slice of apple strudel. She had to admire its tenacity though, the way it cut its losses with seemingly no ill-will, just moved on to the next table in the hope that food might find a way down to its level.

Her foster parents had had the same breed, and really anyone who wanted such an ugly dog, well, there had to be something wrong with them, didn't there?

Last night, as she'd lain in bed in her cold hotel room, listening to the rattling screech of the trams, feeling their vibration rocking her bed frame, the frayed cotton duvet cover rough against her skin, she'd thought about what had happened with Jaap.

How they'd kissed, briefly.

And whilst she'd initially felt elated, even after he'd had to rush away, the feeling had worn off and memories crowded in, as if trying to take control, stopping her enjoyment.

She'd spent years trying to hide from her past, she could see that now, as if human memory could be erased so easily, and not burrow down into the very fabric of her being, like poison slowly seeping though her, shutting down vital systems one by one.

All of her relationships had failed because at some level she didn't trust, *couldn't trust*, any man, even though she was drawn to them. All that energy spent pushing down the pain and anger, and a million other feelings which didn't even have names she could articulate – and maybe it would have helped if she'd been able to name them, maybe they would have lost some of their power? – had somehow meant she'd eventually driven all the men she'd met away from her.

And that was not fair. The physical pain and revulsion had left her long ago, but the throbbing torment had been a constant anchor which her life had become tied to. Her emotions had become as frozen as the canal she'd walked back along from the station.

Of course, she'd pretended, laughed, got drunk, but none of it had rung true, it was as if she were watching herself, a dead being trying to take part in the world of the living. She'd see people, couples her age, laughing together, light, carefree. People in the bars she used to go to, people in restaurants, in the queue at the supermarket, walking down the street, sitting in parks, and felt like she was a freak, someone who couldn't relax, enjoy life.

She felt like she'd missed out.

It wasn't fair. Her life had been taken away from her, and now, now that she'd finally woken to the fact, and now that she was for the first time being honest with herself, she felt entitled to some kind of compensation.

She played out the scenarios, hunting him down, maybe a short burst of violence – and now that she thought about it, had she joined the police as she'd subconsciously craved justice? – the payback that he so deserved.

Maybe, she'd wondered when she'd finished crying – sitting up in bed, arms hooked round her legs, her bare shoulders being pinched by the cold air – now that she'd admitted to herself, come clean after so many years, that would be enough to release her, to set her free, liberate her.

*And where does Jaap fit in all this?* she wondered.

The clatter of cutlery brought her back, and she noticed the time. She needed to question Haak and she couldn't wait any longer. Adrijana was somewhere out there, that had to be her focus now. She pushed away her bagel, two round bites all that had been taken, and checked her phone.

Still nothing.

*I'm done waiting*, she thought as she paid the bill and headed back to the station. *He'd better be ready now.*

# 81

'You can take time off,' said Smit.

Jaap felt like the phone was about to implode in his grip.

'I have to keep going. If I don't I'm going to go mad.'

He didn't feel that. Didn't feel anything at all. Which he knew was partly the shock. But mainly it was certitude. He was going to find whoever killed her. And he was going to make them suffer.

'Okay, I can understand that. But the moment it gets too much you give me a call, understood?'

# 82

Tanya glanced at her watch; the lawyer had been in with Ludo Haak for nearly an hour now, and she was getting impatient. He'd turned up first thing in the morning and, judging by his clothes, tanned skin, and total arrogance, he was in the big league.

How did someone like Haak – everything that she'd seen in the file on him had led her to believe he was a very minor piece of DNA in the rich primordial soup of Amsterdam's criminal class – afford a lawyer who looked like he spent most of his time on yachts moored on the Riviera. She could see him, standing with loose shorts, a shirt flapping undone in the soft breeze, champagne glass in one hand and several long-legged bronzed women fawning on him.

*Maybe by burning down people's houses with them inside and kidnapping their children, that's how*, she thought, just as the lawyer emerged, his expensive cologne, woody, spicy, overpowering, billowing out from him like the blast from a hot oven. But that wasn't it. Someone else would be paying for this, the most likely candidate being the Black Tulips.

If Haak was a bag man for them they'd be none too happy about him being arrested, they'd want him out of there, and wouldn't think twice about hiring an expensive lawyer.

They'd have money to spare.

She stood up and walked towards him, hoping she looked more confident than she felt, though there was a kernel of anger too, something she'd better watch when she was in there with them both. Kees saw her move – he'd been over at his own desk having a whispered conversation – and hung up, making his own way through the collection of desks. Jaap had said Kees should be in on the interview if he hadn't made it back from the funeral, and she'd accepted, knowing that it was always better to have two, even though she didn't feel that comfortable around him.

She wished Jaap had made it back in time, and thought about when he'd had to rush off. Something to do with his sister, but he'd been in such a hurry she didn't get an explanation.

Then De Waart stepped out of the cell followed by Haak.

A uniform un-cuffed Haak and started to lead him towards the stairs.

'Hey, what are you doing?' called Tanya as she started across the room. De Waart looked at her, he and the lawyer exchanged a word, and then De Waart moved to intercept Tanya.

'I need to question him,' said Tanya as De Waart blocked her way. Over his shoulder she could see Haak, the uniform and the lawyer disappearing down the stairs. She tried to sidestep round him, but he moved and caught her upper arm, his grip ferocious.

'You're not going to question him, because you're the one who fucked up his arrest.'

Tanya squirmed her arm free.

'He's holding a little girl, you can't just let him walk out.'

'Like I said, it's you who let him walk out. He's making a complaint. Apparently he's got witnesses who'll testify that excessive force was used in his arrest, and they'll file for police brutality as well.'

'That's bullshit, he attacked me.'

'All I can say is you fucked up, bad. And talking of which you've been ordered back to Leeuwarden, someone called Lankhorst called and said we had to send you back right away. Sorry.'

He smiled.

# 83

'And what reason did they give?'

Jaap was on his way back from the funeral, waiting for Roemers' call, when Tanya had got hold of him. Driving with one hand on the wheel he'd had to fumble in his pocket to get his phone. The car swerved, not helped by the snow.

'De Waart said they're filing charges against me for police brutality, they've got sworn statements from a bunch of people that I beat Haak up when I arrested him.'

Jaap cursed inside; she should have told him about the nightclub, given him the chance to go with her.

'Okay, listen –'

His phone beeped twice in his ear, and when he looked at the screen he saw the battery was dead. *Shit.* He forgot to charge it overnight.

Hardly surprising.

Moving again, he grabbed the car's radio and tried to get through to her at the station, but he finally got the message back that no one could find her, and she wasn't answering her phone.

# 84

*So that's it, is it?* Tanya raged to herself. *Nobody gives a shit?*

She felt twisted up with anger now, what was wrong with these people? Couldn't they see what was going on here? But then a thought occurred to her: Haak wouldn't be leaving for another twenty minutes; the paperwork always took at least that long to process.

Tanya ran out of the building, scanning round for a supermarket or clothes shop. She found one five minutes away, grabbed the first coat she could find, dark green with a large hood and fake fur trim, and ran back to the station, halting about fifty metres out, hoping she hadn't taken too long.

The cold was intense, and the snow, which had started falling vertically, was now angling towards her, the flakes aiming for her face. She tried to call Jaap but his phone was off. She wondered about calling Kees, but just as she was about to she saw Haak emerging from the glass doors with his lawyer.

They stood for a moment looking up at the snow as if they'd never seen such a thing before. He and his lawyer exchanged a few words, and a handshake.

Then Haak's head went down and he started walking,

west towards Centraal station. She followed, pulling her hood tight as she passed the lawyer. There were enough people around walking in both directions to hide amongst, but also enough to lose sight of him. She'd done some trailing as part of her training, but for one thing they hadn't done it in the snow, and for another no exercise really prepared for reality.

Her feet kept slipping on the ground. The snow was starting to settle now, but she couldn't let up the pace, Haak was walking fast, shoulders hunched.

By the time he reached the station there were two trams waiting to leave. She could see that he was heading for the number 16, and had to quicken her steps, making it just in time as the doors closed, the bell clanging in her ears. As the tram pulled away her phone started ringing, she fumbled in her pocket and managed to turn it off, Haak would certainly recognize her voice if she answered.

The tram was packed, the windows coated with people's breath, and at first she couldn't see him. Just as the tram started to slow down for the next stop – metal wheels screeching against metal tracks – an old woman, sitting to her left, leant forward and tugged at her coat, Tanya looked at her and followed the woman's gloved hand, a single finger pointing down to the floor. Tanya was standing on a leather lead which joined the woman and her small dog, a ridiculous creature with a top-knot holding a bunch of straggly white fur aloft. She shifted her foot, the old woman tutted, as if she'd never seen such rudeness in all her life, and stood up ready to get off.

Then she could see him; he was by the door in the middle carriage, ready to alight.

Tanya had to push her way off, through the four or five people who were trying to get on, and she was afraid Haak would sense the commotion and look up – new clothes weren't disguise enough for close contact – but he just carried on walking towards Damstraat.

The snow was getting heavier, thick enough to muffle the sounds of the city, swooping into her eyes and settling on the fake fur trim. It looked like he was heading to De Wallen, the red-light district centred in the old medieval centre, but if so he was going a roundabout route.

She'd have to be careful, it was always busy – she'd read it generated billions of euros each year – and it would be easy to lose him there. He turned the corner; she was about ten metres behind him so she increased her speed, and, just as she went round the corner her left foot shot out like she'd stepped on a rollerskate.

Her arms automatically tried to compensate, flapping out in large circles, but it wasn't enough to stop her flying back, and smashing her head on the ground, her lungs paralysed from the hard impact.

She heard someone laugh, then hands were reaching down to her, and other voices, more sympathetic, were asking her if she was okay, was anything broken, and wasn't this snow slippery? Then she was on her feet, thanking whoever had helped her whilst scanning the square, willing his head to come into view, the wound on her leg throbbing, as if the fall had opened it up.

Nothing.

She started moving again, hoping that he would suddenly appear. Her heart, already pumping from the shock of the fall, pulsed harder. Was that him there? Just over by the stand selling roasted chestnuts? Almost sprinting now, oblivious to the danger of falling again, she kept her eyes trained on what she'd just seen, but as the gap narrowed she could see it wasn't him.

Stopping, another sweep around with her eyes.

Too many people.

Too much snow.

# 85

As soon as he got inside Jaap managed to borrow a charger.

He tried to get Tanya on the phone, but she wasn't answering so he left a message to call him straight away. He couldn't believe that Haak had been released. The chances of him resurfacing now he knew they were on to him were zero.

*Where is she?*

The office was quiet, only two other Inspectors in, and he leant back in his chair. It was only just gone nine in the morning, but it could have been midnight, at least based on how he felt.

Jaap had started doing push-ups before going to the funeral, trying to jam all the anger into each movement. He'd ended up sobbing on the floor when his muscles had finally given out.

He'd heard that the act of burial was important for the living, the ceremony meant to help people move on, feel that some kind of conclusion had been reached, a full stop.

But clearly all that kind of thing was bullshit.

Andreas and his Karin. Both innocent in their own way. Neither had deserved to die.

He had work to do. Haak was the link. He knew, from Haak's reaction last night, that Haak knew both about Andreas' death and the Black Tulips. But he was less sure that Haak had pulled the trigger himself. The way he saw it was that Friedman and Zwartberg had decided, at some stage, to turn their hobby into a lucrative sideline, maybe with the help of Korssen. If Korssen was connected to the Black Tulips, a potential source of smuggled children, then Haak could have been a go-between, someone who actually delivered the children.

And maybe the Black Tulips had been short, a shipment delayed, and Haak thought he could make a bit of extra money. So he took a child that he'd previously handed over to the Van Delfts, killing the couple in the process. He'd know that there would be no records for any bought child so he should be relatively safe. That all worked. But it left open the question of who had killed Friedman and Zwartberg, and who, now that Haak was free again, might be on track to kill him as well. It had to be someone who had been abused or who knew about the abuse, maybe even as far back as Zwartberg's time in Maastricht.

But it wasn't Haak who had killed Karin, he'd been in custody. It was someone else. Someone who was pulling Haak's strings.

And Haak now was back in the wild, and had to be caught again, so that Jaap could find out who the puppeteer really was.

*And where the hell is Kees?* he thought as he reached for his phone. But it just rang out, not even going to voice-mail. Then he remembered the legal secretary hadn't got back to him with the details of who paid the rent at 35 Bloedstraat. He called her only to find she'd gone home sick yesterday and the person answering the phone didn't know anything about it.

He threw the phone; it caught on the charging lead and slammed into the floor.

Heads turned.

Downstairs he asked the desk sergeant if he'd seen Tanya, discovering she'd left just before Haak had been officially released.

He'd not known her for long, but he felt like he *knew* her.

*She's not*, he thought, *following him, is she?*

# 86

The man in the balaclava checked his watch again, and found that less than a minute had passed since he'd looked at it last. His foot was drumming against the branch he was perched on, and he noticed he'd been holding his breath again. He consciously breathed out, trying to relax his shoulders, and it worked, for a moment, before the muscles tightened again.

The message had been clear, stating time and place, but there was no guarantee that Haak would come.

Something told him he would though: the photos which he'd got hold of and threatened he'd show to the police if a substantial amount of money wasn't delivered today.

The snow was getting heavier now, but that wasn't a bad thing. He'd chosen this spot because it was out of the way – who'd be walking around the woods of Amsterdamse Bos on a day like today? – but any extra cover would be welcome.

He heard something off to his left, a twig snapping, muffled by the snow. And all his senses zoomed into focus as a figure stepped into the clearing.

He smiled.

His bottom lip, dry from the cold, split.

# 87

Tanya'd been following him for forty minutes since nearly losing him in Dam Square.

He'd walked to a tiny bar just off Sint Jacobstraat – she'd been worried that he'd go out the back, it had been too small a space to risk going in – so she had to wait outside, trying to look in the window from across the street without being seen. Relief had shored her up when he emerged only ten minutes later, started walking again, heading into the narrow streets of De Wallen. She'd been forced to wait again as he chose a booth – the prostitute swishing the curtain closed the moment he entered – until he emerged quarter of an hour later with a swagger.

Then he'd appeared to be killing time, wandering round slowly, occasionally checking his watch. But about twenty minutes ago purpose entered his steps again and he'd caught a tram then a bus all the way out to Amsterdamse Bos.

And now, as she tried to keep him in sight through the trees, she was convinced this was where he was holding her. Maybe he'd constructed a small hut out here, or just a tent. In either case Adrijana would be freezing.

But there was something about his movements which

told her he wasn't at ease. He kept stopping, looking around, as if nervous, and she'd had to dodge behind trees on several occasions, her heart thudding in the stillness.

Finally he reached what looked like a clearing, and after scouting round it, and apparently finding nothing, stepped into the misshaped circle which was quickly gathering snow, his footprints trailing him.

*What is he doing here?*

He stopped in the middle and checked his watch.

*He's meeting someone, that's what it is.*

She glanced over her shoulder, easing her gun out of her holster, and in the split second when she looked back up another figure had dropped out of a tree on the edge of the clearing, the branch he'd been on reverberating, flicking more snow to the air, and run at Haak, his hand raised, a knife glinting.

She was up, running before she even knew what she was doing, branches ripping at her face, but Haak turned, just in time to receive the blade.

It slipped into his throat with ease.

A curved arc of slick blood, like a fountain, was the only colour in the scene.

# 88

It was over. Their last chance gone.

Snow was starting to melt on his shoes, Jaap could feel it soaking through to his toes, and it kept on falling.

He remembered one of Yuzuki Roshi's favourite phrases, *no snowflake ever falls in the wrong place.*

He looked across to where the three crime scene officers were trying to erect a shelter, Haak's body already covered in a thin layer of snow. He was surprised that the residual body heat hadn't stopped it settling, but then he'd died, according to Tanya, nearly an hour ago and the air temperature was well below freezing.

The wood was quiet, the snow muting everything, the only sounds the soft crunch of footsteps and the swishing of material as the tent finally went up. Not that there was going to be much gained from an examination they didn't already know. Tanya had tried to chase Haak's killer through the wood but he quickly lost her in a dense patch of evergreens which protected the ground from snow, leaving no trail to follow.

She was standing off to his left – shoulders hunched despite the hood, her nose red – moving gently from one foot to the other. He felt a pang of regret about having to dash off last night, and he wanted to tell her about Karin. But he stopped himself.

'You okay?'

She nodded.

'He was our last link,' she said, her voice tailing off.

How was he going to get Andreas' killer now? How was he going to find out who killed Karin?

He pulled out his phone and dialled Kees – he'd not been able to contact him all morning – but this time he answered.

'Where've you been?'

'Just working on some stuff.'

'I've been trying to call, did you not have your phone on you?'

'I, errr, forgot to turn it on.'

A lie, as it had rung out each time he'd called.

'So have you got anything?'

'Yeah, Friedman and Zwartberg, they worked at the same school.'

Maastricht. Where Andreas was brought up. The photo, the one he still had in his jacket pocket, must have been taken there.

'Have you cross-referenced this yet?'

'With what?'

'The list from Grimberg. Are you telling me you haven't got it yet?'

'Tanya was in charge of that, I don't know if she got it, but if she has then she didn't give it to me.'

'Okay, you try and get it. I'll be back in about half an hour, but call me straight away if you get anything.'

He put his phone away, hands finding pockets against the cold.

'Anything?'

'Might be getting somewhere. Did you get that list from Grimberg?'

She shook her head.

'He didn't answer, and I didn't have time to go round there with all this going on.' She shuffled a bit of snow with the toe of her boot. 'She could be anywhere,' she said, staring straight ahead, her voice flat.

Jaap didn't want to say it, but he knew he should.

'There's a good chance she's already dead.'

'No! She's not, I can feel it. She's alive, she's . . .' her voice choked off. Jaap put an arm out towards her shoulder but she shrugged it off and walked away.

Jaap looked over to where Haak's body lay, the photographer ready to begin. Each flash froze snowflakes in the air round the body. It reminded him of Kyoto. He wished he was there now, and that none of this had ever happened.

He pulled up his collar and stared out at the trees. He'd had cases like this before, where after days, sometimes weeks, he'd hit a brick wall. It was part of the job, you had to learn to let them go, and those Inspectors who didn't learn never stayed for long. Old unsolved cases eating away at them until it became unbearable. Some recognized it for what it was and got out, others just couldn't, until one day, in sheer frustration and rage, they stepped over the mark, beat someone up so badly that nobody could ignore it. Career over. With no pension.

Was that going to happen to him? Karin and Andreas were dead, but should he, could he, learn to accept it?

He'd learnt about life and death in Kyoto. Or he thought he had. Now he wasn't so sure.

'Inspector?' Jaap focused his eyes. One of the uniforms who'd been at the scene when he arrived, taller than Jaap, was standing in front of him, 'Are you okay?'

Jaap shook himself.

'Just thinking.'

The officer, twenties, built like a marine, with a thin moustache covering his top lip, pulled out a cigarette and offered one to Jaap, who refused.

'Weird job, isn't it?' he asked blowing smoke out.

'Yeah, sometimes I don't know why we do it.'

'I know what you mean, someone asked me recently if I'd been bullied at school, and if that was why I'd joined up,' he laughed.

'You don't look like you were bullied at school.'

'No, quite the opposite, I just felt, because of my size, I kind of had a duty to protect others, you know what I mean?'

Jaap looked out across the clearing.

He did know what he meant.

Then something struck him. Something someone had said a few days ago.

He pulled out his phone, dialled Kees, who answered on the third ring.

'Have you got hold of Grimberg yet?'

'He's not answering, I'm just heading there now.'

'Meet me at the west end of the street his office is on, and find out his home address as well. And this time *do not* go in without me, understand?' He hung up without waiting for a response.

The uniform looked at him, catching the urgency in his voice.

'Thanks,' said Jaap before starting towards Tanya. He told her what he thought was going on, and was interrupted by his phone. Roemers' voice.

'I've got it. It's a computer owned by a shipping company.'

'What are they called?'

'BSC.'

'BSC?'

'Stands for Baltic Shipping Company, they've got an office up at the port.'

Jaap hung up. Tanya looked at him.

'Anything?'

He wanted to tell her, but knew she'd be unable to wait, that she'd go after it right now, and he couldn't allow that. It would be too dangerous.

'It might be, you finish up here, then give me a call when you're done, I may have something by then.'

And then he turned and ran back through the woods to where he'd parked his car.

# 89

'He's all yours.'

Tanya turned; she'd been staring into the trees, and looked back at the body. She was feeling numb, though she wasn't sure if it was just from standing around in the freezing cold for so long, or something else. She looked at the body, under the tent, footprints wheeling round the area in psychedelic swirls.

'Thanks.'

She made her way back, the snow almost a centimetre deep now, and knelt on one of the sheets which had been laid by the body. Someone handed her latex gloves, which she snapped on and went to work. There was nothing unusual: wallet with cash and no ID, a large key ring, a crushed pack of cigarettes.

Nothing which was going to help her. She stood up and bagged the items, dropping the keys into the snow. Not that it mattered, what were they going to do, lift prints off them? She pulled them out and dusted them off. Then she went through the wallet again, separating out each note. In between two was a scrap of paper, folded in half; it looked like a receipt for the cigarettes. But on the back, scrawled in blue biro, was an address.

And a number.

She took out her phone, her hands trembling all of a sudden, and punched it in, getting it wrong twice. Finally it was right and it rang seven times before going to answer machine, a man's voice saying the Baltic Shipping Company was closed until the following Monday.

Baltic Shipping Company.

Jaap had said BSC on the phone. It had to be the same thing.

And he hadn't told her, had just rushed off.

*Does he not trust me?* she thought. *Or is it some chivalrous thing, now that he's kissed me he thinks I need to be looked after?*

A voice she recognized barked out her name and she looked up just in time to see Bloem striding across the clearing to her. His face was red, but it wasn't from the cold.

*What is he doing here?* she thought, even though she knew the answer.

'Well, Sergeant *van der Mark*.' He twisted her name, pronouncing it in tones of deep sarcasm. 'I'm glad I've managed to catch up with you. Thanks for returning my calls.'

'Listen, I know where the girl is being –'

'No. Enough of this shit. You've caused no end of trouble' – his eyes gleamed at her. He was enjoying this – 'and you're coming back up to Leeuwarden with me. Right now. And if you don't end up on traffic duty for the rest of your career, well . . .' He left it hanging.

Tanya looked back down at Haak, the man responsible for kidnapping Adrijana. The little girl who looked like her and, like her, no longer had any parents, no one to care for her. But her eyes wouldn't stay on him, and she glanced off into the woods, the snow even thicker now, visibility reducing.

'Okay,' she sighed. 'Just look at this one thing.' She squatted by the body. Bloem looked at her, then bent down. As he did so she shoved him forward, grabbed his arm, and cuffed him to Haak's cold, dead wrist.

And then she ran, Bloem's curses following her into the trees like shotgun blasts.

# 90

When he saw it, the police car nosing into the street like a silent predator, his stomach lurched as if the whole world had suddenly tipped sideways.

The snow had attracted him, the softness of its descent, and he'd wandered over to the window to watch the eddying flakes, to take a moment to breathe, to live.

He'd been having moments like that recently, when everything seemed beautiful, the merest of things catching his attention; the liquid pattern in a particular cobble stone when the sun burnished its smooth surface, the intricacies of a bit of fabric, rich in the tiny details of weave and colour. And he'd found himself staring, marvelling at their beauty, as if he'd never seen anything so wonderful.

Which in a sense he hadn't, or at least not as far as he could remember. He must have been observant as a child. All children were, all had that capacity for intense concentration on an object which to them looked fascinating but to an older child, or adult, was merely commonplace.

And now he was like a child again, a second birth, a new person, the skin which had been containing him, trapping and squeezing, trying to squash him into nothing finally split, allowing him to emerge blinking into a fresh world.

And it was a surprise, the opposite of what he'd been expecting, what he'd resigned himself to. When he'd decided to kill them both it felt right, but he hadn't anticipated any pleasure, it was just something he had to do, no question, it was inevitable, it was coded in his DNA, it was revenge, it was justice. He didn't think there would be any release, or any closure to use that overworked phrase that the characters on TV dramas always talked about.

But closure he'd got, and he was revelling in it. The first hint of what was to come had been when he'd watched Friedman die, watched the eyes flicker madly, as delicate as butterflies, before they suddenly stopped, frozen, and the light drained from his irises even as his grip round his neck tightened, feeling the panicking pulse in his jugular, there one minute, gone the next.

Then Zwartberg two nights later. Satisfaction had overcome revulsion.

And then only an hour ago, when the knife had punctured Haak's flesh, so easy until the tip of the blade hit against the neck bone, that he'd really started to fly.

And so what if that woman, that police officer had seen it all, he was wearing a balaclava, and he'd easily lost her in the woods. There was nothing there to link him.

Now he just had to get the fourth one, the one who was working for the Black Tulips, and he'd really be free.

There was work to be done, he still didn't know who he was. But he was going to find out. He was going to make sure of it.

So the shock he felt when the patrol car turned up was

like a battering ram to his skull. He tried to tell himself that the car was there for another reason, but as he watched, he saw the person at the wheel was the policeman he'd seen the other day. He tried to think how he knew, but then his mind kicked into gear, coming up with a single word.

*Run.*

# 91

Jaap leapt out of the car.

He ran towards where Kees was parked right on the corner, the window sliding down with a quiet hum as he approached to reveal an empty passenger seat. Then Kees.

'So what's this about?'

'I think Hans Grimberg's our man.'

'Why?'

'He was probably a victim when he was younger, his accent's from Maastricht. He's the right sort of age, he'd have been a teenager during the time Zwartberg was there, probably Friedman too, and he said something, about how abuse can affect everything the victim does, how they behave, what job they get –'

Jaap's phone was ringing in his pocket; he pulled it out and was about to answer but movement in the street caught his attention.

A figure emerged monastically, hood up, from the door to Vrijheid Nu.

'I'll follow him,' Jaap said to Kees as he pocketed his phone unanswered. 'You check in the office.'

The figure had just turned the corner, heading north along the Singel canal, and Jaap broke into a run, or as

386

much of a run as the conditions would allow. As he rounded the same corner he could see the figure had started to walk faster. It must be Grimberg, though he couldn't have seen Jaap. He increased his pace and once he was within a few metres, as if by some remnant of an ancient defence mechanism, the hood turned, recognition sparking in his eyes.

Grimberg was off, bounding, his hood pushed back and ballooning in the airflow, jostling past the few pedestrians who were out, their indignant cries muffled by the snow, Jaap following. At the next block he skidded round the corner, and took off back towards Herengracht. Jaap expected him to charge over the bridge, but instead he turned north, running up the stretch of canal lined with houseboats.

It was a mistake.

Because heading down Herengracht were headlights, a car blocking the way. Grimberg saw it, hesitated for a moment then dived off to the right, jumping over the rail of the last in a line of barges.

Jaap followed, catching his foot and crashing into the wooden wall of the cabin. By the time he'd made it to the end Grimberg was over the rail and on the ice, thick now with snow, stumbling across, bent over like a hunchback, trying to keep his centre of gravity low.

Down on the ice, even more slippery than he'd thought, he started to close the gap when Grimberg went down hard.

Jaap was within a few feet of him now but he realized that something was wrong. Grimberg was flailing, trying to get up, twisting round. Then he saw it – the impact had split the ice, still not frozen hard enough to withstand a battering.

Water was seeping out of a hole broken by Grimberg's weight, melting the snow in a circle, a dark wound. A few more feet and Jaap was there, grabbing his hood, trying to pull him back, but Grimberg's thrashing was opening the hole more, and he was starting to slip into it. The water was reaching Jaap's feet now, licking them like a hungry predator, and no matter how hard he pulled Grimberg was drawing him in.

Then a cry from behind him, Kees, yelling 'Get back!' over and over like it was the only phrase he knew.

That broke the spell.

Jaap released his grip and started to edge away, afraid that any quick movement would cause more ice to split.

Grimberg was in the water now, arms slapping on the ice, looking for purchase, but doing more damage, one blow from his left hand releasing a jagged split like an electric snake, racing towards Jaap. He tried to turn, run back but he could feel the water on his ankles – so cold it stopped his lungs from working. He threw himself forward, landing on his front a few metres from the barge.

He felt something – his phone – crunch against his hip.

A rope with a lifebuoy swung down and smacked him in the side of the face, he grasped it, Kees shouting at him to hold on to it, climb up.

'Get me something to pull him back with!' he shouted up to Kees.

'Just get up here before it all goes!'

'Get something!'

He hauled himself up to his feet, and took the few

steps remaining to get him to the boat's hull, the ice holding, slipping the lifebuoy round his waist.

Kees' footsteps on the deck above him, moving fast then stopping suddenly. A pole flew down, clanging against the hull beside him, the reverberations shaking his back. He grabbed it and flipped the end over like he was a pole-vaulter. The curled hook landed by Grimberg, just short of his grasp.

Grimberg didn't need to be told what to do; he tried to heave himself up, but Jaap had to edge forward again to make sure he got it. The second he was sure Grimberg had a good enough grip he pulled and pulled until every muscle in his back and neck felt as if it was going to snap.

# 92

Smit looked at the bit of paper in his hands.

'I can't believe it.'

'Neither could I, but it's there in black and white,' answered De Waart. 'And there's more, look at this.'

He flipped open his laptop and played a short CCTV clip.

Smit rose from the chair, closing the laptop which De Waart had placed on his desk, and paced towards the window. He stood there for a few moments, hands behind his back, rocking slightly on his heels before he turned back.

De Waart waited for an answer.

# 93

Once they'd got him on board the boat, shuddering like he was receiving a steady stream of electric shocks, they knew they had to get him warm, and quickly.

'Knock on doors,' said Jaap, and Kees was off.

He started dragging Grimberg towards the shore side of the boat, and then down the gangplank on to the road. Kees emerged from a house and ran over to help.

Inside, the young woman – an Eastern European maid, he guessed from the accent – gestured to the front room and they got him into the warm and ripped his sodden clothes off. She brought towels, they dried him off, and roughly dressed him in some oversized clothes she brought down from upstairs. Kees found the kitchen and made some hot coffee.

'You shouldn't give him that yet,' the maid said, 'I think it can do damage, too hot.'

Kees glared for a moment, and left the room, returning with the same cup a few moments later.

'Half filled with cold water, will that be okay, do you think?'

Grimberg, the shaking subsiding now, sitting on the

floor, a thick woollen jacket draped over his shoulders, reached out and took the cup, sipping at it gently.

'Thanks.' His voice was a croak, his eyes stayed on the ground.

A car horn sounded in the street.

'Get a paramedic team here. And a car.'

Kees left to make the call.

Once he'd gone Jaap sat, not wanting to look at Grimberg.

'You know I did it?' asked Grimberg finally.

'Yes.'

'So you know *why* I did it?'

'I think I –'

'Then you'll understand, I've already served a sentence, for something I didn't do.'

'Let's take the whole thing from the beginning.'

Grimberg shifted slightly, putting his cup down. The colour was returning to his face, and he ran his hand through his hair, pushing it back off his forehead. He looked straight at Jaap, who had to struggle to return the gaze.

'It started when I was thirteen, I was at school and . . .' He paused, a slight shudder running through his torso. '. . . that man was our football teacher.'

'Friedman.'

He nodded; the name still seemed to hold a sway over him.

'He . . . well, I don't need to spell it out, do I?'

Jaap shook his head.

He knew.

And he didn't want to hear it.

'The thing is, he was charismatic, and everyone wanted to be on the team, and I guess he took advantage of that.'

'Were you the only one?'

'I thought so at the time, but clearly I wasn't.'

'And you didn't tell anyone?'

'Of course I didn't. He trapped me, made me think that if I told anyone they wouldn't believe me. That's how these people operate. And then he left, two years after it had started, and I thought I was free, thought I could get over it, forget it all. So I went to university and tried to be a normal student, and I kind of succeeded in beating it, you know? The pain gradually went away but it left me with a feeling that I had to do something, if not for myself, then for other kids who'd gone through the same thing. So I went to work at the charity.'

'And then one day Friedman walked in?'

'I couldn't believe it, the sheer fucking hypocrisy of it. I was sick for three days, I couldn't keep from throwing up. I guess the damage he'd done to me hadn't really gone away, I'd just become used to covering it up, hiding it from myself.'

'How come he didn't recognize you?'

'I was thirteen at the time, I look different now, and the amount of children he abused? Christ, they probably all look the same to him.'

'And your name?'

'I changed it, when I went to university, I thought it would help me escape my past.' He forced a laugh. 'New name, new person, right?'

Grimberg was still shivering, but it was subsiding. Jaap's muscles felt tight from the pull.

'You were at school with Andreas Hansen?'

'That name rings a bell, I think he was in the year above me?'

A lie, Jaap was sure, but he'd let it pass, for the moment. In a way he didn't want to know.

'So you decided to do something about Friedman yourself?'

'I didn't decide, I had no choice. He hadn't recognized me, so I was free to do what I wanted.'

'And where does Zwartberg fit into this?'

'I'd only meant to kill Friedman. I thought that by leaving his phone at the scene the police would get the others. And I hung him up because I wanted him to be shamed, even in death.'

'So why did you kill the others?'

Grimberg swallowed.

'I . . . it was so easy. Once I'd done it. I thought it would be hard, killing someone. But . . . afterwards I realized that I had the power to make a change. I could stop these people, all of them. I guess I kind of hoped someone would catch them first, stop me from doing it, but part of me didn't want that.'

'How did you find out about the others?'

'I'd started to watch Friedman, following him, trying to find the best place to get him, and I saw him with Zwartberg.'

'In De Wallen?'

'Yeah, they'd meet at a place in Bloedstraat. I'd followed Friedman one night, he'd left the house late, walked there. He went inside and I waited down the street, and a few hours later Friedman came out, followed by this other guy. So I hired someone, to do a bit of digging, just to find out who this other guy was.'

'What, like a private investigator?'

'Yeah, I didn't even know they really existed, but they do. Mainly divorces, I guess.'

'And you weren't worried that they might be alarmed when the people they were hired to track started getting killed?'

'I never met them, so they didn't know who I was. They were reluctant at first, but I paid them well. In cash. They insisted on that.'

'So they found Haak as well. Anyone else on your list?'

'There's one more, he's the worst one, he controlled the whole thing.'

'Who is he?'

'I don't know what he's called, but I know that he's connected with a gang –'

'The Black Tulips?'

'Yeah, but the people I hired? They got scared, said they were dropping it. And I never heard from them again.'

'Give me their details,' said Jaap. Grimberg told him and Jaap wrote it down.

'You should have come to us,' said Jaap.

'I didn't have a choice, I had to do it.' His voice rose, roughened with anger. 'There was Friedman, this predator, ruining people's lives for his own pleasure. Raping them. Raping them just as he raped me. You'd think there'd be some kind of punishment for that, wouldn't you?' He stared at Jaap. 'But there wasn't. He inherited a business which gave him enough money to live in this millionaire's house. Where he could fuck people, fuck kids, for god's sake. It wasn't right. It just wasn't fucking right.'

'And now?'

Grimberg looked down at his hands, scratching his left forefinger with his thumb. The sound of a chair being scraped across a floor, a faint radio, voices raised in joy or anguish he couldn't tell, and his own breathing filling the room. Grimberg's eyes rose to meet his own.

'If they were here right now, I'd do the same again.'

Kees walked back in and nodded to Jaap.

What Grimberg had been through was unforgivable. But his duty was to find murderers and bring them to justice. The role didn't have room for subtlety, for moral judgements as to cause or effect.

He motioned to Kees, who unzipped his coat and reached for his cuffs. Kees stepped forward and Grimberg looked at him, then slowly raised his hands. But just as the cuffs were about to slide over his wrists he grabbed Kees' arm and pulled him forward. Kees lost his balance and fell on top of him with a grunt.

Before Jaap could react Grimberg had Kees' gun, slipped from his holster as he'd fallen forwards, and was pointing it right at Kees' temple.

Grimberg rose slowly, making sure Kees did the same, all the time keeping the gun jammed into his head. In a split second when Grimberg's eyes had left Jaap he pulled his own gun out, aimed it right at Grimberg's head.

Just as he had years ago in a similar situation.

And that had not turned out so good.

'I was punished before I'd done anything wrong,' Grimberg said, his voice stronger now, 'so now I've made up for it. Does the order things happen in really matter?'

'Put the gun down, then we can talk about this.'

Grimberg glared at him.

'Talk about it? What's there to talk about?' He was shouting now; Kees flinched. 'You don't give a shit about what happened to me, you don't give a shit that the people I killed were evil, that they deserved to die!'

'Just put the gun –'

Grimberg shoved Kees towards Jaap.

Grimberg's mouth opened in a silent scream and he rammed the gun between his teeth.

# 94

The windscreen wipers were working hard, squeaking, and the tyres weren't gripping too well as she pulled up at one of the port entrances, the car sliding forward, despite her low speed. She couldn't believe Jaap hadn't told her about the shipping company, and that he hadn't answered her call once she'd given Bloem the slip. Did he not trust her, was that it? Did he want to rescue Adrijana himself? Or was it because of what had nearly happened last night? He now felt he had to protect her?

*Or am I just being paranoid?* she thought.

As she killed the engine and got out of the car she could see Bloem, cuffed to Haak, bellowing like a stuck cow. There was going to be hell to pay for that. But right now she didn't care.

The important thing was Adrijana.

The only thing was Adrijana.

# 95

The clean-up team had arrived, and Jaap and Kees were stepping out the front door when two uniforms Jaap didn't recognize appeared in front of them, blocking their way.

'Rykel?'

Jaap and Kees exchanged a glance, the tone of voice out of place.

'Inspector Rykel. Yes?'

The first uniform held up a pair of cuffs, dangling the loop from a finger.

'You're under arrest.'

# 96

*Is this for real?* thought Kees as he heard the news exploding round the station.

Smit hadn't seemed that impressed when he'd told him about the call he'd had from Roemers. He'd expected action, congratulations, being put in charge of the case, but all he'd got was a tepid reaction and a curt thank you.

And yet now he'd had Jaap arrested.

He knew he'd made a mistake, and then when that fucking priest had looked at him as if he knew exactly what was going on in his head, well . . . it had sealed it as a bad deal.

Now he felt sure it would get out that he'd been spying for Smit. And Smit wouldn't protect him, he couldn't give less of a toss, he saw that now. He'd been played.

By that fat fuck of a Station Chief.

He was finished.

His relationship with Marinette was over, his career was over, and that would probably mean, just to top everything off, that he and Carice would be over as well.

He'd fucked up, and he knew it.

But even if he was finished, there was one thing he wanted to do. Find the woman who, if he'd managed to catch her on the first day, might have been able to stop all of this from happening.

Because when he thought about it, the whole situation he found himself in could have been avoided had she not run.

And, well, he wanted some payback, payback for being knocked out yesterday. He turned to leave the building but as he passed the front desk the Sergeant called out to him, waving a phone.

# 97

Tanya had been trying his phone every minute for the last ten, but it kept just going straight to voicemail. *Damn.* She really needed to talk to him.

*Maybe*, she thought, *someone at his station knows where he is.*

She called, asked to speak to him, and, after a long pause in which she wondered if the connection had been lost, heard a voice.

'Inspector Terpstra.'

'Hey, Kees, It's Tanya, I'm trying to get hold of Jaap but he's not picking up?'

'Yeah, uuh, he's kind of busy at the moment.'

'Look, can you get him, it's really important.'

Another pause.

'I can't right now.'

'When will he be free?'

'Could be a while, he's just been arrested.'

'What? Why?'

'I'm ... I'm not really sure.' Tanya knew him well enough to know he was holding something back. She knew Jaap hadn't wanted Kees to know about what he was up to, but now it looked too late.

'Shit. Is this because he's been investigating Andreas Hansen's killing?'

'It could be, I guess.'

*Did Kees already know?* she thought. *Was it Kees who ratted on Jaap?*

'Can you get a message to him, it's really urgent, I think I've found her.'

# 98

Kees put the phone down, his head swimming.

He was feeling sick, guilt seeping throughout his body. His career was over, the level of mistrust from his colleagues once they learnt of his deception would make his life hell.

*At least*, he thought to himself, *Judas got paid some silver. All I got were vague promises about my career.*

But he owed Jaap now, or at least he felt he did, and went back upstairs, cursing himself for his stupidity.

The atmosphere in the office was tense, the news that Jaap was being held in one of the holding cells had ricocheted round the office like a wrecking ball, and nobody quite knew what to do. Some were openly questioning why he'd been arrested, others were more circumspect, not wanting to get involved in case it was serious.

Which, the general consensus said, it had to be as none of them had ever seen a colleague of theirs, one of them, being treated like a common criminal.

And of course Kees got the brunt of the questions, and each time he had to say he didn't know any more than they did, it had felt like he was nailing himself to a cross, knowing that his denials would be remembered when the truth came out.

He had to talk to Jaap, give him Tanya's message. And whilst he was there, he might as well come clean. It probably wouldn't help, his career in the police would be finished now anyway, but it was, he saw, the right thing to do. Face up to it, to his mistake.

His mouth felt dry.

# 99

Jaap had been in this very cell so many times over the last few years that he couldn't even begin to count. Faces, crimes, interviews, some clear, others blurring together, joined only by the seam of their stupid repetitiveness.

But he could remember them in broad terms, because there were distinct categories of reaction, those who broke down almost straight away, the ones who thought that cockiness would see them through, finger-pointers who blamed everyone but themselves, those who raged, against the police, their lawyers, their victims, fate itself.

But the category who had always spooked Jaap were the clams, the ones who just sat there, immutable, immobile, resolute in their refusal to engage with any of the tactics, empathy, shouting, bargaining.

*That's what I should do*, he thought as the door opened and De Waart stepped in, his face grave. Jaap thought he could glimpse something underneath it though, triumph maybe.

'It's a sad day for all of us, Jaap.'

'What the fuck am I here for?'

'Didn't they tell you when they arrested you? Maybe you can get off on a technicality.'

'They said evidence suppression, but that doesn't mean anything to me. This is just about you, isn't it?'

De Waart shook his head, a teacher disappointed by his protégé.

'It's about the law, Jaap. It's about following orders, it's about not doing anything so stupid as tamper with evidence from a case which belongs to another Inspector.'

Jaap stared at him, trying not to show the realization which was starting to form in his head.

'Because when you played with Andreas' phone at the morgue – we have the CCTV tape by the way – you were fucking with *my* investigation.'

'This is bullshit.'

'No, I'll tell you what's bullshit. What's bullshit is that you've just chucked away your career, and you did it by fucking with me. I'm checking with the phone company, see what it was you deleted. But it's kind of irrelevant anyway. We'll drop the charge of evidence suppression. You want to know why?'

Jaap didn't respond, thinking that at least he'd deleted the same message from his own phone.

'Well, I'm going to tell you.' He cracked the knuckles on his left hand. 'We're actually upping the charge. To murder.'

'What are you talking about?'

'The gun that killed Andreas has turned up. It was in your houseboat, Jaap. And when they ran a fingerprint check' – he held his palm out and waggled his fingers – 'the only ones they found were yours.'

# 100

Jaap looked around, at the scuffed and scratched concrete walls, the smell of sweat and fear saturating the air, and wondered what he could do. It was because of Andreas that he was here.

*No it's not*, he told himself, *it's because of my inability to let go. It's because I stubbornly believed that I had to find his killer, that I was the only one smart enough to do it.*

Suddenly he wanted to kick something, tear the bench from the wall and smash it on to the floor. He'd been set up. Whoever was behind this had planned for everything. If they failed to kill him, twice, they still had a backup plan. Frame him.

And if he couldn't prove otherwise he was going to have all the time in the world to go over and over his mistakes. A week ago he was on track to take over from Smit, and now . . .

It was as if he'd learnt nothing in that year.

Desire causes suffering.

And attachment was a form of desire. He'd become too attached to revenge. Sure he'd called it justice, to himself, but really it was vengeance.

He'd become attached, and now he was suffering.

Simple.

He sat back against the wall, his head against the cold concrete, closing his eyes, the anger from a moment ago gone.

Why could he not figure it out?

Yuzuki Roshi had often told him to be the master of his own mind, not be mastered by it.

He started counting his breaths, trying to let go of his thoughts.

His pulse gradually slowed, as did his breathing.

CCTV.

The planted journalist.

And Andreas' phone call to the station.

He'd spoken to someone, the length of the call proved that. Jaap had assumed they'd made Andreas wait whilst they tried to get in contact with him, but what if Andreas had spoken to someone, told them what he'd texted Jaap?

*Why*, he thought as he heard voices moving down the corridor towards his cell, *didn't I think of that before?*

A key scraped in the lock.

Jaap looked up, expecting to see Smit, but it was Kees who stepped in, closing the door behind him.

He looked nervous.

# 101

Kees needed to swallow, his Adam's apple felt like a tennis ball stuffed down his throat.

Finding the cell – at least they'd put him in on his own – he'd asked the Duty Sergeant to let him in.

Jaap was sitting on the bench, his back straight against the wall. His eyes were closed and he looked weirdly calm.

'I –' started Kees but Jaap cut him off as his eyes opened.

'This isn't going to reflect on you, you know.'

'Sorry?'

'They know you had nothing to do with it.'

Kees, confused, didn't know what to say.

'You look confused.'

'I am,' said Kees, cautiously, sensing that there was a glimmer of hope.

Or it might just be a trap.

He needed to swallow; he fought the urge, then tried to hide it with a cough, the noise sounding strange in the cell.

'Sorry, I should have trusted you right from the start, told you what was going on.'

Kees, unsure if he could trust his voice, had to ask, 'So what is going on?', still not sure if he was out of the woods.

'They checked the CCTV tapes at the morgue and saw me messing with Andreas' phone, I deleted a message he'd sent me.'

*That's what De Waart was asking me about.*

'So . . .' Kees tried to keep the relief out of his voice. '. . . it was Inspector De Waart who had you arrested?'

'Who else?' Jaap looked at him. 'And someone planted a gun, with my prints on it, at my houseboat. The same gun that killed Andreas.'

'Listen.' Keen now to get away from the topic, inside a voice kept repeating, *He doesn't know, he doesn't know.* 'Tanya just called for you. She says she's found the girl, at some shipping company?'

'Where is she?'

'She's there now.'

'On her own?'

'I think so.'

Jaap considered this for a second.

'Okay, there are two things I need you to do for me.'

'Yeah?'

'You heard about the press conference, about the journalist who made those accusations? Well I tried to find out who it was, but he didn't work for the paper he said he did.'

'So it was a set-up?'

'Exactly. Whoever killed Andreas planted him there, to make it harder for us to investigate his death. Now that Haak is dead, finding that journalist is the only way we're going to get them. That journalist would have entered the building by the front, see if you can find someone who doesn't sign in. He might even have been brought in as an arrest.'

'Okay, and the second thing?'

Jaap looked at him as if trying to make a decision. The light overhead started buzzing and flickered once, before dying completely.

'The second thing could land you in a whole lot of trouble.'

# 102

Tanya watched as the man pulled out his phone.

He started speaking, something foreign, then laughed. As he hung up he took one last drag on his cigarette, the smoke getting lost in the falling snow. He tossed the butt and ground it with his heel like he was an actor playing a tough guy in a film. Then he unzipped and pissed a pattern in the snow, before shaking, zipping back up and walking away from the door he'd been guarding ever since Tanya had turned up.

She pulled her head back round the edge of the shipping container she was crouching behind and felt for her gun. Taking one last look around, the rows of containers like a strange city, the man's footprints showing the direction he'd gone in, she dashed across the twenty metres to the door, a small lamp high up on the brick wall framing it in a yellow triangle. The door itself was metal, the surface dull and dented, the number '17' sprayed on in black, and beneath the letters 'BSC'.

Unholstering her gun, she reached out her hand, slowly closing her fingers round the handle, as if it could be startled, and began very slowly to turn it, afraid that the man would have locked it.

But he hadn't, it turned freely, and she inched it open, not breathing, her ears straining to hear anything from inside. There was nothing. So she pushed it open a bit further, just enough to get her head in. A large cavernous space, stacked with even more shipping containers and stairs leading down off to her left.

She slipped in and closed the door softly behind her, scanning for movement. The stairs creaked as she descended, even though she was placing each foot with as much care as she could. At the bottom there was another door, marked 'Private', and this was ajar, no light showing from beyond. She pushed it open and tried to peer into the darkness, and then crept along the corridor, one hand against the freezing rough concrete, the other holding her gun down by her side.

A little voice started to whisper to her.

*You shouldn't be here on your own.*

Then her hand hit metal, another door. The noise caused something to move on the far side. She stopped dead still, holding her breath, waiting to hear it again. But nothing came, and a minute or so later she decided to push on.

The door opened easily, total darkness inside. Her fingers connected with a light switch on the wall, she threw it, stepped back into the corridor and raised her gun, holding it with both hands. Her eyes reacted to the light, and she had to fight to keep them open.

There was movement, scuffling sounds, but no gunshots or voices. The picture came into focus as her eyes adapted; there were figures, three, bound and gagged, huddled together against the far wall, their eyes bottomless pits of fear.

Two young women, about eighteen Tanya guessed, and in between them a younger girl, shaking her head, feet scrabbling uselessly on the floor.

She had red hair.

It was her.

## 103

Seconds before Kees smashed his elbow into the glass panel protecting the fire alarm he reflected that maybe he'd simply swung from one extreme to another, from rat to rebel. The piercing sound cut through the air and he rushed down a flight of stairs to the car pool, got into one, and waited, fingers drumming on the steering wheel.

# 104

The officer on duty, Laurens, knew Jaap well. He'd been surprised when the two officers had marched him down, demanding that he be put in a cell. But he'd followed orders, just as he'd always done.

His job was to make sure the prisoners didn't kill each other, or themselves, or escape.

Or die in fires.

The alarm was splitting the air; there'd been no warning of a drill. He had to get the prisoners out of the building, and he had four cells, with nine people in total, ten including Jaap.

He hesitated for a second, then made up his mind.

He unlocked the door.

'Listen, I need a hand getting some prisoners upstairs.'

# 105

All three of the girls were tied to the pipes which lined the back wall.

Tanya scanned the room; there was no one else there. She shut the door behind her, holstered her gun, and approached them.

'Police,' she whispered. 'I'm here to help you.'

All she got was scared looks, she repeated herself in English, and one of the girls nodded.

She untied Adrijana first, loosening the filthy rag cutting into the sides of her mouth, and undoing the ties holding her wrists to the pipes. The pipes themselves were almost too hot to touch. Tanya wanted to hold her, tell her it was going to be all right but she knew they didn't have much time.

'I'm going to get you all out of here,' said Tanya as she reached across and freed the other two girls.

'They told us' – the older girl, with shorter hair, started speaking – 'we'd have jobs, and, and . . .'

'Shhh. It's okay, we just need to get you out of here now. How many men are there around?'

The second girl answered.

'Only one is here at a time, they sometimes go off for while, but never longer than twenty minutes.'

Tanya tried to count, how long had it taken her to get here, five, ten?

They needed to go, so she helped them all to their feet and told them to follow her, back along the corridor, and up the stairs, Tanya going first, holding Adrijana's hand.

All seemed to be quiet in the warehouse.

She grouped them together.

'If anything happens out there you're all to run, do you get that?'

They all nodded, and Tanya took a deep breath.

She cracked open the door.

The muzzle of a gun kissed her lips.

# 106

Jaap raced through the parked cars to the driver's side, yanking the door open.

'I don't want you coming with me, then they'll know it was you,' he said as he slid into the seat, reaching for the key.

'It's all right, I want to —'

'No, I'm not letting you ruin your career. You could be a good cop. If you get help — stop the coke.' He stared at Kees. 'Get out now, and no one will ever know.'

Kees thought quickly — Jaap was right, he'd probably get away with it. And he had someone of his own to chase. He got out and handed Jaap his phone.

'Is it on here?'

'Low res, the best I could get from the surveillance camera.'

Jaap shot the car out of the underground car park, the motor roaring. He tried to look at the tiny screen playing a grainy picture whilst driving, too fast, in thick snow, but gave up after he scraped the side of the car against a parked van, sparks like a miniature firework display.

He reached the port, and parked by the police car that he guessed was Tanya's. He flipped Kees' phone on again.

He watched the video, fast forwarding. But the faces all looked familiar. He took it right back to the start again. And then he saw something which made him stop. His stomach plummeted. But somehow he wasn't surprised.

He grabbed his own phone. Niels had been at the press conference, he'd be able to confirm what Jaap had just seen.

'Niels, it's Jaap, I haven't got much time so just listen. I'm going to send you a picture, look at it and call me back.'

Once he'd sent it he snapped the phone shut, got out of the car, and followed the footprints, already filling in with fresh snow.

His phone started buzzing in his hand. It was Niels.

'Yeah?'

'Well, I recognize both of them. One of them is Inspector De Waart,' said Niels.

'And the other?'

'The other is that journalist you were asking after. Is there a story in this for me?'

'There might well be, I'll call you.'

The so-called journalist had got into the building without a press pass because De Waart had pretended he was an arrest. It had to have been last minute. It was sloppy and De Waart must have known the risk he was taking, but was under enough pressure to go with it.

He thought of De Waart, his switch from aggression, to friendliness, and back again. It should have told him something. He'd been watching Jaap right from the start. It might even have been him who broke down his houseboat door, came for him in the night with the intention of putting a bullet in his head.

And Karin.

Had that been him too?

The gun he'd left on the table.

It was the gun he'd killed Andreas with.

De Waart had been one step ahead the whole time, paying the premium on his insurance policy.

*The fucker*, he thought as he reached a shipping container where she'd obviously waited, the marks in the snow clear. *He's played me all along.*

He peered round the corner. There was a door just across from him, and two men standing outside, their bodies tense, waiting. The one nearest, who had a dirty blond ponytail, was holding a gun in his hand, and when the door in front of him opened slowly, he poked the muzzle into the gap, before the other man, short dark hair and a black leather jacket, lurched forward and grabbed Tanya by her hair.

Jaap wanted to move, but the gun was trained on Tanya's head the whole time and he couldn't risk it.

*Move it*, he willed the man.

The first man opened the door further and Jaap could see two young women. And a girl. She started screaming.

The second man stepped forward and slapped her.

The screaming stopped.

They took Tanya and the girls back into the building, and as soon as the door closed Jaap sprinted across, following her footprints.

*It was these*, he thought as he ran, *that gave her away.*

He waited at the door, ear pressed against the freezing metal, and pushed it open as slowly as he could. Once inside he could hear footsteps, the noise echoing up from a staircase. Jaap paused for a moment, quickly checking the rest of the area before descending, weapon drawn.

Stepping off the last tread Jaap just caught sight of the door at the far end closing. Twenty seconds and he was outside the same door, listening again. He could hear Tanya's voice, but couldn't make out the words. Then one of the men barked something at her, and she fell silent for a few seconds before a scream of pain rang out.

*Tanya.*

He kicked the door in and sprang through shouting 'Police' so hard his vocal cords felt ripped.

The room was small, pipes rising up out of the floor along the back wall, and the captives shoved against them. Jaap could see the ponytail standing over Tanya, her hair wrapped round one of his hands as he yanked her head back, his arm raised ready to pistol-whip her.

He spun round, releasing Tanya, flipping the gun handle deftly back into his hand.

Bad déjà vu. He was back in that tenement block, the woman slumped on the floor in an ocean of blood, Andreas' voice telling him not to fire, and the man in front of him grinning.

Jaap fired, the sound deafening in the tiny room. He could see the women covering their ears, and the man juddered, his gun arm flailing and releasing the weapon, which flew up into the air in an elegant curve, heading towards Tanya.

*There were two men*, but before he could do anything he felt a rush of air behind him, then a sickening crunch.

# 107

Tanya watched as Jaap shot the first man, and the gun flew out of his hand. It arced downwards towards her and she twisted round, trying to catch it.

It fell just out of reach.

She strained to grab it and a movement caught the corner of her eye.

Her fingers scrabbled on the concrete floor until she managed to clasp the barrel and pull it towards her. She looked up just in time to see Jaap slump forward, revealing the second man, pointing his own gun right at her.

# 108

'Just fucking get on with it,' yelled Kees as he shoved a drunk back into the cell.

The man stumbled on the steel threshold, put his arms up and smacked into the wall. He was turning round, presumably to complain, when Kees slammed the door shut on him.

*I need to get out of here*, he thought. *Now.*

The station was still in chaos, and he'd been roped into getting all the suspects back into their cells by Smit. There were eight more suspects waiting to be ferried back from where they were being held outside. But all he could think about now was getting to the woman's address before she split. She must've noticed her wallet was missing, and she'd probably figure that it could lead back to her.

*Fuck it*, he thought, as he reached the ground floor.

He ducked out the back, just as he saw Smit stepping off the stairway, talking on his phone. Kees wasn't sure if Smit had seen him or not.

Getting to the address would have normally taken about ten minutes, but the snow slowed him up, and by the time he got there, a terraced red-brick out south, he was sure she'd be long gone. He wanted to hammer against the door but managed to make himself press the bell instead. The snow was falling heavily now, starting to settle properly.

The door opened a crack, and he recognized her, despite only seeing a tiny portion of her face. She tried to slam it shut but he was stronger and forced his way in. She was running up the stairs, then she tripped and he managed to grab a foot and haul her back down. He could smell her perfume, and her fear. She tried to lash out at him, and he had to pin her arms back on the stairs, kneeling on her thighs until she screamed, and spat in his face.

Then she started sobbing, and her muscles relaxed, and he knew that she was beaten. He yanked her to her feet and marched her into the ground floor room, shoved her on to a sofa, and pulled the roller blinds down on the window leading out to the street.

'It's not what you think . . .' she managed between sobs, her face buried deep in her hands.

'No? Running away from the scene of a murder, then assaulting a police officer, me, at a place connected with the first murder? How is that not what I think?'

She looked up at him, her face puffy with tears, eyes red.

'That was you in the . . . the loft?'

'You're the one who knocked me out, gagged me and then put me in a box – you tell me.'

'I couldn't really see, it was dark and I was petrified.'

'*You* were petrified? I think you'd better start telling me what's going on.'

# 109

Silence.

A pulsing universe of pain radiated out from the back of Jaap's head.

Maybe he was dead.

That's what the hexagram had warned against: darkness, maintain light.

But if he was dead why could he feel pain?

In Kyoto, Yuzuki Roshi had always said, 'Just sit.'

And so he'd sat.

He'd sat, and tried to let go of his thoughts, tried to forget what he'd done. But it didn't work; the more desperately he sought to rub out the memory the more vivid it became, growing in intensity until he felt like screaming.

He and Andreas were just at the end of a long shift when a call came out, a report of a domestic disturbance in process. They were only a few blocks away. Andreas had wanted to leave it, Jaap called back and said they'd go.

But by the time they got there it had turned into more than a domestic.

The neighbour who called it in, a woman with tired, frightened eyes, filled Jaap and Andreas in. The shouting had blown up five minutes before, but it was the scream which had made her pick up the phone.

Jaap pushed the door open with his foot, gun outstretched.

A man was standing in the main room.

With a knife.

Held to a woman's throat.

He'd already made a gash stretching from her wrist to her inner elbow. He looked up, like he'd been expecting someone, and Jaap could see from his eyes he was on something strong. Probably crack. Maybe other stuff too.

'Stay back.'

His voice confirmed it. The woman whimpered.

Jaap could see she was pregnant, blood from her arm gushing over her rounded stomach.

They didn't have long, she was losing blood.

'I told her not to do it. But now it's all fucked up.'

'I'm sure we can sort it out, but first I need you to put down the knife,' said Jaap.

'You don't understand, it's too late. And I told her not to do it.'

Andreas was outside calling an ambulance whilst Jaap tried to calm the man. And for a while it seemed to be working, the man started lowering the knife from her throat.

The knife moved down.

Then Jaap realized why, he was simply moving the knife, down towards her stomach.

The crackhead must have seen realization in his eyes.

He sped up the movement, down, then out ready to stab back in.

Jaap fired.

Fired until the clip was empty and the crackhead had

slumped back against the wall, dragging the woman down with him.

Jaap ran across the room, the floor sticky with the woman's blood which had flowed from the cut on her arm.

She didn't seem to be moving.

He looked down and saw why.

Seven for the crackhead.

One stray for the woman.

*All this time*, he thought, *and I still can't let it go.*

Maybe he was dead now, maybe this was his Karma. Waiting for a real shitheap of life to be reborn back into. Payment for the woman's death.

He heard a weird sound echo round him, a kind of muffled wail.

It was only when his body started shaking, and he felt two liquid streams tickle his cheek as they dribbled down, that he realized he was crying, as if the tears were a strange currency of regret, trying to make payment for his mistakes.

The woman's death.

Andreas' death.

Karin's death.

When it subsided, the sobs becoming more and more spaced out until they finally stopped, he tried to sit up again.

Something had changed, he could feel it. As if the tears had strengthened him. He couldn't do anything about their deaths. But he could make sure whoever was responsible was held to account.

He didn't want to leave it to the laws of Karma, or fate, or whatever.

And he didn't care if it was revenge more than justice.

*What's the difference anyway?* he found himself thinking.

He opened his eyes; his left felt gummed up, didn't open fully. It was pitch black, and for a moment he panicked that the blow had somehow made him go blind. But he could smell, there was a damp, metallic tinge to the air, and it took a few moments for him to work out he wasn't in the same place he'd been when he passed out.

He'd known, a split second before the impact – some sixth sense kicking in too late – what was about to happen.

*Stupid,* he thought to himself, *really fucking stupid.*

He listened, wondering where he was, if he was alone. The sound of his breath was all he could hear, and something was jamming into his hip. Trying to move his head made the pain, if that was possible, worse.

Jaap mentally scanned his body, checking that it was all there. After a few moments he came to the conclusion that nothing was missing, but that his hands were tied with some kind of thin cord – biting into the flesh when he tried to separate them.

He tried to sit up, his feet scuffling against the floor, sliding, finding nothing to push against. Shifting his whole body sideways he tried again, and this time he found something with his foot. He pushed against it and managed to get himself into a seated position.

The wall was cold on his back; he put his head back slowly, and could feel the tender spot where he'd been hit.

*They've locked me in a shipping container,* he thought.

A moment of panic rose, and he tried to calm himself by breathing deeply but it didn't help. Here he was trussed up. He could be on a ship headed out to Russia for all he knew. His body would be discovered by customs officials in a few weeks' time.

Footsteps rang out, reverberating madly through the air. Someone was walking on top of the container. They passed right over him, and continued, before stopping when they reached the end. Suddenly Jaap remembered that he'd shot the man hitting Tanya, he'd seen him recoil just before being knocked out, which would mean it was the other man he was dealing with. The shorter man.

Bolts slid, something turned, metal on metal, and the door swung open. A man, short as Jaap had guessed, stepped into the container and walked towards him. Jaap couldn't see his face, the light was behind him. He gave Jaap a kick in the ribs with the tip of his boot, winding him and knocking him down. Then he grabbed Jaap's legs and started pulling him towards the door. Jaap struggled, tried to kick his legs apart, but the man turned round and stamped on his stomach.

After that he let himself be dragged.

Outside the snow was coming thick and heavy, and made the sliding easier, though it rode up into his jacket, making him gasp for breath. The sky was dark, but the dock was lit at intervals by pale fluorescents, the falling snow only visible in their pyramids of light.

Jaap lifted his head, muscles in his stomach shooting pain from the effort. He could see where they were headed, a ship, the massive dark hull looming up from the concrete edge, rust stains dripping down from the bilge holes, and he knew that if he had to do something it would have to be soon. But he couldn't think of anything, his brain seemed paralysed.

Everything swayed, seemed to go to a point, and he passed out again.

# 110

Up the gangplank.

The man struggled, strong as he was, with Tanya's weight, his foot slipping in the snow, compacted from whoever he'd brought up here before.

*It must've been Jaap*, she realized.

Her hands were bound, as were her feet.

The man's phone rang; he paused, pulled it out and answered, listening for a minute.

'Okay, you get rid of them. Get rid of all three. And I'll finish dealing with this bitch.'

*He's going to kill them*, her mind screamed. *Do something, do it now!*

She lunged on to her side, curled herself round one of the vertical poles which dotted the gangplank, and pulled her feet back trying to off-balance the man, just as he was pocketing his phone. He tried to compensate, shooting his foot out behind him to stop the sudden pull, but it slipped and he loosened his grip slightly, his arms automatically trying to correct his balance. He let out a yelp which would almost have been comical in another situation.

Tanya took the opportunity, flailed both her legs free and slammed her right leg into the man's chest. Pain seared through her thigh as she felt the stitches tear open. He toppled over backwards, hitting the surface hard, sliding down head first on his back. His phone fell out of his pocket and over the side.

It was seconds before she heard the splash.

She rolled back into the centre of the gangplank, hauled herself up, and looked down to see the man, sliding fast, smack his head into one of the same poles that had given Tanya her chance. She lunged down the ramp, needing to get to him before the man had a chance to get up, pull a weapon.

But as she got closer she sensed he wasn't moving.

When she reached him, she could see that in hitting the pole, the rest of his body had splayed round to the right, the neck at an unnatural angle. She crouched down to check his pulse. It was there, but it faded even as she pressed her fingers into the man's throat. She looked at his face, a snowflake landed on one of his open eyes.

The eyelid didn't blink.

She watched as the flake melted.

Snapping out of it she frisked the body for weapons. Her hands found two tucked into the man's jeans, one of which was her own. She took both, jamming the second into her coat pocket. She found a penknife on a key ring, her fingers so cold it took her several attempts just to get the blade open.

It took even longer to free herself, the blade small and blunt, cutting through the rope one fibre at a time.

Once loose she shook as much watery slush out of her jacket as she could; the snow had collected as she'd been dragged and had melted against the flesh of her back making her shiver.

*Or is that fear?* she thought. *Fear of what they've done to Adrijana. And Jaap.*

She followed the trail up on to the deck where it turned left, heading for the stern. The snow helped keep her footsteps quiet, and as she approached the open deck she slowed down.

Peering round the corner she could make out a figure, about ten metres away.

It was Jaap. Her heart thudded.

He was kneeling, facing away from her. She scanned for other figures. She couldn't see any. She crossed the space, the metal deck slippery under the snow.

Jaap flinched.

'There's someone else here, and they're going to kill them. We need to go,' she said to him as she undid the gag wrapped tightly round his mouth but before he could say anything she felt intense pain in her leg.

It was only when she looked down at the slick of blood oozing out of her thigh, melting the snow like lava, that she became aware of the noise of the gunshot.


Jaap heard the shot.

He saw the spurt of blood, and twisted round just as De Waart stepped out from a doorway on the first floor of the control tower, his gun trained at Jaap.

Tanya moaned next to him, both hands clutching her leg, trying to stop the bleeding. He hoped the bullet hadn't hit an artery, but the volume of blood said otherwise. Then she was quiet. Jaap could tell she'd passed out.

De Waart walked slowly to the left, down the steps to the deck, moving the gun closer until Jaap could see the dark bore hole, and behind it the face with impassive eyes.

'I'd like to confess,' De Waart said, voice calm, an eerie smile on his lips. 'I'm going to kill you, just like I killed Andreas. And your sister. But I'd like you to know I hadn't meant to kill her, I thought she was you.'

'You think you can cover up their deaths? You think that no one's going to ask questions?'

De Waart smiled, and relaxed his gun arm downwards.

'I thought about that. But I've already written a report showing that it was Grimberg who killed Andreas and your sister. These abuse cases, very sad, but . . . volatile.'

'And no one's going to wonder about my death?'

'Oh, that's easy. I'll tell them I killed you,' said De Waart smiling again. 'I'll say that you were attacking your girl-friend here, must have been the grief which tipped you over the edge. Such a shame I wasn't able to stop you kill-ing her. If only I'd arrived a few seconds earlier. Tragic really. But then with your history . . .'

Jaap's heart was slamming hard against his chest, he thought it would break through his ribs. De Waart was probably right, and presented with an easy solution no one would look any deeper.

His mind raced so fast it felt slow. He wanted to say some-thing, but one look at De Waart's eyes told him that it was pointless. Nothing he could say would make a difference.

Nothing could change what he was. So Jaap just held his gaze.

Everything became clear, as if he'd been back in Kyoto, sitting, emptying his mind.

He wanted to live. For himself, for Tanya.

But he knew he was going to die. He thought of the

woman he'd killed, the guilt he'd been living with over the years.

He closed his eyes.

*I'm going to die*, he thought, *I need to forgive myself.*

'What the fuck,' asked De Waart as he stepped forward and raised the gun again, 'are you smiling about?'

The shot had rung out less than a minute before Kees reached the corner.

He'd made his way up the gangplank, but had turned right towards the front of the ship, skirting round the deck on the far side. It was a detour which had added several minutes, and he hoped the shot didn't mean he'd made the wrong decision, got there too late.

Kees crouched at the corner and listened, the thick snow not only making it hard to see but softening sound as well. Which had been good for his approach, but was less useful now. He wanted to look round but needed to establish what was going on first.

There was a man's voice up ahead, but he couldn't tell what he was saying. Then a second; it sounded like Jaap.

Kees looked at his knuckles holding the gun out in front of him. They were white. And it wasn't because of the cold.

*Fuck it*, he thought.

He slowly rolled his head round the corner, the metal of the ship's wall freezing against his cheek. Snowflakes blurred his view, but he was pretty sure there were three figures down on the deck. Tanya was lying, one of her legs bloody, and Jaap was kneeling next to her with his hands behind his back, looking at a figure standing just in front of him.

Kees couldn't make out who it was. He might be able to get a better view if he retraced and came round from the other side.

*That's going to take me too long*, he thought.

Then he saw the figure step right up to Jaap and raise the gun, pointing it in his face.

Before he knew he was even doing it, Kees found he'd sighted the man. The trigger's resistance was at the last point before it gave, like a foot on the clutch.

His finger twitched.

He felt the recoil.

The figure's head blossomed red.

*Friday, 6 January*
*16.38*

Tanya lay in the back of an ambulance.

She looked down as the hi-vis paramedic gently lifted the blood-soaked fabric of her trouser-leg and started cutting through it.

Beyond him, outside the back doors, uniforms floated through the snow. Blue lights flashed.

She'd passed out just after the shot had hit her leg. When she'd come round Jaap was bending over her, and Kees was also there. They'd said something, about who'd shot her, but she hadn't really heard, all she could think about was Adrijana and the two other girls.

She'd tried to get up, tried to explain to them what was going on, but she couldn't speak, and they'd not let her move. She remembered lashing out in frustration, hitting Jaap. Then she must have blacked out again.

'Where are they?' she asked, and found her voice was working now.

The paramedic was intent on his job, bare arms as hairy as a chimp's, latex gloves already covered in blood.

Her blood.

'Looks like you've got another injury on this leg?' he

said as he split the trouser-leg open down the front and saw the stitches.

'The girls, did they find them?' she asked again and tried to sit up.

'Careful,' said the paramedic. 'You don't want to be moving right now.'

He probed around, trying to find the entry wound amongst the gore. Grabbing a wipe from a box attached to the wall behind him he started to clear away some of the blood. Tanya flinched, her whole leg jerking back with the pain when he found the spot.

She watched the top of his head as he bent closer, shifting continuously to get a better look. His hair was cut military short, but she could still see the whorl of his crown.

'Cute,' he said. 'Though it looks like one of the two heads is now missing.'

Tanya raised her head and glanced down. The bullet had obliterated part of her tattoo.

'Wait there,' he said to her with no trace of irony, as he clambered out of the ambulance.

Tanya tried to shift her leg, but it made the pain worse. She had no idea how long she'd been out. But she was sure it was too late. She could hear the paramedic having a conversation with someone; he seemed to be saying she needed to get to the hospital quickly.

Everything in the back of the ambulance began to distort, and she leant her head back on to the stretcher.

Footsteps crunch-squeaked through the snow outside.

She opened her eyes – she hadn't even realized they were closed – and lifted her head.

At the open doors stood Adrijana.

They stared at each other for a few moments, before Adrijana climbed into the back of the ambulance and walked alongside the stretcher.

She laid her head on Tanya's shoulder, her little arm curved round her neck.

Jaap had watched as the red-haired girl got into the ambulance, just as Kees stepped over to him, still clutching his gun.

'Maybe now you could tell me what the fuck just happened?'

Jaap looked at Kees; he seemed shaken, a look to his eyes he recognized all too well. It was the same look he'd seen for years in the mirror. He suddenly felt the day crush down on him, the snowflakes turned to lead.

He wanted to tell Kees, but not yet. He needed to get it clear in his own head first.

'Seriously, they're going to be asking a lot of questions,' said Kees. 'I heard Smit's on his way over with an internal investigation team. And the first thing they're going to want to know is why I shot a senior Inspector.'

Jaap's legs were feeling unsteady, but Kees had just saved his life, and he figured he owed him a full explanation.

'Okay, but do you want to put that away first?' Jaap motioned to the gun.

Kees brought his hand up and looked at it like he'd never seen it before. Then he stuffed it in his jacket holster.

'You heard Andreas and I were working on that case with the Black Tulips?' asked Jaap.

Kees nodded.

'Well, we knew what was going on, but we hit a brick wall. But you know what Andreas was like, he wouldn't let it go, and the night he was killed he texted me to say he had a way in. Friedman.'

*If only I'd gone with him*, he thought for the millionth time. Jaap's hands were in his pockets, he could feel them trembling. His toes gripped the soles of his shoes in an effort to stay steady.

'But whatever it was alarmed someone in the gang.'

'De Waart?' said Kees, not looking at Jaap.

'Yeah. Andreas called the station looking for me. When he couldn't get hold of me I reckon he talked to De Waart. Andreas must have told him about Friedman. They didn't get on at all, but they were both cops so I guess Andreas didn't suspect anything. De Waart panicked, and arranged to have him killed.'

'But if De Waart knew Andreas had connected Friedman to his case he could have got you pulled off it, made it part of his own investigation into Andreas' death,' said Kees, still not looking at Jaap.

'Yeah, but it was risky, he'd have to explain why he knew, that he'd talked to Andreas. It probably wouldn't have mattered, but I think it was such a shock he didn't really think it through, he just wanted to neutralize the threat as soon as possible.'

Jaap paused, watched the blue lights freeze the snowflakes in the air for micro-seconds at a time.

'It was him who broke into my houseboat that night. He'd have known Andreas was trying to contact me, that's why he kept trying to press me, see what I knew, see if —'

A voice called out Jaap's name from behind him, and he turned to see a uniform running through the snow, feet slipping, clutching a phone.

'You're needed at the hospital,' the uniform said, out of breath. 'Saskia Hansen's gone into labour.'

# 112

*That's a month early*, thought Jaap.

Then another thought jack-knifed him.

*It can't be . . .*

Jaap saw the paramedic start to close the ambulance doors, the little girl being taken out by a female uniform.

He had to get to the hospital, for Saskia. He glanced over to the ambulance. Tanya was laid out on a stretcher.

'Hey,' he called out, starting towards the ambulance. 'I want to ride with her.'

The paramedic shook his head.

'It's better if you don't. You can follow, it'll be more comfortable.'

'I'm going with her,' said Jaap as he climbed in, past the paramedic. He could smell blood and disinfectant.

The paramedic shrugged his shoulders.

'Okay, fine. But don't touch anything.'

The paramedic reached out to slide the door shut when a hand from outside appeared and pulled it back open. Kees stood with snow swirling around him.

'I'm coming too.'

'No, seriously. How are we all supposed to fit in here?' said the paramedic.

'Easy,' said Kees. 'You're getting out and riding up front.'

'I've got a patient to look after, and you're delaying her treatment so —'

'It's fine,' said Tanya.

They all turned to look at her.

'Really, I'll be okay. If Kees wants to come that's fine. It's not far, is it?'

The paramedic looked at all three, shrugged, and got out.

'Let's stop pissing around then and get going,' he said as he walked round to the front of the ambulance.

Kees got in, slid the doors shut, and then banged twice on the metal wall.

The ambulance started, the wheels spinning for a few seconds before they caught, lurching forward.

'Not going to wait for Smit then?'

'He can come get me himself,' said Kees. 'And anyway, I still need to know what really happened. We three probably need to get our stories straight. It's going to be fucking chaos out there, and I'm the one who's most at risk.'

Jaap could see Kees was on edge; he hoped he could control it. He hoped he wasn't high right now.

'Okay,' said Jaap. 'You heard about my sister?'

Kees nodded. Tanya shook her head.

'De Waart was waiting for me, at my houseboat,' said Jaap, feeling like he was listening to someone, not doing the talking himself. 'Karin turned up, and he killed her. He said back there it was by mistake, but I'm not so sure.'

Neither Kees nor Tanya said anything, then Tanya reached her hand out to Jaap's. He realized he was about to cry again.

'And all that stuff about you killing Andreas, I heard the

gun that shot him was found at your place, with your prints?' asked Kees.

'So you think I did it?' Jaap said, anger throttling his voice.

'Hey, easy. I'm just asking about what I heard.'

Jaap felt his hand being squeezed by Tanya; he could see Kees was looking at their hands.

'I met with him that second day, and he left his gun on the table. I stupidly picked it up and gave it to him when he tried to leave without it.'

Kees breathed out slowly, releasing pressure.

'You know what? I'm glad I wasted the fucker.'

Tanya's hand was still on Jaap's, but it felt odd now.

He'd thought it was going to be simple, thought that he and Tanya might . . . But if he was right about the timing of Saskia's pregnancy things were going to get complicated . . .

'So I checked his pockets back there,' he said addressing Kees, trying to distract himself from the thoughts slamming round in his head. 'He had two phones, and one of them was the last on the list, he was the one controlling Friedman and the others. He got himself put on the case, and arranged for a fake journalist to smear Andreas' name. There are people higher up for sure, but I think we'll find he was the head here in Amsterdam.'

The ambulance slid round a corner; Tanya winced as the trolley she was on slammed against the side, her grip tightened on his hand. A box of syringes fell off a shelf behind Jaap.

'So how long was he doing this for?' she asked, once Jaap and Kees had secured the trolley.

'I don't know, must have been for quite a while for him to react like that, he obviously had a lot to lose.'

'Is there going to be enough to get the rest of the gang, the people who actually smuggle the girls in?' asked Tanya.

'Now they know which shipping company to look at it should be easier.'

Jaap looked out the back window. It didn't tell him anything.

*Are we getting there yet?*

'I thought I told you not to come?' said Jaap turning to Kees.

'Yeah, well, there's a story attached to that. You know the woman who ran from Friedman's house that first day?'

'The one that apparently looks like your girlfriend?'

Kees winced.

'Ex-girlfriend, more like. How did you hear?'

'You hear all sorts of gossip when you're in prison.'

'I guess so. Anyway, she was the one who knocked me out at the loft. I figured that she was involved somehow, maybe worked for them. So I tracked her down after you left, but it turns out she wasn't involved, or at least not in the way I thought.' He reached up and rubbed the back of his head. 'She was a private detective, hired by someone, and she'd come across the stuff that those two produced.'

'It was Grimberg who hired her,' said Jaap.

'I guessed that, though she said it had been anonymous. Anyway, she'd got to the stage that she knew Friedman and Zwartberg were involved in something heavy. She found the loft, picked the lock and knocked me out thinking I was one of them.'

'Why didn't she come to the police?'

446

'She was going to, but she recognized someone when she turned up at the station.'

'De Waart.'

'Must have been. She'd seen him meet with Zwartberg a couple of times. So she got scared, basically.'

The ambulance came to a halt, Tanya's trolley juddered.

'Looks like we're here.'

# 113

'. . . Hansen. H-A-N-S-E-N.'

The woman at the front desk was unmoved by Jaap's urgency. She looked up the name with what seemed to Jaap maddening slowness, eventually finding a ward number on the fifth floor.

He ran over to the lift and hit the button repeatedly, the numbers indicating that it currently resided on the ninth floor. Eventually it started to move down, stopping at number six, and then it was on the move again, only the next number to appear was seven. Jaap cursed and hit the button repeatedly, then gave up and tried to find the stairs.

By the time he reached the fifth floor his lungs felt as if he had been breathing in mustard gas. He ran down the corridor, checking off the numbers in his head, and he could hear someone, a woman, screaming.

Was that Saskia? He couldn't tell, the human voice seemed to lose its personal characteristics when pushed to the extreme. Maybe, and he was surprised with the clarity of the thought which popped into his head, it was nature's way of making sure that a cry for help was always answered, not on personal grounds, but as a matter of duty for the survival of the species.

As he neared the number he was looking for the screaming got louder, and when he burst through the door, it increased in volume twofold.

The doctor, clad in green, jumped as the door flew open, but he didn't say anything, he could tell from the wild look on Jaap's face why he was here, and he turned back to the bed.

# 114

Tanya lay her head back on the pillow.

The material was starched so hard it only gave in patches, the smell of fabric conditioner surrounding her. It was quiet, an occasional call for a doctor mixed with the soft snoring from the old woman who was the only other occupant of the room. Nurses periodically opened the door, spilling light in from the corridor, and left again, letting the door swing shut.

They'd stitched her up – her leg now looked like a horror version of snakes and ladders – and told her she was lucky, that there was nothing to worry about.

But that wasn't true. She'd already had a visit from an officer telling her she was going to be booked for assaulting Bloem; they hadn't decided on exact charges, but he'd made it plain that they were going to do everything they could to make sure she was punished severely.

And then there was Adrijana. People had been congratulating her for saving her, but as she'd lain in the ambulance having her leg cleaned, the local anaesthetic just dulling the pain, not eradicating it, she realized she'd only managed to put her in just as much danger again.

She would now get swallowed up in the same system which had placed her with her own foster parents.

Taken into care, so the phrase went.

Of course she knew that not every foster parent was a child abuser, they couldn't be, but all she could think about was her own experience. She wrestled back and forth, slipping from end to end on a see-saw.

She had done the right thing.

If it wasn't for her who knew what would have happened, but the pictures in her mind, images from her past, kept getting mixed up with images of Adrijana.

The door opened and Jaap walked in, coming over to her bedside.

They looked at each other.

'Jaap, can I ask you something?'

'Sure.'

'When we were out there, and De Waart was about to shoot us, you were smiling.' Jaap nodded. 'What were you smiling about?'

'I thought you'd passed out?' he said, looking away from her.

'I had, but I must have come round for a second. And I'm sure you were smiling.'

# 115

'So then what happened, you came in to save the day?'

Kees sat back on Carice's sofa, his hand accepting the cold beer she held out before flopping down beside him. Candles dotted the room, soft music crept from hidden speakers.

'Yeah, I did actually.' He took a swig, focusing back on Carice.

'And you shot an Inspector?'

He shrugged like it was no big deal, like he regularly shot people. He hoped Carice couldn't see the bottle shaking in his fingers. He tightened his grip.

'He was about to shoot Jaap.'

'Did you kill him?'

He relived the moment he'd pulled the trigger and watched De Waart's head explode.

He'd always wondered what it would be like.

Now he knew.

'Yeah,' he said before downing the last of the beer. 'You might even get the autopsy.'

'Great, piling up the work for me.' She shifted, stretched her leg out, her foot landing slowly in his lap, toes burrowing. 'It could be like some TV series, a partnership between us. Each week you kill someone off and I fake the autopsy, keep the suspicion away from you.'

He thought back to the conversation he'd had with Jaap in the station car park. Jaap had told him he needed to get help and he was probably right. There were places you could go for that, people who'd been through it and could relate, could help you get off the stuff.

He saw De Waart's head bursting like a ripe water-melon, played in slo-mo in his mind again.

He felt like he needed a line right now.

'So is there anything I should look out for on this one?' She tipped her head back and took a sip of her own beer. He watched her long pale neck flickering in the candle light.

He really needed a line. Hell, he needed a whole motor-way of the stuff.

'Not really, just that he doesn't have much of a head left.'

# Epilogue

A sliver of dawn started to ease on to the horizon, pushing up the night's hem.

Jaap was awake, staring out of the hospital window, Saskia asleep in the bed next to him, exhausted, emotionally drained, drugged to the eyeballs. The snow had stopped at about three in the morning; he'd been watching the flakes for hours, like white petals, or feathers floating down from a ripped pillow.

He'd only slept in episodes, partly as the chair wasn't really designed to be sat in, let alone for sleeping, but partly because he was wired, too much having happened in such a short space of time, and he needed to digest it all. Needed to let his mind run though it, neutralize it.

He'd found Andreas' and Karin's killer, but there was no real satisfaction in that.

Andreas was still dead.

Karin was still dead.

And on top of that the discovery of the photo of Andreas had opened up a whole other avenue of sorrow. He didn't want to think about how Andreas had lived, carrying that secret around with him for years, eating away at him.

But maybe it hadn't, maybe he'd got over it, somehow managed to move on.

They were dead and that was it, more victims in a long

line of victims, and for the first time he had a feeling for the futility of what he did.

He heard footsteps approaching outside and looked up to see the door open slowly, Smit's face appearing as the gap widened. He jerked his head towards the corridor before disappearing. Jaap joined him, closing the door quietly as he left.

'All okay?' Smit motioned to the door.

Jaap nodded, feeling a distinct lack of interest in Smit's question.

'Good.' Smit coughed, looked down the corridor to where a nurse was fiddling with a saline drip on wheels. 'I've talked to Kees so I know what happened. I'll be giving a press conference later on this morning.'

Jaap could picture it already, Smit talking about the exoneration of Andreas from the child pornography claims, the swift result in Friedman's, Zwartberg's and Haak's deaths and the busting of a child porn ring at the same time. Add to that the saving of a kidnapped child and Smit had just the kind of results he needed to secure his next career move.

But with De Waart, an Inspector working under him, to have been so heavily implicated with a criminal gang, and then guilty of murdering a fellow officer, that career move wasn't going to happen.

'We are going to need further investigation into De Waart's death though,' continued Smit. 'I'm not sure anyone can be sure that he was really involved.'

'He admitted to me that he was, he told me he was going to kill me like he'd killed Andreas and Karin.' Jaap was trying to keep his voice down, but the nurse had looked up at them.

Smit took a step closer.

'Keep your voice down.' He looked around him before continuing. 'The thing is, we –'

'The thing is, you're trying to cover it up because you don't want it known that De Waart was bent, on your watch.'

'Inspector Rykel, I have a duty to the department here. A story like that is not going to help anyone, you know that. We'll have the press all over us, and I'm not going to allow that to happen. I've dropped the charges against you –'

'Those charges were never going to stick, you know that.'

'– and I've taken off all mention of them from your record. But . . .' He leant closer; Jaap could see something white crusted at the side of his mouth. '. . . if this story comes out then I'll know where it came from. Charges can be reinstated. So think hard before you do anything.'

Smit turned and walked down the corridor.

'You're going to say he was killed in the line of duty, aren't you?' Jaap called out after him. 'Make him a hero.'

Smit didn't stop walking.

'And what about my sister? And Andreas? You're happy to leave that listed as unsolved?'

Smit turned back.

'There's more than enough evidence that it was Grimberg –'

'That was De Waart covering his back!'

'So where's your proof?'

'He confessed. To me.'

'Witnesses?'

Jaap felt like he was burning.

Smit turned the corner, and was gone from sight.

Jaap stood for a moment, before pulling out the photo he had of Andreas as a teenager.

He studied it for a moment, then ripped it into tiny pieces, his hands shaking as he did so, and dropped it into a bin marked 'Sharps'.

He made his way to Saskia's room and sat back in the chair.

Maybe Smit was right, exposing De Waart would only make all their jobs harder.

And it would end his own career in the police, but he wasn't sure he cared.

He could call Niels. He pulled out his phone.

But it wasn't just him any more.

Saskia had told him just after the birth. That time last spring. She'd lied to him about the timing. The birth wasn't premature.

Glancing out the window he could see the light revealing a soft world, corners rounded off, the lone tracks of a dog or fox in the park just across the street. Everything looked clean, pristine, a beautiful world for a newborn to enter, and suddenly he wished that he could keep it just as it was, its stillness, its clarity, its sheer peacefulness for ever.

Keep it for his daughter, who'd just mewed softly like a kitten, cocooned in Saskia's arms.

He rummaged in his pocket, looking for change. Then he pulled out his I Ching, took a deep breath, and started flipping coins.

# Acknowledgements

My thanks to Simon Trewin at WME for guiding me with both skill and humour, and to Rowland White at Penguin for the kind of enthusiasm which I'm sure all writers crave – to both of you I am truly grateful. I'd also like to thank Nick Lowndes for his killer eye for detail and calm demeanour in the face of a writer who likes to tinker right up until the last moment.

I was lucky enough to have three people read early drafts of the book, and I received from Benjamin Evans, Gordon Weetman and Kylie Fitzpatrick encouragement and excellent advice. In Amsterdam Feico Deutekom and Marjolein van Doorn offered a warm welcome back to the city I'd spent several years in during the early 2000s, and even if we disagreed on seagulls, their help was invaluable. I still made some stuff up though where it suited the story, and for that I'm entirely responsible.

Thanks also go to both my parents who have always been behind me, giving support regardless of the recklessness of some of my ventures, and my wife Zara who is my first reader, and so much more.